The O...
"PU...
(New York Times bestse...

PRAISE FOR
DARKLING

"The most fulfilling journey of self-discovery to date in the Otherworld series . . . An eclectic blend that works well."
—*Booklist*

"Galenorn does a remarkable job of delving into the psyches and fears of her characters. As this series matures, so do her heroines. The sex sizzles and the danger fascinates." —*Romantic Times*

"The story is nonstop action and has deep, dark plots that kept me up reading long past my bedtime. Here be Dark Fantasy with a unique twist. YES!" —HuntressReviews.com

"Pure fantasy enjoyment from start to finish. I adored the world that Yasmine Galenorn has crafted within the pages of this adventurous urban fantasy story. The characters come alive off the pages of the story with so many unique personalities. . . . Yasmine Galenorn is a new author on my list of favorite authors." —*Night Owl Romance*

PRAISE FOR
CHANGELING

"The second in Galenorn's D'Artigo Sisters series ratchets up the danger and romantic entanglements. Along with the quirky humor and characters readers have come to expect is a moving tale of a woman more comfortable in her cat skin than in her human form, looking to find her place in the world." —*Booklist*

"Galenorn's thrilling supernatural series is gritty and dangerous, but it's the tumultuous relationships between all the various characters that give it depth and heart. Vivid, sexy, and mesmerizing, Galenorn's novel hits the paranormal sweet spot."
—*Romantic Times*

continued . . .

Night Huntress

YASMINE GALENORN

BERKLEY BOOKS, NEW YORK

THE BERKLEY PUBLISHING GROUP
Published by the Penguin Group
Penguin Group (USA) Inc.
375 Hudson Street, New York, New York 10014, USA
Penguin Group (Canada), 90 Eglinton Avenue East, Suite 700, Toronto, Ontario M4P 2Y3, Canada
(a division of Pearson Penguin Canada Inc.)
Penguin Books Ltd., 80 Strand, London WC2R 0RL, England
Penguin Group Ireland, 25 St. Stephen's Green, Dublin 2, Ireland (a division of Penguin Books Ltd.)
Penguin Group (Australia), 250 Camberwell Road, Camberwell, Victoria 3124, Australia
(a division of Pearson Australia Group Pty. Ltd.)
Penguin Books India Pvt. Ltd., 11 Community Centre, Panchsheel Park, New Delhi—110 017, India
Penguin Group (NZ), 67 Apollo Drive, Rosedale, North Shore 0632, New Zealand
(a division of Pearson New Zealand Ltd.)
Penguin Books (South Africa) (Pty.) Ltd., 24 Sturdee Avenue, Rosebank, Johannesburg 2196,
South Africa

Penguin Books Ltd., Registered Offices: 80 Strand, London WC2R 0RL, England

This is a work of fiction. Names, characters, places, and incidents either are the product of the author's imagination or are used fictitiously, and any resemblance to actual persons, living or dead, business establishments, events, or locales is entirely coincidental. The publisher does not have any control over and does not assume any responsibility for author or third-party websites or their content.

NIGHT HUNTRESS

A Berkley Book / published by arrangement with the author

PRINTING HISTORY
Berkley Wal-Mart edition / January 2009

ISBN: 978-0-425-23038-1

BERKLEY®
Berkley Books are published by The Berkley Publishing Group,
a division of Penguin Group (USA) Inc.,
375 Hudson Street, New York, New York 10014.
BERKLEY® is a registered trademark of Penguin Group (USA) Inc.
The "B" design is a trademark of Penguin Group (USA) Inc.

PRINTED IN THE UNITED STATES OF AMERICA

10 9 8 7 6 5 4 3 2 1

To Keeter and Luna, both now over the Rainbow Bridge.
Samwise and I love you and miss you.
And when Lady Bast called,
we handed you over to her with love and tears.

ACKNOWLEDGMENTS

Thank you and much love to my husband, Samwise. This is the twenty-first published book you've seen me through. Thanks also to my agent, Meredith Bernstein, and to my editor, Kate Seaver—the best team I could have. I also want to thank my cover artist, Tony Mauro. You've taken my words and brought my characters to life on canvas. That's a rare gift and an inspiration.

To my Witchy Chicks—thanks ladies, for being such a great support system. Scritches and love to my little "Galenorn Gurlz," who offer me their love, their fur in my printer, their fur on my clothes, their purrs of encouragement, and nose-licks and head-bumps when I'm down and need their support. Most reverent devotion to Ukko, Rauni, Mielikki, and Tapio, my spiritual guardians.

Thank you to my readers, both old and new. Your support helps keep us writers in ink and fuels our love of storytelling, and believe me, I appreciate each and every wonderful note you send, whether it be via MySpace, e-mail, or snail mail. You can find me on the Net at Galenorn En/Visions: www.galenorn .com, at MySpace (www.myspace.com/yasminegalenorn), and you can contact me via e-mail on my site. If you write to me by snail mail (see website for address or write via publisher), please enclose a stamped, self-addressed envelope with your letter if you would like a reply. Promo goodies are available; see my site for info.

Ever has it been that love knows not its own depth until the hour of separation.

—KAHLIL GIBRAN

Do not look upon this world with fear and loathing. Bravely face whatever the gods offer.

—MORIHEI UESHIBA, *THE ART OF PEACE*

CHAPTER 1

The late-April night was unseasonably warm, so I'd left the window open a couple inches. Just enough for a breath of fresh air to pass through. From the bed, I gazed up at the moon, which glittered a quarter past full. A low bank of clouds—illuminated silhouettes against the sky—rolled through, streaking the moon with their long fingers of ink. I slid out from between the sheets and silently crossed to the window, padding softly over the braided rug that Iris had recently found in a little vintage store.

Lifting the window just enough so I could lean my head out, I peered into the shadows of the backyard. My sister Camille was out for the night. She was staying with her husbands, Morio and Smoky—a fox demon and a dragon, respectively—in the woods near Smoky's barrow. They were casting yet another spell to bring home one of our own. Trillian, Camille's alpha lover, was still missing. We knew he was alive, but that's all we knew. He'd disappeared, and from all accounts, a goblin contingent nabbed him back in Otherworld, which spelled potential disaster . . . for both Trillian and for us.

Menolly, my other sister, should be just getting home from work. She ran the Wayfarer Bar & Grill. The driveway wasn't visible from my window, so I couldn't see whether her Jag was parked there.

I turned back to the bed. Chase had decided to stay the night, and he was sprawled out across the mattress, sound asleep, cover thrown to the side. The man was hot-blooded, which made him very amenable during the nights when I yanked all the blankets away and curled up in them, leaving him naked. *Speaking of naked,* I thought. Chase was obviously enjoying whatever dream he was having. Either that or he was dreaming he was a sundial. I licked my lips. Time to wake him up in a very special way. If I was careful . . .

I slowly climbed back on the bed and leaned down to cautiously trace my tongue along the length of his erection.

"Erika?" he muttered.

I frowned and paused, tongue still poised against his skin. Who the hell was Erika?

"Delilah, come quick!"

The door slammed open. I lurched, Chase jumped, and my fangs scratched an inch-long razor-thin gash, leaving a delicate red line as a few drops of blood oozed out. *Oh shit!*

"What the fuck are you doing?" Chase yelled, his voice unnaturally high as he scrambled away. The expression on his face was *not* the one I'd been going for, that was for sure.

"Chase! I'm sorry—"

"Oh, Christ!" His foot got caught in the quilt, and he went tumbling over the side of the bed. He hit the floor with a thud, swearing a blue streak.

I rushed to his side as Menolly snorted from where she stood by the door, wreathed in light from the hallway. Blood burbled out of her nose and dripped down to her lips.

"Can you maybe remember to knock next time?" I stared at her, shaking my head. "I take it you just had dinner?"

She coughed, and I caught the glint in her eye. It went against every instinct I had, but I managed to repress my own laughter. I felt bad for Chase—especially since I'd been the one to inflict pain on him—but I felt like Lucy Ricardo caught in the middle of one of her harebrained schemes.

I didn't dare let him see me smile, though. My detective had been going through a rough spot the past few days, and his sense of humor had taken a hike. His job—or rather, jobs—were driving him nuts.

Not to mention that Zachary Lyonnesse—a werepuma with whom I'd slept one time and who was constantly trying to woo me away—had been hanging around the house more. His visits had increased since he got wind that, for the past month or so, Chase had been too busy to drop over most nights. Zachary hadn't put any pressure on me, but I could sense the tension that still ran between us. We tried to pretend it wasn't there—or at least I did—but it was hard to ignore the chemistry, even though Chase was the one who held my heart.

Chase had been irritated, that much I knew, but he'd been smart enough to steer clear of pushing an ultimatum on me. And that was a good thing, because I genuinely liked Zach, and we *had* to work together as we formed the foundation for the growing Supe Community.

I reminded Chase time and again that I loved him and wouldn't stray without talking to him first. But the fact that we'd only managed to have sex four times in the past six weeks didn't help. We were both pent-up, frustrated, and feeling out of sync.

Menolly delicately stepped over the pile of clothes that had grown in the middle of the room. I wasn't much on laundry baskets, even though Iris kept bitching at me. I know, I know, being a werecat, I should be fastidious and tidy, but it just wasn't going to happen. I always meant to do better, but the truth was that I was a slob, and no matter how hard I tried, I'd always be one.

As she plucked a tissue from the box on my dresser and patted her nose, Menolly's gaze flickered back to us. Her pale blue eyes—almost gray, really—grew luminous in the dim light as she stared unabashedly at Chase. The tip of her tongue reach out to trace her lips.

I was about to give her a good what for when I realized it wasn't his nether regions she was focused on. Nope. She could smell his blood. Menolly was a vampire, and while she did a good job of keeping herself in check, when she was startled, her steel-clad grip on her emotions could slip a little.

Chase noticed her intensified scrutiny at the same time I

did. "Stop right where you are!" He hurried to pull the sheet over his groin. "If you think you're sticking your fangs in my . . . *anywhere* in me, you've got another think coming!"

She reined herself in. "Sorry, didn't mean to stare. Just . . ."

"Menolly . . . remember where you are," I said, slowly standing.

She glanced at me, then back at Chase, and shook her head. "Really, I didn't intend to be rude. You okay, Chase?" Without waiting for an answer, she whirled back to me, and a goofy grin spread across her face. "You need to come downstairs, or you'll miss everything!"

"Miss what?" I scrambled for my sleep shirt and dragged it over my head. "What's going on? Do I need to get dressed? Are there demons in the yard? A goblin brigade marching through our kitchen? Another unicorn visit?" Knowing our luck, it could be multiple choice: Take your pick, any and all. Or something worse.

"No, no brawls tonight." She clapped her hands. "I just got home. Iris is up. Maggie said her first words, and she's awake and babbling up a storm. Most of it's nonsense still, but she really can say a few things! Iris is recording it on the camcorder. So hurry up and get your ass downstairs."

As she shut the door, Chase pushed himself to his feet. He fumbled for a moment, then sat on the edge of the bed, staring at his penis. The blood had stopped, but the thin red wheal left a reminder of where my left fang had lacerated him.

I winced as I rooted around in the pile of clothes, looking for my slippers. "That's gotta hurt."

Chase glared at me. "You think? Ever decide maybe you should warn a guy first? We already tried that maneuver before, and I've got the scars to prove it, thank you very much." He sighed. "I'm okay with forgoing blow jobs, you know that. So Delilah, honey, what on earth gave you the idea to try it again?" He gingerly examined his wounded pride, shaking his head.

I let out a little growl. "You don't have to act so pissy. I wasn't planning on giving you a *blow job*. I was just teasing you awake so we could have a little late-night fun. Everything would have been okay if Menolly hadn't come in. Great gods, we've barely touched each other—" One look at his face, and I stopped that train of thought. Best not to go there right now.

"I *said* I'm sorry. Let me get the antibiotic ointment." I stalked into my bathroom, which was right off the bedroom, and brought back a tube of unguent. He relented and let me slide a thin layer down his skin.

As I gazed into his eyes, he leaned forward and kissed me. Slow, deep, with tenderness. I was tempted to catch Maggie's first words on the morning rerun. Maybe we could get in some hot sex without hurting him any further. But then Chase abruptly pulled away.

"Come on, let's get dressed." He slid into a pair of burgundy boxer shorts and the velvet robe he kept in my room. "This is about the only good news we've had in a while. We don't want to miss it."

As I found my slippers and slid them on, he headed out the door, and I scurried to catch up. Chase adored Maggie, that I knew. But for him to forgo sex for something like this . . . there had to be something going on. And whatever it was, he obviously wasn't letting *me* in on the secret.

Iris had the camcorder in hand, while Menolly knelt beside Maggie. Menolly had taken our baby calico gargoyle under her wing and played substitute mama as much as possible. We all loved the little twerp, but a special bond had grown between the vampire and the gargoyle. Maybe because they were both out of their element—both adrift, thanks to the demonic envoys that walked the world.

Maggie looked a lot like a cross between an imp and a large cat. Short, downy, calico-colored fur covered her body. She had pointed ears and whiskers, but her wings were still far too small to support her, so she couldn't fly yet.

The baby 'goyle could barely walk, actually. She'd taken her first steps a few months before. Maggie had a long tail, with a devil's tip at the end, and it, too, was covered with fur. With Menolly's help, she'd gotten the hang of using her tail to balance herself. Now she could stand for several minutes without leaning against the coffee table and even walk a few steps, but after that things got shaky, and her wings would flail, and she'd land on her butt. She never hurt herself when she fell, but her bewildered little *moophs* always managed to get her a treat of some roast beef or a little more of her cream drink.

Maggie gazed up at me with yellow topaz eyes as I knelt in front of her. Would she speak in English? The Fae dialect we often used among ourselves? Or something else?

I glanced up at Iris. "Well?"

Iris, a Talon-haltija who lived with us, shook her head. "She's taking a break, I think. I swear, the moment she said one word, she opened up like the clouds, and she's been babbling on ever since. I wasn't sure whether to disturb you, so I waited till Menolly arrived home." She lifted the camera again and zoomed in on Maggie as I reached for her.

Maggie shook her head at me. "No!"

Surprised, I sat back, waiting.

"No sit. No sit. Deeyaya no sit on me."

I stifled a laugh. Maggie had already proved extremely sensitive to anything remotely decipherable as ridicule. "I think she's got that backward, but she's definitely talking. That's for sure."

Menolly perched on the edge of the coffee table. "Yeah, and she knows all our names. When I walked in, she called me Menny."

"Menny!" Maggie looked extremely proud of herself. "Menny, Deeyaya, Camey? Where Camey?" She glanced around, a confused look on her face.

"Camille will be back in a while," Menolly said, slipping her hands under Maggie's arms as she lifted her onto her lap. "Who's that?" She pointed to Chase. Chase had spent a number of hours babysitting Maggie.

Maggie giggled and clapped. "He-man! He-man!"

I looked over at Chase. "What the . . . is she trying to say *human*?"

"*He-man!*"

Chase blushed red, right to the tips of his ears. "I don't think so."

"Then why is . . . oh good gods, did you teach her that your name is *He-Man*?" I snorted as he rolled his eyes.

"Well, it seemed like a good idea at the time." He appealed to Iris for help, but she just pressed her lips together in a winsome grin. "I didn't think she'd remember it," he said, "let alone repeat it."

Menolly arched an eyebrow. "We found out your secret, Johnson. You want to play superhero. At least we know she's developing along normal lines . . . I guess. The demons may have treated her like livestock, but she can grasp basic concepts—" She paused as a crash echoed from out back. Then again, the echo of something breaking, closer to the house.

"Delilah, come with me. Chase, Iris, wait here." Without another word, Menolly handed Maggie to Iris and slipped out of the living room.

I followed her to the kitchen. She held her finger to her lips and eased the back door open. Silently, thanks to my catlike nature, I tiptoed out behind her. We paused on the porch. There it was again: another thud and the sound of breaking tree limbs.

Tapping Menolly on the shoulder, I motioned for her to step back. As she did, I focused on my core, my center where all facets of my essence fused into one, then split apart again.

The world began to fold, the shadows deepened into gray scale, as I spiraled into myself. Limbs and torso melding, blending, breaking apart to re-form. The metamorphosis never hurt, though nobody believed me when I told them. At least, it didn't hurt as long as I shifted slowly and smoothly.

Hands and feet to paws, torso shrinking, spine lengthening, all was a whirl of change and transformation. I rolled my head back, luxuriating in the feel of the magic as the waves rolled through my body, claiming me into a different form.

A whiff of mist, the scent of bonfires in the distance, but now was not the time for Panther. The Autumn Lord, my master, was still and silent. No, now was the time for Tabby to emerge. As my golden fur quivered in the wind, I flicked my tail and blinked, then raced out through the cat door.

In cat form, I could go exploring without drawing too much attention to myself. Whoever was playing havoc in the woods that lay boundary to our land didn't need to know we were onto them, and chances were they wouldn't notice me in my cat form.

As I padded over the silent earth, the scent of late spring threatened to cloud my senses. It was hard to keep hold of my instincts when playing the tabby. Every flutterbug tempted me, every scent that might be dinner or a toy made me want to race off and explore. But I was on a mission, I reminded myself, even as I spotted a daddy longlegs and promptly smacked it with one paw. I sniffed it, then gobbled it up before racing over toward the noise.

In my half-Fae, half-human form, the sound had been loud enough to hear. Now it was almost deafening. I lowered myself into stalk mode and slinked forward, keeping to the shadows. I was downwind, so unless whatever it was had an extremely keen sense of smell, it might not notice me.

As I crawled through the grass, practically on my belly, I began to sense a presence nearby, one that I recognized. It was Misha, a mouse that I'd formed a semblance of friendship with. I still chased her, but it was all in fun, and she said it kept her alert and alive. She'd saved my butt when my tail got stuck in a patch of cockleburs during the winter, and we'd managed to transcend our instincts and forge a weird but viable alliance.

Now she slipped out of her hole and came running over to me. "Delilah, there's something on the land that shouldn't be."

In my Were form, I could talk to animals and understand them. Oh, it wasn't the same form of vocalization that I used as a woman, but there's a common speech recognized by most animals: a combination of body language and sounds.

I gave her a slight nod. "I know, but I'm not sure what. I haven't picked up a scent yet, and I was just going to investigate."

She shuddered. "Nasty thing. Terribly nasty thing. Big and dark. It eats mice and rodents and other small creatures, so you'd better be careful. Sticks them in its dark mouth and chews, chews, chews them up."

I paused. Maybe *not* such a good idea to head into this in cat form. "Have you ever seen anything like this before?"

Misha sniffed. "No, never. Terrible beast. It drools. Gray, it is, and looks like a broken two-legs. Not so tall and not so wide, but ugly, and hair stringing down its back, and its belly fat and bloated. It has fur, it does, but not in the right places. *Not Friend.*" Creatures, animals, and birds were divided into two distinct categories in Misha's world—*Friend* and *Not Friend.*

She scurried back toward her hole, pausing for a moment to glance back at me. "Be careful. This creature, it could snap you like a twig." And then she vanished into the earthen lair, back to her children.

I waited until she was safely underground then crept forward again, one paw step at a time. If this thing were capable of catching and eating small animals, I had to be careful. I could be killed in cat form easier than when I was hanging out on two legs. As I neared a bend that would lead me into the wood, onto the trail toward Birchwater Pond, I paused, one foot in midair. The sound of bushes rustling and boughs breaking echoed from up ahead. Whatever it was, it was a lot closer than before.

As I neared the source of the noise, the wind shifted just enough to sweep an overwhelming odor my way—dung, cloying like sickly, overripe fruit. And testosterone—thick and musky. Atop the fetid fragrance rode the scent of someone who delighted in administering pain. Animals can smell the intentions of beasts and humans, and I could sense this creature was cruel. He reveled in torment. Misha had been right. This was one vicious dude, whatever he was.

I brushed aside a stand of tall grass with my paw, silently peering between the blades. From where I crouched, I could see into a small clearing. Moonlight struck the ground, breaking through the wispy clouds, illuminating the dell enough for me to see the source of the disturbance.

A creature that stood about four feet tall was clawing at two prone tree trunks. One had fallen atop the other, probably during the last big windstorm. A whimper drifted out from between the downed trunks.

Wait a minute—I knew that sound! It was Speedo, the neighbor's basset hound: He occasionally escaped from his yard and wandered onto our land. As I tried to figure out where he was, I saw that he'd wedged himself into an opening between the fallen firs and couldn't get out. But his woodland cage was also his saving grace. The creature, whatever it was—and I suspected Demonkin—was having trouble. While he could reach his long, twisted hand into the opening, Speedo seemed to have enough room to back up, just out of reach.

It wouldn't be long before the demon figured out that if he moved the top log, he'd be able to access what lay below. And below was Speedo, obviously a Happy Meal just out of the demon's reach. The hoser wasn't too bright, but even the dumbest demon couldn't possibly be stupid enough to ignore the obvious, at least not for long. Poor old Speedo was a goner unless I did something.

I sized up my opponent. Going in as a cat would never work. He'd eat me in one gulp if he caught me. I could probably take him down by myself, but I'd have to shift fast. While in midtransition, I was helpless, and if the demon noticed me then, it would be all over.

Silently backing away, I hid beneath one of the nearby fir trees in a bushy patch of maidenhair fern and huckleberry. The thorns on the huckleberry would hurt when I transformed, but I'd been through worse. Thank the gods we weren't under a full moon, or I'd be trapped in cat form until morning.

Sucking in a deep breath, I envisioned myself metamorphosing back into my two-legged body. Golden shag haircut, six foot one, athletic, a few scars here and there from all the fights we'd been in over the past few months, emerald eyes, just like my eyes when I was a cat . . .

As I clung to the image, I began to shift and willed the transformation to come fast. For once, my body obeyed me. With a dizzying *whoosh* I hit the ground as my collar changed back into my clothes. It hurt a little—I had shifted too fast— but it wasn't anything I couldn't handle. Sort of like being spanked all over with a rubber mallet. As soon as I was sure I'd fully transformed, I ripped out of the huckleberry bush and shook off the fern fronds entangling me.

"Get out of here, you ape!" I raced toward the demon at full tilt, ready to kick butt. The moment I'd made the full change, my sense of dread and fear had shifted to *I'm pissed off, and you better make tracks!*

The demon lurched around, staring up at me with a bewildered look on its face, but his puzzlement lasted just long enough for him to raise his ugly claws and slash at me. I dodged the attack. Barely. The ugly brute was a lot faster than he looked. I'd almost been snagged.

"So you think you're going to rip my new jeans, do you?" I'd just bought three pair of the coolest indigo low-rise jeans from my favorite store the other day, and I wasn't ready to punk them out yet. "Think again, Bubba!"

I pivoted on one foot, lashing out with the other to land a kick right in the middle of his grubby face.

"Crap!" My leg shuddered as it made contact. It felt like I'd just kicked a brick wall. Well, maybe not brick, but damned close. The demon might look like a little pissant, but he was resilient. This was going to be more of a challenge than I'd first thought. Worried, I took aim again. Again, my foot bounced off him, this time with a kick to the stomach.

"Watch out!"

The unexpected shout startled me, but being used to combat situations, I obeyed and dove into a somersault. Good thing, too, because the creature opened his mouth right as I ducked and let out a long belch of flame. I heard the crackle of dry tinder as I rolled to my feet and spun around.

A small patch of debris from a downed log was on fire. Next to it was standing a tall man with pale skin and dark hair, wearing a leather duster.

The demon seemed to think that facing *two* opponents wasn't such a hunky-dory idea, and he turned tail and went crashing through the woods, away from the path. He had to be heading toward one of the boundary lines that divided our land from a protected wetlands area.

"Roz, be careful! He's hard to kill," I shouted as I gave chase.

"I know, you twit," Roz shouted back as he raced past me. Very few creatures were faster than my sisters and me, but Rozurial was one of them. He was an incubus, technically a minor demon, but he roamed in that nicely shadowed ethical region into which we'd all slipped. He was definitely on our side, but no mistake—he was an incubus to the core.

Since he was helping us against Shadow Wing, the demon lord bent on taking over both Earth and Otherworld, we conveniently overlooked his cavorting with—and seducing of—nubile young maidens. And nubile older women. And nonnubile women. Roz liked women of any type, age, shape, size, or color. His greatest delight was in seducing the ones who considered themselves in full control. He loved seeing strong women capitulate to his charms. Apparently, he was good at what he did, but I had no intentions of finding out for myself.

I dodged around a burnt-out tree stump, hoping to hell the fire behind us wouldn't go anywhere except *out*, and then hurdled over a clump of three fallen trees. Roz took them without a single hesitation, his duster flying out behind him as he gracefully sailed over the moss-laden trunks.

After a moment, he stopped and stared into the undergrowth. "I can't smell him anymore. The scent of cedar's too thick."

I sniffed the air. Yep. Cedar, it was. Cedar and fir, and the moist scent of soil still slightly damp from the recent rain. Cocking my head, I tried to pick up any sound. My hearing was keen, like a cat's, though in my half-human, half-Fae form, not quite so much. Small creatures were rustling through the tall grass. A jet soared overhead in the darkness, and somewhere in the distance, the faint sound of rippling waves from Birchwater Pond heralded an incoming breeze. But no sound of the demon.

"Damn it, we lost him." I looked around once more, trying to decide if it was worth giving chase. But chances were he was long gone. He might come back or maybe not, but there was no doubt in my mind he'd broken through Camille's wards. Unfortunately, she wasn't here to alert us. We had to do something about that. Create some sort of warning system so that if she was out, the rest of us would know the wards had been breached.

I shook my head, disgusted. "Can't even kill a simple demon. I'm getting soft," I muttered.

Roz moved to put his arm around my shoulders but stopped when I shot him a warning look. He knew the rules; he was welcome in our home as long as he kept his mitts off Camille and me.

He'd put the skids on his pursuit of Camille after a run-in with Smoky. All it had taken was one misplaced hand on Camille's ass while the dragon was watching to squelch any more attempts. As a dragon, Smoky could crisp Roz with one belch, but even in his six foot four wantonly gorgeous human form, Smoky was stronger than the incubus. He'd grabbed the demon by the scruff of the neck and dragged him outside, where he proceeded to beat the crap out of him. It took Roz two weeks and a lot of ice to heal up from Smoky's thrashing.

But Roz still flirted constantly with Menolly, and she flirted back. Kind of. He'd tried to get in my pants a few times until I threatened to give him a nasty bite where it counted most. Now he left me alone except as a buddy.

"Don't chide yourself," he said. "That was a bloatworgle. You couldn't have killed him without help. They're lightning-fast even with their potbellies and scrawny-looking limbs." He motioned toward the trail. "Come on, let's go make sure the fire's out and then report what we found."

"A *bloatworgle*? Demonkin, I presume?"

Roz nodded. "Yes. Mainly grunts. They tend to congregate over here Earthside, a lot. I think several nests of them were hiding out when the portals were closed against the Subterranean Realms. They've kept the line going, it seems. But they're usually found in deep caverns and barren mountain passes, so I'm not sure what the hell this one's doing here."

What the *hell* was right. Great, just great. Yet another monster I'd never heard of, and the thing was still on the loose. What had it wanted?

Regardless of what Roz said, there was no doubt in my mind that the bloatworgle had been sent here. Either another Degath Squad of Hell Scouts had broken through, or the demon lord Shadow Wing had something else up his pointy little tail. Either way, it looked like we were headed right back down the rabbit hole.

CHAPTER 2

On our way back, Roz and I made a quick sweep around the outskirts of the driveway and gardens to assure ourselves that nobody was hiding near the house, but we found no one lurking except a few scattered mice, raccoons, and other denizens of the animal realm.

Back inside, I dropped beside Chase, who was sitting on the sofa. Roz sprawled in a chair next to Menolly. Iris had taken Maggie off to bed and was now in the kitchen, heating water for tea.

"Our visitor was a demon. Roz says it's a bloatworgle. I have no idea what it wanted, except that it was about to make a snack of Speedo. The creature has a hide as tough as seasoned leather. We lost him, unfortunately." I slumped back against the sofa. "He got away through the undergrowth. By the way, he can belch flame. Nice touch, huh?"

"Bloatworgle?" Chase grimaced. "It look as nasty as it sounds?"

"Worse." I glanced over at Menolly. "Heard of them before?"

She shook her head, but as Iris returned from the kitchen, the house sprite said, "Bloatworgles? Heavens, it's been a while since I've run into one of those. They were all over the Northlands. When I moved back to Finland, I noticed quite a number there, too."

"Northlands?" Menolly and I chimed at the same time.

"You lived in the Northlands like Smoky?" There were a lot of things we didn't know about Iris. It had taken a good six months or more to pry out of her that she was a priestess of Undutar, a Finnish goddess of mists and ice. She still wouldn't—or couldn't, as she put it—talk about it.

Iris nodded, and her veiled look told me the door for discussion was closed and locked. "Yes, I lived there for a good share of my early years, after I grew out of maidenhood but before I came to work for the Kuusis. There were a host of bloatworgles, kobolds, and other dark dwellers there. They're endemic to a number of places besides the Subterranean Realms, so there *is* a chance that this creature has no connection to Shadow Wing."

"Not likely," I muttered. "Given our track record? Given what we're up against? No, I don't think we should discount the probability that this was a scouting mission."

"Maybe, but Karvanak already scouted out our land, and he answers directly to Big Bad himself," Menolly said. "Let's face it, we've moved up the ladder. Shadow Wing isn't going to throw grunts at us now that he's got one of the spirit seals."

That put a chill on the conversation. One of Shadow Wing's generals, Karvanak—a Rāksasa who had managed to thwart our last mission—had managed to steal the third spirit seal. Not good. Not good at all. We weren't sure just what Shadow Wing could do with one seal, but our battle was a lot more dangerous than if we'd managed to keep it out of his grasp.

Nine spirit seals. Nine gems that had originally been one. An ancient artifact, the spirit seal had been forged and then broken. The break had signaled the Great Divide that parted the realms, making it much harder for the demons to break through to Earth or Otherworld.

If all nine parts are reunited, the portals separating the

realms will shatter, leaving the worlds open and vulnerable as movement between them would flow freely again. We've managed to find two spirit seals, now safely hidden away for safekeeping, but we're racing against time. Shadow Wing, the Demon Lord running the Subterranean Realms, is also after them, and he plans to use them to rip open the veils and send his armies marching through to raze both Earth and Otherworld, turning them into his own private hell.

My sisters and I and a ragtag bunch of friends are the only ones standing in the way. We're on the front line, facing the devil himself.

When we first came Earthside from Otherworld, we'd considered the assignment tantamount to exile. The OIA, the Otherworld Intelligence Agency, had made it clear that we weren't very good at our jobs. Our half-human, half-Fae bloodline skews our powers, and so our superiors thought they'd found a way to keep us out of the way without firing us.

But a few months after we'd arrived, Shadow Wing began to make his move. At the same time, a civil war broke out back home, and our father disappeared from the Guard Des'Estar.

Chaos rules our lives now, and we're stuck here, fighting against a force that could decimate millions, both human and Fae. Our opium-dazed queen from Y'Elestrial, our home city, has put a bounty on our heads, so we can't go back home. At least not to *our* city. Our allies are few and fragile. A bizarre mix including FBHs (full-blooded humans), Fae, demons, Cryptos, and a dragon, none of them necessarily getting along with the others.

And then there's my sisters and me.

Half-human, half-Fae, we're a mismatched set at best. Currently we live in Belles-Faire, a seedy suburb of Seattle on the outskirts of the city.

Camille's a witch, pledged to the Moon Mother. Sexual and passionate, she recently married Smoky, the dragon, and Morio, an Earthside fox demon. She's also bound by a magical sexual union to Trillian. He's Svartan, one of the dark, charming Fae, and he disappeared while looking for our father a couple months ago. Camille's powers are sketchy at times, often backfiring on her, but as the eldest, she looks after all of us and holds the reins when it comes to dealing with the organization of our little band of ragtag guerrillas.

Menolly, my younger sister, was tortured and turned by one of the worst vampires in history. We managed to dust him into oblivion, but the scars that cover Menolly's body will live on for eternity. She's recently gotten active in vampire and Earthside Supe politics and is in the process of setting up an underground police state to keep tabs on the bloodsucker activity in the area.

And then, there's me, Delilah. Werecat by nature, my golden tabby nature has been with me since birth. But in our quest for the second spirit seal, my path crossed with one of the Immortals, the Elemental known as the Autumn Lord. One of the Harvestmen, he's an avatar of Death. In return for his help, he claimed me as one of his Death Maidens. Shortly after my transformation, another Were form began to emerge: a black panther, over which I seem to have no control.

At first, I thought the new form had shown up because of the Autumn Lord, but then the idea was broached that I might have had a twin who died at birth. If so, I could be inheriting her powers. Camille has no clue whether this is true, and our father's nowhere around to ask, so I've pushed the thought to the back burner. But sometimes, I can't help but wonder—did I have a twin, or not? And if so, what had happened to my sister? Why did she die?

"What's our next step?" Menolly asked.

Chase yawned. "I don't know about you, but I have to get another hour or two of sleep. I'm wearing two hats at work, remember. Since Devins was killed by the troll, I haven't had a chance to breathe, let alone take more than a scattered handful of days off. Plus the FH-CSI is in the middle of an overhaul, and I have to be there to supervise." The Faerie-Human Crime Scene Investigations team was Chase's brainchild, and he was in charge of the unit. Nationwide, all FH-CSI units had been based on the prototype he'd started here in Seattle.

"Go on up," I said, pressing my lips to his lightly. As I lingered in his embrace, he searched my eyes, and I thought I saw a flicker of doubt there. Suddenly nervous, I pulled him to me and leaned into the kiss. After a second's hesitation, he returned my kiss, but he was holding back. I could feel it. Too tired and nervous to ask him what was going on, I merely said, "I'll be up soon."

He pushed himself off the sofa. He was my height—six one—and as swarthy as I was fair. Chase's curly hair was slicked back close to his head. He couldn't wear it long, and long wasn't his style anyway, but his dark eyes gave him a slightly dangerous look, and he was trim and kept himself fit. He was sporting the beginnings of a mustache and goatee, and I rather liked the new look. Impeccably neat, he loved designer suits and polished shoes. We were opposite in so many ways, but our differences only added to the spice. Or so I liked to think.

As he hit the stairs, I turned back to the others. "We have to talk to Camille. There has to be some way for us to get a warning when her magical wards break. Maybe Morio and I can figure out something. I'm getting pretty good with some of the Earthside tech stuff, and Morio's good at merging it with magic."

"Vanzir's due back first thing in the morning," Menolly said. "He's been scouting around the past few days, and I got a call from him while you were out of the house. He said he's found something that we need to attend to. We'll need Camille and her boys, because I won't be able to go in with you on this one. Vanzir said that the best time to take them on is during the day. Whoever *they* are. I put in a call and left a message on Camille's new cell phone."

Vanzir was a dream chaser demon who'd been in the service of Karvanak, the Rāksasa. At the last minute, Vanzir had turned sides and defected to us. He wasn't fit to join the Boy Scouts, not by any means, but he didn't want Shadow Wing infiltrating Earth. I wasn't quite clear on exactly why, but apparently the dream chaser had his reasons, and he was oath bound to Iris and my sisters and me. If he turned on us, he died.

"I guess I'd better get some more sleep, too. How can we

make sure the bloatworgle doesn't come back and try to get in the house?" I winced as I stretched. My body felt achy and sore, like I'd lost too many nights of sleep and had been drinking too much caffeine—neither of which I was prone to do.

Menolly motioned at the stairs. "Go to sleep, Kitten. You too, Iris. Roz and I'll watch over the place until sunup. Rest deep. I have the feeling you're going to need it."

As Iris trundled off to bed, and I trudged up the stairs, I wondered just what Vanzir had roped us into now. Over the past few months, it felt like we'd gone from killing a handful of bad guys here and there to constantly patrolling the city in search of demons and vampires and monsters.

If that wasn't enough to deal with, rogue portals had been opening on their own, allowing denizens from Otherworld to come through unannounced, and they weren't always user-friendly.

To top it off, the Earthside Courts of Fae were rising again with Titania, Morgaine, and Aeval at their helms, and there was a tension in the air between the Fae from Otherworld and those who lived Earthside. Neither side fully trusted the other, and I prayed that we wouldn't end up with a civil war of our own right here in Seattle.

Life had gone from being simple and fun to one bloody nightmare after another. I sighed as I hit the landing leading up to my suite of rooms on the third floor. There was no going back. That much I knew. We couldn't go home again, either figuratively or for real. And the latter thought made me want to weep.

By the time I rose at five forty-five, Chase was gone. He'd left me a brief, crisp note but hadn't woken me up to say good-bye. I frowned. This was too much. Whether he liked it or not, it was time we had a talk.

As I clattered downstairs, I found everyone in a state of preparation. Camille was sitting in the kitchen, along with Morio and Smoky. They were an odd pair, her husbands were. Morio was on the shorter side, Japanese, with a long, sleek ponytail. He dressed in grays and blacks, a perpetual twinkle lit his eyes, and he was deeply devoted in our fight against the demons.

Smoky, on the other hand, was an almost-albino six four, with ankle-length silver hair that moved on its own. His gaze could freeze boiling water, and he was single-minded in his focus on Camille. He helped us out, all right, but if Camille hadn't been around, I had the feeling he wouldn't have given us the time of day.

The three were sitting around the breakfast table, discussing tactics and strategy in hushed whispers.

Menolly was asleep in her lair, of course, and Maggie was snoozling in her playpen. Roz was helping Iris set the table. Over in the corner, flipping through a stack of papers that looked like old maps, was Vanzir.

The dream chaser looked human, all right. With platinum-blond hair that was slicked back in a shag, and a lean, gaunt face, he looked like a heroin-chic rocker, but the fire in his eyes gave away his demonic heritage. He wore jeans and a sweatshirt, and the sentient collar encircling his neck beneath the skin was proof that he'd undergone the Ritual of Subjugation. If he broke his oath, the collar would burn him to a crisp.

I poured myself a glass of milk and darted out of the way as Roz carried a platter of pancakes and bacon to the table. Iris followed with a dish of scrambled eggs. As I slid into my chair, I leaned over to tap Vanzir on the knee. I didn't particularly like him, but he'd turned out to be true to his word. Whether it was from the threat of annihilation or not, I wasn't sure, but since he was holding up his end of the bargain, I did my best to be polite.

"What's shaking?"

He gave me a lazy look. "I was waiting for you to wake up."

"Well, I'm awake. Let's have it," I said as I speared a stack of pancakes. Iris had made a towering platter of them, and she must have fried up two pounds of bacon, all of which would be gone by the time we were done with breakfast.

Sitting between her two men, Camille slathered her pancakes with butter and syrup and dug in, leaning over the table so she didn't drip syrup on her boobs, which conveniently acted like a catch tray.

"You buy a new bra? You look especially perky this morning." I jabbed my finger in the direction of her chest and snorted. "Honestly, with as much as you have to go around, it's a good thing you've got two men!"

"Three," she said automatically, her face clouding over.

"Three," I said softly. "I'm sorry. I never forget about Trillian, trust me."

"Neither do I," she whispered.

My little attempt at humor had landed as flat as roadkill. I cleared my throat and turned back to Vanzir, who was delicately wiping his mouth. He ate very little, and I wondered just what his natural form of food was. I didn't bother asking. I might not like the answer.

"Go ahead. We're listening."

Getting nods from around the table, he said, "Okay, I've located a nest of venidemons. Not sure how they got here, but they're usually only found in the Sub Realms. Nasty buggers, though."

Shit. Venidemons—venomous demonic blowflies from the Subterranean Realms. They were nearly as big as my head and were damned fast for their size. Using their needlelike stingers, they injected a butt load of toxic soup into the bloodstream. Along with the toxin, which paralyzed within seconds, was a mess of eggs, which hatched within twenty-four hours and began nibbling the victim from the inside out.

"Damn parasites." Camille grimaced. "Hate parasites."

Smoky tenderly reached over to brush back a lock of her hair. "I won't let them hurt you," he said, then went back to his own breakfast.

She arched her eyebrows and gave me a quick grin. If Smoky had his way, she'd be secreted away in that barrow of his, safe from all unwelcome visitors—and other suitors. Sometimes the Stones were right, though, and we couldn't get what we wanted. So Smoky had settled for joining our exploits, even though he had little interest in anything other than whatever he happened to fancy at the time. Dragons made great mercenaries, if you paid them enough. Apparently

Camille's hand in marriage had been enough to ensure his help.

"Crap," I said. "I suppose we have to wipe them out. Are they under guard or being left to their own devices?"

He nodded. "Unfortunately, yes. They have a guardian. I'm not sure what it is—could be a ghost or a wight. Whatever the case, their guardian is both powerful and from somewhere other than the Subterranean Realms."

"Oh great." I stabbed another piece of pancake. "That sounds just delightful—" The phone rang, putting a stop to my rant. I jumped up and grabbed it. "Hello?"

"I'd like to speak to Chase Johnson." I didn't recognize the voice, but it was clearly a woman and unsettlingly smooth and sexy.

I stared at the receiver for a moment, then asked, "Sharah?" even though I knew full well it wasn't her.

"My name is Erika. I'm looking for Chase Johnson and was told he might be at this number." Again, the husky, breathy voice that reeked of sex and designer wear and cognac.

Wait a minute—*Erika?* Hadn't that been the name Chase had muttered during his sleep, before I put the fang on him? *What the . . . ?*

I paused for a second, debating on what to say. "I'm sorry, Chase isn't available. He's probably at work. May I take a message?"

She laughed, and her laughter conjured up images of sultry summer nights. "No, I know where his office is. Thank you, anyway." There was a sudden catch in her voice, and she added, "I take it this is Delilah? Chase's *friend*?"

I held my breath and counted to three. "Girlfriend. This is Chase's *girlfriend*. And you are?"

For the first time since she'd spoken, Erika's voice took on an edge as she said, "I'm Chase's ex. We used to be engaged. Oh well, thanks anyway. I'll catch up to him in a bit."

And then the line went dead.

I stared at the phone blankly before slowly replacing the receiver. Chase had never told me he'd been engaged. He'd never told me about any serious relationships in his past. I shouldn't be jealous. I was half-Fae, my father's blood almost guaranteed me freedom from jealousy. But there it was, simmering in the pit of my stomach. A little worm that wanted to find this Erika, whoever she was, and claw her eyes out. And why the hell had Chase been dreaming about her? Had he seen her already and not bothered to tell me? Or was it some weird coincidence that made fate seem like a first-class bitch?

Whatever the case, I couldn't worry about it now. We had a nest of venidemons to go after before I could give in to the green-eyed monster that was *really* bedeviling me.

CHAPTER 3

"Iris, is Henry taking over the shop today?" Camille asked as we geared up for battle, which basically meant arming ourselves with anything we thought might come in handy.

Henry was an FBH whom Camille had hired to help out at the Indigo Crescent—her bookshop—during times when neither she nor Iris could get there.

As part of our OIA cover stories, we'd been assigned jobs when we first arrived Earthside. Camille ostensibly owned the Indigo Crescent, a bookshop. I ran a low-budget PI business, D'Artigo Investigations. And Menolly had clocked in at the Wayfarer Bar & Grill as a bartender on the night shift.

Now, Camille really *did* own the Indigo Crescent, my PI business was spotty at best, and Menolly had taken over as owner of the bar. If the HR department at the OIA ever returned to its former bureaucratic glory and turned their attention back Earthside, they were going to be in for a bit of a shocker.

The Talon-haltija nodded. "Yes. And I asked him to stay all day. Since your wards were broken by the bloatworgle, I've decided to do a little research on my own and find out what I can. I know there are natural repellents to bloatworgles and their kin, but it's been so long since I had to protect the Kuusis' land that I can't remember what they were. Bruce and I are meeting for lunch. So I thought that I'd run over to the Alysin te Varden Lending Library before our date and find out what I can. I'll take Maggie with me."

One of the newest Fae-oriented establishments in Seattle, the Alysin te Varden Lending Library was named for an elf who'd been killed down in Portland, Oregon. A group of Freedom's Angels gang-raped her, beat her senseless, and left her to die. And die she did. Our cousin Shamas had managed to help catch the culprits. The DNA evidence proved them guilty, but the men mysteriously turned up dead in jail before they could stand trial.

The library was a joint enterprise between three OW Fae, who hearkened from the Southern Wastes in Otherworld, three members of the newly risen Courts of Fae: one Seelie, one Unseelie, and one of the newest Court, one of the dusk Fae. In addition, two members of the Rainier Puma Pride and two members of the Elliott Bay Orca Pod had joined the effort.

The Elliott Bay Orcas were the newest band of Weres to come out of the supernatural closet. They were killer whale Weres, and with the rise of the Supe community project I was spearheading, they had not only made themselves known but had taken the reins on a restoration project to clean up Puget Sound.

The King County government could no longer look the other way when it came to polluting the bays and inlets, not now that everybody knew sentient creatures lived there. Of course, there had been an influx of membership to the Guardian Watchdogs and Freedom's Angels groups from über-right-wing anticonservationists, but that was only to be expected. For every swing of the pendulum, there was an equal and opposite reaction.

Together, the Fae and the Supes had created a lending library of books related to their races, most of which had lain dormant in hidden alcoves for hundreds—sometimes thousands—of years. The volumes had been reprinted and were being distributed. While the Freedom's Angels held book burnings, the lending library idea was catching on in major cities around the nation.

"That's a good idea," Morio said. "While you're there, see if you can dig up any information on wights and specters. If this thing guarding the venidemons proves to be a greater spirit and we can't deal with it, then we might need the information." He slid into a lightweight quilted jacket and tightened his ponytail.

Camille was wearing an outfit that was downright modest. My guess was that she didn't want to give any unnecessary encouragement to the venidemons. She'd changed into a pair of black tights, a knee-length black rayon skirt, a turtleneck sweater, and a stunning red patent leather belt. She was wearing lace-up granny boots to cover her lower legs. Smoky joined her, in his usual white jeans, pale blue shirt, and ankle-length white trench. Somehow, he never managed to get dirty, no matter how mucky the fight or how bloody the job.

I was dressed in heavy jeans, a pair of motorcycle boots, a long-sleeved knit tank, and my leather jacket. Roz was in his usual black duster and jeans, and Vanzir slid a heavy denim jacket over his jeans and T-shirt. We were outfitted for battle and ready to go.

"Where's the nest, and how many are we facing?" I asked, grabbing my backpack and keys.

Vanzir shook his head. "I don't know how many. I couldn't get an accurate count. At least fifteen, though. The nest is in an abandoned house down near Boeing. It's set back on a couple acres of land, and it looks like it's been up for sale for a long time."

I sighed. "I don't like this, not at all. We're heading into a dangerous situation without any real idea of how many opponents we're facing, what their capabilities are, and who's leading them."

Camille smirked. "You mean, it's business as usual."

"Funny woman . . . funny woman! Okay, come on, let's go get this over with." I sheathed my long silver knife in my leg holster. "Iris, you taking a cab to the library, or what?" Iris was too short to drive, and we hadn't had the time to order a new car retrofitted for her specific height needs. It was on our to-do list, though.

She shook her head. "Siobhan's picking me up. She's bringing us a bucket of clams, and I'm giving her some spring lettuce and baby carrots."

Siobhan Morgan was one of our friends. She was a selkie—a wereseal—who passed in human society. Still firmly in the closet, she was a good ally if we needed someone to dig up info not normally given to Supes or Fae. She was also very happily pregnant, and because she'd managed to conceive, her boyfriend, Mitch—also a selkie—had been allowed by the Pod elders to ask her to marry him. They were scheduled for a July wedding, and their baby was due in November.

"Okay. Just keep your eyes open when you're outside. And keep an eye on Siobhan, too. The wards are still down; anything could wander onto the land."

Camille sighed. "I'll recharge them when we come home," she said. "But until we can figure out a way for somebody besides Morio or me to tell if they've been damaged or negated, it doesn't really do a lot of good. If the bloatworgle managed to break them, then he's either got a lot of power, or he had help. Otherwise, he couldn't get through."

"My guess is the latter," Morio said. "Those wards were strong."

"Well, I guess we can't put it off any longer. You bringing the unicorn horn?" I asked. Camille had been gifted with a rare magical item and had been doing her best to learn to wield it.

"Yes." Camille nodded. "But I don't want to use it unless I have to. Given that I can only charge it up under the new moon, I don't want to drain its powers unless these critters are more than we can handle."

"I guess this is it, then. Vanzir, you and Roz come with me. Smoky and Morio will go with Camille. You got a map for them?"

Vanzir handed Camille a Google map, and she, in turn, handed it to Morio, who always took care of the details like directions. We headed out to the cars. I waved as Camille and

the boys climbed in her Lexus, then I swung up into my Jeep.
Roz rode shotgun; Vanzir sat in the back.

Belles-Faire was on the northern outskirts of Seattle.
When traffic was light, we made good time into the heart of
the city. When it was heavy, we could be stuck in gridlock for
hours. Luckily, at this time of the morning, rush hour was
almost over.

I swung over onto I-5. The freeway would be the quickest
way to reach south Seattle, past Georgetown—a graveyard of
railroad tracks and boxcars—into the Industrial District. Built
over the mudflats that once lay beneath Elliott Bay and over
covered landfill, the area was prone to liquefaction, and during
earthquakes, the buildings were easily damaged.

As we headed down the road, I glanced toward the west.
Storm clouds were moving in. We were heavily into the spring
rains, and Mandy Tor, the loopy meteorologist on K-Talk, was
predicting a heavy drenching for the area by early afternoon. I
trusted Camille's and Iris's take on the weather more than
Mandy's, but both of them concurred: We'd be soaked through
before afternoon tea.

"Vanzir, tell me again," I said, steering my way between
two huge semis, one hauling diesel, the other hauling gasoline.
Yeah, that would be a nasty combination in a wreck. Big boom.
Big bonfire. "What did you say about the venidemons? What
are their weaknesses?"

Vanzir had filled us in before we left the house, but I'd still
been fuming over the call from Erika and had only half
listened. He leaned forward, resting his elbows on the back of
Morio's seat. "Venidemons are extremely dangerous, but they
do have one major weakness. They're prone to ice and snow
damage. If it gets too cold—say subfreezing—they can't fly.
Makes 'em sluggish. They die if it falls below minus ten."

"I take it that's . . . what's it called . . . Fahrenheit?" I
quickly switched lanes to skirt around a slow-moving RV.
Camille was right behind me, her Lexus mirroring us like a
steel-gray shadow.

"Right."

"Perfect! Smoky's heritage is directly from the Northlands.
His father was a white dragon, his mother a silver, giving him

a dangerous mix of ice, snow, and electrical attacks. At least we have him on our side," I said.

"We should have brought Iris," Roz added. "She's proficient with ice and snow magic."

Damn it, why hadn't I thought of that? Or why hadn't Camille? We were so used to leaving Iris in charge of the house that sometimes we forgot how handy she could be in a fight. "Why didn't you say something back at the house, dork?"

The incubus winked at me in the rearview mirror. "Because nobody asked." He laughed when I sputtered indignantly. "Don't get your panties in a wad. I didn't say anything because what she's doing is valuable, too—and we *do* have the dragon with us. We don't have a lot of manpower to go around, lately, not with Trillian missing, and we have to make the best use of who's available and what resources we have handy."

I winced. He was right. We had more help than when we'd begun our fight against the demons, but more issues kept cropping up to dilute our firepower. Shamas, our cousin, couldn't fight with us because Chase desperately needed him on the FH-CSI team. Some of the Weres who'd been showing interest in joining us had, instead, thrown their lot in with the Supe Community Council, which had its own concerns.

As for the vampires, they were focused on working with Wade and Vampires Anonymous to take over control of the Seattle area and put an end to any feeding frenzies that might rise up. A couple of the bloodsucker clubs were fighting back, Dominick's and the Fangtabula in particular, and Menolly had warned us that tensions were building toward an eventual showdown.

I couldn't blame them entirely. After all, we still hadn't told many of the Supes and vamps about the demons yet. It just wasn't news we could spread around indiscriminately. If the FBH population got wind of the demon threat, panic would rage through the streets, and then we'd have massive chaos to cope with. Which would lead to the military interfering when there really wasn't a lot they could do. At least not with their armaments as they were.

Even nukes weren't always effective against some of the demon hordes. But we'd play hell trying to convince the government to lay down their automatic weapons and pick up silver swords.

I managed to cross three lanes of moderately heavy traffic in time to veer onto our exit as we headed into the heart of industrial Seattle.

The city here was less than pristine. The buildings were as gray as the sky, stark concrete and metal, with parking lots that held a thousand cars. Train tracks ran everywhere like a crazy jigsaw puzzle. If we followed the road we were on long enough, we'd wind up curving north again, toward the lower ports of Seattle. But before we got that far, we needed to turn south onto Lucile. From there, we'd wend our way through the narrow streets until we came to Finley Avenue SW.

The Industrial District looked a lot different during the day than it did at night. During the daylight, all the concrete and metal was just depressing. At night, the area was downright spooky. It didn't help any that the district had become home to a number of the Supe clubs, including the infamous Fangtabula, one of the most popular vampire clubs in the Pacific Northwest.

Roz jabbed his finger toward the building, which had been painted with bold black-and-white stripes and was as solid as a bomb shelter. "Menolly sure doesn't like that club."

"She's right not to. The owner's trouble." I shook my head. "Terrance isn't an old-school vamp—he doesn't get into the whole black-cape-goth-boy thing—but neither is he a good candidate for the newest member of Vampires Anonymous."

"Why?" The incubus blinked as we passed by the nightclub. There were no signs of life, nor would there be until after dark.

"Terrance likes to live on the edge. Menolly told me that she has a bad feeling about him—that she can easily see him becoming another Dredge, give or take a thousand years. Rumors are the club caters to blood whores, but there's no evidence to prove it. There's nothing we can do to close them down. If he walks on the wrong side of the law, he's been covering his tracks damned good."

"What makes you think there's anything shady going on?" Roz asked.

I bit my lip. We'd been keeping an eye on the Fangtabula for over a month now. "Tales have trickled out about some questionable parties involving underage FBH girls. Whispers of rape and blood feasts, but nobody ever seems to remember the details, and there's nothing Chase can do to check them out without official complaints. The vamps would smell undercover cops a mile away, and they'd make sure everything was under wraps. So Menolly and the VA group keep their ear to the rumor mill, hoping for something we can pounce on."

I swung onto Finley Avenue. Camille turned right behind me. Vanzir leaned forward again. "Three blocks down, to the left. Pink house with brown trim, weathered paint, two-story. The venidemons are in the basement, along with their ghostly sentinel."

The house could have been any weathered house in a run-down neighborhood, but as I pulled up to the curb on the other side of the street, the hairs on the back of my neck began to rise. Even if I hadn't known about the venidemons, my body would have told me that something inherently evil lurked here. As I sat there, staring at the flakes of pink that were peeling from the siding, I had the distinct impression we were being watched by something behind the windows that were covered with heavy gray drapes.

Camille pulled in behind my Jeep as I opened my door and swung to the ground. Followed by Roz and Vanzir, I headed back to her car. Camille and the boys emerged from the Lexus to meet us.

She motioned to the house. "Bad. It's bad. I've never encountered a venidemon, but I didn't think they were as nasty as the vibes I'm getting."

Vanzir shook his head. "They aren't. I mean, they're bad, and they can be deadly, but this . . . this is bigger. Maybe it's coming from the spirit, but don't count on it. I think we'd better be prepared for the worst."

"The worst would be Shadow Wing, and this isn't anywhere near what his power would feel like," Camille said.

"Well, that's one thing in our favor." Roz leaned against the car. "But I smell trouble ahead."

Camille nodded. "You and me both."

Smoky and Morio glanced at her. "Battle order?"

Camille motioned to me. "You fight better than I do, but I'll need space to cast spells. Same with Morio, so he and I should stay on the same side."

I nodded. "I'll take the left, along with Roz. Morio and you take the right. Vanzir, you and Smoky follow. Both of you are fast and can speed past us if you have to."

"Sounds good," Roz said, opening his duster to examine the arsenal he routinely carried like some psychotic peddler. I had no idea how he ever made it past a metal detector. He ruffled through the inner pockets of his walking armory and held up a couple of white orbs that looked suspiciously like golf balls. "These are ice bombs. They'll send a bone-chilling wave of frost in front of us. Once we get in with the venidemons, I'll toss one. It should give us a little edge; the spell lasts for at least sixty seconds, and it will take them a while to regroup."

"It's cold and drizzly. I can try for a spell of freezing rain. Morio?" Camille closed her eyes and began to prep for invoking the moon magic.

Morio shook his head. "I'll send a wave of confusion through them. That should add some chaos to the party."

"I guess we're ready." I glanced at Smoky and Vanzir. "I'm using my silver dagger as usual. Roz has his pick of weapons. Smoky, I've seen you fight; I don't even need to ask. Although if you have something in the icicle range, that would be good. Vanzir, I take it you'll be hands-on?"

He nodded. "I can use minor fire spells, but they'd just lap it up like candy."

There was nothing more to say. "We're ready, then. Shall we?" They waited, so I swung in front, together with Camille, and we headed across the street. "I guess the front door is as good as any entrance," I muttered.

Camille snorted. "Just so long as we don't have to ring the bell and play Avon lady. I'm not giving my makeup secrets to a bunch of blowflies from hell."

"What about Tupperware?" I let out a snort of nervous laugh. We were in the yard now, cautiously approaching the house. "I have the feeling we're being watched," I muttered.

"I know we are," she countered. "And you can bet they're ready for us, so I suggest we just get our butts in there and clean them out."

As we came to the porch, I glanced at the men. "Good to go, boys?" Everyone nodded. "Then let's play exterminator."

Camille was right: They knew we were coming, and we *knew* they knew, so there was absolutely no use pussyfooting around.

I raced up the stairs, spinning as I came to the door. My motorcycle boots were good and heavy, with thick soles and steel-clad heels. Letting out a war cry, I rammed my foot against the door, grinning as the wood around the lock splintered. A flurry of dust came rushing out as the door slammed open. Woohoo! My kickboxing lessons at the gym were paying off in a big way.

I leapt into the room and darted the beam of my flashlight around, my nostrils flaring. Something smelled nauseating. Camille dashed in on the other side, leaving room for the men to enter. All of a sudden, light flooded the room as another crash ripped through the air. Camille had grabbed one of the curtains and yanked it hard, tearing down the rod and all so that the entire room was filled with the overcast shimmer from outside.

Well, that would take care of any vampires who might wander into the living room, that was for certain. And possibly any light-sensitive specters, too. The room was large, with scuffed hardwood floors. Motel art hung crooked on the wall, and the paint was chipped in several places. Two archways, one on either side of the back wall, led out of the room.

A broken-down sofa sat in one corner, along with a table filled with so many filthy take-out boxes that I almost lost my breakfast. They smelled putrid, and there were maggots crawling on some of them, but in the back of my mind I knew that they weren't what was causing the horrid stench. A very nasty thought crept into my mind, one I didn't want to explore, but it wouldn't go away.

Camille and the boys glanced around the room. "Nothing here," she said. "Let's spread out." She motioned to Smoky and Morio. "We'll take the right arch. Delilah, you guys take the left."

Roz and Vanzir slid in behind me as we headed toward the left archway. I mirrored Camille's actions, flattening myself to the wall next to the entrance. As I edged my head around the corner, I saw a long hallway. Empty. There were several doors on either side.

Camille did the same, then pulled back and shook her head. "Kitchen," she mouthed. Given that all of us had exceptional hearing, it was as if she was talking at a normal volume. Unfortunately, chances were our opponents also had acute senses. "Looks empty. There's one door, which probably leads out to the porch."

"I don't want to split up," I said, motioning to her. "Come on, we're doing this together." I was leery of traps.

"How well can venidemons hear, anyway?" Camille asked.

Vanzir frowned. "I don't know. Hell, I don't even know if they have ears or *can* hear. But the ghost or specter or whatever it is, is probably aware we're here."

"We'll go together." I stared at Camille. She usually took the lead, but I had a strong premonition about this, and I wasn't in any mood to be proven right. When she frowned, I added, "Please, just listen to me on this?"

Slowly, she nodded. "Whatever you like, Kitten. I'm not getting a whole lot of guidance on this, except for the creepy feeling I got coming up the stairs. What about you, Morio? Smoky?"

Morio closed his eyes. "Squirmy. The energy feels like it's squirming. It's all over the place, and I can't pin it down."

Smoky stared at the walls. "There's Netherworld energy here, along with demon stench."

Netherworld energy. That confirmed it. Ghosts, specters, and wights were all from the Netherworld. Although the Netherworld was linked to the Underworld, there was a big difference between the two.

The Underworld was usually a peaceful—if somber—place where a number of spirits journeyed after they left their mortal forms behind. The Netherworld, on the other hand, was filled with wandering souls and angry dead and generally pissed-off spirits. Of course, the undead also included vampires and ghouls, but they seemed to hang out with the Demonkin.

Somebody really needed to write a handbook on how to keep track of who was stationed where. Actually, if I remembered my OIA training right, they'd taught a class on the subject, but for the life of me, I couldn't remember anything from it.

"That seals it. We stick together." I motioned to Camille, and we swung into the hallway, Roz and Morio right behind us. Vanzir and Smoky brought up the rear. As we edged toward the first door, I swallowed my fear and put my hand on the knob. I looked at the others.

Camille gave me a nod. "Do it."

"Here goes nothing," I said, yanking open the door. As I did, a cold shaft of wind gusted past, and my skin broke out in goose bumps. I stared into the room, thinking I'd been prepared for just about anything, but this took the cake. Nope, no way had I expected to stumble onto a portal first thing. Wide open, the portal led right into the heart of a glacier by the feel of the energy pouring through. Oh yeah, this was going to be a fun ride.

CHAPTER 4

"Holy crap, where the hell does this lead?" Morio said.

Smoky cleared his throat. "At first I thought it was the Northlands, but the energy is tainted, not clear. I'm thinking the Netherworld."

"Oh shit," Vanzir said. "Then we're open to invasion from a bunch of spooks of the worst kind. They might even be able to summon the venidemons, though I'm not sure if that's what happened in this case."

"Great." I stared at the shimmering energy, wondering just how big of a zap it would give me if I touched it. "So the spirit world has decided to take up residence over Earthside, too."

Camille folded her arms over her chest and stared nervously at the opening. "Who are we going to call in to watch over this one? I don't know many Supes who are very effective against denizens of the Netherworld. It's not quite the same as a troll or goblin, whom you can take out with one good thump over the head. Spirits can be dangerous on so many levels."

I squinted, trying to think of anyone who might be able to help. "I can ask Venus the Moon Child. He might know of somebody." The shaman of the Rainier Puma Pride was an incredibly powerful Were, and if anybody would know how to deal with ghosts and spirits, it would be him. He'd been intensively trained when he was young, and I had the feeling he'd traveled to Hell and back more than once.

"Good idea," Morio said.

"Meanwhile, that just leaves us with finding the venidemons and whatever creep's protecting them. Considering where we think this portal leads, well . . . it could be anything or anyone." I glanced down the hall. "Want to make a bet the venidemons are belowground? If I were a giant demonic blowfly, I'd hide in a basement."

"Ten to one you're spot-on, babe," Roz said, winking at me. "Now to find the staircase down."

I ignored him, not feeling up to playful banter. Another portal meant more havoc to guard against. And the Netherworld wasn't some scenic spirit amusement park. No, there were creatures there that could swallow your soul and spit it back out, blackened and empty.

Slipping past him, I motioned to Camille. "You take the right side of the hallway; I'll take the left. Peek in the door and slam it if something tries to get out. Everybody be on their guard. For all we know, we could be facing a spirit demon."

Vanzir shivered. "Could be a spirit demon. They scare the hell out of me, and *I'm* a dream chaser. Some of them eat any psychic energy in their paths, which means Morio and Camille better be alert and ready to run. If it *is* a spirit demon, whatever you do, don't let it touch you."

Camille shuddered. "Why?"

"If one touches you, they can latch onto your psyche, and you'll play hell trying to dislodge them. That's how they feed. Psychic leeches, you might call them. Only they're a damned sight smarter than any leech you'll find in a swamp, and a whole lot deadlier."

I held up my hand. "In that case, Roz, you switch places with her. Camille, I don't want you and Morio in front; you two stay back a little. I'm not taking any chances losing either of you to a spirit demon." Camille started to protest, but I waved her silent. "Listen, you're far more valuable alive than dead. Got it?"

She gave me a grin. "Got it, General. Okay, while we're

waiting, maybe Morio and I can tune in on whatever's going on. If it is a spirit demon, maybe it will sense our energy and show itself. By the way, how do you kill one of them?"

Vanzir rolled his eyes. "Don't you girls know anything about demons?" When we stared at him blankly, he shook his head. "Besides the fact that you want to kill us all? A spirit demon can be killed, but the worst way to attack it is through magic. It eats up spells like candy. They're just fuel. Silver is always good. You can actually hit them on the physical plane and it will affect them if you have a silver weapon. And an experienced enough witch can trap them—"

"Of course!" Morio snapped his fingers. "A Snare spell. If they wander into it, the energy creates a barrier they can't absorb, and yet they can't free themselves. Kind of like when a spin-bug traps a spider in its own type of web, which it attaches to the spider's guy wires and spins in a parallel direction."

I stared at him. "Spiders, huh? I don't even want to think about spiders."

Morio grinned at me. "Subject makes you a little jumpy, does it?"

I shuddered. We'd fought a bunch of werespiders some months back. Hobo werespiders, at that. I still got creeped out every time I saw a brown arachnid scuttling across the floor. Luckily, the Spider-Be-Gone spell that Queen Asteria's technomage had cast on our house was still doing the trick. The Elfin Queen knew how to pick her helpers.

"Yeah," I said. "So what's a spin-bug? I've never heard of one. We don't have them in Otherworld."

Smoky spoke up. "Spin-bugs aren't endemic Earthside, either. Nobody knows where they came from, actually, though I've heard they can be found in some of the older Fae barrows."

"That's right," Morio said. "The spin-bug's a spider-eater. It looks like a cross between a praying mantis and a centipede, and it spins a web out of its butt, just like a spider. It usually hooks its own web next to that of a spider's and waits in ambush. The spider thinks the webs are connected and tries to scuttle over to put the bite on the spin-bug. Everything looks safe enough, but the moment the spider touches the spin-bug's web, boom, it's stuck."

Camille leaned against the wall. "So the Snare spell is like the web. It looks like magical energy the spirit demon can eat, but when he gets in the middle of it, he can't touch it, and he can't get away. Essentially, he becomes a sitting duck."

"You got it," Morio said. "And then we pick him off."

"Can you cast one?" She frowned, thinking. "I have a vague idea of how it might be done, but there's no way in hell I'd trust my magic unless I knew precisely what to do. Even then, I'd be on red alert."

Morio let out a long sigh. "Theoretically. I'll need your help, and we can't do it here in the hall, and it can't be done on the run. We have to set it up somewhere quiet so I can concentrate."

"The living room?" Camille glanced back down the hall at the archway. "We could put the curtains back up to make it more inviting to those in the spook division."

The youkai gave her a nod. "Let's go—"

"Hold on!" I vigorously shook my head. "Nobody's going anywhere without group consensus. We don't even know if it's a spirit demon we're facing. What if you're wrong? What if it's something that decides to double around and take you two on while you're focused on setting up the spell?"

"What if we're right, and we have no other way to combat the creature?" Camille asked.

A sudden thump put an end to our bickering. "Oh crap, what's that?" I spun around as a second thump landed squarely on the door at the end of the hallway. It shuddered. Whatever was back there was big. At that moment, I noticed the padlock holding the door shut. The door opened out into the hallway— the hinges could easily be busted through.

"The lock looks flimsy. Maybe whatever it is, isn't so tough after all."

"Don't count your chickens," Camille said. "The lock's been charmed."

Oh hell. If it was magically enhanced, then there was no

telling what was behind the door. Whatever it was, it wanted out, and from the way the wood was splintering around the hinges, it was about to get its wish. I headed down the hall.

"Come on! That thing's coming through. Get ready." Roz and I stood in front, leaving enough space through which Morio and Camille could aim their spells. "What's a spirit demon look like, anyway?"

Vanzir pulled out a nasty-looking kris blade with a bone hilt. I flinched. That thing was likely to leave a bad scar, if it didn't cut off whatever appendage it managed to hit.

He saw my grimace and let out a snort. "What? You expect me to use silver? Or some hoity-toity fancy-assed dagger? I'm a demon, girl, even if I don't look the part. Get used to it." His gaze met mine, and his eyes swirled with a kaleidoscope of colors and took on a wild, rough look. It never failed to give me the shakes.

"Just answer me," I said over the repeated slams against the door. Either our friend's keeper was out of the house, or whatever we were about to face was being given a pep talk before being freed to attack us.

"Spirit demon. Check. The best way to differentiate between a ghost and a spirit demon is that it will have glowing eyes the color of fire. The thing has a hole—a vortex, actually—where its heart should be. The hole looks like a whirling fogbank, and it's about the size of a small melon. That's where it leeches energy. Tendrils come through the hole and fasten themselves into the aura of its victim. Holy crap, that was a big one!" He jumped as the door shuddered.

Whatever it was, it was almost through. I thought about breaking the lock to get it over with, but who knew if it had been booby-trapped? And to get close enough to break the lock would put me in the danger zone. No, better to let the mountain come to us rather than go to the mountain.

Camille apparently didn't think so, though. She moved toward the door. "Let's just get this over with."

"Stop right where you are." When she turned to look at me, I said, "Listen: I'm a werecat, right?" She nodded. "We know when to make the jump and when to sit and wait. Be patient. I know it's hard, but trust me, my instincts are not saying attack first. There's a reason that nobody's opened the lock and let it out on us."

And when I said it, I knew it was true. Whatever was behind that door was so nasty that its keeper had no intention of getting close to it. I glanced at Vanzir. "Are you sure you didn't see anything when you came spying here yesterday?"

He shook his head. "I knew this place was overrun with a bad miasma, but I had no idea there was anything like this here. I thought we were facing a bunch of venidemons and their guardian, that's all," he muttered. I could tell it bothered him that he wasn't prepared for this, so he was probably telling the truth. And he was oath-bound not to lead us into a trap. He'd be dead by now if he had lied. His symbiont collar would have strangled him.

At that moment, the door gave way to one particularly nasty thud, and we all jumped as a creature lurched out. The thing must have been a good seven feet tall at the shoulder. With three heads, it looked all too much like a very nasty mutant Rottweiler with large, bared teeth. It saw us and raised one of its heads to let loose with a long, piercing howl.

"You shall not pass," said the second head, while the third growled.

"A hellhound!" I tried to get a grip. Tabby wanted me to bolt, and Panther wanted me to tear the creature apart. I fought to stay in control and not shift.

"Crap!" Morio immediately dropped his bag and stepped back. "I'm going in as my true form. None of my spells will work against a hellhound."

As he began to shift into his full demonic form, Camille yelled out, "Hellhounds don't like the cold, either!"

Smoky pushed past her in a blur and was on the creature as I managed to bring myself back to the edge of control. The dragon's hands—now bearing long talons instead of fingernails—swiped at the three-headed dog and left a row of deep scratches along one side of the hellhound's back. As Smoky leapt away to avoid being bitten, I rushed in, my dagger raised.

The hellhound's left head—the one that had ordered us to back off—snapped at me. I managed to avoid the long teeth, but he laughed and said, "Fair meat for the children."

"Don't be so hasty, dogface!" As I headed in, I saw Morio racing by. He was a good eight feet tall in full demonic form. His eyes glistened golden topaz, and his body was lightly covered with a downy fur the color of burnished copper.

Morio's face was still close enough to his own to recognize, except his nose had lengthened and turned black and shiny. Steam puffed out of his nostrils, and a row of needle-sharp teeth gleamed as he opened his mouth. The fox demon walked on feet, not paws, and his hands were still human, though they were fully furred and tipped with curved claws. A cock the size of my favorite vibrator hung heavy from his loins.

"Holy crap," Vanzir yelled. "I wish *I* could do that!" He swung with the heavy kris, slashing at the haunches of the hellhound. He managed a strike with the last few inches of his blade.

Morio was on the hellhound now, which stood on its hind legs to engage him. Camille let out a short scream, and I saw the blur of her skirt as she raced by, her own dagger out and ready.

I took the opportunity to drop and roll, right against the hellhound's feet. One good strike, and I hamstrung his right back leg. He let out a loud yowl from his right head as I rolled away again. I came up in time to see the youkai and the hellhound in the grips of a duel to the death. The hellhound was close to Morio's demon size, and they were probably evenly matched for strength.

"Out of the way, girl!" Smoky pushed me aside and landed a long swipe of talons down the left side of the hellhound, leaving five bloody lines that dripped smoking blood to the floor, where the drops ate into the wood, leaving burn marks.

"Its blood is acidic," I shouted, spinning around to look for an opening.

Camille leapt away with a short scream, her fingers smoldering where she'd struck with her dagger and missed, hitting the side of the beast with her hand. She dropped the blade and leaned over, moaning. "Damn, it's worse than iron."

As the hellhound turned its attention to her, Smoky let out a low growl that set the entire hall to vibrating and moved in. We all edged away, recognizing his breaking point. All except Morio, who dashed forward to drag Camille out of the way.

Smoky threw back his head, his long braid coiling around his shoulders like a snake. His eyes took on the look of frozen glaciers and tundras long forgotten by the sun, and he raised his arms, letting loose a chant that was both impossible to understand and impossible to ignore.

Within seconds, the temperature of the air dropped a good thirty degrees, and his hands were vibrating, his talons gleaming like icicles. The hellhound turned away from Morio and Camille as Smoky thrust his hands forward and grabbed the sides of the center head. His face contorting, Smoky growled as the head froze—turned to pure ice—and shattered in his death grip.

The hellhound's other heads both shrieked—whether in surprise or pain I'm not sure—and it backed away, the stump of the center head covered with a frozen pool of the acidic blood. But once Smoky was pissed, he stayed pissed until the object of his anger had taken a nosedive into oblivion or until he'd decided he'd done enough damage. That much we'd learned about the dragon. And when somebody hurt Camille, there was no escaping him.

Smoky flew at the creature—a blur of white and silver—landing beside it with a heavy thud. He laughed then, his eyes crinkling in delight as he tore through the hellhound's hide, gutting it.

The hellhound let out one last howl as a cloud of smoke emerged from its belly. Within seconds, the creature, entrails and all, vanished in a puff of ashes and blood.

I stared at the spot on the floor where it had stood, then looked up at Smoky. The delight in his eyes, the joy of battle, died as quickly as it had appeared. He hurried to Camille's side as I raced over to join them. Morio was already examining her hand.

She was on the floor by now, gritting her teeth as Morio probed the wound. The acid had burnt through to the bone in one small spot. Smoky smoothed her hair as I shushed her cries.

"Damn it. I'm sorry," she said, shaking away angry tears. "I missed, and my hand landed against one of the cuts on the creature."

"Great Mother, that's a nasty wound. You can't stay here. We'll just have to come back another day—" I started to say, but she shook her head.

"No! We can't let them regroup. Find me something to wrap this up with, and I'll just stay near the back." She glanced over at Roz, who was digging through his coat. "You got any more of that salve you carry around with you?"

He held up a little jar. "Here," he said, opening it and slathering a good spoonful over the open wound. "This will stave off the worst of the pain and infection for now. Just don't get it dirty." He pulled out a small roll of gauze from another pocket and began to wrap her hand.

"You're not only a walking armory, but now you're an infirmary, too?" I couldn't help but smile. "Someday, I want to see everything you keep hidden in that coat."

He gave me a long look. "Everything?" he said softly with a smirk.

"Give me a break. You know what I meant." I let out a sigh. Once an incubus, always an incubus. He'd never change. I was just glad he was on our side. "Okay, change of plans. Camille, in back with Smoky. He can protect you best if we come across another big beastie. Morio, up front with me. Roz and Vanzir, take the middle."

Vanzir pointed at the open door where the hellhound had busted through. "All right, but I think we found our nest. This is the door to the basement, it looks like, and there's definite demonic energy radiating up the stairwell."

I peered down the stairs. The light was dim, probably only a twenty-five-watt bulb. The stairs vanished into the darkness below. The scent of dung and fetid meat and sour milk rose from the depths.

"Cripes, that's a nasty scent. My stomach's testy enough as it is," I said as I moved to the edge of the staircase. "I guess we go down?"

Vanzir nodded and handed me a broom he found in the corner. "You might want to test the way as you go, in case there are any traps or broken steps. The last thing we need is for you to go crashing down the stairs and break your neck."

With that thought to cheer me up, I grabbed the broom, and we headed into the basement, one step at a time.

CHAPTER 5

My dagger in one hand, broom in the other, I stood at the top of the steps. I gingerly tapped the first one with the handle of the broom. The light flickered, the bulb old and ready to die. I glanced back at Morio, who followed me.

"Do you have a light spell in case that bulb goes out? I don't want to go plunging into dark water, so to speak." Truth was, I didn't want to go down into this basement at all. For one thing, I was worried about Camille. For another, the thought of taking on poisonous creepy-crawlies didn't interest me at all. Especially not after our run-in with the Hunters Moon Clan a few months ago. And third, well, I was hungry. My stomach rumbled at that moment, as if punctuating my thoughts. I ignored it.

Morio nodded. "I can use my fox fire. But if the light goes, everybody stop where you are. I can't very well cast a spell while I'm tumbling down the steps."

"Good point." I cleared my throat and glanced over my shoulder. "Well, here goes nothing." I put my foot on the first step. A little squeak, but nothing too terribly untoward. I gathered my breath and tapped the second stair. The third. The fourth. I was about to tap on the fifth when the light suddenly vanished. The bulb had burnt out.

"Everybody stand still." Morio's voice came out of the darkness.

I felt like I was poised on the edge of a chasm. The stairway into the basement was well over fifteen stairs down, because that's as far as I could see when the light was still flickering. There might be another door waiting for us, or maybe a hallway or maybe a guard lurking in the depths below. I tried to reach out, to sense danger, but all of my senses were on overload.

Morio shouted and the dark well exploded into light as a green phosphorescence flickered from a foot-long wooden dowel he was holding. It lit up the passage a little better than the dim bulb had, though everything took on an eerie hue. I grimaced, thinking about all the late-night monster movies I'd made Menolly sit through with me. What we were facing was ten times worse, but still, images of nubile young women creeping down into underground tombs without a stitch of protection plagued me.

As I tapped my way down the next ten stairs, I had to duck my head as I passed beneath a crosshatch of beams that stretched over the stairwell to form a low overhead. I was the tallest one here except for Smoky—and Morio, in his demonic form. My head almost skimmed the bottom of one of the beams. Roz was two inches shorter than me, and Camille and Vanzir quite a bit shorter than that.

"Heads up," I called back. "Low beam—watch yourself." As I ducked to avoid another, a cobweb dangling from the beam brushed against my shoulders, tickling my neck. As the hanging dust catcher caught me off-guard, I let out a little shriek.

"Holy crap. *Spiders.* What the hell are they doing here? I hate spiders." Truth was, I was on the verge of developing arachnophobia.

"What kind of webs?" Camille said from the back.

"The wrong kind," I said grimly. "Keep your eyes peeled for hobo spiders."

Morio grunted. "This is their kind of hangout, all right. I thought most of the Hunters Moon Clan was dead, though."

We'd fought a powerful clan of werespiders not long back. Though we'd tried to take them all out, no doubt some had escaped, and they weren't likely to be very happy with us.

"We can't be too sure about that. Just keep your eyes peeled."

As we descended into the lower region of the basement, more steps came in view and, about eight more feet down, a door at the end of the stairwell. Nestled next to the door was an alcove. I could already smell the stench of rotting meat coming from it. It was of the size and shape to house the hellhound, and a thick silver chain told me that the creature had served as a guard dog. The chain was smooth, the links strong and unbroken. Somebody had unleashed him to come after us. Whatever it was hadn't stuck around to open the door at the top of the stairs. I figured they were probably as scared of their sentinel as we had been.

The door itself looked reinforced. As I neared it, the energy reached out and slapped me in the face. Hell. The door had some sort of heavy iron alloy in it—too much for our comfort zone.

"Crap. Iron. I can't touch it. Camille can't, either. Morio, what about you?" I paused on the step, not wanting to go any farther until we'd decided what we were going to do about it.

Morio stared at it. "I shouldn't have any problem with iron. Smoky?"

"I'd like to see the piece of iron that could stop me," said Smoky, his voice low.

I stared at him for a moment. "Pretty sure of yourself, aren't you?"

He sent a frozen glance my way. "Are you questioning me?"

Backpedal time. "Nope, nope . . . not in the least." Camille's husband or not, he was still quite capable of smashing little—or big—kitty cats, and I had no desire to put his patience to the test. Unnerved by the entire afternoon, I turned to Roz. "And you?"

"Well, I bloody well don't like iron, but I'm not going to fry from it. At least not now," Roz said. He edged his way past me and bent to study the lock.

I turned to Vanzir, and he shook his head. "Demons like

iron. We use it a lot, actually, down in the Subterranean Realms. Iron, lead, uranium . . ."

"What?" Smoky sputtered. "You have uranium down there?"

Vanzir shrugged. "It's like a drug for some demons. We resonate with the energy, though I don't miss it all that much. Most of us are immune to its dangers. Some demons are hooked on it, and there are even uranium Elementals that wizards have managed to conjure out from the metal."

I blinked twice. Uranium Elementals? Great, that's all we needed over Earthside: a bunch of crazed uranium Elementals running around poisoning people. "Lovely . . . just lovely."

Roz suddenly stood up. "I can blow this lock."

"Won't that bring the house down on us?" This day was just getting better and better.

"Not if I use just the right amount of explosives. I suggest that you turn away, though. There's bound to be smoke and a little shrapnel. In fact, maybe you'd better retreat up the stairs a little ways." He opened his duster and pulled out two smalls vials, one filled with black powder, another with red. "Myocian powder and alostar compound," he said, noticing my gaze.

I immediately motioned everybody up the stairs. "Go halfway up," I said, pushing against Morio's back. Myocian powder and its companion, alostar compound, were made by the dwarves in the Nebelvuori Mountains back in Otherworld and had all the perks of gunpowder. When mixed in just the right proportion, it was extremely volatile. A single tap from a pen-sized mallet could set it off.

When I was a little girl, I'd seen a dwarf who lost his leg to a myocian land mine. The goblins had been using them in a crusade against the dwarves. The dwarves had opened up bounty season on goblin skulls, and shortly thereafter, the goblins had withdrawn their efforts to infringe on dwarven lands. The land mines ended up as a tool for mining operations.

"Where in the world did you get that crap?" Camille said, wincing as she leaned against Smoky's shoulder. It was obvious she was in pain, but I knew she'd refuse to leave until we were finished.

"I picked them up in a little mining shop in Terial. They have everything you could hope to purchase to make your spelunking adventures complete." He laughed, shooting a smoldering glance her way. "I like spelunking, if you know what I mean—" Smoky glowered, and Roz lowered his eyes. "Uh . . . never mind."

"That's better," Smoky said, relaxing a little as he sat down on the step behind him and pulled Camille onto his lap. She winced, then rested her head on his shoulder.

Roz finished shaking a few of the grains of the black powder into the lock, then cautiously added a pinch of the red. He took out a thin, pencil-length rod, and with a shake of the hand, it expanded to four feet long. It was narrow but solid, and as he backed away to the bottom of the stairs, he reached out and delicately aimed toward the keyhole.

"I get it," I said. "I see what you're doing."

"Yes, well, I strongly advise everybody to turn around. You don't want to be facing this direction when it blows." He twisted at the waist, turning his face toward the stairs, and we heard the scrape of metal on metal. There was a sudden hush, then a loud explosion, and the stairwell filled with dark, greasy smoke.

Coughing, I turned around. "Eww . . . that's nasty." The residue from the smoke began to settle on our clothes, leaving an oily silt behind. But the door was unlocked and standing ajar. I glanced back at Smoky. Spotless. As usual. "How the hell do you do it?" I asked.

He gave me a puzzled look. "Do what?"

"The coat, the jeans, the shirt . . . you're never dirty. You never get muddy, dusty, filthy, or, apparently, oily. What the hell kind of laundry detergent do you use?" I stared down at my own jeans, which now sported several lovely looking grease spots. "I want some of it."

He just grinned, saying nothing as he helped Camille to her feet, and they started down the stairs. "Why do you suppose nobody's come after us?" he asked, his smile fading. "We've made more noise than a band of drunken Vikings on a rape-and-pillage mission."

"And just what was the hellhound doing?" I started to ask, but Vanzir shook his head and held up his hand.

"He's right. And my only answer is that I don't think there *is* anybody here to stop us. I think there's some sort of revenant or specter protecting the venidemons, watching over them as they hatch. I'm figuring we're heading into a nursery. Want to make a bet they were counting on the hellhound to stop anybody trying to get through?" Vanzir studied the hallway. "There's demonic energy coursing down the hall like a river gone wild."

Camille closed her eyes, then shuddered. "Vanzir's right. It's undulating like a wave. There's demonic energy everywhere down here."

"Then we'd better get a move on. If you're right," I said, looking at the dream chaser, "then the protector of those venidemons is waiting for us at the end of the road. Along with the venidemons themselves."

"Remember, they're dangerous even when just hatched. They may not be able to inject their eggs at larval stage, but they can still do a lot of damage," he said. "Whoever has the cold spells ought to go in front with you."

"I don't want to leave Camille unprotected," Smoky said.

Morio turned to him. "I'll watch out for her. You're needed up here." When Smoky hesitated, he added, "I'm her husband, too. You know I'll protect her with my life."

Camille let out a long sigh. "Get up there with Delilah, you butthead. Morio can help me." When Smoky didn't budge, she added, "I'll be all right. I'm not stupid enough to put myself in the front lines as wounded as I am, but I'm not in danger of keeling over this second. Yeah, my hand burns like hell, but I'm not dying."

He gave a resigned shrug and then traded places with Morio.

"Butthead?" I mouthed, flashing him a wide grin.

Smoky snorted. "What can I say? You know Camille."

Suddenly, I missed having Chase with us. Missed the usual comfort of our relationship. I bit my lip. Every couple went through hard times; I'd learned that by watching Camille and her lovers. But right now, I envied her easy ways and confidence. I had no idea what I was doing. I tried my best, but being part of a couple was still new to me.

Hell, *I* was still new to me. Since our visit to the Autumn Lord, everything in my world had gone topsy-turvy, and it seemed like the rules changed every time I turned around. One thing was for sure, though. Chase and I were going to have a long talk after this mess with the venidemons was over, and that included him telling me about Erika.

Shaking off my frustration, I turned to the others. "Are we ready?" Everybody nodded. "Then let's get a move on."

Vanzir pushed the iron door open, holding it wide. After we all filed through, he slowly eased it shut behind us and caught up to the front.

The corridor through which we crept was dark, but thanks to Morio and his fox fire, we could see to the end where the passage turned to the right. I soon realized this wasn't just a basement. It looked like a network of tunnels and had probably been added long after the main house was built. Which meant that one of Shadow Wing's scouts probably bought this place and turned it into a hideout for his network of spies to use for . . . well . . . whatever they were up to.

The walls of the passage were damp and slick with mildew. While the tunnel itself wasn't heated, I could sense a heat source emanating from somewhere up ahead. As we neared the end of the passage, I motioned for everyone to stop and crept forward to the edge, where I peeked around the corner.

About fifteen feet farther, the tunnel came to an end. Directly at the end was a door, this one iron, too, and that's where the heat was emanating from. I swung around the corner and led them down the hall.

Vanzir placed his hand on the iron. I winced, but he seemed okay with it. "Behind that door—the venidemons are there."

"Roz, you're going to have to get us through that door. And when we meet up with the specter or whatever's guarding them, be on the alert. A run-of-the-mill ghost wouldn't bother us, so it's got to be something worse. And with that portal to the Netherworld, you know it's going to be nasty. The hellhound could have come from either the Subterranean Realms or the Netherworld, so . . ."

Roz glanced at Smoky. "There's one way we can get the jump on them. But I don't know if Smoky's willing to do it. I'll give it a go—but then again, we have no way of knowing what we'd be getting into."

"What do you mean?" I glanced around at the dragon, confused. "What's he talking about?"

Smoky eyed Roz with a cool stare. "Surely you jest. Without knowing what's on the other end, we could be dropping them into a lake of molten lava, or a nest of larvae where they'd be immediately attacked."

Camille let out a little gasp. "So that's how you get around so fast," she said to Roz. "I knew about Smoky but . . . how can you . . ."

Smoky cut her off. "Enough. We're not attempting it, so let it drop for now." I was about to say something, but he shook his head at me. "Save your questions for later. Rozurial, attend to the door. If you don't, then I'll remove the impediment."

Roz gave him a shake of the head. "You're too full of yourself. Never mind!" He held up his hands when Smoky took a step forward. "I'll take care of the door. No problem. No worry." He pulled out his vials of myocian powder and alostar compound.

"You've been holding out on me," I whispered to Camille. "You care to dish it up later? That is, if you can tear yourself away from Moe and Curly here."

"Sure thing. It just never came up until now." She winced, clutching her hand again. "Shit, this hurts. I just want to take care of those bugs and get the hell out of here."

I glanced at Roz, who was backing up, his extendable rod in hand. "I think you're about to get your wish. Battle order: Smoky and me, Roz and Vanzir, Morio and Camille."

Just then an explosion rocked the hallway.

"Stand to the side," Smoky ordered, throwing the door wide. By the force in his voice, I knew he meant business. We all jumped to the side as a huge gust of wind came rattling

down the hall from behind us, following him into the room.
There was a loud screech, and then the smell of ozone filled
the air and I saw snowflakes swirling out the door.

I raced in after him. Smoky must have cast some sort of
freeze spell, because the minute I entered the room, I saw a layer
of snow and frost dusting what looked to be a dozen nests across
the floor, all filled with venidemons in various stages of growth.
Some were wriggling larvae, like giant tube worms from the
ocean's depths. Others were full-grown blowflies, and I saw that,
indeed, they were as big as my head. They all moved sluggishly,
though, and I saw a couple try to go airborne, but they couldn't
seem to flutter their wings fast enough to gain any height.

A deep chill ran through my body as if I'd just walked into
a freezer. Smoky's spell must have dropped the temperature to
thirty degrees, and it had managed to slow the venidemons.
How long it would last, I didn't know. I suspected we were on
borrowed time, but for now, it gave us the advantage.

A glance told me the chamber we were in was large and
built of solid steel. It was lit by the glow from a granite slab
that rested in the center of the floor. The rock was glowing
orange, and I knew without a doubt that if I touched it, I'd burn
my hand to a crisp. The slab wasn't molten, but looked well on
its way. The chill had overcome it for now, though, and the heat
was sputtering, trying to melt the frost surrounding it.

A shallow pit had been dug next to the granite, and inside
the pit was a jumbled mishmash of remains. Remains of
what—or rather, *who*—I didn't know, but a tennis shoe rested
near a pile of bones that were still covered with all too juicy
bits of flesh and muscle still attached. There were other
tattered remnants of clothing, and other bones—some cleaned
to a high sheen, others still ripe—and I fought back my urge to
empty my queasy stomach.

"There goes my appetite," I muttered.

A shift in the light caught my attention, and I turned,
dagger raised. The silhouette of a man was headed our way.
He was almost invisible, and would be if he turned sideways.
In the flickering of Morio's fox fire, I spied the barest glimmer
of a face in the inky depths of the shadow. Skeletal, it was
frozen in a steady stare aimed directly at me.

"Great Mother Bast. It's a revenant!" I whispered a quick prayer to the Mother of all Catkind for protection as I backed up, bumping into Roz, who was standing right behind me.

Smoky let out a long breath. "The cold won't stop him. He'll just find the frost a nice change."

Rare entities, revenants tended to inhabit the Netherworld and Earthside haunts more than Otherworld ruins, but I knew what they were and what havoc they could wreak. A single touch from one was enough to give an FBH a heart attack. While they didn't have the same effect on the Fae, they were capable of doing significant damage.

Camille glanced at me, then at the shadow. "What can we do?" she whispered, her voice raspy with fear. She glanced at Morio.

He grabbed her good hand. *"Reverente destal a Mordenta."*

She nodded and placed her feet square, sliding her injured hand inside the pocket of her skirt. I wondered if she was looking for the unicorn horn, but when Morio began a low incantation and she fell in sync with him, I knew they were up to some sort of death magic.

Smoky looked ready to pull her away, and I grabbed the sleeve of his jacket. He swung on me, his eyes narrowing, but I pointed toward the shade. "We need all the help we can get. Do something—anything! I've got nothing. I'm no good against these things."

Roz was frantically pawing through his duster. Vanzir pushed his way between the revenant, which was headed my way, and me. "It can't really hurt me that much," he said over his shoulder. "Stay behind me."

I let out a long breath, hoping that we could dispatch the spirit before the venidemons cleared the frost out of their brains. Fighting both at once would be a disaster.

Smoky glanced at me as I pointed toward the nests. One of the flies had shaken off the snow and was almost aloft. He shook his head. "I can't use that spell again for a while. Weather magic is taxing, especially in my human form. I'll attack it if it comes this way."

He was nervous. The thought that something might actually frighten the dragon hadn't occurred to me before, but one look at his face told me his fear was for us, not himself. And *that* made me downright terrified.

Just then Vanzir whirled and shoved me back, sending me careening across the room. I blinked. What the fuck? And then I saw that the revenant had attacked him, trying to reach around to grab hold of me. As he grappled with the shadow, his arms went through it, and the spirit darted around him and once again was heading my way.

Cripes! I steadied myself and looked for a place to run. Why was it so interested in me, anyway? What the hell was so special about me? As it bore down, Smoky raced by and took a swipe at it, but his taloned hand just flew through the revenant, too. And then I was facing it—the creature from the Netherworld. As it reached out, I heard Camille scream, and everything began to grow fuzzy. Something was happening to me. The room went caving in as my body contorted, twisting in on itself, folding, melting, re-forming into new bone and muscle and sinew.

And then I found myself on all fours—four big black feet, four silken furred legs—and my breath came thick and frozen in the chilled room.

And *he* was standing behind me, his jet hair streaming down his shoulders as a woven garland of burnished maple leaves flamed in a wreath around his head. His eyes were as I remembered them: twin diamonds in a black velvet tapestry. His cape—covered with a kaleidoscope of leaves and flame— fluttered around his black boots. Frost fell from his heels, and the scent of graveyard dust and old books and crackling bonfires embraced me. He tightened his grip on a silver chain that I now realized was attached to a collar. *My collar.*

The Autumn Lord turned to the revenant, who cowered in his presence. "Down, dog," he said, and his voice rocked the room. "My Death Maidens are not for the likes of you."

As the spirit backed away, I glanced up at my master, and he leaned down. "Delilah, my dear one. I have a task for you. And no specter from beyond the grave is going to interfere." With a rough laugh, the Autumn Lord waved his hand, and the shadow vanished in a shriek of twisting color.

CHAPTER 6

A job? Through the heady scents that buffeted my senses, the words echoed in my ears. And then I felt myself begin to shift again. Within seconds, I was standing before the Autumn Lord in a cloud of mist and sparkling smoke. I couldn't see the others, but from experience, I knew they were there, that we'd just shifted into a slightly different dimension.

After I'd regrouped from the sudden shift into panther form and back, I looked up at the Autumn Lord. Elemental Lords were always tall, it seemed, always towering above even someone of my height.

I hadn't actually seen the Autumn Lord, except in dreams, since I'd faced down and defeated Kyoka, a thousand-year-old evil werespider shaman. I genuflected. After all, though not my own choice, the fact was the Lord of Autumn was my new master, and I bore a tattoo in the shape of a black scythe on my forehead that linked us, that would forever remind me of it. I owed him respect.

"I'm not sure what to call you," I said.

He gazed down at me, a strange light dancing over his face. From this angle, he was handsome, darkly enticing, and I felt my breath flutter in my lungs. Was this why his Death

Maidens who served him after their deaths were also his wives? Charisma, he had, but it was entwined with such otherworldliness that I couldn't even consider whether he was handsome or not.

"No one knows my name, not a name such as you have, but I will give you one you may use. For your lips and my ears only." He leaned over, and his lips grazed my ear, sending a shiver of fear through me that almost verged on arousal. "You may call me Hi'ran," he said, then brushed his fingers across my lips.

I could barely breathe as the cold chill of his flesh sent sparks through my body. "Hi'ran," I repeated, mesmerized by the feel of his touch. I opened my mouth, just enough for his finger to graze the inside of my lip.

"Hush and listen. You will never speak my name to another living soul, nor to any who are dead or walking beyond the grave. It is your link to me and exists only between the two of us."

As he spoke, a mist drifted out from his fingers and entered my lips, and I felt it swirl in my mouth, the taste of cigar smoke and brandy and crackling hearth flames. I sucked it deep into my lungs, and the energy flowed through my body, heightening all of my senses. I wanted to fall into his arms, to feel his lips on mine. He was so alien and yet so seductive. And then the mist seeped into my throat and onto my tongue, and I knew I'd never be able to say his name aloud to anybody, nor write it down, nor transfer it in thought. It was our secret—and ours alone—and would remain hidden for the rest of my life.

And then he pulled away. I couldn't tell if he'd felt the same desire as I had, but he raked his gaze slowly over my body, then settled on my face again. "I have a task for you. You are to journey back to your homeland—to the forest of Darkynwyrd—and there you must search for the panther's fang."

Panther's fang? Darkynwyrd? I frowned. This wasn't sounding so much fun after all. Darkynwyrd was a feral woodland back in Otherworld, where not-so-nice creatures made their home. It wasn't on my list of must-see places.

"What's the panther's fang?"

Hi'ran gave me a soft smile. "*Panteris phir*. An herb endemic to the forest there. You will bring it home with you and plant it in your garden. Tend to it, nurture it, and once a month, under the new moon, make a cup of tea from it and drink it. This will aid you in controlling your shifts into panther form as the herb builds up in your system." He backed away. "Do this before the next new moon. And remember, Delilah. You are bound to me. You are the first of my living emissaries."

With that, he vanished, and I found myself standing among the others. They were in the midst of fighting the venidemons, and suddenly Camille, who had been relegated to standing beside the door, shouted, "She's back to herself!"

I was about to say something when a buzzing echoed on my right. I swung around to find myself facing a full-grown venidemon. It was hovering near my face, and I saw its abdomen curve under, its stinger ready to jab as it aimed for my chest.

Holy crap—maybe Hi'ran had eliminated the shade, but apparently he trusted we could take care of the venidemons ourselves. Time to rumble.

I snatched up my dagger and, with a loud shout, brought it down, cleaving into the rapidly approaching tail end of the venidemon. The damned sucker was tough. I couldn't slice clean through, but the gash sent the blowfly hurtling toward the floor. It let out a piercing shriek, and I stabbed it, like a kid pinning butterflies to a display table. One down, but a glance around showed me there were plenty more for the counting. I whirled just in time to take on another.

Out of the corner of my eye, I watched as the others left a trail of muck and guts as they fought their way through the demons' nests.

Smoky was making tracks through a nest of larvae, swiping with his talons at the wriggling maggots. As he sliced through them, they wailed, keening so loudly I wondered if they could be heard up on the street.

The second venidemon darted back and forth, trying to get the jump on me. Irritated, I tossed my dagger from hand to hand.

"Come on, sucker, come and get me!"

Apparently, venidemons didn't take much to goad, because it changed tactics and made a beeline straight for my side. Instinct won out, and rather than swing with my dagger, my right foot shot into the air, meeting the big bug in the face. It bounced back, but I could tell it wasn't hurt—merely stunned. I lunged for it with my dagger and met the creature square in the midsection. It went down like a fly facing a can of Raid.

"Delilah, give me a hand!"

I glanced over my shoulder to see Morio fighting off two full-size venidemons struggling to get past him to Camille. She was trying to draw down energy; by now I could tell the look on her face when she was invoking the Moon Mother. But it looked like her pain was preventing her from focusing.

"Incoming on your left," I shouted over the roar of the fight and the shrieks as the blowflies and their larvae bit the dust one by one. I took on the venidemon aiming for his left side, and he turned his attention to the one on the right. We finished them off in good time.

"How many more can there be?" Camille asked, giving up on the spell. She looked miserable, and I wished to hell she'd just back out of the room and play it safe outside.

I motioned toward the rest of the room. "Still too many."

Vanzir was battling it out with a nest of the half-grown bugs. They fell left and right as he waded in, eyes blazing, striking double-handed with a pair of serrated steel daggers that he'd unsheathed from his boots. He smashed the smallest of the venidemons under his heels, grinding them to a pulp.

Roz was fighting a trio of full-grown bugs that were trying to guard a nest of larvae. While he was holding them at bay, it was obvious we were on the losing end of the battle.

I raced over to Smoky. He'd just finished off the last of the larvae in the nest he'd been fighting. "We have to do something. There are still too many—"

He gave one quick look around the room and nodded. "Get everybody out of here. I'll take care of it. But you have to head upstairs immediately and get out of the house. Do you understand me?" As I nodded and started toward Roz, he grabbed me by the wrist. "And you damned well make sure your sister is safe. Hear me?"

I stared up into those glacial eyes and froze. Camille was as good as bought and sold. I could see it in his face. Smoky owned her. And while I had no doubt he loved my sister, there was also little doubt that *anyone* he didn't approve of would go down screaming if they hurt her.

"Let go of me, Smoky. You know I'll protect her, you idiot." I swallowed the lump forming in my throat. I couldn't let him cow me down. Camille wouldn't put up with it, and Menolly sure didn't. I wasn't about to, either.

He let go. "Of course I know that. Now move. I'll put a stop to this mess."

I raced over to Roz and grabbed his arm. "Come on." He didn't question me, just turned and followed, dodging to avoid the venidemons now swarming toward us. Vanzir saw me run past and with a quick look at Smoky, joined us. Morio was already guiding Camille down the hall toward the stairs. As we passed the room with the portal, I glanced in and saw glowing eyes peering from out of the swirling vortex, but we didn't have time to stop. Whatever Smoky had planned was going to be good, I thought. Good and probably explosive, considering *who* he was. Or *what*, rather.

We weren't disappointed. We'd just reached the top of the stairs when the floor began to roll in waves under our feet. The house shook like we were on Earthquake Alley. We were, actually—the whole area was geologically unstable, and there were volcanoes aplenty around to prove it—but I knew this wasn't an actual temblor. A dragon quake, yes.

"Head for the door," Morio yelled over the sound of the freight train that was our deliciously gorgeous dragon hunk.

As he swept Camille into his arms—she was stumbling now, the pain and the quake threw her off balance—I wondered just how far Smoky was going to go. It felt like he was ready to pull the rafters down.

Roz and Vanzir brought up the rear, making sure we were all on the front lawn. Roz pushed Vanzir toward us, then raced back up to the front door. "I'm going back to help him."

"Don't be a fool! You'll be crushed." I shook my head, pointing to the spot beside me. "Get out of there now, Roz!"

"Quit worrying about me. Look after your sister." He vanished back inside. I was about ready to follow him when Camille grabbed my arm. For someone about ready to faint, she was pretty damned strong.

"Leave them. They both can escape easy enough." She moaned, holding the wrist of her hurt hand. I sat beside her. The ground was still trembling, but from where we sat, the waves were weaker. Whatever Smoky was doing was muffled by the dirt.

I unwrapped the makeshift bandage Roz had applied. The wound was festering, despite the salve he put on it. "You're infected. We have to get you home. In fact, I've got half a mind to run you over to the FH-CSI medical lab. The elves can probably cure this faster than Iris."

I peered closer at the wound. Yep, right to the bone, and it looked nasty. Thank the gods this hadn't been inflicted by the venidemons, or she'd have a nasty batch of eggs in there by now.

"I think I'll take you up on that," she said, wincing as I replaced the bandage.

"What did you mean—they can both escape easy enough? What do you know that I don't?" I peered at her. She blushed. Yeah, she was holding out on me. "Tell me, or I'll tell Smoky that you kissed Roz." I was joking, but she paled.

"Oh Great Mother, don't do that! Smoky would kill him! And then he'd . . . well . . . never mind."

She backtracked so fast I knew something was up, but she didn't look afraid. More like embarrassed? Camille didn't embarrass easily, which meant Smoky had found a way to corral her—not an easy task. I decided to let it go.

Finally she sighed. "Don't say a word. This news could be used against them, and we may need it as a secret tactic someday. Smoky travels through the Ionyc Sea. That's how he gets around so fast. And Roz apparently knows how Smoky gets around and does the same. He tried to encourage Smoky to take us all in through the iron door that way."

"The Ionyc Sea? That's what that was all about? I had no

idea. Kind of scary . . . wait a minute! Oh Great Mother, has Smoky taken you through the Ionyc current?" The thought of traveling through the astral worlds like that terrified me. The energy was so volatile, like riding through a patch riddled with land mines.

The Ionyc Sea wasn't exactly on the astral, but it held the astral, etheric, and several other planes of existence together, yet created a buffer zone so they'd never merge. If the differing energy fields clashed, it could cause a major explosion on the scale of creating a black hole, or—if enough of the energy collided—a black-hole universe. Think differing forms of antimatter and matter coming into contact . . . so not good, according to Captain Kirk as well as the elementalist wizards we'd grown up listening to.

The Ionyc Sea was harsh, and few creatures could traverse it. Some, especially those who wielded the forces of ice and snow, could create barriers around themselves and swim through it, stepping outside of time.

She nodded. "It's not so bad. Rather strange, actually. He was very careful, though. Nothing to worry about."

"And Rozurial can travel through the Ionyc Sea, too? That makes sense in a weird way." I frowned, wondering what else our wonder boys had up their sleeves.

"Yeah, though I have no idea how he manages it," she added, leaning against my shoulder. I put my arm around her and held her tight. "He's a demon—an incubus. I don't know enough about the Ionyc Sea to know what gives him the strength to forge—"

She was cut off by a sudden roar as the house imploded on itself. As we watched, the walls and roof came crashing down, tumbling into a chasm as the ground around it opened up. I leapt up and pulled Camille to her feet. Along with Vanzir and Morio, we made tracks across the street to where our cars were, staring at the gaping hole that was covered with dust. A moment later, fire erupted and blazed into the sky. The gas mains must have burst, or at least sprung a leak.

"Smoky!" Camille cried out, but I held her back when she would have gone running toward the fire.

"I'm right here. Don't worry yourself," Smoky said,

stepping out from behind the car. He hadn't been there a moment before, and neither had Roz, but now the incubus joined the dragon. Smoky opened his arms, and I gently pushed Camille into his embrace. He folded her inside his coat—clean and tidy as always—and kissed her head softly. "You were worried about me?" he whispered.

She nodded and blubbered something I couldn't make out. As I turned away to watch what was left of the house burn, Roz sidled up beside me.

"I wish somebody would worry about me like that," he said, a grin on his face.

"Try again, you liar. You know you aren't cut out for a steady girlfriend." But I flashed him a return smile. "What about the portal?"

"We put a temporary seal on it. Aimed the gas pipe directly at it and lit the fuse. The Netherworlds are cold—icy cold. The fire from the gas acted to . . . well . . . almost cauterize it. It won't hold, but for now, it's shut." He glanced over at Smoky. "The big doofus isn't so bad, once you get to know him," he added.

I thwacked him on the nose. "Yeah, just don't try to pick up his wife, and you'll be safe." With one last look around—the sound of sirens was growing louder—I motioned to the cars. "Come on, let's get the hell out of here. We're heading to the FH-CSI. I want them to check out Camille's hand. Everybody's going, so nobody run off anywhere."

As we drove away, it occurred to me that we still didn't know who was responsible for opening the gate for the venidemons, but thanks to our little altercation, I now had a new task, one that I didn't dare ignore: go to Otherworld and find myself a *Panteris phir* plant. Joy of joys. I wasn't a gardener at heart, but maybe Iris could help me keep it alive.

I glanced in the rearview mirror, making sure that Morio, who was driving now, was keeping up with us. A flash—brief as quicksilver—and I was staring at the Autumn Lord, then the mirror showed only road and Camille's Lexus again.

Hi'ran might not be a demanding master yet. But my master he was, whether or not I wanted it that way. I'd damned well better get used to it. Avatars of Death generally didn't take no for an answer. But Hi'ran . . . the memory of his fingers on my lips stayed with me, and I could still taste the mist that had tied my tongue. Once again, the thought of sliding into his arms crept through the back of my mind, but I pushed it away. Didn't I already have enough trouble on my plate without inviting Death to play footsie?

CHAPTER 7

By the time we pulled into the parking lot at the Faerie-Human Crime Scene Investigations offices, I'd shaken off my daydreams about the Autumn Lord and was focused on getting help for Camille. We headed toward the building. Halfway there, Camille collapsed. I knelt down, pressing the back of my palm against her forehead.

"She's got a fever. Get her inside!"

Smoky swept her up and with long strides headed into the building. I was right on his heels, along with Morio. Vanzir chose to wait in the car, along with Roz. We raced through the front entrance where Yugi—a Swedish empath recently promoted to lieutenant—caught sight of us. One look at Camille, and he waved us through.

The morgue was in the basement, three stories belowground, but the healing facilities were on the main floor. As we rounded the corner into the medical wing, the receptionist caught sight of us. She was a youngish woman who looked fully human, but somewhere a few generations back, one of her ancestors had been an Earthside Fae. She punched a button and called for Sharah over the intercom. Sharah came running out of the break room.

"Exam Room One," Sharah said, dashing ahead of us. We followed her into the sterile room. It was painted a pale green, which was supposed to be soothing but just made me depressed.

Smoky laid Camille on the table while Sharah washed her hands and slipped on a pair of nonlatex gloves. Latex bothered her skin, as it did many of the elves. "What happened?"

"She was attacking a hellhound when some of his blood got on her. Her hand's been burned through to the bone on the side." I hovered, worried. "She wouldn't leave until we finished mopping up the joint, even though I tried to get her to back off."

Sharah glanced up at me. "That sounds about right," she said as she unwrapped the bandage. The wound was really festering now, and pus oozed out of the deep hole. "Mother Arachne, look at that."

"Will she be okay?" Smoky asked from the foot of the table, arms crossed, a pensive look on his face. Morio stood beside him.

"She probably fainted from the pain. I imagine it must be incredibly bad, considering the look of this wound. Did you know that the acid in the hellhound's blood is used by the dwarves up in the Nebelvuori Mountains to etch designs on their magical swords?" She glanced up at us. "It's a prized commodity there. You could have made a small fortune if you'd managed to gather the creature's blood before it vanished."

"We weren't exactly thinking along monetary lines," I said.

Camille began to stir as Sharah cleansed the wound, lowering the injured hand into a basin that contained some sort of foaming solution. Wisps of white smoke curled up as it bubbled around the wound. "I hear you," she said. "The infection is topical—on the surface. I don't think it's had time to work its way into her bloodstream. She's a lucky woman," she added, glancing up at me. "Another half hour, and she'd be on her way to dead. And a very painful death it would be."

Suddenly feeling faint, I leaned back against the wall. It hadn't occurred to me that the wound could be fatal. Painful, yes. Disfiguring perhaps. Fatal had never entered my mind. Smoky blanched, turning pasty white, and Morio caught his breath with a sharp hiss.

As Sharah inspected the deep hole in Camille's hand, my sister stirred and moaned. Her eyes fluttered open, and she blinked, looking confused.

"Hush," Sharah said. "You fainted from the pain, but you're going to be okay. Now, if you'd just tell your doting husbands and sister to get the hell out of here, I can take care of this a lot better without them hovering over my shoulder." She flashed us a grin but nodded toward the door. "Get moving. She's going to be okay, though she'll have to wear a dressing for a while. She may end up with a nasty scar, but she'll be all right."

Before I could get to her, Smoky brushed past the elf and leaned over, planting a long, gentle kiss on Camille's lips. "I'll be right outside," he murmured. Not to be outdone, Morio followed suit.

As they reluctantly left, I brushed Camille's hair away from her head and kissed her forehead. "Get better. I'm going to go find Chase. I'll be back in a little while." I headed for the door, adding, "If she gives you any guff, Sharah, just let me know."

Sharah laughed. "No problem. Go on now. I think Chase is in his office."

With a last look at Camille, who looked totally out of it, I swung out the door and headed back to the waiting room. Smoky and Morio were sitting on one of those uncomfortable, too-low sofas you always find in hospitals. They were talking in hushed whispers. I gave them the thumbs-up and headed through the labyrinth of hallways to Chase's office.

The knowledge that Camille was going to be okay lightened my mood. I felt ready to have a long talk with Chase. We would work through whatever was bothering him. I'd never been in a relationship before, except with other cats when I was in cat form. Cat connections are of an altogether different nature. Considering that I was involved with an FBH, I thought I was handling things pretty well, though I knew Menolly didn't think we had a chance. Camille kept whatever she felt to herself.

Chase's door was closed, and I barged in without knocking, like I'd done so many times before. "Hey love, surprise!"

What I saw stopped me cold. I started to sweat, my hand still on the doorknob. A lovely brunette, petite with big boobs and dressed to kill in what was probably some designer getup, was sitting on his desk, her legs spread wide, with Chase standing between them. His left arm encircled her waist, while his right hand stroked her clit. His pants were down around his feet, and he was sliding his cock into her pussy. At the sound of my entrance, he thrust so hard she let out a little shriek.

"What the *fuck* is going on?" I heard the sound of my voice before I realized I'd said anything.

"Oh God, I'm coming!" The woman dropped her head back and let out a long moan as Chase jerked around, his eyes wide and frightened. The woman pulled him tighter, writhing against him.

Chase quickly disentangled himself, trying to straighten his jacket. His penis poked through. He obviously still had the boner from hell.

"Who is she? Tell me!" As I swung toward her, the woman scrambled off the desk, tugging at her skirt hem. She smoothed it out, but not before I'd had a chance to catch a glimpse of bare butt, a sight I really didn't need at the moment. She gave me a satisfied smirk.

"This isn't . . ." Chase started to say, then stopped. He hung his head. "I'm not going to lie to you. This is exactly what it looks like. This is Erika. She's . . . we were engaged five years ago."

Chase had told me he'd never had a serious relationship. Apparently he'd forgotten that little fact. So, lie number one.

Furious, unsure what to say, I just stared at the two of them. Erika patted her hair back into place, now looking bored and vaguely annoyed. Chase was staring at me, his dark eyes haunted and luminous.

I wanted to run over and throw my arms around him, to beat the crap out of Erika, to stake my claim. But the truth was, I didn't have any right to do that. I'd slept with Zachary, the werepuma. But Chase had said I was enough for him. He'd never mentioned wanting somebody else. He'd lied to me. And I hated liars.

After a moment, I found my voice. "How long has this been going on?"

Chase dropped into the chair next to his desk. He looked over at Erika. "Maybe you'd better leave. I need to talk to Delilah."

She gave me a snotty look, then picked up her handbag and swished out the door. "Call me when you're ready for dinner," she said over her shoulder, and I knew she wasn't talking to me.

I waited till she'd closed the door behind her and then turned back to Chase. "When were you going to tell me about her?"

He squirmed. "I don't know. Maybe never. She's leaving at the end of the month. I'm sorry you had to find out this way, honey."

"Don't you *honey* me," I whispered, wondering if Mother had ever gone through this with Father. We girls had always assumed he'd been faithful, and Mother had never given us reason to doubt him. But I'd just learned a painful lesson about assumptions, and it made me question a lot of things I'd believed.

Father was full-blooded Fae, and the Fae were seldom monogamous. Had our parents had their bouts of jealousy and temptation? Father was a handsome man, it was hard to believe no woman had ever tried to entice him away.

Chase gulped. "Erika came into town a few weeks ago. She called me. I haven't seen her in years, and I thought we'd just have dinner and let it go at that. But she said she was sorry she'd let me go. She missed me. I *told* her I was involved with you, but she didn't care. She came here for lunch the next day . . . and . . . things . . . just escalated."

I tried to control my voice, to remain calm. "Do you love her?"

He jerked his head up. "*Love* her? No . . . no. Whatever love I felt for Erika vanished a long time ago. She's just . . . I was so horny, and you were . . ."

"And I was what? Conveniently not around? Did it ever occur to you that you could call me to come over here for a quickie at lunch? You know I would have." Now I *was* mad. He couldn't even come up with a good excuse.

When he didn't answer, I slammed my hand into the wall, taking care not to leave a dent. "So you're telling me you've been fucking her because it's too much trouble to call me? That you're just too horny to wait for me to drive over? Spare me!" I shook my head as the tears threatened to well up. Angry at myself for caring, I dashed them away. "At least I had the guts to tell you about Zachary right after it happened. And I didn't keep on fucking him."

Chase jumped up, eyes blazing. "You never promised it wouldn't happen again—"

"I told you that if it ever happened again, I'd tell you first. I'd give you the chance to decide whether you could handle it or not. I've never gone behind your back on anything—"

"Bullshit!"

"What?" I strode over to the desk until we were inches apart. "What the hell are you saying? Are you calling me a liar?"

"Get real, Delilah. You and your sisters are always hiding information from me. Or you just conveniently forget to tell me things I should know. How do you think I feel around you and your little band of superheroes? Camille and her hot studs, Menolly and her blood-crazed friends. All of you make your own rules, and every time I protest, all I hear is 'Maybe we should go home and leave the demons to you, Chase' or 'Oh, grow up and deal with it, Chase.' Do you ever *really* consult me? Do you even give a fuck about this world? Or are you just hiding out here because of the death threat your psycho queen slapped on your heads?"

I couldn't believe my ears. Did he really believe what he was saying? How could I have spent the past six months with the man and never tripped over the resentment he was spouting? Because that's what was coming to the surface. His words were tainted with it, full of anger and envy. Unable to respond, I simply stared at him. For a moment, I thought I was going to shift, and I almost welcomed the transformation, but as I stood there, I realized that nothing was going to happen.

He closed his eyes and leaned against his desk, deflating slowly. "I'm sorry. I went too far. I know you care, I know you girls have a rough time . . . I'm just . . ." Letting out a long sigh, he said, "I don't have an excuse, Delilah. I was frustrated about the way things have been going. Everything's crazy, and it all seems linked to you girls. I guess Erika . . . she reminded me of a simpler time. She was here, willing, and I wanted her. So . . . I fucked her."

Numb, unable to feel anything but a searing shame that I couldn't even understand, I sought for words, but they were scattered and would not come. Finally, I turned away.

"I've got to get out of here," I said. "Menolly will call you if something comes up. You can always call Iris or Camille. I've got to . . . I just . . . I'm going to leave, and I don't want to talk to you for a while."

"Delilah, you can't go. We have to talk about this." He ran to my side and reached out to grab my hand, but I jerked away, standing frozen. I didn't want him to touch me, didn't want to feel his hands on my skin. "Don't go. Please stay. *I'm sorry.* I'm sorry I didn't tell you."

I shook my head. Maybe he was, or maybe he was just sorry I'd caught him. Either way, I didn't want to know. Not now. Maybe not ever. "I'm going to walk out this door and down the hall. Please don't follow me."

"Delilah—no!"

As I stepped through the door, I paused, avoiding his gaze. "By the way, you should know that Camille's in the infirmary. She almost died today fighting a hellhound. And just FYI, if we didn't love our mother's world and the people in it, we would have left it long ago. We've all paid the price in pain and injuries. We face death every time we go out there."

"Delilah . . ."

His whisper broke through my anger. I whirled around, glaring at him.

"If we didn't love it here, we *would* have left it to the hellhounds and the demons and the wackos that walk the streets. The perverts Menolly takes out so they never hurt anybody again. The same ones you and your men can't catch or can't put away. So *fuck you*, Chase Johnson. Fuck you and your insecurities and your lies. You want an open relationship? Fine! You knew I wouldn't object. But I want it aboveboard and honest. At least my father's people have enough honor to tell their lovers when they take someone new. Can you say the same?"

He held out his hand. "Delilah, please . . . can't we just talk?"

I'd had enough. I wasn't sure whether it was Erika herself or the lies that bothered me more. And I knew it would take a while before I could sort everything out in my mind. If we were to have a chance, Chase and I needed a break. I shook my head.

"Maybe in a week or two. But for now, let's just call a truce. A break. As I said, phone Iris or one of the others if you need to talk to us about official business, but don't contact me. I need to think. And so do you." With that, I shut the door behind me. I cried all the way down the hall.

CHAPTER 8

~⊰≈⊱~

Camille was sitting in the waiting room with Smoky and Morio by the time I'd washed my face and composed myself. Chase hadn't come after me, and while I didn't expect him to, I halfway wished he would have.

"You guys ready? We need to get out of here." Other than my voice sounding throaty—like I'd been around too much smoke or had spent all night yowling with the neighbor cats— I didn't look any different, and I wanted it that way. I'd tell Camille everything when she felt better, but I didn't feel like exposing the situation with Chase to Smoky or Morio.

Camille took one look at me and narrowed her eyes. "What's wrong—"

Oh great gods, that intuition of hers. I flashed her a pleading look, hoping she could read my expression.

She cleared her throat. "I'm ready. I have to keep the bandage on for a week, but Sharah says I'll heal up. I can add another scar to my repertoire, though. And it's not going to be all that pretty."

"Scars or not, you're beautiful," Morio said, helping her up.

When Smoky went to carry her, she shook her head. "I'm not an invalid. I'm tired of being carted around like I broke my leg. I needed help earlier, but Sharah cleaned out the wound and used a healing powder on it, and she also gave me a much-needed boost of energy in the form of zaybarz."

Zaybarz . . . yum . . . they were delicate elfin wafers, and they provided a much-needed shot of energy to the system, although it was short-lived. Excellent for that middle-of-the-battle fatigue. I wondered if Sharah might have one to spare but decided I didn't want to hang around any longer than necessary. Best to avoid running into Chase again.

Smoky acquiesced for once, backing away as she shakily maneuvered toward the front of the building. He followed a couple steps behind, and I found myself getting a little irritated. She was my sister; I should be by her side, not him. I flashed a nasty stare at his back and caught Morio looking at me out of the corner of his eye. He dropped back to walk beside me.

"Are you okay, Delilah? Did Smoky do something to piss you off?" he said, his voice barely audible.

I frowned, then sighed heavily. "No, no. Something happened—something that doesn't involve him, or you, or even Camille, and I guess I'm just looking for a place to vent." Swallowing back tears, I gave him a little shrug. "It just sucks. I really need to talk to Camille, but she's had such a rough time that I don't want to make her feel worse."

The fox demon shook his head, his dark eyes glittering with understanding. "She won't mind. When we get home, Smoky and I'll go buy takeout for everybody, and you and Camille can have a long talk. That work for you?" He gave me a sweet smile that made me choke up again.

Maybe Camille was onto something. Maybe I shouldn't be dating FBHs. I might be part human—all too human—but maybe I needed somebody who understood the Fae side of me. Or the Were side, I thought, my mind flashing to Zachary. He'd predicted a depressing outcome to my liaison with Chase, too, but I'd thought it was just jealousy. Now I wondered if he'd just been trying to spare me heartbreak.

I managed to eke out a smile. "Thanks, Morio. Camille's a lucky woman. I hope she knows it."

His eyes crinkled, and he let out a short laugh. "Oh, she

does. Trust me. Camille never lets Trillian or Smoky or me feel like we're just window dressing. She may not show it to the world, but she's got a terribly romantic side."

I nodded, then took a deep breath and quickened my pace until I was walking at Camille's right side. Smoky glanced at me. Whether he had overheard my conversation or whether he just sensed my need, he dropped back, leaving me to steady my sister as we headed to the parking lot.

Camille glanced at me as I helped her over to her Lexus. "Something happened. I can tell. You need to talk about it?"

"Yeah," I said, "but not here. Morio said he'd take Smoky, and they'd go get dinner after we get you home. Maybe we can talk then, if you're feeling up to it?" Sometimes I still needed my older sister's advice. Menolly and I'd relied on Camille ever since our mother died. Camille smoothed over the frayed edges; she picked up the pieces and put them back together again. She was the glue that held our family together. Maybe that's why we indulged her whims most of the time.

"No problem," she said, wincing as I helped her slide into the passenger seat. "It's a good thing Morio has a license. I'd hate to see what Smoky would do behind the wheel." She flashed me a big old grin.

"He'd probably end up behind bars." I laughed, then sobered. "Thanks, I needed that chuckle." I kissed her on the cheek before heading back to my jeep, where Rozurial and Vanzir were taking turns playing some sort of Game Boy game. I hopped in the driver's seat, motioned for them to fasten their seat belts, and started the engine.

"She going to be okay?" Roz said quietly, as if he could sense my mood.

I nodded. "Yeah, she'll be fine. But I'm all talked out, so if you boys don't mind, can we limit the conversation on the way home? I'm beat and tired and not feeling very good."

"Sure thing," Vanzir said. We made the rest of the trip in silence.

* * *

Iris hadn't returned from the library by the time we got home. Roz took the hint when I asked him to make himself scarce. He mumbled something about checking out a lead he'd thought of regarding who had summoned the venidemons, and he took Vanzir with him.

I impatiently waited as Smoky tucked in Camille on the sofa. Only then did he allow Morio to drag him off to the store. The dragon hated going shopping, but he was getting accustomed to it.

As soon as they left, I dropped into the rocking chair and stared at Camille, who immediately pushed off the blanket and propped herself up on the cushions.

"You'd think I was dying," she said. "I love the dude, but damn, he's overprotective."

"Just wait until you find Trillian." I winked at her, not feeling up to chatter but realizing she was as bereft as I was, although for entirely different reasons. "I can hardly wait to see the fireworks when he finds out you've married both Morio and Smoky. And that you expect him to join in the fun."

She sniffed. "You know perfectly well that Trillian's straight. And so is Smoky."

"And Morio?" I was killing time, and I knew it. When I finally told her about Chase, it would make it all too real.

"The subject's never come up. I can tell you that if he tried to put the moves on Trillian and Smoky, they'd eat him alive. And *not* in the good way." She shrugged. "Now, will you tell me what the hell happened? You look like death warmed over."

"Two things, actually. First, and we'll talk about this later when Menolly wakes up, the Autumn Lord has ordered me to go back to Otherworld, to the forest of Darkynwyrd in search of a plant to help me control my shifting into a panther. He insists that I do so now—as in yesterday." I expected her to nix the idea, but instead, her eyes lit up, and she pushed herself to a sitting position.

"Home?" Camille's voice trembled. "If we went back home, then Morio and Smoky and I could test our bond to see if it will lead us to Trillian. We've been working on strengthening the soul link. I had no idea when I agreed to marry them in the binding ritual that the chain created would turn out to be such a strong force. Kitten, I can *feel* it if they're too far away from me. It's like part of me feels stretched. Kind of freaks me out, to be honest."

"That would be nerve-racking. So you don't object to the trip?" It was good to know I could count on her, and the thought of having Morio and Smoky along was also reassuring.

"Hell no, I'm so there. Menolly probably won't be able to come. I'd rather not journey into the Darkynwyrd forest during the night, so she's stuck here." Camille rubbed her head and slid back onto the pillows. "The pain reliever Sharah gave me is making me dizzy. Now tell me what else happened— because this sure wasn't what was making you cry."

Voice shaking, I spilled out the whole story. "I can't believe I feel so betrayed. Isn't our father's blood supposed to cushion us against jealousy?"

Camille laughed. "Oh Kitten, honey, no. No. Our father's blood only gives us that *potential*, but it's so much more complex than just blood. And think—you're part cat. You have territorial issues. That's the only reason I haven't gone out and picked up a few kittens. I knew we couldn't bring a cat into the household because you'd hiss and spit and make a fuss and pee on the floor instead of in your litter box. Which—speak of the devil—Iris is complaining about again."

"Oops." I rolled my eyes. Back home, there had been servants to take care of the mess. Although when Mother was still alive, we'd been assigned chores so we'd learn how to fend for ourselves. Mother had never objected to the outside help, but she objected to *lazy layabouts*, as she called the idle rich. "You'd think I'd learn, but I don't need it every day . . ."

She shook her finger at me. "Yes, but we've had this talk before. I suggest you get your butt in gear and sift it today, or she's going to dump the whole thing outside and just leave you adrift next time you transform. Back to the territorial issue— you may befriend other cats outside, but the house is your territory. Just like Chase is your territory. Erika's an intruder, and you don't like her horning in on your domain one bit. Hell, I'm surprised you haven't marked him."

I blinked. Territory? Now there was a word I understood. "Is that why I feel like I'm running a double standard?

Because I slept with Zach and I expected Chase to understand. Well, I didn't expect him to understand, I just wanted him to. But for me . . ."

"You're queen of the pride. You have to approve the other members of the harem if your mate brings somebody new home. Chase deprived you of that right. And don't forget, he lied to you. I knew better than to trust Johnson—right from the beginning when he was trying to get under my skirts." She narrowed her eyes. "You want Menolly and me to have a little talk with him?"

I jumped. If Menolly summoned Chase in for a little talk, he'd come away skinned and boiled. That I knew for sure. Menolly was still overprotective of me. Camille had eased up on the Delilah's-a-naïve-little-girl attitude ever since I'd bitched both of them out about it a few months back. She'd backed off and was letting me fight my own battles when it came to love and life. Right now, I wasn't certain I liked it any better than I'd liked being coddled. There was something to be said for having the hard knocks in life cushioned.

"No! I mean, not yet. Let me think for a while. Menolly said she didn't think my relationship with Chase would work out, and I wondered why at the time. I doubt she would have predicted this." In fact, I was pretty sure she thought *I'd* be the one unhappy to keep the relationship on an exclusive level.

Camille let out a sigh and leaned back. She closed her eyes. "Damn, my hand still hurts. Those hellhounds are a bitch. But at least we know what we're in for, should we run up against one in the future."

She squinted at me. "Listen, Kitten. Don't let Chase throw you. You're beautiful, you're passionate, you possess every quality a man could hope for. He's either a jerk, or he screwed up big time because he thought with his cock first, instead of his heart. We both know the blood runs south with men whenever they see a pretty face and a winsome body. Either scenario could be the case—but *you* have to decide which one to accept."

"I guess," I said, thinking it over. "Do you think we should just take a break, put some breathing space between us to think?"

"Well, we have to work with him, so you two are going to have to remain civil." She grinned. "If you really want my opinion, I think you should spend some time with someone more our speed, if you get my drift. Maybe you'll find that dating an FBH isn't going to work for you. Or maybe you'll realize you really do love Chase, and then you'll have to find a way to confront what happened today. Come what may, you owe it to both of you to give both sides of your heritage a chance. You have one very willing and gorgeous man waiting in the wings, you know."

She was talking about Zachary. Zachary Lyonnesse, who had made it abundantly clear he still wanted me. My stomach lurched. Should I chance creating more of a rift between Chase and myself? Or was it already there, done damage? Would I get along with Zachary better? Would we connect on a level Chase and I never could—on a Were level, even though his Pride didn't consider me a *real* Were because of my heritage? I headed toward the kitchen.

"Where are you going?" Camille readjusted the blanket and sleepily closed her eyes.

"To make a phone call," I said. She was right. It was time to explore other options.

CHAPTER 9

━━◆◆◇◆◆━━

Zachary sounded surprised to hear my voice, but when I asked him if he wanted to get together for dinner on Sunday, he jumped right on board.

"What about Chase? Won't he object?" he asked.

I stared at the receiver, wondering just how to answer. "Chase and I aren't playing footsie right now." I hadn't intended on telling Zach anything about what happened, but before I knew it, the whole sordid scene spilled out.

Zach let out a low whistle. "He screwed up big time. Tell me, what bothers you most?"

Even Camille hadn't asked me that. I thought for a while. "The lies, I guess. The subterfuge. The sneaking around. I can't stand sneaks. They piss me off and always have. When I was little, K'sander—a child in my school before my mother yanked me out and taught me at home—befriended me, then he stabbed me in the back. He found out I was afraid of water, told the other children about it, and they tossed me into the pond out back of the Y'Elestrial palace."

"Holy crap, why did they do that? Kids can be such little shits," Zach said, growling a little.

"We were always tormented because we were half-human.

Trust me, while our parents loved us, we didn't have many outside friends. The three of us grew up unusually close for sisters, and we've stayed that way. Anyway, I couldn't swim, and I almost drowned."

I closed my eyes, remembering that afternoon. I hadn't liked water before, and since then, I hated getting wet. A daily shower—or on rare occasions, a bath—was the limit to any liquid frolicking I might do. Rain was okay, but I still didn't like it much.

"What happened?" Zach asked. "How did you get out?"

"Camille saved me. You have to understand, even before Mother died, Camille always looked after us. She followed me home after school to make certain I was okay. K'sander swore up and down that he had nothing to do with it, but the truth came out. His parents didn't even punish him. The fact that he'd lied hurt worse than the kids dumping me in the pond."

"Honey, you deserve so much better than that. I'll pick you up at seven on Sunday. We'll go out to the Keg Steakhouse. Afterward, how about a walk through the woods at your place?"

"You're on," I said, hanging up. Inside, I was a mass of knots. I'd just made a date with Zachary. If Chase found out— but then again, Chase had no place to talk. I ruthlessly kicked him out of my thoughts. I was going to enjoy my evening with Zachary, and Chase could fuck Erika all he wanted if he needed company. Apparently, she served him on a moment's notice far better than I did.

By the time Iris arrived home, Menolly was awake and puttering around the kitchen, fixing Maggie's dinner. They both listened silently as Camille and I ran down our encounter with the venidemons, the hellhound, and the shade, and Camille's resulting wound.

"Shit, you really got roughed up," Menolly said, examining Camille's hand. "I wish I could have been there. I'd have sent that hellhound back to hell in a handbasket. You sure you're going to be okay?"

She poured the warmed cream, sugar, sage, and cinnamon into a bowl and set it down on the floor for Maggie, then prepared the ground meat with which we were supplementing her diet. *The Care and Feeding of Woodland Gargoyles* had made it clear that it was time to introduce Maggie to solid food.

"For the hundredth time, I'm going to be fine," Camille said. She pointed to the raw slice of meat Menolly was mincing. "How's she liking the lamb?"

Maggie had—like any toddler—developed some inexplicable likes and dislikes. She loved chicken and turkey but hated fish. She gobbled up beef and buffalo but was hesitant about pork, and there was no way in hell we could get her to touch liver or other organ meats.

Menolly shook her head. "She's eating it so far, but I don't think it's going on her favorites list any time soon. Does the book say she should get any vegetables or fruit?"

I picked up the volume from where she'd tossed it on the table. It was so well-thumbed that we'd need a new copy soon. It felt odd to read in our native language again after reading predominantly English for well over a year, but Mother had taught us both English and Spanish when we were young, along with the various Fae dialects. All three of us were well-versed in multiple languages.

"Let's see." I thumbed through the chapters. "Sleep . . . play . . . hey, have you tried to teach her how to use her claws yet? It says here she should be learning the basic rudiments of hunting through play, though she won't be ready for a real hunt for years to come."

Menolly shrugged. "I tried, but she seems reluctant to take a swipe at anything. I used a dead mouse, but she showed little interest in it, either as a toy or as food."

That was strange. Gargoyles were notorious carnivores, and in the wild they fed on game primarily. I skimmed over the feeding section. "No sign . . . oh here—she needs berries for roughage, and they recommend giving her wildcress and grasswort once a week. In the wild, the mothers chew it up for the babies and regurgitate it." I grimaced. "I don't think I want to chew either one of those, let alone feed it to Maggie afterward. I might urp up hairballs, but that doesn't mean I enjoy the process."

Camille laughed. "That's what food processors are for. What's the closest thing to wildcress and grasswort over here Earthside?"

Iris piped up from the rocking chair where she was ensconced with a light afghan and a cup of orange spice tea. "Watercress and wheatgrass, I expect. I can buy some next time I'm at the market. I wouldn't wild craft it around here because of all the pesticides and chemicals used on the roads and orchards."

"Sounds good," I said as the phone rang.

Menolly wiped her hands and picked up the phone while Camille and I took turns feeding Maggie the ground meat, one spoonful at a time. Menolly whispered something, then took the phone and disappeared into the hall. Must be Wade, the president of Vampires Anonymous. While they'd dated a little, they'd ended up just friends. Menolly had become extremely active in local vampire politics, especially since offing her sire, though she said there were a number of vamps who disapproved of her actions.

"You say Smoky and Morio are bringing dinner home?" Iris said, frowning as she stared at the clock. "Do you know what they're getting? I'm not sure whether to get out soup bowls, chopsticks, or plates."

"If Smoky has anything to do with it, plan on pizza," Camille said with a shake of the head. The dragon had developed a pizza fixation over the past month, and we'd eaten it every time he'd been in charge of bringing home food. He'd shaken off every gentle hint to perhaps go for Chinese, or hamburgers, or even fish and chips.

At that moment, the door slammed open and Vanzir and Rozurial strode in. Vanzir looked ready to bust. "Man, have I got some information for you—" he started, but I waved him silent.

"Wait till Menolly's off the phone. Meanwhile, go take off your coats. Dinner will be ready soon." We'd gone from eating alone to big family-like dinners. Iris loved it, but sometimes I missed the privacy we'd had for so many months. Between Chase, Smoky, Morio, and—until recently Trillian—and then the two demons, and occasionally Bruce, Iris's leprechaun boyfriend, we had somehow expanded our evenings alone to lively discussion roundtables. Fun, but right now, I wasn't feeling very social.

I was about to excuse myself when Smoky and Morio meandered in. Instead of the predictable pizza boxes, Morio was carrying a large bag from Chang's Golden Palace, a Chinese restaurant about ten minutes down the road. It had recently opened up, and I'd been wanting to try their food.

"Dinner's on," Morio said.

"Thank the gods you convinced him to get something other than pizza," Camille said as Iris pulled out plates and chopsticks. As she set the table, Roz and Vanzir helped her. Menolly came strolling back into the kitchen and slowly replaced the receiver.

She turned to me. "So, when were you going to tell me?"

"Tell you what?" I stared at her, wondering what bee she was hiding in her bonnet this time.

"Tell me that your dick of a boyfriend decided to expand the explorations of his penis. That was Chase. He told me what happened. I'll give him this—he knew better than to lie. So, your detective's developed a yen for his own kind? Good riddance." She hovered up by the ceiling, her eyes flashing dangerously. "You want I should spank him a good one?"

Smoky blinked. "Chase strayed? Without asking permission?"

Camille swiveled her head to stare at him. "They aren't married, dude. Chill out, this isn't our affair."

"They may not be married, but from Chase's tone, I gather he knows he screwed up," Menolly said from her perch near the ceiling.

Iris cleared her throat. "Dinner's ready. I suggest we leave Delilah's business to Delilah for the meantime. I believe Vanzir had something to tell us?"

Oh yeah, the night was just getting better and better. I flashed Iris a grateful look and pulled out a chair, sliding into it with a thud. "Thanks, Iris. I'm going to say this once, and one time only tonight. The last thing I want is a bunch of unsolicited advice. I'll handle this in my own way, and it doesn't include any spanking, crisping, groin kicks, or any other attacks. Let me attend to my own affairs. I'll call Chase when—and if—I'm ready to, and until then, you can tell him I'm not available if he calls. Of course, if there's an emergency, we'll get the job done, but right now, butt out of my private life. Everybody."

The room fell silent until Camille let out a snort. "Good girl," she said as she piled her plate high with pot stickers, rice, almond chicken, and an egg roll.

Menolly glared at me. "Kitten, you tell me everything. I can't believe you were planning on keeping this a secret from me. Chase has no right to treat you like this—"

I jumped up. "See? This is why I didn't want to tell you. Camille, I told. Okay? She's leaving my decisions to me lately, and I appreciate it. You, on the other hand, still act like I'm five. If you'll remember, I'm older than you— Oh what's the use?"

Seeing her expression, I knew it was hopeless. Dropping back into my chair, I grabbed the nearest box of takeout. "You never listen. Just let it go for now, okay? Vanzir, what do you have for us? And it better have nothing to do with boyfriends, love, or sex."

He gave me a sympathetic smile, but the light in his eyes was cold. Sometimes it took me a moment to remember he was a demon, after all. Not human, not Fae, but a dream chaser demon who had, up until recently, entered humans' dreams and dined on their life essence, leaving them weakened and terrified from the constant barrage of nightmares he brought with him during his soporific visits.

"I was hanging around the Bloody Gin, when I overheard somebody talking about Karvanak," he said.

I grimaced. The Bloody Gin was yet another vampire-owned bar that welcomed shadier customers. Like Dominick's and the Fangtabula, they'd resisted every attempt by Wade and Menolly to get them on board with the mission statement of Vampires Anonymous.

And Karvanak was a Rāksasa—a Persian demon. He'd stolen the third spirit seal from us during our last big battle. Vanzir had defected at that point, but we'd still lost the seal, and Camille blamed herself, though there wasn't much she could have done. Rāksasas were greater demons who had far more power than we did.

Even with the horn of the Black Unicorn—a gift Camille had received from the Dahns Unicorns—she'd been unable to withstand the demon's demands and had lost the seal to him. Chalk one up for Shadow Wing. We were determined it wasn't going to happen again.

"Just what did you hear?" Menolly asked, leaning close.

Vanzir gave her a long, studied look, and she backed away just enough to tell me she still didn't fully trust him. None of us did.

"I overheard a goblin tell a vampire that Karvanak was offering big money for any clue to a great treasure, a gem that was priceless. The goblin seemed to think it was some sort of ring or something, but I'll bet you anything that Karvanak's putting out feelers, trying to find the fourth seal." He crossed to the silverware drawer. "Anybody else need a fork? I can't use chopsticks."

"Me, please," I said, raising my hand. Smoky did, too. Menolly stared at the food like she was both starved and ready to throw up. I had to give her credit. Sitting through dinner, watching all of us eat while she could never touch food again, had to be rough, but she did it for the cause.

"How does that help us, though?" Iris asked.

Vanzir handed me a fork and one to Smoky, then sat back down, a smile slowly spreading across his face. "It helps us because I also spent some time today talking to a couple of modern-day prospectors whom Karvanak at one time had thought to employ. They weren't interested in scouting out the mountains for him, and rather than tell them as to why he wanted their help, he just passed by the rejection and let them go."

"Prospectors?" I asked. "They spend a lot of time up in the Cascade Mountains?"

He nodded, the grin widening. "Oh yeah, and they were eager to make a quick buck today, especially when Rozurial laid on the charm. We found out several interesting things, including that one of the men ran across a cave a few weeks ago. A cave that's *haunted*. But before he managed to escape the cave, sans his buddy, he caught sight of a necklace being guarded by what sounds suspiciously like a passel of wights. A ruby set in gold. And it was glowing like a firefly in June."

A ruby? I glanced at Camille. "Is one of the spirit seals—"

She nodded. "A ruby? Yes. Did the dude remember where the cave was? And, more important, did he tell Karvanak about it?"

Vanzir shook his head. "Yes, and no. And he won't ever have the chance to spill his guts, either."

"You didn't—" Iris gasped and almost fell off the high stool that boosted her to the table. "You didn't kill that poor man, did you?" she asked, steadying herself.

Roz cleared his throat. "Chill, pretty wench. No, Vanzir did not kill the guy. Neither did I, though we thought about it. After all, Karvanak can't very well extract information from a dead man, now can he? But I charmed him and talked him into going to sleep, and Vanzir slid into his dreams and ate up the memory. There's nothing for him to tell now, so he should be safe enough. And so should we."

I stared at my plate, my appetite starting to return. "That means that we know where the fourth spirit seal is, but that Karvanak hasn't got a clue. We can snatch it up and send it back to Queen Asteria."

"No shit, Sherlock," Vanzir said, but his eyes crinkled, and the cold fire went out of them for a moment. "We're one up on Shadow Wing's cronies this time. Let's just make sure we keep it that way."

Suddenly hungry, I filled my plate and began chowing down as we sorted out our plans. We were too tired tonight, and tomorrow we had a trip to OW to make. But come tomorrow night, we could drive up into the mountains and search for the cave. And—with a little luck—we'd find the seal before anybody was the wiser.

CHAPTER 10

For the first time in ages, I crept into bed alone, not knowing if Chase would ever be in it again. At first, exhausted though I was, I tossed and turned, unable to sleep. I thought about getting up, sneaking downstairs to watch late-night trash TV with Menolly before she had to go to work. But she was still pissed at me, and I didn't feel like answering any questions about Chase right now. So I padded over to the window seat and shifted into cat form. I hopped up on the cushioned bench and curled into a ball, staring out at the moon.

Sometimes life made more sense when I was in cat form. I was still me, my emotions still ran freely, but life on two legs didn't seem quite so important or quite so painful. I inhaled deeply and let it out with a soft purr. So Chase was screwing around. Did it really matter? In the long run, would it matter at all? We were a long way from winning the war against the demons, and who knew if any of us would be around in a year? We might all be dead. Or my sisters and I might be called back to Otherworld. Chase might just be a blip in the road map of my life.

I stood, stretched, and turned around three or four times, trying to find the most comfortable position. As I rested my

head on my paws, settling in for a much-needed doze, there
was a faint knock on the door, and then it opened and Menolly
peeked around the side. She glanced around the room, looking
puzzled, until she caught sight of me.

"Kitten? Hey, Kitten, what you doing over here, furble?"
She silently crossed the room and, in one swift motion, sat
down on the bench next to me. I glanced up at her, not sure I
wanted to change back just yet. She caught me up in her arms.
When I was in cat form, I was especially sensitive to Menolly's
scent. She reminded me of Hi'ran. Her fragrance was that of
graveyard soil and old bones and dusty rooms long hidden
from the sun. She smelled slightly sweet, like overripe fruit,
but it was so faint that most people would never catch her scent
on the wind. But the Fae—and Weres—we could smell the
undead.

Sometimes I still got creeped out by the thought that my
sister was a vampire. Our family had been ripped apart by her
death and rebirth. Camille had managed to keep it together
until help arrived, and one thing Father never knew—nor did
Menolly—was that I'd been there. I'd seen the whole thing,
but I'd been in cat form, and when she came bursting through
the door like a bloody terror, Camille had grabbed me up and
tossed me out the window, whispering for me to flee, to get
away.

I'd run for help but had been so frightened that I couldn't
change back, and it had taken Camille's piercing screams to
summon aid. Long after she'd managed to lure Menolly into
the safe room and lock her up—a room Father had made in
case we were ever overrun by trolls or goblins—Camille had
continued to scream.

When I realized that she hadn't followed me out and that I
was useless in going for help, I'd doubled back and climbed
up the tree next to the living room. I watched as Camille raced
to the door, still screaming, and out into the streets.

After that, I lost track of what happened, but it wasn't long
before Father arrived home, along with several members of
the OIA. By then, I managed to shift back, and I came in like
I'd been away all afternoon. I was too ashamed to say I'd been
there but hadn't lifted a finger to help Camille. She never told

anybody, and for that, I was grateful. Later, she tried to convince me that she understood, but I couldn't forgive myself for letting her down.

Now, of course, things were vastly different, but the memory of what Menolly had first looked like when she burst through the door, a murderous rage filling her face, covered from head to toe in blood—both her own and her victims along the way—stuck in the back of my mind. No matter how hard I tried, it was an impossible image to erase. Camille had managed to get past it, but I still couldn't. So I tried to spend extra time with Menolly, to overcome the web of fear that still wove itself around a corner of my heart.

Menolly scooped me up in her arms and chucked me under the chin, scratching softly. I shook off my worries and settled into her arms as she cooed over me gently.

"Kitten, I know you can hear me. I know you can understand me. Chase called again a few minutes ago. He wants you to call him; he wants to talk to you. He said he'd be up for another hour or two."

She paused, then let out a long sigh. Menolly didn't have to breathe. When she did so it was purely for effect, though sometimes I suspected she used breathing exercises to cope with the bloodlust when it hit her. With a scritch between my ears, she whispered, "You should call him, you know. Get this straightened out one way or another."

Obviously, she wasn't going to let this go. I leapt out of her arms and padded softly toward the bed. I was going to have to talk to her sometime, it might as well be now. But before I could shift, I felt a lurch in my stomach. Damn it. Why *now*?

My body shook as I began to hack. It was like having a hair caught in your throat and trying to spit it out, only I didn't have fingers and I couldn't feel around inside my mouth to grab hold of it. I backed up, yowling once—loudly—before I began to cough and then it was there, slimy and thick. Struggling to expel it from my throat, I strained, coughing loudly.

Menolly sighed. "Hairball? Oh, Kitten, I'm sorry. I'll make sure Iris grooms you more. Or I can brush you if you like. Let me know which you prefer." As she spoke, I opened my mouth, and the glob of gunk ricocheted out of my throat, onto the braided rug. It would have to be the rug. It was always the rug, or the bedspread, or the pillow. Never the floor. *Nope*, no matter how hard I tried, I could never land one on the hardwood floor, where it would be easier to clean up.

As soon as the hairball was free, I shifted back. I'd had enough playing kitty cat for one night. I stretched and yawned as I shimmered back into bipedal form and blinked. Menolly grinned at me as she cleaned up the hairball for me.

"Playing nudist, I see?" She ran her eyes up and down my body in an exaggerated leer.

I glanced down. Oh shit, I'd changed into cat form when I was naked. No wonder I hadn't been wearing my usual collar. "Very funny," I said, grabbing my sleep shirt and yanking it over my head. It was chilly, so I fished out the magenta pajama bottoms to match and slid into them, then hopped on the bed and crossed my legs. I searched through the nightstand drawer until I found my stash of Snickers. Tearing open the wrapper, I bit into the gooey treat, sighing as the taste of chocolate coated my throat.

I stared at the candy bar. "Sometimes, our mother's people get it right, and when they do, they get it right in a big way."

Menolly shrugged. "I wouldn't know. At least not now. But I remember when Mother brought home the bag of chocolate Kisses from one of her trips. We were what . . . I don't remember . . . little, though. Camille had barely started her training with the Coterie of the Moon Mother. They were good, I remember, but almost too sweet for me."

"Nothing's too sweet for me," I mumbled, taking another bite of the chocolate bar. "You aren't going to let it drop, are you? About Chase?"

She shook her head. "You need to talk to him. One way or another, you have to come to terms with this."

"I thought you said we were doomed." I stared glumly at the pattern on the comforter. I'd picked out one with a swirl of roses and ivy, and now I thought maybe I should trade it in for a SpongeBob bedspread, or something with monkeys on it. Something whimsical to make me laugh.

"I still think you are, but that doesn't mean you can leave it like this." She stood up. "Whatever happens, I'm here for you.

But don't push me out of the loop, Kitten. I love you, and I care about you. Even when I'm being a total badass bitch." She kissed me on the forehead and headed toward the door, stopping to peer over her shoulder. "By the way, while you and Camille are back in OW, if you get the chance, try to scrape up a few toys for Maggie. Something she'd like to play with that would at least introduce her to her home world. I want her to know both Earthside and OW culture."

I nodded, smiling, but said nothing. Menolly was playing mama to Maggie. She was following in the steps of our own mother, but if I told her that, she'd pooh-pooh it. I finished my chocolate and turned off the light, sliding under the covers. Finally, somewhere near midnight, sleep caught up to me, and I fell into an exhausted, dreamless slumber.

Camille, Morio, Smoky, Iris, and I stood at the entrance to the Hydegar Park portal. One of the random portals to open up over the past few months, it was in the corner of a small, two-block-square park that the city had let grow wild. Luckily, the park was seldom used, and we'd gotten away with assigning an elderly—but still powerful—elf to watch over it.

Sent by Queen Asteria, Mirela dressed like a bag lady so as not to attract attention and spent her days in the park. At night, she cast a temporary seal on the portal, but it never held for long; the energy of the portal dissolved it. By morning the seal dissipated, and Mirela was once again camped out in the park, watching to make sure nothing nasty got through. In case it did, she had a cell phone and our numbers, and we'd hear about it in under five minutes.

The portal led straight to Darkynwyrd, problematic because the dark forest bordered the Shadowlands and shortly thereafter, the Southern Wastes. Should the beasties who prowled the woods there realize that the portal had opened, there would be plenty of creatures who would take delight in crossing over to wreak as much havoc as they could.

That was the problem with goblins and trolls and any number of other denizens of Otherworld. The more trouble they caused, the more butt-slapping, back-patting bullshit went on back in their native watering holes. It was like a men's locker room, only worse. And the women were just as bad. I'd only met a few goblin wenches, but they were just downright nasty.

Camille waved at Mirela. "Hey, we're ready. Anybody around this morning?"

Mirela shook her head. "Nobody stirring but the birds, and even they have been uncommonly quiet. There's a storm brewing—thunder, it feels like, and lightning, and heavy dark clouds coming this way."

Iris sat down beside her on the bench. "You're right about that. I've sensed it since I woke this morning. Camille, you'll probably be able to, too, if you close your eyes and focus."

We'd decided to bring Iris with us because she was an expert with plants, and she'd be able to ferret out a *Panteris phir* plant without any problem. Maggie was tucked away in Menolly's lair, and we'd left Rozurial to watch over the place. Vanzir had been sent packing for the day. Not that we didn't trust him, but we preferred to err on the side of caution.

The elf motioned to the two trees that created the framework for the portal. Sometimes portals were erected between standing stones, other times they were dependent on trees or cave entrances or even large boulders. In Hydegar Park, one of the trees was oak, the other cedar. Guardians both, and sentient, though they would not speak to me. I could sense their watchful natures, observing us, taking in all that went on around them. Earthside forests kept to themselves. Compared with our woodlands back home, they were quiet and sometimes sullen, resentful of those who had destroyed wide swaths of thicket and copse.

The energy flowed between the trunks, alive and vibrant and new. The portal had been dormant for who knew how long, for at least a thousand years, and had woken to life a few weeks back. Rogue, independent of the spirit seals, the new portals' opening signaled a breakdown in the energies dividing the realms. Even if we found all the spirit seals, even if we regained the third one from the Demonkin, who knew how long the system would maintain itself?

Aeval, Morgaine, and Titania—the three Earthside queens

of Fae—insisted the Great Divide had been a colossal mistake on the part of the Fae, that it had altered the energy holding the realms together in such a manner that backlash was inevitable. Perhaps they were right.

Smoky examined the trees. "The energy isn't stable. I think this could close on its own at any time. We run a risk traveling through it."

"We have no choice," I said. "If we use Grandmother Coyote's portal, we'll have a long journey to travel to reach Darkynwyrd. This should hold up for the trip there. And the trip back. I hope."

The fact that the dragon considered it risky made me nervous. Smoky wasn't afraid of much. In fact, the only real things I'd seen him wary of were the Autumn Lord and—to some extent—the werespiders. But I wasn't about to nix our plans now. I needed that plant. I didn't want to find out what would happen if I disobeyed a direct order from Hi'ran.

Camille shrugged. "We might as well give it a try. If we get stuck over there, we'll just have to find another portal to come home through. It's not the end of the world."

I flashed her a silent thank-you and marched up to the nexus point between the tree trunks. "Here goes nothing," I said and, seeing the others were behind me, stepped into the swirl of light.

CHAPTER 11

❦

Walking through a portal is a little like putting on a suit of armor and gallivanting between two giant magnets. It's like being torn to tiny bits within the blink of an eye. Then, suddenly the magnets disappear, and a whirlwind spins you back into one piece again. The whole experience isn't really painful, but it's definitely dizzying.

I hadn't been home in a long time. When Camille and Menolly made the trip to Aladril a few months back, I'd been jealous as hell. Now it was my turn. Too bad our destination was Darkynwyrd, but at least with Morio and Smoky to back us up, we weren't in as much danger as we would be otherwise.

The smell of the air made me homesick. Usha trees and night-blooming khazmir flowers and the scent of clean. No acid rain, no pollutants in the air save for woodsmoke.

As we traipsed out of the portal, I found my thoughts turning to Father. Where was he? Lost, like Trillian. That much we knew. But was he safe? Hurt? Captive? His soul statue was still intact, which meant he was alive, but other than that, we had no idea where our father had gotten himself to or what he was doing. Aunt Rythwar was missing, too.

Our family had been torn apart by Lethesanar's drug-crazed civil war, and all we could do was hope that the Queen's sister, Tanaquar, won the battle for the throne soon and put Y'Elestrial to rights. Considering everything Lethesanar had put our family through, a dark little part of my heart hoped she'd end up with her head on a pike at the hands of her own torturers. I tried to shake it away, but I couldn't help the way I felt. I just didn't like the *way* it felt.

Once outside the portal, we found ourselves in a narrow strip of grassland that lay between the lower foothills of the Qeritan Mountains and Darkynwyrd. The Qeritan range divided the Shadowlands from the Elfin lands.

Considering the nature of the Shadowlands—and the Southern Wastes beyond them—the elves were lucky the mountains formed a barrier. As it was, they kept a tight watch on the mountain passes during the summer. Winter offered a reprieve. Few travelers could safely make it through the tall peaks. Anybody from the southwest who wanted to visit Elqaneve was forced to take the long way around, and the long, arduous trip wasn't worth the trouble to most raiders looking for a minor skirmish.

Smoky glanced around and immediately wrinkled his nose. "I smell a wyvern. Filthy imposter." He frowned. "It passed this way a few hours ago. Wyverns move quickly, so it should be long gone. I hope."

"Not looking for a strafing battle, eh?" I blinked, assuming an innocent smile as he shot me a withering look.

"Not looking for a battle at all, thank you." He moved toward the back. "I'll cover our backs. Morio, you assume the front, along with Iris, since she knows what we're looking for. Delilah and Camille, take the middle ground."

Morio obeyed without question. He'd obviously accepted Smoky as the alpha male. I wondered just how the whole marriage thing would play out for Camille when—*if*—we found Trillian.

Iris made her way up beside Morio. She nodded to the youkai. "I'm ready. I know what *Panteris phir* looks like, but I can guarantee you that we won't see a single plant until we near a stream or pond. It grows near water in the thick shade, so we'll have to enter the forest proper in order to find it." She had donned a pair of thick leggings and a tunic that reached to midthigh. She was wearing a leather vest, leather knee and elbow pads, and she'd dug up an old bicycle helmet.

"You look ready for skateboarding," I said, shooting her a grin.

Iris rolled her eyes. "Don't laugh. It can get rough over here, especially around this area. I'm not the best in a fistfight, and though I'm not *that* fragile, I *can* get hurt. I figured the leather and helmet would offer me some protection in case we run into trouble. Camille, did you bring the unicorn horn with you?"

"No," Camille said with a shake of the head. "I didn't want to bring it over here. There are too many mages here who would happily kill me to get hold of it. I hid it in Menolly's lair for the day. We shouldn't need it. There aren't any demons over here. At least not of the caliber we're facing Earthside. And we can mop the floor with goblins and their ilk."

Iris nodded. "Good thinking. Well, let's get moving. I've never been to Darkynwyrd in all the times I've visited Otherworld," she added.

"You were born and bred Earthside," Morio said. "Like I was. When did you first come visiting over here? I'd barely heard of it until Grandmother Coyote summoned me over from Japan."

"I'd like to know the answer to that, too. Iris seems to have a lot of secrets hidden behind those winsome eyes," I added with a grin.

Iris glanced back at me and snorted. "That I do, my girl. Consider I'm much older than you—well, chronologically. We Talon-haltija live a long, long time, like many of the full-blooded Fae, and I've reinvented myself several times over. Or rather, my life has been reinvented for me.

"As to Otherworld," she continued, lowering her voice, "I found out about this land when I was very young. My . . . a friend from long ago in my past used to bring me here on picnics and for visits. He was born here. We met in the Northlands." She fell silent, and I recognized the look. We'd get no more information out of her on that subject.

As we approached the shadow of the tree line, a strange

silence fell over the strip of meadow that acted as a natural boundary for the edge of the forest. I could still hear the birds singing away in the trees, but they sounded strangely muted, as if somebody had turned down the volume on the stereo.

Most forests in Otherworld were warm and welcoming. Darkynwyrd was another matter. Silver fir and alder, willow, yew, hemlock, and elder, the trees were all sentient, and they were all watchful, keeping guard over the dusky forest. Their trunks were tall and broad, with burls in the gnarled bark that looked like faces. They watched as we entered, and the hairs on the back of my neck stood up. I scooted close to Camille, who silently reached out to take my hand.

The branches stretched over the narrow pathway, forming a lattice above us, a canopy of leaves and boughs. Emanating a slightly fetid smell, they were thick with webs strung between the limbs.

Leshi spiders thrived in the arboreal garden, and here and there I caught sight of the fat, shiny orb weavers. The size of a silver dollar, they were slick, with jointed legs and round abdomens, and their venom could paralyze a grown man. I'd heard tales of lone wanderers who had entered the forest and stumbled into webs strung across the path, their skeletons later found hanging in a cocoon of spider-silk. Darkynwyrd wasn't safe for solitary travelers unless they possessed strong magic or, at least, strong talismans for protection.

Scattered among the trees were large patches of thorny brambles and skunkwort, yungberry bushes—the berries were often used in magical trance work—and eisha flowers, which were harvested for love and lust potions. Darkynwyrd was a treasure trove of magical spell ingredients and herbal remedies for healers and witches and sorcerers, but the trip to harvest them could be a dangerous one. The leshi spiders were bad enough, but the forest was also thick with venomous snakes and sharp-toothed wyrerats. And then there were the goblins and trolls and other, darker beings.

Just the knowledge that we were journeying into the forest our father had warned us never to enter was enough to set me shivering. I clutched Camille's hand, trying to stave off my nerves. She looked all too calm and collected.

I frowned. "Aren't you scared?"

She shook her head. "There's tension here, yes, but consider what we've been through this past year. What could be worse than facing down demons? Than facing Dredge? Or Kyoka? Goblins are a nuisance, but we can kill them easy enough. Trolls? We took out two dubba-trolls just a month or so ago. I've been practicing death magic. And look at you: You've been marked by the Autumn Lord. You've faced one of the Harvestmen himself. Why should you be afraid?" She laughed. "I'm more worried about running into Lethesanar's armies than I am about what dangers we face here."

I stared at her, thinking she was sounding more and more like Menolly every day. But she made a good point. After what we'd already been through, why should I allow a simple forest to scare me? And we had Smoky with us. The dragon would never let anything happen to Camille without wiping out the enemy first. He'd burn down the entire forest rather than let it harm his prize.

With a snort, I said, "You're right. I guess it's a holdover from childhood. All those years we were warned never to come here, never to venture into the dark wood. Father couldn't have foreseen where we'd be today." I drifted off, thinking for a moment. "Do you think we'll find him? That we'll ever see him again?"

Camille sobered. "I don't know, Kitten. I hope so, I desperately want to believe we will. Just like I have to believe that I will find Trillian. If there's no hope, then what good is it all? We can't ever let our guard down, but we have to hold on to the belief that we'll be reunited with the ones we love. And look—cousin Shamas found his way to us. We thought he was dead, but he's fine, and he's on our side. If someone targeted by an assassin triad of Jakaris can survive, then Father and Trillian have to be able to fight their way back to us."

Morio glanced back at us. "Trillian is far more savvy than you think. He's a survivor. Whatever happened, you can bet that he'll get out of it and take control of the situation. Remember, he lived in the Subterranean Realms for years before the entire city of Svartalfheim relocated to Otherworld."

As we trekked through the woodland, which stretched for a good two hundred miles before opening into the Shadowlands and the Southern Wastes, I fell into the rhythm of the forest. If I closed my eyes, I could feel it breathing around us. I sank into the cadence of Darkynwyrd's pulse and slowly let go of Camille's hand. She was right. What did we have to fear? We'd hardened up since we first left Otherworld. We were far more dangerous, far less trusting. It was harder to catch us in a trap and harder to take us down.

In some ways, we were walking in our own shadow land back over Earthside. The majority of humanity had no idea how close to danger their world was. And we were standing on the front lines, holding off the battle. We'd lost our sense of what it meant to be carefree when Menolly was first turned. Dredge had ended our hopes for a normal life.

And then, when we were assigned Earthside, we'd run smack into Demon Central, and any lingering Cinderella dreams had vanished like so much smoke. We were the true dangers here. Dangerous to any of the creatures who might seek to stop us, to interfere, to harm us. I straightened my shoulders and took a slow, clear breath.

"I smell water," Iris said, pointing to the right. "Can you hear it?" she asked me. "Your hearing is better than mine."

I listened, and so did Camille. There, faint but definite, the sound of water lapping against the shore. "Yes," I said. "I don't know if it's a stream or pond, but I hear it."

"I smell it, too," Camille said. "It's not a stream; it smells like lake water."

I moved up beside Iris and stared at the veritable fence of undergrowth that we faced passing through. "Stickers and briars. Lovely. Should we go on and hope we find a clearer trail ahead?"

She shook her head. "I have the feeling no matter how far we go, we'll have to wade through the thicket to get to our prize."

Morio agreed. "It probably just gets worse the farther you head into the forest. And we don't want to be here when it gets dark. Or at least, I don't." He glanced nervously over his shoulder. "It's one thing to battle it out in the daylight, but night brings out the undead, and I can feel them here. The wood is thick with spirits."

"Okay, then. Let's do it," I said, turning to Iris. "Since I'm taller, let me go first. Morio, move back with Camille. I'll break the trail."

I pushed ahead into the thicket, using my silver dagger to sweep aside the brambles. Iris was faring pretty well; the leather of her vest and knee pads didn't catch on the thorns, but some of the brambles were at eye level with her, and I had no intention on letting her get an eye poked out on my account.

I glanced over my shoulder. "Smoky, keep a close watch on the back end. We don't want anybody sneaking up on us when we're caught in a patch of thick thorn bushes."

As I plowed through the brambles and waist-high ferns, it occurred to me that, as nervous as the forests over Earthside left me, they were a walk in a nicely groomed park compared to Darkynwyrd. Camille had gone a long way to calming my fears of the wild wood, but I wasn't stupid enough to blow off the dangers that we faced coming here. We might have a dragon with us, but should a wyvern come screeching down from the skies, we'd have a fiery battle on our hands, and none of us would come out the better for it, Smoky included.

As I brushed my dagger through one patch of berry bushes, the faint sound of chanting echoed to my left. Somewhere, up ahead, somebody was singing. Or . . . they were casting a spell. I slowed, motioning for everybody to be quiet, and gestured for Camille to join me. As she slipped up beside me, I nodded to where I heard the chanting coming from and whispered, "What is it? Can you tell?"

She closed her eyes, listening. I could sense her reaching out on the astral, trying to touch the magic. She must have made some sort of contact, because she jerked suddenly, her eyes flying open. She clapped her hand to her mouth and stumbled back into Morio's arms, as he kept her from falling.

As soon as she had regained her balance, she whispered frantically, "We have to get out of here. Now. No time to explain. Either turn back or turn the other way."

Undecided—we'd come so far already—I finally turned to the right and plunged ahead, forging through the undergrowth as fast as I could. Whatever it was, it was bad, because Camille didn't spook very easily.

We'd forged on for another ten minutes when there was a shift in energy, and the already-dim path grew darker, the sunlight blocked by a great shadow. I jerked my head up, expecting to see a wyvern winging overhead, but there was nothing there. Just a shadow. A gloom that rested between us and the latticework of sky shimmering between the tree branches and webs.

"What is it?" Iris said, her voice low.

"I don't know," Camille said. "I sensed . . . back there I sensed something connected to the Corpse Talkers. It felt like some rite. Trust me, we do not want to witness whatever dark rituals they pursue."

"Corpse Talkers?" I shuddered.

> *Lips to lips, mouth to mouth,*
> *Comes the speaker of the shrouds.*
> *Suck in the spirit, speak the words.*
> *Let secrets of the dead be heard.*

As children, we'd sung the rhyme to chase away the bogeys, but like so many nursery rhymes, legend had its foundation in fact.

Only the women of their race ever became actual Corpse Talkers. Only the women were ever seen. It was rumored the mysterious race of misshapen Fae lived in some underground city built of bone and ash. Able to speak for the dead, Corpse Talkers offered their services for a bloody price, and they were worth every penny—worth every heart that they ripped from the victims to seal their communion with the dead. Always cloaked in long robes, only their glittering eyes showed through the gloom of their hoods.

"You'd better stay well away from them," I told Camille.

Witches and Corpse Talkers dare not touch one another. If their powers collided, the resulting sparks could produce an explosion big enough to blast a good-sized crater in the ground. Along with good-sized shrapnel wounds in anybody who happened to be near.

As I spoke, the shadow grew larger, looming closer over our heads. Hell, and double hell. Please, don't let it be one of the Corpse Talkers. We had no idea how they journeyed. They might be able to fly, or teleport, or maybe even run as fast as Superman for all we knew. What I did know is that stumbling in on one of their private rituals in the middle of Darkynwyrd couldn't be good.

The sound of water grew louder, and I caught a glimpse of an opening up ahead. We were almost through this patch of undergrowth. With a glance at whatever apparition was tailing us from above, I poured on the speed. I could hear Iris struggling to keep up. She was fast, but she couldn't match my stride.

With a sudden grunt, Iris said, "What the—"

I swung around, dagger at the ready in case she was being attacked, but just then Smoky passed by me, Iris hanging over his shoulder, a surprised look on her face. Camille pushed me forward.

"Hurry, let's get out of the wood. Whatever's winging overhead means us no good, I can tell that from here. We have to be able to— Oh shit!" She jumped back as the shadow took a nosedive and landed right in front of her.

Whatever it was, was transparent, but enough ripples in the air told us *where* it was. I could see the faint outline of wings, as well as a tail, before it took a swipe at Camille. She jumped back, landing in the middle of a briar patch.

Morio tossed his bag on the ground and began to transform, towering up and over all of us, even Smoky. Eight feet tall, the youkai was letting go all the stops as he shifted into his natural shape.

Camille steadied herself and began to call down the Moon Mother. The Moon Mother was stronger here for my sister than back over Earthside.

A blast of energy shot forth from her hands toward where the intruder was standing, hitting him square in what looked probable to be his torso region. It was still hard to gauge whether the creature was bipedal or not, but then the blast ricocheted off the creature and landed in a patch of dry wood to the south and burst into flames.

"Crap! Fire!" I lunged forward but stopped when our opponent began to shimmer into sight. The energy ball must have disrupted his invisibility, because we were suddenly facing our opponent—and one hell of an opponent it was. A weird crossbreed, he looked to be. A centaur with huge wings. His parents must have been one heavy-duty mixed marriage, I thought, moving forward, dagger high and ready.

Morio engaged him from the front as I approached his left flank. As the youkai grappled with him, locking grips with the muscle-bound arms of the winged centaur, I swiped my dagger alongside the silken brown fur of his butt. A long gash opened up under my blade, and he roared. I was about to lunge again when he raised his back left foot and let fly, hitting me square in the gut and knocking me back. I flew through the air to land at the foot of a yew tree.

"Delilah! Are you okay?" Camille swung around.

I couldn't answer—he'd knocked the wind out of me. As she made her way to my side, Smoky came racing back, a blur of white and silver as he dragged his claws across the right side of the beast, leaving five long, bloody gashes in his wake. Iris was right behind him, chanting something as she pulled out a small box and opened it. She swallowed whatever was in there, then blew in the direction of the battle, and a hailstorm of ice began pounding the shit out of the three men: Smoky, Morio, and our adversary.

Morio backed away, and Smoky ignored the hailstones as if they were dust mites, but the centaur let out a loud groan and froze, a thin layer of frost covering his body.

Smoky glanced over our way. Camille helped me up, and my lungs seemed to be working again, though my stomach felt like it had French-kissed a sledgehammer.

"We don't have much time. Kill or capture?"

I thought as quickly as my pain-racked gut would let me. What would Menolly do? The centaur might be able to give us some information, yes, but he'd attacked first rather than ask us who we were and why we were here. I swallowed the feeling of guilt that rose in my chest.

"Get rid of him. He won't talk to us. He was out for the kill, and he's not going to make any deals. Even if he did, how could we trust that he wouldn't hunt us down again, this time with a few more of his buddies?"

Smoky nodded. I could tell he approved. The same with Camille, and Morio . . . and Iris. I turned away, feeling older, feeling too harsh for my skin. This was what it meant to be a soldier. This was what it meant to be in a war. Shoot first, ask questions later. Take no prisoners. The one time we'd tried—with Wisteria, a floraed member of the dryad family—things had gone horribly wrong. She'd escaped and led Dredge to us. And that had been beyond bad.

I swallowed my fear and turned around. "Wait. I should do it."

They looked at me, and I could see concern filling Camille's face. "Are you sure, Delilah?" she asked.

I bit my lip, glad she hadn't used my pet name. "I've killed before. It's not like I don't have blood on my hands. I have to get over being squeamish. I have to accept that we're never going to go back to the days when life was gentle, when Mother was alive and there to cushion all our problems. You tried, Camille. The gods know, you tried so hard, but you can't stand between us and the horrors we now face. You're only one woman . . . and the dangers are so great . . ."

She reached up to cup my face with her hands. "Kitten, we've never faced life without pain, even when Mother was alive. We were always beat up, always picked on. We've never known gentle. Let's face it, gentle isn't in our nature, and it's not in our destiny. We have to take those moments when they come, hold them dear, and enjoy them because they're ephemeral and fleeting." She motioned for Smoky to join her.

Morio had shifted back into his human form, and he gave me an encouraging smile.

Stepping up to the winged beast, I looked into his eyes. He was still frozen, still paralyzed by Iris's spell. I looked for something to stay my hand, some sign that he might have made a mistake. But then I saw the light there: the treacherous light that filled the eyes of the goblins and demons and other shadow-bound creatures we faced. His teeth were sharp, pointed, like a row of needles, and I understood then.

He really was *hunting*—for his dinner. He was a sentient beast, and in this jungle—in this woodland—it was eat or be eaten. I placed my dagger against his neck and swiftly slashed across the skin, wanting to scream as I did, wanting to shout out, "This isn't me!" but I knew that it was. *This was who I was*.

Delilah of the silver blade, Delilah, the Death Maiden; Delilah, the Night Huntress who prowled in the dark under the moon. I had always skirted my predatory nature, but when I was in my cat form, it came to the surface. And in panther form, it roared to life. As much as I tried to avoid thinking about it, I loved the chase. I loved the hunt.

As the winged centaur toppled to the ground, I turned away, wiping my blade on my jeans. I glanced at the others, unable to smile but unable to cry.

"Let's go. The lake sounds like it might be ahead, through that patch there. Be on your guard. These woods are treacherous and deadly." As we set out, a refrain in my head played over and over again, whispering, "And so are you, Delilah D'Artigo . . . and so are you . . ."

CHAPTER 12

~~~

The thicket broke about twenty yards from where we were standing, opening up into a clearing around a small lake or large pond. I wasn't sure which, and I didn't care. Whatever the case, water made me nervous. As we tumbled out of the briars and vines, the scent of brackish water filled my lungs, and I winced. Whatever the source, it wasn't free-flowing, or it wouldn't smell like that. Camille winced, too.

"Good gods, that's an awful smell. Look—the surface is covered with algae." She pointed to the water.

We could easily see the other side, but there was no way in hell you'd pay me to cross it without a sturdy boat. For one thing, I couldn't swim. Not really. For another, the lake was covered with a thin slime of greenish algae. Pond scum. Delightful. Oh yes, I wanted to go mucking around in that Jacuzzi just about as much as I wanted to get into a four-legged race with Speedo, the neighbor's basset hound. Speedo not only bayed all night long, but he told me secrets I really didn't need to know. Such as his owners had a thing for spanking. Each other—not him. Too much information, I'd told him, but he was intent on figuring out just what they enjoyed about being smacked on the butt when it was so clearly a punishment for him when he forgot his manners and piddled on the carpet.

After a quick check around the immediate vicinity, which produced only hazards of the normal kind, namely spiders, snakes, and a snarling tuskwort, Smoky and Morio stood back, letting Iris take over.

Camille and I sat on a log. We were as good as useless when it came to hunting herbs. Camille grew an herb garden, but it was tidy and neat, and she knew what everything was because the seedlings had come with labels. I was hopeless when it came to plants. I didn't even like eating them. Vegetables weren't my forte, and Camille had to bribe me to eat my broccoli and carrots.

Morio walked alongside Iris, while Smoky kept a watch over the forest, making sure we weren't taken by surprise by anything nasty. The morning wore away into noon, and the sun was shining, though not particularly warmly. As we listened to the low thrum of insects, I realized that we weren't hearing the incessant pounding of traffic, or the blaring of the television or stereo, or even the hum of electricity that rolled through the wires.

"I haven't heard it this quiet since . . . since we first left." I leaned back, closing my eyes, savoring the silence.

Camille nodded. "I know. I miss this. But I'd miss things from Earthside, too. I'm afraid that if I was forced to choose where to live, I'd have a hard time making up my mind. I'd probably pick Otherworld, of course . . . but . . ."

"But Mother's homeland has rubbed off on you," I said, giving her a rueful smile. "Me, too, I'm afraid. And Menolly likes the dark city streets." I kicked a stone with my foot, watching it roll down the embankment, into the pond. "Do you think we'll ever come back here to live? Permanently?"

Camille frowned. She stared at the water, breathing so softly I could barely see the rise and fall of her chest. Finally, she said, "I don't know, Kitten. Truthfully, I don't know if any of us will live through the coming war. We've had a lot of close calls already, and who's to say that one day . . . one slip and . . ." She shrugged. "I think we should just enjoy each day as it comes."

"One day at a time, huh? I didn't know you were a philosopher," I said, grinning.

She blinked. "A year ago, I wouldn't have been. But with everything that's happened . . . Today we revel in the fact that we're home in Otherworld, even if it is only to hang out in Darkynwyrd. Tomorrow, we'll enjoy being home with Maggie, in the city. It's the only way I can see for us to keep our sanity."

Iris waved from a patch of thick grass, twenty feet to our left at the edge of the water. "I found it! Delilah, come here."

I slowly rose, dusting my hands on the butt of my jeans. "How's your hand doing? You aren't getting too tired, are you?" I asked as I reached for Camille, offering to help her to her feet.

She jumped up on her own, shaking her head. "It stings, but it's healing. I'll be okay, Kitten. Don't worry about me. Sharah knows what she's doing. Now go talk to Iris."

While she joined Smoky on guard duty, I meandered over to where Iris had parted a large patch of wild grass. She was pointing to a large plant. The leaves reminded me of a geranium's leaves—scalloped and fuzzy, not shiny. The smell was musky, thick and close, rising from tiny purple blossoms on spiked flower heads. The plant was a good three feet high, and almost reached Iris's chin.

"This is the *Panteris phir* plant? Looks a lot like rose geraniums. Siobhan has them on her balcony." I knelt beside the plant, examining it. The roots were thick and ropy, the stalk of the plant had lignified for the first foot out of the ground, and I had the feeling that as it grew, the remainder would turn woody and hard, too.

"Aye, this is the *Panteris phir*. Panther's fang, when you translate it from the language of the northern elves. This is a potent plant, Delilah, and you can't take the entire thing, or it would punish you for doing so. You must take several cuttings—I'm positive I can get at least one of them to take root—but you have to leave an offering in its stead." She produced a trowel and a pair of cutting shears from her backpack. "I can't do this for you. You were told to harvest it yourself, and so you must do it."

"How do I do that without hurting the plant or cuttings?" I stared at the plant, not quite knowing how to go about this.

"You have to give it an offering, and then I'll show you where to cut." She produced a plastic bag that had a few holes punched in it. There was a paper towel inside, and she poured a bit of water over it and wrung it out.

"We wrap the cuttings in the moist paper towel and then tuck it into the plastic and zip it closed. That will keep it alive till we get the cuttings home and root them in water. When they're ready to plant, we'll create a special place in the garden for it. You'll also want to take home enough of the leaf for your tea until your plant is strong enough to withstand monthly cuttings. It only takes a small pinch to infuse a cup of water."

I considered the plant. What could I give it, in return for part of its body? And then I glanced up at Iris. "My blood and hair? Would that be an acceptable offering? After all, I'm tearing up part of its body and taking it with me."

She smiled, gently. "You've learned a lot, Delilah. Yes, that would be most appropriate. By the roots. That will strengthen the cuttings' connection with the mother plant. Go ahead, then, and say whatever comes into your head that feels appropriate."

Still uncertain, but feeling my way through what felt like the right course of action, I took my blade and gouged a hole next to the root system of the plant. I held up a small lock of hair and cut it with the dagger, slicing unevenly through it so that I had odd, uneven bangs on the right side of my head. I dropped the hair in the ground, pushing it deep, hoping no one else ever found it. Hair and blood were potent forms of magical connection. I knew that much from listening to Camille.

Then I held up my hand and slid the blade down my palm, cutting an inch-long gash in the fleshy pads under my fingers. It wasn't deep, but it bled enough for my purposes, and I held my hand over the hole and let the blood trickle over the lock of hair.

"My blood and my hair I offer to you in exchange for your children, for part of your body. May we both find strength in this communion." I couldn't think of anything else, and it sounded good to me. I shot a glance at Iris, who nodded.

"Very good . . . that should be fine."

"You don't think anybody will come along and find my hair, do you? I know witches and sorcerers can use hair to bind people to their will. We have no idea who might be watching from within the forest." I pointed to the edge of the woods. "There may be some creature worse than the winged centaur in there right now, listening and waiting."

Iris considered my words, and as I filled in the hole with dirt, she marked a rune on top of the soil and held her hands over it. "Sink deep. Bind and protect. Curse any who would misuse this offering." A flash of light crackled from her hands to infuse the rune, and it glowed briefly, then vanished. "That should take care of it until your hair has a chance to decompose and go back to the land. Now, here. You hold the stem like so, and then cut on a diagonal—no—not like that, look at how I'm holding the knife."

As she guided me through the steps, I tried to focus, but my thoughts kept slipping back to the fact that we were in Otherworld, and we would soon be returning Earthside, and we hadn't found Father, Trillian, or any clue as to whether I'd had a twin at birth. The latter wasn't nearly so important as the former two, of course, but still . . .

"No! Now, look at what you're doing," Iris said, reaching out to shift my hand position by a quarter inch. "See how the angle changes the direction of your cut?"

I nodded. "Yes, I'm sorry. My thoughts are a million miles away."

"Well, better to focus on the here and now. Do one thing at a time, and you'll never end up having to redo anything."

I let out a long breath, then inhaled deeply and tried again, this time keeping my thoughts on my work.

We were finished by midafternoon, and it was time to head back. As we aimed in the general direction of the path, once again I forged a trail using my dagger as a makeshift Weedwacker. I couldn't decide whether I was happy to be leaving or not. It wasn't that I liked Darkynwyrd. I'd be altogether delighted when we emerged from the shadowy depths. But once we worked our way through the woods, it would be time to head over Earthside. That's where my heart was torn.

I really wanted to stay in OW for a while. To go someplace comfortable and lean back and relax. But thoughts of Menolly and Maggie, Chase and our home Earthside intruded, and I realized that *home in Seattle* meant almost as much to me now as did *home in Y'Elestrial*.

Indecision flickered: *OW, Earthside; OW, Earthside . . .*

Hell. I snorted. When I really thought about it, I realized that I had no idea what I wanted. As usual. When Iris first came to live with us, she was always complaining that when I was in cat form, I'd stand at the door mewing until she opened it. Then I'd stop smack in the middle of the threshold, unsure whether I wanted in or out. That's why she installed the cat door.

As we stumbled out from the overgrowth onto the main path, Camille looked around, frowning. "Hey, we're not where we were when we went off the trail. I don't recognize this point in the path. Want to make a bet we overshot and are farther up the road, deeper in the forest than we were when we headed toward the pond for your plant?"

I gazed at the surrounding trees. "You're right. Which means we have more distance to backtrack. I hope it's not too far."

Iris, who was excellent with navigation and directions, made sure we were heading in the right direction, and we set off. The sun—and Morio's watch—told us that it was three P.M. If we hadn't traveled more than a mile or two off course, we'd reach the meadow and the portal around five and be home in time for dinner.

As we rounded a bend in the path, Camille stopped, pointing off to the right. There, tucked back about twenty yards along a dirt path, sat a small cottage. Surrounded by a sturdy wooden fence, the land enclosed within had been cleared, and in place of the knee-deep brambles, a vegetable garden and an herb patch thrived. Large crystals guarded the gate—one to each side—and even I could sense the magic that ran between the smoky quartz spikes. They stood a good three feet high, points aimed toward the sky, and must have weighed several hundred pounds each, easily.

A figure standing near the fence stared at us. I reached for my dagger, but Camille suddenly let out a shout and raced toward him.

"What are you doing? Are you out of your mind—" I started to say, but she was waving. The man—a Svartan by the look of him—waved back. He was ruggedly handsome, looking far less civilized than Trillian, but the jet color of his skin glimmered appealingly, and his eyes were the same pale blue as Trillian's. His hair was far shorter, barely skimming his neck, and he had a good mustache and goatee going.

Of course, the moment Camille raced off, Smoky was right on her heels, as well as Morio. I glanced at Iris, shrugged, and we followed, jogging to catch up.

Camille was babbling like a fountain on overdrive. "Darynal! I can't believe it's you." She skidded to a stop two yards from the gate and looked at the crystals. "You got any wards up that I should know about?"

He flashed her a lazy grin. "If it isn't Trillian's woman. Camille, it's been a long time, you gorgeous wench. I'm not surprised to see you, though." He leaned on the fence post and closed his eyes, waving his hand over a sigil painted on the front of the gate. "There, it's safe now. Come in, and bring your friends."

Camille motioned for us to follow her. Smoky looked none too pleased. Frankly, neither was I. Any friend of Trillian's was bound to be suspect. But we silently filed through the gate and joined them at the house, where Darynal opened the door and stood back, waiting for us to enter.

As soon as I stepped through the door, I looked around, searching for any signs that this was some sort of a setup. Maybe my sisters had been rubbing off on me too much, but I didn't trust someone whom Camille hadn't seen in over a year. And far more time than that, if Darynal thought she was Trillian's woman, unless the two men had talked in the past few months. Camille and Trillian had broken up several years ago, before Trillian showed up Earthside, and they picked up where they left off.

Too much could happen in that amount of time. Allegiances could be formed . . . and broken.

There were three rooms that we could see. A kitchen, living room, and what was probably a bedroom. Built from sturdy logs, the cabin had a solid feel to it, a ruggedness I'd never associate with Trillian.

A row of antlers attached to the walls provided handy tines to hold various bags and clothing. *Functional trophies*, I thought. A faded, overstuffed divan and chair sat at one end of the living room, a rough wooden desk and chair at the other. A bookshelf filled with scrolls and volumes buttressed the desk. Apparently Darynal could read.

The fragrance of soup drifted in from the kitchen, and my mouth watered. We hadn't eaten in hours. I sniffed, the scents of carrots and warm beef broth filling my lungs. Maybe Darynal wasn't such a bad sort after all. I mean, a man who could make soup that smelled like heaven in a pot couldn't be all bad, could he?

"That's not beef soup I smell, is it?" I blurted out, my stomach rumbling.

Camille shot me a long look that spoke volumes about my lack of manners, but Darynal just grinned.

"Indeed it is. Delilah, isn't it? Won't you all join me for a late lunch?" He nodded toward the kitchen.

"How do you know my name?" I said, freezing.

"Trillian told me all about you," he said.

So he had talked to Trillian within the past few months. "Then you've seen him lately?" I asked.

Darynal inclined his head. "He stays with me sometimes, when he comes back to *Artanyya*."

Artanyya . . . the Svartan name for Otherworld.

"He isn't here now, is he?" Camille glanced around, a wild hope flickering on her face that maybe somehow we'd lucked out, that maybe Trillian was alive and well and staying with his best buddy.

But Darynal quashed her hope with a quick, "No, I'm sorry. He isn't here right now. I'll fix the soup and bread," he added, heading into the kitchen.

"I'll help," Iris said, following him.

As soon as they were out of the room, Smoky turned on Camille, his eyes practically glowing. "Who is he? What connection do you have with him?"

"Those are supposed to be my questions," I said, chiming in. "How do you know we can trust him?"

She shushed us both. "Trillian and Darynal are blood-oath brothers. They're bound by a pact they forged in childhood. They didn't just oath-swear, either. They bound themselves before gods. If Darynal plays turncoat on Trillian, he'll be struck down by his own oath. And vice versa. Trillian told me they decided the pact was necessary just in case times came to this. I guess life in the Subterranean Realms, even within their own city, wasn't easy. This way, they knew they'd have someone they could trust even in the darkest hours."

If that was the case, then Darynal had to treat us with courtesy, considering Trillian and Camille were bound together. I relaxed my guard, and so did Smoky. Morio arched his eyebrows and slowly wandered around the room, glancing at a sheaf of papers on the desk.

"Darynal's a trapper, isn't he?" he asked. "Here's a receipt for twenty wild fox pelts." He shuddered and looked away.

Camille nodded. "I'm sorry, but yes, he is. He's not at all like your usual Svartan. He prefers to remain solitary, and he's a mountain man at heart. He traps, he hunts, and he fishes. He keeps bees, I believe, and Trillian told me that he also makes the best apple cider in the world."

"Trillian is telling the truth," Darynal said as he entered the room. "Lunch is ready. Please join me in the kitchen."

We followed him into the large room where we found a rough wooden table laden with food. The benches were covered with padded cushions. As I swung my leg over the bench and glanced around the kitchen, I realized that Darynal's home felt cozy. The garlic braids hanging on the wall, the baskets of beans and potatoes and tubers, the fresh loaves of hearty grain bread, all made up for the roughness of the décor.

Lunch consisted of bowls of spicy beef-barley soup, a platter overflowing with soft, rich bread and butter, a jar of the sweetest honey I'd ever tasted, and mugs of foaming apple cider, steaming with nutmeg and cinnamon. It was the best meal I'd had in a long time. The food in OW was richer, more flavorful . . . most likely due to the lack of additives and depleted soils that plagued Earthside.

As we ate, Camille grew quiet. She glanced up at Darynal, and I knew she was thinking about Trillian. Finally, I decided to ask what she couldn't bring herself to.

"Darynal, have you seen Trillian lately? He's missing, and we're worried." I gave a meaningful glance toward Camille. "She's been frantic."

Darynal's head shot up and he frowned. "*Missing*? Trillian's not missing. I saw him three days ago. Unless . . . did something happen since then?"

"Three days ago!" Camille jumped up. "What do you mean? He's been missing for several months now, and I've been terrified!" She backed away from the table. "I've been so scared that the goblins got him . . ."

"You mean he didn't tell you? I thought for sure . . . uh-oh . . ." The look on Darynal's face said it all. Trillian wasn't missing, Trillian was still around, and Trillian had let us go on thinking he was in danger on purpose.

Camille looked like she was going to cry, but then, the tears disappeared somewhere between her eyes and her cheeks and I could see the fury starting to rise. Darynal had said it, all right: *uh-oh. Uh-oh* was what happened when Camille got angry. And Darynal could sense the impending storm, too.

He raised his hands. "Hey, it's not my fault. I assumed he'd told you what was going on. He never said he didn't."

"I hope Trillian told you about my temper, because I want you to understand that it's far better that you tell me everything. *Now*. If you don't . . ." With each word, Camille stepped forward, and Darynal took a step back.

"Oh crap." Darynal scooted around behind the table. "Hang on, woman. Don't blame the messenger. I had no idea that Trillian had actually managed to keep this a secret from you. I'll tell you. After all, he didn't tell me not to. I doubt he ever believed it would take this long, or that you'd end up on my doorstep. Just don't aim one of your misguided energy bolts at me. Please!"

Obviously, Darynal knew about Camille's wayward magic.

"Then spill it. *Now!* Why the hell did Trillian lead me to think he'd been captured by the goblins? Why the hell did Queen Asteria tell me that he'd disappeared? What's going on?"

With each question, my sister got louder. I glanced at Iris, relieved that Camille wasn't mad at us. Iris seemed to concur, a faint smile lining her lips.

Smoky cleared his throat. "The lady asked you some questions. I suggest you answer them immediately. In case you hadn't figured it out, I'm a dragon. I'm also Camille's husband—"

"One of her husbands," Morio interjected.

"Yes, yes . . . *one* of her husbands, and I don't take it kindly when people ignore my wife." The dragon smirked as Darynal squirmed.

"Stop! I said I'd tell you. Just leave my house—and me—in one piece. Great gods, Trillian was right. You don't take prisoners, do you?" Darynal slid back onto the bench and motioned for Camille to do the same. He gave her a strange look. "First, I had no idea you were married. Somehow, I don't think Trillian knows, either."

"I married Smoky and Morio to forge a soul bond so I could use their powers to search for Trillian, since we thought he was captured and in danger." She stopped, blanching. "You mean I got married for no reason?"

Smoky cleared his throat. "I think we've just been insulted," he said.

Morio sniggered. "Sounds like it."

"No, no—but—" Camille shook her head. "Just stop it, you two." She turned back to Darynal. "Okay, the truth, and let's have it now. Where's Trillian, and why did he drop off the face of the world?"

Darynal let out a long sigh. "You didn't hear this from me. Understand?" When she nodded, he leaned his elbows on the table. "I don't know everything involved. I can't; it would be too dangerous for Trillian. But he's been back and forth through Darkynwyrd for the past moon cycle. He was on the trail of your father, but something happened. Something very bad. Lethesanar got wind of what was going on, and she sent out a tracking party to follow him."

I paled. "Oh hell, so it was true. A party of goblins found him?"

"Not quite. They almost caught him, but he managed to get away. However, it became clear that Trillian had to vanish. So he went underground in order to continue the hunt for your father. Apparently, whatever information your father ran across can make—or break—the war. Both Lethesanar and Tanaquar are searching for him. The key he carries can turn the winds of war."

We sat back, mulling over that one. A highly secret mission that involved not only Camille's lover but our father. And if Trillian was in danger, Father was in far more danger.

"Why don't they keep a watch on your house? Isn't Trillian afraid that you'll be kept under observation?" I asked.

Darynal laughed. "No . . . I am known to be a goblin sympathizer. I do business with them, I publicly support the goblin king. Trillian comes and goes by the dark of the night, and he's a master of disguise. But you must not stay long. I cast an illusion spell on the gate when you entered to keep prying eyes out. But I can't hold it for long, and Trillian must not find you here, either. He can't have any distractions right now, Camille. He has to focus on his mission."

The look in his eyes said it all. Trillian couldn't afford to divide his attentions right now, and if he knew we were looking for him, he'd have to double his efforts to hide.

"If we find him," I said slowly, "then we chance exposing him to the enemy, and we chance putting our father in worse danger."

"Precisely. Please, eat your lunch and go. Don't look for him, don't search for him. If something happens, I promise, I'll let you know, but unless I show up on your doorstep, assume he's alive and well. Leave him to what he does best." Darynal paused, then reached out and lifted Camille's chin. He leaned forward, almost lip to lip, and gazed into her eyes. Smoky tensed.

"Trillian adores you. He worships you. He would never just run off and leave you worrying if the balance of war weren't so perilous. Can you let him do his job and not interfere?"

Camille swallowed slowly, then nodded. She licked her lips, almost looking frightened. "I hate this. I hate this with every fiber of my being. But I'll let him be. Just . . . I love him."

Smoky leaned forward and firmly but gently disengaged Darynal's hand from Camille's chin. "Enough. We understand. We'll let him do his job, and Morio and I will keep Camille occupied until Trillian is able to return. We should leave now. Our very presence puts the operation in jeopardy."

Morio stood up. "Smoky's right. Thank you, Darynal. At least you were able to put our minds at ease. We know more than we should, but rest assured—the information will not leave our lips. And we won't tell Queen Asteria that we know, either."

I eased over to Camille's side. She murmured a thank-you to Darynal, then gave him a quiet hug. He kissed her forehead, almost like a big brother might do, and then glanced over at me. "You're still hungry. Here, drink this up before you go," he said, holding out my soup bowl.

I grinned at him. "You're all right, I'll say that for you." I quickly chugged down the rest of my soup and gratefully took the chunk of buttered bread, and we left the house.

As we quietly slipped out the gate and hurried away as fast as possible, Camille remained silent. I knew she was mulling over this little twist in her mind, and she'd talk when she was ready. Meanwhile, I nodded at Iris, and we pulled ahead of Camille and the boys.

"This is a fine kettle. Camille bound herself to those two, and she didn't need to," I said, fretting a little. The wedding had bothered me on some level I couldn't quite catch, even though I adored both Smoky and Morio.

Iris let out a long sigh. "She would have done so eventually. You know so, if you look deep into your heart. What bothers you, my fine tabby, is that things are changing. You've had your sisters all to yourself for so long, and you don't want to see anybody or anything interfere with that bond. You don't seem to realize yet that families can expand. That's the cat in you: territorial, wanting your people to stay your people. You have to get over the fear that Camille will abandon you. She's going to stay right by your side, honey. You know that, if you'd only let yourself see it."

I stared at her, unable to answer since my mouth was full of bread. As I silently ate the rest of it, I wondered if she was right. I'd hated the fact that Trillian had returned. But was that so much because he was Trillian, or because my sister so willingly let him back into her life? And Smoky . . . and Morio . . . could it be that I really wanted things to stay the same?

As if reading my mind, Iris added, "You know, life can't stand still. People and relationships must evolve. Look at you; you bear the Autumn Lord's mark, and you're only now beginning to understand what sweeping changes that will bring into your world. Don't begrudge Nature and her relentless drive to move forward. It's the way of all things. Even death is a transition, a progression. You can't freeze time, Delilah. You can't bring the past into the present. Everything moves and shifts and turns. It's up to you whether you will face the changes or be left in the dust."

I hung my head, staring at the trail as we hurried along at a brisk pace. She was right, and yet I didn't want to face all the changes that were happening. And the most immediate—the one closest to my heart—was Chase. What was I going to do? He wanted me to call him, but what could he say? Was he going to tell me how much he enjoyed fucking Erika? Or that she meant nothing to him? That he wanted a threesome? And I had a date with Zachary.

And in the larger scope, we had a spirit seal to find and keep from the demons. Screw relationships; saving the world was hard enough without emotions interfering.

Life had been so much simpler when I'd been ignoring men in favor of running around on all fours. I was sorely tempted to retreat to that state, to say *fuck you* to loving anybody except in a family manner. But as Iris's words ran through my head, I knew I couldn't go back to the way I'd been. So where did that leave me?

As we broke into the meadow, the sun was lower in the sky, and the birds were chirping loudly as a contingent of clouds headed toward us, an army in gray, set to loose a volley of rain overhead. I shook myself out of my ill-disposed reverie and headed toward the portal. We needed to get home and, as much as I loved Otherworld, right now, I wanted to get back to Maggie and Menolly. And with a little luck, I'd think of an answer to my problems with Chase.

CHAPTER 13

We got home right around dinnertime. Vanzir and Rozurial were hanging out in the front yard, playing a game of gin rummy at the picnic table Iris had ordered so we could eat outside during the summer. They ran over to the car as we drove into the yard.

"We found it—we found the cave," Roz said, rushing over to my side. "We know where the spirit seal is, and there isn't a moment to lose. Karvanak nabbed the prospector, and while Vanzir's memory steal should hold, we can't take any chances. We need to go out there tonight and claim the spirit seal."

Shit. I was tired. So was everyone else. But Roz was right. In a war, sleep came second. Winning battles came first.

"Yeah, you're right. Camille? What do you think?"

"Same thing you do. Why couldn't this happen *after* we got some sleep? But hey, at least Menolly can go with us, and that's always good. If they'd found the location tomorrow morning, we'd have had to go without her. As it is, we wait another couple hours, and she'll be up and raring to go. Meanwhile, we can catch a few z's." She yawned and looked at her hand, which was still wrapped in a bandage. "This wound hit me harder than I thought, but if I can just doze for a while, I'll be fine."

I nodded, a little concerned. Our half-Fae blood usually helped us heal up without a problem, but the wound had been a nasty one. Actually, when I thought about it, we'd all had a rough year.

"Sounds good to go. Iris, any chance you can have a quick meal waiting for us when we get up? Something light but protein-rich and sweet?"

She nodded, weary herself. "Not a problem. Since I'm not heading out to the hills with you, I can rest later, after you leave. Meanwhile, I'll get the herb cuttings tended to until you have time to plant them."

I turned back to Roz and Vanzir. "So, tell us what we're facing."

"The seal's located in a cave up in the Snoqualmie foothills. Rumors say the cave is haunted. I wouldn't dismiss them lightly. There's some sort of spiritual activity going on up there, although I sense demons better than ghosts," Vanzir said.

He slipped the pack of playing cards into his pocket, then continued. "Karvanak won't cut us any quarter. If he can break through the memory seal I performed, he'll jump on the information. Either way, the poor guy is dead. Either the Rāksasa will break his mind, or he'll break his body."

Shuddering, I followed them into the house.

Iris immediately slipped downstairs to fetch Maggie, then returned to the living room and handed the gargoyle off to Smoky, who frowned but took her anyway.

"Since you're going to be sitting here talking, I might as well put you to work. You can watch the baby while I make dinner." Iris brooked no rebuke, and Smoky, along with every other member of our extended family, obeyed her.

Maggie *moophe*d and promptly planted a slobbery kiss on the dragon's cheek. Smoky grinned as a lock of his hair rose up to tickle her under the chin. Maggie loved to play with Smoky's hair, and he would tease her with it like he might tease a cat with a string.

With a chuckle, Iris scurried back to the kitchen, and the clanging of pots and pans promised that dinner would be ready when we woke up. I glanced at the clock. Another ninety minutes, and Menolly would be awake.

"To bed," I said, heading for the stairs. Camille trudged along behind me, followed by Morio, who looked as tired as we were. They peeled off at the second floor, giving me a small wave.

"See you at the table," Camille said as they disappeared into her bedroom.

I dashed up to the third floor, gauging the most effective way to fall asleep. So tired I didn't even bother to undress, I shifted form, then jumped up on the bed and curled up at the bottom. I always slept better as a cat, and sure enough, within moments, I was drifting off into a deep, utterly wonderful, catnap.

"Delilah, Delilah? Time to wake up!" A woman was lifting me into her arms, and still half-asleep, I purred as she started a delightfully luxurious ear-scritch around my head. After a moment, I shook myself awake and looked up into Menolly's eyes. I let out a loud *purp*, and she tossed me lightly on the bed, where I leisurely transformed back to two legs.

I stretched and yawned. "Oh, that felt good. How long did I sleep?"

"I made the others give you and Camille two hours instead ninety minutes. That extra time can play a big difference in reflexes and alertness. Feel good enough to go for it tonight?" Menolly was dressed for the woods: jeans, long-sleeved turtleneck, a denim vest, her lace-up-to-the-knee Doc Martens boots. She gave me a toothy grin, and I could smell blood on her breath.

"You ate already, I take it?" I grimaced and shook my head.

"Shit. Breath stinking again?" She rolled her eyes.

"Yeah. Here. Try this. I keep telling you to start carrying one around." I tossed her a pocket-sized Listerine breath spray. Mint. *Strong* mint. I loved it, because it reminded me of catnip without making me do something stupid. My sisters knew my little secret: Catnip—be it tea or the herb—was as potent for me as tequila was for some FBHs, even when I was in two-legged form. I never told anybody else because I didn't want any practical jokers trying to see how far they could push it.

Menolly couldn't drink or eat anything but blood, but the breath spray didn't bother her like food. She gave herself a few good squirts until I couldn't smell the blood anymore. Holding up the spray, she asked, "Can I keep this?"

Nodding, I glanced down at my outfit. Grungy, yeah, but where we were going, it wouldn't matter. "Think I'm dressed okay? It worked over in OW this morning. I might as well wear it tonight. I'm just going to get filthy again. I know it. I'm about as much of a klutz as Smoky is a clean freak. Have you noticed that he never seems to get dirty?"

"Oh, yeah, and I dare you to ask him how."

"Already did." I snorted. "He just gave me that smart-assed grin of his. Maybe Camille can get it out of him. He's sure a close one with information, that's for sure. You think he's told her his real name yet?"

"Ha! I doubt it. After all, he *is* a dragon." Menolly grinned. "Come on, Kitten. Iris is holding dinner. Camille and Morio should be at the table by now."

As I clattered down the stairs, my sister silently gliding behind me, I could smell the aromas of hamburgers and fresh fruit. My mouth watered, and I bounced into the kitchen, suddenly feeling jazzed. So what if we were on the tail of one of the spirit seals? We'd come through. We always did. Well, not always, but we had the jump on the fourth seal, and this time, we wouldn't let Karvanak win.

Iris handed me a burger and a thick slice of melon as I slid into a chair. Camille and Morio were already eating. Smoky was leaning over a map with Roz, and Vanzir was sitting in the corner. Menolly reached into the playpen and hoisted the Magster onto her hip. Maggie gurgled something and planted a fat kiss on Menolly's cheek.

"So here's the plan. We've got a forty-minute drive to the Skattercreek Road turnoff." Roz traced the route along the map as I leaned across the table to watch. "Once we get there, the grade takes a steep incline, so we'll want to take vehicles that can weather the conditions. Your Jeep should do fine. Camille, leave the Lexus at home. Same with the Jag, Menolly."

As his gaze flickered over to Menolly, a little bell went off in the back of my mind. Something was going on between them. Or was going to, even if neither one realized it yet. Of course, Roz had been trying to get in Menolly's pants for some time, but had my sister decided to open the gates to her garden? They would be one hell of a match, for sure. The incubus and the vampire.

I decided to keep my mouth shut. So did Camille, though she caught my gaze and arched her eyebrows.

"So if we take my Jeep, there are . . . how many of us?" I counted. Smoky, Roz, Vanzir, Camille, Menolly, and me. "Six. I can fit that many, but it will be a tight squeeze."

"We better just take my SUV," Morio said as the phone rang.

Menolly moved to answer it while I shrugged and nodded. "Fine by me. I don't feel like driving anyway."

I had just taken a bite of my burger when Menolly handed the phone to me. I stared at it, hoping it wasn't Chase. Menolly shook the receiver at me, and I finally wiped my hands on my jeans and took the damned thing.

"Yeah?" Not too friendly, but it might be Chase, and I wasn't ready to play nice-nice. But I shouldn't have worried; it was Zach.

"I'm in town, and thought I'd see if you were up for a movie." His pleasantly growly voice was thick and rich as usual, and my body responded to the deep baritone.

I sucked in a deep breath. "No can do. Not tonight. Say, how would you like to take a trip with us? We can use all the help we can get."

A pause, then a low sigh. "Spirit seal or demon or both?"

"Spirit seal. Demons aren't quite onto this one yet, and we'd like to keep it that way. You feel like taking a road trip out toward Snoqualmie?"

He laughed. "Delilah, by now you should know that if *you're* involved, I'm up for anything. I'm about twenty minutes from your house. I'll be there as soon as I can. Don't start without me."

As I handed the receiver back to Menolly, I felt a smug sense of satisfaction. Zachary wasn't scared to help us. Zach

wouldn't let us down. I told the others we'd have another pair
of hands on board.

"Good," Camille said, licking the ketchup off her fingers
and reaching for a napkin. "Iris, if we have any cookies, now
would be the time to spring them. I always crave sugar when
we're on a job."

Job . . . I blinked. "You know, I never thought of it before,
but you're right. That's what all this has become, hasn't it?
More so than the bookstore, than my supposed PI business . . .
more than the Wayfarer Bar & Grill. *Your mission, D'Artigo
sisters, should you choose to accept it: Hunt down and
procure the magical spirit seals before the demons get to them.
If you should fail or be caught, Earth and Otherworld will
suffer a horrible fate . . .* "

Menolly snorted. "Not quite as poetic as Jim Phelps, but
hey, it works in a pinch. Look at it this way, Kitten. At least
we're not stuck behind a desk. Now, *that* would be hell."

Good to his word, Zach arrived fifteen minutes later as we
finished tracing out the route. I opened the door to find him
standing there, looking all tidy and polished. Zach was tall.
Even taller than Smoky, by an inch. At six five, he towered over
my six foot one. His blond hair was cut into a collar-skimming
shag, and he sported a perpetual five o'clock shadow.

Lean and muscled, Zachary was one of the golden boys:
good-looking, rugged, all-American. Except for the fact that
he was a werepuma on the Council of Elders for the Rainier
Puma Pride.

I leaned toward him, inhaling his mingled scents of leather
and dusty sunlight. We'd slept together once, and though I had
sworn it wouldn't happen again, now I found myself considering
him from a whole new angle.

He seemed to sense something was up, because he leaned
down and softly kissed me on the forehead. My knees
quivered. His lips found their way to my lips. My pulse revved
like an engine on steroids. He brought his hand up to my hair
and gently pushed it away from my face.

"What's going on?" he said. "Is it over between you and Chase?"

We were ready to go. We had work to do. Not the right time for a long, insightful talk.

"I don't know," I said. "Right now, help us retrieve the fourth seal. Then, if you don't mind a late-night dinner, we can talk." I knew I was inviting Zachary to play more than tea party, and I knew that *he* knew it. It was my choice. Chase had chastised me for doing the exact same thing he'd succumbed to. Double standards weren't on my menu, and if he now felt free to play without permission, I'd take my cue from him.

He stroked my cheek. "Whatever you desire."

As he pulled back, Camille slipped by, smiling brightly when she saw him. "Good to see you, Zach. Glad to hear you're joining us. We can use all the help we can get."

We clattered down the steps and converged on Morio's SUV. Menolly shoved Zach toward the back door. "Get in, puma boy. Fight now. Talk later. You, too, Kitten."

With a last look at the house, where Iris stood holding Maggie in her arms, I scooted into the backseat next to Zachary, shivering as the warm, musky bulk of his thigh pressed against mine. Oh yeah, it was going to be one hell of a night.

CHAPTER 14

◆━◆

We'd made the drive out toward Snoqualmie before, to a battle involving some butt-ugly werespiders and an ancient shaman who put the *E* in evil. This time I prayed we wouldn't be facing anything quite so gruesome. After all, spirits and ghosts couldn't be as frightening as werespiders, could they?

Then I remembered the revenant and what it was capable of. I shrank back in the seat, wondering if there was any chance in hell we'd catch a break and get through this without a fight.

At least the night wasn't as cold as it had been in December. And we *knew* we were on the tail of a spirit seal. That alone cheered me up. If we could find the rest of the seals before the demons did, maybe we could put a stop to Shadow Wing's plans. Relieved to see my optimism wasn't dead after all, I leaned back and closed my eyes, enjoying the feel of the car as it purred along the miles.

Thirty miles east of Seattle, Snoqualmie was nestled in the foothills of the Cascades, towering mountains of fire and ash. The Cascades were the home of Mount Rainier, a majestic volcano who was merely biding her time until she blew again. Her sister, Mount St. Helens, had lost her peak back in 1980 with a thunderous explosion that killed nearly sixty people. When Rainier went, if she blew big, so would a huge swath of the population who lived right in her path. The land around the Pacific Northwest was alive, all right. Alive and churning beneath the layers of rock and soil and forest.

Snoqualmie's main claim to fame, other than a mountain pass by the same name and a ski resort, was that the city had played host to the filming of *Twin Peaks*, an odd show I'd watched on reruns a few times and found disconcertingly spooky. Considering what we faced on an almost daily basis, I couldn't explain what about the show creeped me out so much, but it was a good scare, unlike the kind in which we always seemed to get entangled.

We had to pass through the Eastside in order to get to Snoqualmie. A conglomeration of cities—Redmond, Bellevue, Woodinville, Kirkland, Issaquah—each had their unique charm. The Eastside was the heart of high-tech in the Northwest, with software companies dominating the area, led by Microsoft. And the area itself was developing at a rapid rate. Bellevue's skyscrapers were giving Seattle's tall towers a run for their money. As we drove through the glittering wash of lights and concrete, I held my breath, thinking how different this was from my home.

And yet . . . and yet . . . Otherworld had its own brilliance and towering palaces and marbled buildings that we seldom saw over Earthside. And the magical lights of the eye-catchers glittered as brilliantly, though not quite so neon, as the scattered lights within the glass-and-steel buildings. Just replace the hum of electric wires and cell phone towers with the buzz of magical energy, and the two realms weren't so different after all.

As we sped down I-90 and then turned off on exit 25, the trees grew tall and thick on either side of the freeway. The towering firs loomed dark over the landscape, and the undergrowth was thick and full with burgeoning ferns and huckleberry and scrub holly and wild grasses.

The Cascade Mountain Range and its foothills, running the length of Washington down into Oregon, were a wild region. Mountain lions and bears and coyotes roamed the hills, occasionally venturing into the outskirts of the city, and the land felt rugged and tough. If you weren't up to the challenge, you could die in the mountains in any number of ways, none comfortable to think about.

As the engine hummed, I inhaled deeply, then let out a long sigh. How many times had we raced off to quell a problem in the past six months? How many nights had we spent bashing heads and getting beat up in return?

The problem with rogue portals opening showed no signs of stopping. Cryptos and Fae were showing up everywhere, especially around the Northwest. Guarding the portals that opened into the Subterranean Realms was proving to be difficult, because the OIA had been absorbed into our Queen's army and for now, we were working off the radar.

One thing we had to be grateful about, though, was that the new portals showed no signs of opening into the Sub Realms. The Netherworld, yes, but the Sub Realms—not so much. A blessing we couldn't ignore.

I leaned forward and peeked over Roz's shoulder. He was riding shotgun, while Morio drove, and considering he had the map, it was probably a good arrangement. "You're sure that Karvanak hasn't got wind of the seal yet?"

He shrugged. "As far as we could tell, no. Of course, there's no guarantee, but I don't think he'd be torturing that poor man if he already had the information. He'd just eat him. Rāksasas do that, you know. They eat humans, along with other species."

Shuddering, I slipped back in my seat. "Yeah, I know, but thanks again for the visual. Just what I needed."

Smoky, who was sitting on my right, snorted. "I eat people, too."

"Not like that," I said. "You don't just go devouring innocents, and we know it. Maybe some dragons do, but don't pretend that you're like them."

He narrowed his eyes. "You've got a mouth on you, girl," he said, and it wasn't a compliment by the tone in which he spoke. But I noticed he didn't contradict me.

I glanced over my shoulder at Camille, who was sprawled

in the back, along with Menolly and Vanzir. "Did you bring the unicorn horn?"

She nodded. "We have no idea what we'll be facing. I figured I might as well bring it, especially since my hand's still sore, and it's going to hurt like hell to run energy through it."

Vanzir let out a huff of impatience. "We get the seal, then you take it wherever you need to take it. Then what?"

"We start searching for the fifth one, I guess." I shrugged. "That seems to be our current direction, don't you think?"

Camille shook her head. "I hate to remind you of this, but the demons aren't our only rivals for the spirit seals. I'd say it's a good bet that Aeval, Morgaine, and Titania are probably looking for them, too. And should they find one, I'll lay odds they won't be keen to turn it over to Queen Asteria. The pit of my gut tells me that Morgaine wants to give them to Aeval."

Morgaine. Titania. Aeval. Three brilliant and terrible queens. We'd recently found out that Morgaine was a distant relative of ours, but she didn't seem to put a lot of stock into blood ties unless it benefited her own agenda.

"Get real," Menolly said. "They played you like a Spanish guitar. I grant you that Grandmother Coyote had a hand in it, but I still maintain they somehow put her up to convincing you that it was your destiny to help them."

I gulped. I'd been wondering the same thing, but it never occurred to me to say it to Camille's face. For one thing, no matter what had really happened, there was no changing the outcome. For another, the thought had flickered through my mind that perhaps Camille had been so desperate to believe we had allies that she'd allowed herself to be blindsided.

Whatever the case, with her help, the three nobility of Earthside Fae had reestablished the fallen regime that had been, at one time, the Unseelie and Seelie Courts. Now, Morgaine, Titania, and Aeval ruled over the Courts of the Three Queens. And they weren't just sitting around looking pretty.

"Have you noticed just how many Earthside Fae have been flocking to the area? The Supe Community Council has been paying attention, and rumors are filtering out that there's a growing unease rising between the Earthside and OW Fae. The FBHs are thrilled by the novelty, but they don't see the potential dangers of the situation. We have enough on our plates without coping with yet another civil war between the Fae, this time one between the realms." I shook my head.

"Wonderful." Menolly sounded anything but thrilled. She flicked Camille on the head with her thumb and forefinger. "I still think you were off your rocker to help them."

"You've made that abundantly clear," Camille said quietly. "I've taken a lot of flack for my actions from a lot of people, so maybe, just maybe, my own family can *lay off*?"

Her eyes narrowed. "You *really* think that I acted on impulse? That I didn't know what I was doing? I knew perfectly well. I also know that it will take a miracle for them to allow me to stay on should the OIA ever regroup and the death threat on our heads be removed. I'm as good as gone from the fold, no matter who wins the war in Y'Elestrial. Lethesanar . . . Tanaquar . . . doesn't matter. I'm history to any government who had a hand in the Great Divide. And if you think I didn't consider that *before* I helped Morgaine and Titania free Aeval from the crystal, maybe you're the ones who are blind. When the Hags of Fate tell me to do something, I *do* it. This is bigger than just us. Bigger than Otherworld."

Smoky let out something that sounded like a huff. He was glaring at me, and I had the feeling he was none too happy with Menolly, either. He kept quiet, but I could feel him tensing beside me.

I also felt my own inner equilibrium beginning to blur, and I took a deep breath, trying to avoid shifting. Family arguments always gave me the most stress, and I had a hard time keeping it together when we squabbled.

"The portals," I whispered. "You did it because the portals are breaking down."

Camille glanced at me, looking surprised. "Ten points for Kitten. The fabric that separates the three realms was never meant to be stretched so tightly. The Great Divide was a big, fat mistake, and the OW Fae who participated in it are going to have to acknowledge their error sooner or later. And I don't think we have until *later*."

"Do you think any of them still exist? Beyond Queen Asteria and the Fae Queens?"

"I'm fairly certain there are a few of the forefathers still alive. But that doesn't matter. What matters is that the system is collapsing, and we have no idea how this mess will affect our problems with the demons. Shadow Wing might be able to rip through the portals easier with the fabric dividing the realms breaking apart. We aren't in this alone; the Earthside Fae can help us, but we need to give them a reason to. And not feeling second-class to OW Fae might just be the start." Camille frowned, leaning her head against the side of the car.

I suddenly felt like a heel. I'd been judging her actions as if she'd gone rogue, or—and I'd only admit this in my heart of hearts—a part of me had secretly wondered if she just wanted to get in good with the Fae Queens. Now I stared at my hands, not knowing what to say.

Menolly cleared her throat. "Gee, Sis, you might have told us all this back when it all went down. I thought . . . oh, never mind what I thought. Your heart's in the right place, but I still don't know about your head. But what matters is that we gather our allies and do our best to capture the spirit seals before anybody else does. Even then, I wonder what Queen Asteria is going to do with all of the seals. If they're all in one place, it could spell big trouble if the Elfin city is ever under siege from a bigger foe."

"Oh joy," I mumbled. "Give us something new to worry about, why don't you? Let's just focus on one thing at a time, shall we? We capture the fourth seal, take it over to Queen Asteria, and talk to her about our concerns. Okay?" My head was spinning with all the debate. All I really wanted was to find a nice warm corner and curl up to sleep for a dozen hours or so.

Morio, who had been silent until now, said, "Delilah's right. Everybody just calm down. Grandmother Coyote knew what she was doing, so drop it and quit harassing Camille. We're almost to the exit. Once we take that, we've got another ten or fifteen miles to drive, and we'll be headed up the hillside toward the cave. I suggest you all use the time to catch a little rest. Just close your eyes and doze or something." He sounded pissed—the first time I'd really ever heard a testiness to his voice.

The fox demon was usually impassive, but apparently we'd managed to ruffle his feathers. I glanced at Smoky again, who looked grimly pleased at Morio's words, and decided that the best defense was a quick catnap. I leaned my head on Zachary's shoulder—he'd been listening silently to our debate—and closed my eyes, letting the rumbling of the wheels lull me into a light snooze.

Some twenty minutes later, I was rudely jogged out of my slumber to find that we were heading up a steep grade that was bumpy as all get out. My guess, unpaved and covered by chunky, rough gravel.

As we jolted along, I turned around in my seat. Camille and Menolly looked quiet, both lost in thought. I reached over the backseat and lightly rested my hand on Camille's shoulder.

"I'm sorry," I said softly. "I never meant to imply you didn't know what you were doing. I admit that I thought you did what you did for different reasons, but I was wrong. I'll never doubt your actions again. You've held us together for a long time, and I trust you."

Her eyes glistened. "Thanks, Kitten. I appreciate that."

Menolly rolled her eyes, but she nodded. "Double that from me, too. We're a team, and we have to stick together. Let's leave the infighting to the politicians."

That was as good as a tearful apology from our sister, the vampire, and Camille knew it. She sniffed and dashed her hand across her eyes. "Man, I'm tired. I just want to get tonight over and go home and sleep. I have so much to think about from today."

"Yeah, especially since you know that Trillian's just playing undercover spy again and not really in danger. Pretty shabby of him not to tell you," Menolly said, then glanced at me. She'd gone too far, and she knew it. Menolly was great in a fight, but diplomacy was a long ways from being one of her strong suits.

Camille stared at her, then shook her head. "Don't even go there. I'll deal with Trillian later." Her voice said *case closed* in no uncertain terms.

I turned back around in my seat. What the hell was going on? We'd never been at each other's throats like this. Of course, we weren't really arguing, I tried to tell myself. We were all tired, stressed out, and facing yet another night of battle against some undead fiends.

"Maybe we'll get lucky, and they'll just be a bunch of Caspers," I said, trying to lighten the mood.

Menolly laughed. "Ever the optimist, that's our Kitten."

After a moment, Camille joined her. "Yeah, maybe. For once I'd like to see her optimism pay off. Maybe if we wish real hard . . ."

"And find some ruby slippers!" Menolly added.

"Oh stop it, you two!" But I wasn't mad. At least I had them laughing, and that was a good sign. "Next you'll be telling me to clap really hard or Tinkerbelle will die."

"Yeah, well, Tinkerbelle has it easy, the little slacker," Camille said, snorting. "All she has to do is fly around on TV and look cute. We've got the real world to deal with."

"Speaking of real world, ladies, get ready. We're about to park and go for a little hike. I hope you all wore warm clothing," Roz said. He directed Morio to pull into a turnoff.

As we piled out of the car into the chill evening air, I noticed there was a fire pit nearby. It was rough, a small circular hole that had been lined with chunks of stone. There had been a blaze in it recently, but by the smell of the charcoal, it had rained since then, so it had to be a few days old.

I knelt down beside the ring of stones and examined the debris next to it. A couple of beer cans, a wrapper from a Whopper, a few cigarette butts. "I don't think any demons or ghosts left this stuff lying around."

Roz shook his head. "Ten to one, this was where the prospectors made camp. This road is seldom used. The man we talked to said that it used to be an old logging road but that a new one had been built a decade ago, and now this one's primarily used by hunters and hiking enthusiasts who don't mind a rough jaunt into the wilderness."

Rough jaunt? Delightful. I stood, wiping my hands on my jeans. "What now? Which way?"

Vanzir pointed out a trail, barely discernible through the waist-high grass. We geared up and, following the incubus and the dream chaser, plunged into the undergrowth.

The path immediately began to descend, and at first I wondered if we were really heading the right way. Weren't most caves supposed to be up on a cliff face rather than down in a ravine? But then the path opened out into a narrow walkway that ran alongside a deep gully. The gully overlooked a stream flowing a good fifty to sixty feet below. The drop-off was immediate and steep, with no shoulder to cushion the way should anyone fall. While the trail was wide enough for two to walk abreast, we fell into single file.

I glanced across the streambed. The cliff on the other side of the ravine was covered in timber. From where we were, I could see that the trail led to a narrow bridge that spanned the stream. The bridge was a wooden trestle, the supporting timbers weathered and old. I'd guess at least a hundred years, if not more. No doubt, it had been used by the prospectors and hunters who had wandered through the mountains. The loggers, however, would have had to use a different bridge. I couldn't see any vehicle-accessible road from where I stood.

Zach, who was right behind me, gasped and stopped in his tracks. He pointed toward a ledge on the opposite side of the ravine. I followed his gaze and found myself staring at a magnificent puma. She was a lioness, that I knew by instinct, and she was no Were, just pure, primal feline. And she was watching us—Zach and me primarily. I could feel her stare etch itself all the way into my bones.

Zach leaned closer to me. "She's lactating."

I knew. Somehow, I knew. The mother cat had kittens, and they were probably somewhere near, hidden from prying eyes. I scanned the cliff wall but could see nothing. My gaze wandering back to the mother puma, I took a deep breath and sent a wave of goodwill toward her.

Tears welled up as she leaned her head back and let out a roar. Longing rang in the call, and fear, and anger. Something was wrong. I knew it, and while I wasn't sure what it was, she needed help.

Before I knew what I was doing, I'd pushed ahead of the pack and—with Zach right behind me—found myself racing across the bridge. Camille and Roz were shouting behind us, but my attention was totally caught up by the mother lion. She needed help, and she recognized that we could offer it to her.

As we jogged across the bridge, I saw that Zach had shifted into his puma form. Without a thought, without warning, I found myself shifting, too—this time not into Tabby but into Panther. What the—? The Autumn Lord controlled me in this form. What were his concerns with the puma?

And then I heard him, buried deep in my thoughts, deep in my heart. "She is under my protection, as are all of Einarr's descendants. Her mother was a werepuma who chose to return to the wild and stay on four legs. The daughter cannot shift, but she can recognize shifters. Help her in what she needs. Just because you're a Daughter of the Grave doesn't mean you can't help the living."

In the blink of an eye, his presence withdrew, but I remained in panther form. Zach and I loped along, side by side, in silence. There was no trail leading up to the lioness, but we didn't let that stand in our way. I reveled in my strength and power as we leapt from rock to rock, forelegs touching down even as hind legs pushed off the boulders. We bounded up the cliff, and I felt like I could run forever, intoxicated by the cascade of scents and sounds that washed over me.

The lioness waited for us, unwavering in her gaze. We landed beside her, but she gave no sign of fear. I gently reached out, butting her with my head. A tabby gesture, but one that most cats responded to, big or small.

"What's wrong?" The words weren't in English, or Fae, but she understood them perfectly.

"My cub—she's trapped, and I can't get her out." A flicker of pain raced through the mother's eyes, and I recognized the fear that filled her softly spoken vocalizations.

"Lead the way," Zach said. "We're here to help."

The puma led us back along the ledge to a den. We followed

her inside, and I could hear the mewing of a kit. Another kitten sat in the corner, looking confused and hungry. My instinct was to run over and pick it up, but one look at Mama Puma told me that wasn't the best idea. We wound through a small tunnel until we came to the back wall. There was a narrow fissure near the edge, a foot wide and a good four or five feet deep. The mewing came from within the crack.

I leaned my head down, and in the dark, could make out the other kitten. Somehow, she'd gotten herself down into the crack, and there wasn't room enough for Mama to reach in and pull the baby out. The cougar would get stuck if she tried to rescue her baby. Unless we helped, the kit would starve to death.

Glancing back at the lioness, I said, "I need to change into my two-legged form. Please don't worry. I won't hurt your baby. But it's the only way I can pull her out."

She gave me a bob of the head, as if she were nodding. "My mother was a Were," she said. "I've seen the change happen before."

With her approval, I moved away and focused on shifting back. After a moment, my body began to twist and shift, and within seconds, I was Delilah again, standing on two legs. I cast a quick look at the mother puma, but she seemed good to her word, so I knelt down beside the fissure and leaned in. I scrambled to reach the kitten, who was leaning up against the wall, reaching for me with her paws, but I couldn't quite reach that far down.

Zach sensed my difficulty, and he, too, shifted back into human form. Silently, he caught my legs and lowered me so that I was hanging over the edge of the fissure. The kitten struggled to reach my hands, and then I managed to catch hold of her under the forepaws, and while I held on for dear life, Zach dragged me back out of the crack. The kitten came with me, and as soon as I let go, waddled over to its mother and began searching for a teat to suckle on. The kits were still in that confused, awkward stage: terribly cute and terribly vulnerable.

I looked around for loose stones to fill the fissure, but there weren't enough.

As the mother puma anxiously groomed her baby, I crept forward, slowly, wondering if she'd accept me near her when I was in human form, too. She huffed slightly, but then her eyes met mine, and we were no longer big cat and human, or big cat and Were, but two souls, bound by all things feline, gazing into each other's heart.

"She's beautiful," I whispered in cat. "May I pet her? May I touch you?"

With another soft huff, the mother moved ever so slightly, opening the way for me to reach the baby. I gently laid one hand on the kit's side and shivered as the soft fur ruffled under my fingers. A low trill told me the girl was purring, and I bit my lip, leaning forward to gently kiss the side of the kitten. The mother let out an anxious mew, and I moved my hand to her side, resting my fingers lightly against her fur for a moment as we connected, our auras blending for a brief moment.

Then I backed away.

"We should go," Zach said. "The others will be worried."

Nodding, I slowly backed away, my eyes never leaving the mother's face. She dipped her head again and—carrying her kit by the scruff of the neck—followed us to the front of the cavern.

"You should find another place to stay, Mama," I said softly in cat. "I couldn't make the crack in the ground safe for you. So you'd best find another den that won't swallow your babies."

She blinked, and I knew she'd gotten my message. As we left the cave, I heard her grunt, then settle down as the cubs set to nursing. I glanced at Zach, and he beamed.

"You want one, don't you?" he said.

"Want one what?"

"A kit—a baby." He laughed when he said it, but the look in his eyes told me he wasn't joking.

I stared at him, thinking he was out of his mind, but once it took hold, the idea wouldn't go away. It was true. Seeing the mother with her kittens had resonated inside. I wanted a family. But I didn't just want a baby, I wanted Were babies. Kittens who would understand my feline nature as well as my half-human, half-Fae side. And that was bound to be a problem. Because half-Fae Weres were sterile, as far as producing Were children. I could have a baby, all right, but there was no guarantee that she—or he—would have any chance of coming out Were except by a random roll of the dice.

I let out a soft sigh as we emerged from the cave and began cautiously lowering ourselves down the cliff face to the path below, where the others now waited. I didn't have time to think about this. Not now.

"Well, one thing's for sure," I said to Zach as we joined the others. "Children—of any kind—are going to have to wait. Don't tell the others, please. My sisters don't need to know that my biological clock is ticking. They'd just worry themselves sick for no reason. It's not like I can get pregnant, anyway. We had long-term treatments before we left home, and the antidote is only found in Otherworld. For now, the baby-making factory is closed."

Zach just nodded, but a bright light flickered in his eyes, and he gave me a soft smile. As we began to tell the others what had happened, I wondered what the hell he was thinking.

CHAPTER 15

~~~

Vanzir acted impatient as we explained the situation. I tugged on the hem of my jacket. While the dream chaser was doing his best to fit in, the fact that he was out-and-out demon shone through in a lot of ways and made me uncomfortable. And for once, I wasn't alone.

Before we'd gotten in the car, Camille had confided that the heroin-chic rocker look-alike gave her the creeps, even though he was bound to our side. But we needed all the help we could get, and beggars couldn't be choosy. Especially with Shadow Wing on the rampage. Vanzir knew too much about our operations to set him free. We kept him in the dark about a lot, but he was bound to pick up information from hanging around so much.

I tried to shake off my unease and focus on our goal.

Since we were already over the bridge, Roz took the lead, and we followed him along the increasingly narrow shelf that passed for a trail. We were headed in the opposite direction from the ledge where we'd encountered the puma. I glanced over my shoulder in time to see her watching from behind a scrub bush, and she softly opened her mouth as if to say something, but even with my keen hearing, the only sounds were those of the rushing stream below and the murmur of soft voices as Camille and Morio whispered.

We could all see in the dark, at least to some degree, but Roz insisted we take it slow, and he held a long stick, tapping the ground as we went. There might be large chunks of rock that could turn our ankles, or maybe a sinkhole, or even—perhaps—a rattler, though they tended to be on the east side of the Cascades. But up in the mountains, you never knew.

I caught sight of a faint outline. There was a cavern up ahead to the right, leading into the cliff side and we were headed directly for the blackened opening. As we drew near, the hair on my arms and the back of my neck stood on end.

Camille whispered, "I can feel them. Spirits of some sort. The energy is supercharged here, and I'm not sure what would happen if I were to call in the Moon Mother's power right now."

"Don't try it. Not unless we really need you to," Smoky said, guiding her from behind, his hand pressed against the small of her back. As I watched them, I was suddenly again filled with a sense of loss. Chase should be here; Chase should be worrying about *me* instead of screwing around with his ex.

Zachary seemed to sense my mood. He caught my shoulder lightly with his hand and whispered, "Don't worry. We'll watch out for each other. Okay?"

Feeling a little better, I flashed him a smile, wondering what the hell I really *did* want. But there was no time for self-pity. We were almost there, and I had a responsibility to be on top of my game.

As we neared the cavern, Menolly slipped up next to me. "I don't sense spirits very well, but I can tell you that I don't feel any demonic energy coming from within."

Vanzir heard her and dropped back beside us. "Neither do I. My guess is that Karvanak and his gang haven't found the location yet. We've lucked out," he added, glancing at Menolly. "But I'll tell you this. Some of the shadows who come from the Netherworld put my kin to shame. Revenants and shades are far more dangerous than your standard Rāksasa or dream chaser."

I frowned. Not a good thought. Not a happy thought. Not

one I wanted to entertain, that was for sure. "Do you think there are any spirits or ghosts out there who are as dangerous as Shadow Wing?"

We walked lightly around the subject of Shadow Wing when Vanzir was around. After all, he *was* a full demon from the Sub Realms. He wasn't necessarily angry at Shadow Wing for being the Big Bad he was. Vanzir just didn't agree with his take on breaking through the portals or trying to overpower Earth and OW. When it came down to it, I wondered just how far his reformed status would take him. On the other hand, why else would he undergo the Ritual of Subjugation if he didn't want to change? At least a little? He'd die if he reneged on the deal, and it wouldn't be a pleasant death.

"I don't know. I hope not." Vanzir shrugged. He stared at me for a moment, his disconcertingly clear eyes homing in on my thoughts. Then he reached out lightly, his fingers barely grazing my arm before he seemed to think the better of it and snatched his hand back again.

"I know you don't trust me," he said. "I know you can't figure out what my angle is. I don't blame you. I'd probably feel the same way if I were in your shoes. But I hope that someday you'll be able to believe me when I tell you that I haven't got any ulterior motives. I may have been born a demon, but I'm just not . . . I don't like what I've done in my life. It's not me. I don't fit in the Subterranean Realms, and I don't fit with most of my kind."

Before I could say anything, he hurried ahead to catch up with Roz. I watched him go, then let out a long sigh, not knowing what to think.

Menolly glanced at me, and we both shrugged. She looked as puzzled as I felt. "Who knows?" she said, modulating her voice so low I could barely catch her words. "He might be telling the truth. Meanwhile, we keep our eyes open."

At that moment, Roz stopped and held up his hand, motioning us to come closer. He held his finger to his lips. "Be as quiet as you can. We stormed the house in Seattle and saw just how well that all went down. Let's try for a more subtle approach here."

"You think?" I said, but kept my voice low.

"Yeah, I think." He grinned at me, then sobered. "Here's the deal. We don't have a clear picture of the cavern. The prospector couldn't give us one, but if he's right, the chamber with the spirit seal is off to the left of the main vault. There's a short passage leading to it, but he mentioned a few old sinkholes and shafts. Don't get yourselves lost. If the mining was extensive, there could be a labyrinth of tunnels. The wood shoring them up is bound to be fragile."

Smoky frowned, his brow knitting in a way that made me glad I wasn't Roz. "This is dangerous. I've been in old tunnels like this one before. They can crush you without warning. Walk softly, no loud words, no explosions. Camille, you should hold back on your magic. Morio, your fox-fire light spells will be fine, but nothing that could set up a tremor in the rocks. In other words, we're going to have to face the spirits with spells that don't send out shock waves. Obey me on this one, or you could find yourselves squashed flatter than one of Delilah's toy mice."

I snorted but not for long. He glared at me. Obviously it hadn't been a joke. My smile faded away.

"The man has it down," Roz said. "This is a subtle operation. So think before you speak, and test the ground before heading off into side passages."

Camille glanced at Morio. "Just like with Titania's cave. There were some nasty sinkholes there."

We sorted ourselves out. Menolly and Vanzir would be our first wave. They were the most silent. Roz, Zach, and I would be the second line. Camille and Morio would come third. Smoky would cover our butts and make sure we weren't surprised from behind.

As Menolly and Vanzir disappeared into the cavern, I let out a long breath. *Here we go again*, I thought, and then—motioning to Roz and Zach, who flanked my sides—headed into the darkness.

The air immediately shifted from clear and chilly to murky and damp. It smelled like mold, or slime, or something that had been sitting in the refrigerator a few weeks too long. I managed to catch my breath just before dinner made a repeat visit. I had a strong gag reflex, thanks to the hairball situation, and while I could eat a ton of junk food and watch the weirdest shit on TV, just send me into a room with a strong odor, and I was apt to lose it.

Whatever this was, it didn't smell like any old normal, run-of-the-mill mold. Nope, this was nasty. This was . . . this was . . . sour and fetid and reminded me of the venidemons' lair, though not quite so bad.

"Man, that's rancid," Zach whispered in my ear. "What the hell is it?"

"I dunno, but I'm not looking forward to finding out." A pebble under my foot set me off balance, and I reached out to balance myself against the wall. As my fingers touched the rock, they met with the ickiest, slimiest mess I'd ever felt. It felt like I'd plunged my hand into a melted banana slug or a pile of snot.

"Gross, gross, gross." I managed to lower my voice before I sent my dismay echoing down the hallway. I pulled my hand back and frantically tried to assess whether I'd covered it with something dangerous or just nasty.

Zach leaned in as Roz pulled a tiny, pen-sized flashlight out of his pocket and aimed the dim beam at my fingers. They were covered with what looked like some oozing ichor from an old fifties SF flick, the kind of stuff that comes in a can that parents never, ever want to buy their kids because they know it will either end up in the kids' stomachs or—worse yet—their hair.

Only this stuff smelled worse than skunk juice. Worse than my litter box when I forgot to clean it for a few days. Worse than . . . *What the—?*

I stopped thinking about how it smelled because the slime started to move on my hand. It began to stretch itself out in a fine film. As it wrapped around my fingers and started to slither down my palm like some freak-ass living glove, I let out a little screech.

"Get this crap off me, now!" I didn't care who heard me at this point. Visions of digestive enzymes going to work on my skin crowded my thoughts. I wasn't ready to be assimilated into blob city.

Zach reached for my hand but Roz smacked him away.

"Don't touch it; let me take care of this. Here, you hold the light."

By now, the others, except for Menolly and Vanzir who had gone on ahead, were gathered around us. Roz pulled out a chopstick—what the hell he had a chopstick in his pocket for, I didn't know and didn't ask—and poked at the slime. It reared up, like some bizarre rubbery club, and took a swipe at the long toothpick. Delightful; I was being devoured by Rocky the Blob. Next it would form itself into a tiny boxing glove and start pummeling me.

"I have no idea what the thing is," Roz said as he jabbed at it again with the chopstick, piercing it this time. A burning sensation raced over my palm, and I jumped.

"Stop that! I think it's dripping something on my skin!"

Smoky pushed his way in and leaned down, whispering a few low words I couldn't catch. A thin white mist drifted out of his mouth to cover my hand. It reminded me of Iris's snow and ice magic. As the mist hit my palm, the slime immediately began to pull itself together into a puddle, letting go of my fingers.

"What's it doing?" I asked, both fascinated and repulsed.

"Trying to keep its core temperature high enough to prevent it from freezing," Smoky said. He blew on it again, and the blob crystallized into a white pool of icy gelatin, then froze solid. The dragon gave it a tap, and it shattered. I tipped my hand, and it landed on the floor.

"Is it dead?" I asked, staring at the hundreds of slime shards.

"Probably not. Creatures like this can take a lot of temperature variation. It's some form of ectoplasmic ooze." He examined my hand. "No worse for the wear. Just don't touch the walls if you can help it. There might be other, more aggressive forms of it around."

More aggressive? Not a good thought.

"Where does it come from?" Camille asked.

Smoky glanced around the tunnel we were standing in. "When there are too many spirits from the Netherworld in a small area on the physical realm, the excess spirit energy builds up and takes on a life of its own, usually forming into ectoplasm. When the spirits are strong, it takes on a rudimentary consciousness and becomes a predator."

"How dangerous is it?" I asked.

"That amount of slime could have digested one—maybe two layers of skin off your hand before becoming satiated. At that point, it would fall into a somnambulant state while it grew. If you left it on, it would start in again when it came out of its molt. If you were attacked by a larger amount, it could be a lot worse," he said as he examined the ceiling with Roz's flashlight. "Always check overhead. Ectoplasm can cling to ceilings and roofs."

I squirmed, not quite liking the idea of having a carnivorous slime on me. "Just how many of them do you think there are in here?"

"Hard to tell how many pieces, but there's only one of each variety in any given area saturated by spiritual energy. The slimes hive off into cluster cells—blobs, if you will—but retain a group consciousness," Smoky said, as he turned toward the back of the group.

Before he once again took up guarding our tail, he added, "If you see one that's indigo rather than green, stay away from it at all costs, or we might not be able to save you."

"Of course: viro-mortis slimes! I know what he's talking about now. My father taught me about them when I was young. And Smoky's right," Morio said. "The indigo variety is far more aggressive. They call their sister cells to join them when they find a victim, and the things are faster than you might believe. The indigo variety is unaffected by ice, but fire will char them. Which would mean burning the thing off, which would also burn you."

"Once again, may I say *ewww*?" I shivered and furiously rubbed my hand on my jeans to make sure it was free of the freakish goo. I glanced back at Camille, frowning. She never got slapped with goo. Sure, she got smacked around by demons, fried by hellhound blood, and slashed by vampires, but she never had to deal with the slime monster. All at once, I envied her, even though I knew it was ridiculous. Of the three of us, I was always—and probably forever would be—the one who'd end up with mud on her face and kitty litter stuck to her butt.

We slipped farther along the tunnel, skirting fallen rocks and a few small sinkholes. The pits weren't big enough to swallow us up, but they could give a nasty turn to the ankle. The faint *drip, drip, drip* of water sounded from somewhere in the distance. As we quietly crept along, my mind wandered to the miners who had worked here. They'd dreamed in gold and silver, or perhaps in brilliant Technicolor jewels. How many had truly ever struck it rich?

I was so wrapped up in thought that I didn't notice when Roz motioned for us to stop, and so plowed right into Zach's back, knocking him to his knees. Before I could react, he was up again, flashing me a bemused look as he shook his head when I mouthed, "Are you hurt?"

Roz was standing in an archway. The beams that shored up the opening looked old, weakened by water and time. I strained to listen to the timber and didn't like what I heard: the sounds of age and insects, of wear and tear and splintering wood. Shit, we were in danger here. The sooner we finished and left, the better.

Roz listened carefully, turning his head first to the left, then to the right. His long, curling hair was caught back in a ponytail, and he was wearing his perpetual black Aussie hat with a feather in the band. He'd picked it up in some thrift store after watching *Crocodile Dundee* with Menolly and me on Late-Night Movie Madness, and even I had to admit, it looked good with the leather duster.

After a moment, he turned around. "I think this opening leads into a different dimension. Vanzir and Menolly turned left, that much I can tell. I smell water to the right. And there appears to be a path leading down into a deep chasm. This cave has just officially branched away from anything typical for the area. There shouldn't be any mammoth caves around this area—not like this."

"Should we just walk in? If that's a portal, are we going to be able to get back once we cross the threshold?" I tried to remember everything I could about the portals. Some, like the ones the Fae had set up to guard against the demons, were very restrictive but fairly stable in actual use. Others, like the ones opening willy-nilly, were unbalanced and threatened to close at random.

Roz looked up at Smoky, who was regarding the opening with caution. "What do you think?" he asked softly. Right then, I knew he was worried.

Smoky's gaze flickered to Camille, then to me. "Obviously Menolly and the demon thought it was safe. But then again, perhaps they didn't notice the gateway until it was too late. This entire cavern is unstable. We might as well be carrying a bomb. One wrong move, and we could bring tons of rock down on our heads. Or worse."

Camille sucked in a deep breath. "We have no choice. We have to find the spirit seal, and we don't know where Menolly and Vanzir were headed. Why don't we split up? Half stay here, half go through and see what happens."

I let out a low sigh. "Yeah, I think so, too. You stay here, along with Smoky and Morio. I'll take Roz and Zach, and we'll step through. Once over the archway, we should be able to tell if we're in trouble."

For once, she didn't argue with me, and I wondered if her hand was hurting more than she let on. Usually, Camille played the big-sister card. A lot. But she just looked a little relieved.

Smoky nodded. "Rozurial, if things go wrong, you know how to get Delilah and Zach out. Use it, if you have to."

I caught my breath. "The Ionyc Sea?" I glanced at Roz.

Smoky let out a low growl but said nothing.

I stared at him. "Come on, you know Camille had to tell me."

With a wry grin, Roz said, "She has you there."

Smoky led Camille and Morio back away from the archway.

"If there's trouble," Camille said, "scream—shout—do whatever you have to in order to let us know. If you disappear and we don't see you within a few moments, I'm coming in."

"You are not—" Smoky started, but she brushed away his protests.

"Of course I am, and you can't stop me." She ran back over to me and leaned up on tiptoe to kiss my cheek. "Stay safe, Kitten. I love you. Don't get yourself into trouble."

As she returned to the dragon's side, I sucked in a deep lungful of air and let it out slowly, counting from twenty to one to calm the jitters that had taken up residence in my stomach.

"Are we ready to do this?" I asked.

Roz and Zach nodded. Roz, Zach, and I linked arms and then stepped through the arch leading into the giant cavern.

CHAPTER 16

A crackle warned me that we were headed into an energy field, and then, without fuss or muss, we were through. It was totally different than the portals to OW. I whirled and, much to my relief, saw Camille and Smoky standing there, looking anxious. Morio raised his hand to wave.

I waved back. "Can you still see me?"

Camille laughed. "Yes, thank the gods. We're coming through." They stepped through the archway, and I heard a tiny sizzle of sparks, but nothing untoward happened, and within a few seconds, we were standing together again.

The cavern was huge. My guess was that we were standing a step or two to the left of Earthside's realm—not far enough to totally separate us from our mother's home, but far enough to exist in its own little niche. Even with my keen vision, it was difficult to see the other side of the cave. The murky bottom of the ravine was swathed in a mist too deep to tell how far down it went.

The air here was cooler, more humid than the air in the tunnels, and I noticed the drop in temperature even through my jacket. I borrowed Roz's flashlight and walked over to one of the cavern walls, where I shone the light against the rock. It was wet, slick with water that trickled drop by drop down the sides, and covered with patches of the viro-mortis slime. This time the slime had a purplish tint, and I cautiously avoided getting anywhere near the carnivorous ectoplasm.

"I think we're getting closer. If the spirit seal is protected by ghosts or revenants or whatever, there are probably a lot of them or they're very powerful, because this slime is everywhere. I'm not looking forward to—" A noise stopped me in midsentence.

I stepped away from the wall, and we all listened, on our guard, waiting. After a nerve-racking second, Menolly and Vanzir reappeared from around a corner to our left.

With a short sigh, I let out my breath and relaxed. "Thank heavens. We were just about to come look for you. What did you find?"

Menolly's eyes were wide and glowing red. "We found the chamber with the spirit seal, but it's heavily guarded. There's one shade. Big-time dangerous. But before we can even get to him, we have to wade through at least half a dozen wights."

Wights. Oh shit. Wights were nasty brutes. One foot in the Netherworld, one foot in the grave, they were truly members of the walking dead. Even vampires gave them a wide berth, because wights were so vicious. They were more like animals than intelligent beings, cunning and voracious in their appetite for flesh and spirit. Unlike shades, which devoured the spirit, or zombies, which ate only the flesh, wights fed off both.

They sucked the spirit out of the very bones and muscle as they consumed their dinner, usually while their victim was still alive. There were wights in Otherworld, usually in the dark volcanic ranges of the Southern Wastes and well north of the towering Nebelvuori Mountains, but they seldom ever came near the populated areas, usually feeding off animals and the scant handful of travelers venturing into the mountain passes.

Camille cleared her throat. "Well, do we know what kills a wight?"

"Dragon's breath," Smoky grumbled. "But unless the chamber is as big as this one, I won't be able to transform, and I doubt they'll come out and play, even if we ask them nicely."

"It isn't," Menolly said. "It's a narrow, low passage leading into a smallish cavern. There's plenty of room there for both them and us, but not for a dragon. Wights are undead. If you have some sort of necromantic spell to repulse or turn the dead, Morio, that might help."

We all turned to the youkai, who glanced at Camille. She gave him a slight nod, and he said, "We've been working on that. I don't know if it will work on a wight, though. We've never actually tried it except on a few of the spirits in the known haunted houses around town—"

"Whoa—hold on," I said. "You mean you two have been sneaking around Seattle, exorcising ghosts on the sly?"

"Not exactly," Camille said. "We only just started working on this spell a few weeks ago. So far, we've managed to dissipate a few nasty spirits that were causing havoc. We didn't want to say anything until we knew we had it down pat. And we don't yet."

"No, but we're damn close," Morio said, his eyes taking on a dark, golden sheen. He let out a long breath. "You might as well know that I'm planning to teach Camille how to summon spirits in a few months, but first she has to know how to dispel them, in case something goes wrong. So that's what we've been working on. How to banish spirits. As to how the spell will affect wights, I'm not sure. Maybe nothing, maybe it will help."

I stared at the pair, as did everyone else. Everyone but Smoky, that is. He looked up at the ceiling, and I had a sneaking suspicion he knew all about what they'd been doing. I glanced over at Menolly, and she shrugged.

"So, you two are really immersing yourself in the death magic thing, huh?" Unsure just what I wanted to ask, I finally said, "Why?"

Camille let out a long breath. "Eventually, the work in necromancy will lead me into learning how to use magic against the demons. Morio's going to teach me to use their own magic against them. How to open and close Demon Gates, set up Pentagram Snares, that sort of thing."

"Demonic rites? You'll be practicing demonic magic? Isn't that going a little far?" My hands on my hips, I whirled to face

Menolly. "Tell them this isn't a good idea. I can't imagine what that kind of energy will do to her. She already has the unicorn horn. Why not just focus on that?" The thought of my sister practicing the filthy, scummy magic that demons used made me sick.

But Menolly just shook her head, unblinking. "Let it be, Kitten. Dirty tricks can win a battle. Trust me, if I could learn how to mirror the demons' magic against them, I would. But I don't have the talent for magic. I think we should welcome *anything* that gives us an edge against Shadow Wing and his armies. Who knows what these rogue portals will do? They might start opening up into the Subterranean Realms, and then we'll be facing demons right and left, spirit seals or not."

I fell silent. In the back of my mind, I could hear Hi'ran laughing. The Autumn Lord was *my* form of demon magic. And Menolly—what would happen to her next? What path would she be forced down on this unwanted war that had been thrust upon us?

"I get it," I said, feeling yet another thread break that tied me to the naïve and optimistic girl I'd been a few months ago. "So, back to the subject at hand. Can you try this Spirit-Be-Gone spell on the wights?"

"I doubt it," Morio said. "It's not going to make them roll over and die, I can guarantee you that. We're going to have quite a fight on our hands, so I suggest we have weapons at the ready. And watch out for that shade. They aren't as dangerous as revenants but they're a lot more powerful than ghosts, and they have a touch that can chill all the warmth out of your body and leave you frozen in your boots. We can probably take him, though."

"Famous last words," Smoky muttered. "Let's get a move on."

Menolly and Vanzir led us into a narrow passage to the left, away from the main chamber. As we followed, I wondered what was at the bottom of the chasm. It had been a long time since we'd gone on a hike just for fun. Maybe when this was all over, we could come back and explore it.

"After we pass through this tunnel, we'll come to the chamber with the wights in it," Menolly said, glancing over her shoulder as we wended our way through the passage, taking care not to touch the sides where the slime was thick and waiting.

"There's a chamber near the back. That's where the spirit seal is being protected by the shade," she added. "I have the feeling he won't move to attack until the wights have been dispatched. He seems to be a guardian. And *that* makes me think that he's the spirit of someone who came into possession of the spirit seal centuries ago and felt a duty to remain and protect it after his death."

"That would explain a lot," Morio said. "Shades are often self-appointed guardians. Whether it be of a place, an object, or a person doesn't really matter. If he did possess the spirit seal, he might have grasped the scope of its power—even if he didn't know exactly *what* it was—and knew that it needed guarding."

"What about the wights?" I asked. "How do they play into the picture, assuming that you and Menolly are correct?"

"Wights can be summoned by shades," Smoky interjected. "They can be brought forth from the Netherworld."

Morio stopped, holding up his hand. "Let's discuss this before we get in there. Wights can also be created by a shaman or necromancer who has the power to raise the dead. Could be that when he was alive, the shade had the power to restore life to the dead. Wights are better watchdogs than zombies, and harder to create, so if our spirit did invoke them, then we'd better be prepared for one hell of a showdown."

A nagging thought occurred to me, one I didn't really want to think about. "What if the shade still has the power to summon up wights? What if the shade is still a necromancer? Do magical powers just disappear when you die?" Even with my sister being a witch, I wasn't all that clear on the ins and outs of life in the Spell Zone.

Camille frowned. "That seldom happens. Sometimes when the spirit reincarnates, the magical abilities will come through, especially if they were innate to the soul. When that happens, it can be obvious or latent."

"But is it possible? Theoretically?" I wasn't sure why it mattered so much to me, but I was learning more and more to trust my own instincts. Camille trusted hers, and I was trying to emulate her. Menolly swore up and down that she didn't have any, but I was pretty sure she did. She just didn't know it yet.

Morio spoke up. "Theoretically, yes, it can happen. Although Camille's right; it's a rare occurrence. But yes, we could be facing just such a situation, and if we are, we're in shit-deep trouble, because if he can summon up wights, he can wipe the floor with us."

"Not a happy thought." Menolly glanced at me. "Kitten, I hope you're wrong but, considering the amount of viro-mortis on the walls of this whole cave system, you might be right."

My stomach lurched. Maybe we'd luck out, and I'd been meowing up the wrong tree. Because if we had to face a necromantic shade, we were—as Morio said—in shit-deep trouble.

Morio paused, looking at Camille. She nodded, and he let out a long sigh. "Okay, here's the deal. Let Camille and me go in first. We'll cast our spell the minute we enter the chamber, then jump to the side, and the rest of you can take over. Whatever happens to the wights won't affect you—unless there's one hellacious backlash, and then we're all doomed." He motioned to Camille. "We need to prepare, and quick."

She slipped over to his side, taking his hands in hers as they closed their eyes and began a low chant under their breaths. The rest of us crowded back in the passage, giving them room while trying to avoid the rock walls hemming us in. Camille was more accurate with her death magic than her moon magic, but I was still nervous. The thought of a necromantic spell backfiring was more than I wanted to wrangle with.

As the energy between them built, goose bumps appeared on my arms. My first inclination was to turn and run. This was dark magic, darker than I'd ever felt coming from Camille except when she had sent Geph von Spynne into a tailspin with a death spell. But he'd been attacking us at that point. He'd already killed Rhonda, Zachary's ex-fiancée, and we were next on his list. This—this was a calculated maneuver. I moved closer to Zach, who slid his arm around me.

It was a comforting gesture, and I leaned into his embrace,

feeling his warmth soak through my jacket. I could sense his arousal, though I doubted even he felt it yet. And his desire sparked my own. I wasn't about to start anything in midbattle, but it made sense. Passion and adrenaline run hand in hand. Especially since we'd been through so many life-threatening situations in the past few months.

I pressed against him, and he tightened his embrace, then glanced into my eyes as I slid my hand around and planted it on his butt. He was asking me a question with those golden topaz eyes of his, and I nodded gently, pursing my lips as I flicked my tongue over my fangs. Zach sucked in a deep breath, and his hand slid down from my waist to caress my ass. As my breath caught in my throat, Camille looked up.

"We're ready," she said, and her voice drifted in from a million miles away.

I let go of Zach but squeezed his hand as I stepped away from him.

"Then let's get this show on the road," Smoky said. "Camille, Morio, head in. Delilah, you, Zach, Roz, and Menolly go next. Vanzir, you and I will take the third wave. That will give the fox and our wife time to regain their wits before they fall in behind us."

Without another word, Camille and Morio rushed into the entrance of the cavern, their voices low and haunting in the echo of the tunnel. Their magical chant was rife with passion and pain, and the faint sound of drums echoed on the air currents susurrating through the chamber.

My body hummed in response to the magic. Not prepared for the sudden resonance, I almost fell against the wall but managed to steady myself before I touched the slime molds. My vision ran red, and I pushed to the front, my fear vanishing in the growing cloud of bloodlust. Panther was rising; I could feel her growl deep within my heart, aching to be set free.

Hi'ran. This was his realm, the realm of death and fire and spirits. The Autumn Lord played in this world, and I—his only living Death Maiden—couldn't help but respond to the call of dark shrouds rising from the grave. I had to face the fact that I was as much a part of the shadow as Camille was becoming, and as Menolly had become the day Dredge got hold of her.

I motioned for Zach, Roz, and Menolly to move aside as the world began to shift. At first, I thought I was going to shift as my body wavered between worlds. *Panther to woman to Panther again, with the mark on my forehead swirling.* I felt like I'd just slammed back a handful of speed or had some form of Haste spell cast on me. And then, I was just me, but with Panther fully taking control of my senses.

Racing through the door, I caught sight of the wights. Dark, squat creatures that had once been human, they were leathery, with hair grown wild that covered part of their bodies, like mummies dumped in a fur factory. The lot of them turned as I entered the chamber. Moving like apes, they crouched their way toward us, arms swinging, using their knuckles to propel themselves along, eyes glimmering with the flame of death.

They weren't *right*; they shouldn't be here. They belonged to the realm of the dead, not in the realm of the living. I yanked my dagger free of its sheath, hungry for their blood, hungry to send them back to the grave. I plunged the tip of my blade into a shoulder as the nearest wight clasped my arm with its icy hand. Leaning over, I bit deep, driving my fangs into the flesh, and the wight let go with a screech. As I spat out the blood and fur, it started to back away.

A low roar worked its way up and out of my throat as I leapt and spun, my booted foot catching the creature on the jaw. My kick sent it sailing to the ground. Without a thought, I jumped to its side, driving my heel down on its throat, crushing the larynx as it fought to catch my ankle. Again I kicked, this time catching it in the ribs, sending the wight rolling toward Menolly, who snatched up the creature and smashed it against the rock wall until it fell limp in her arms. She tossed it aside and turned to the next.

The wights swarmed us like bees protecting their queen. I focused on my own little spot in the cave. Again and again, my dagger tasted flesh. Again and again, I kicked and punched my way through the wall of living death. There seemed to be no end to the blood and the stench that rose from the creatures.

As my sixth enemy fell, I watched in fascinated horror as the flesh began to slide away from the bones. No longer held together by magic, it oozed into a primordial soup, a slurry of DNA and blood. Wanting to vomit but still unable to look away, I was too slow. Another wight had crept up behind me, and before I realized what was happening, he fastened his teeth in my ankle and a mind-numbing pain set in as he drove through the boot to the bone.

I screamed, kicking to shake him off, but he held fast. He was determined to bite out a huge chunk of my leg. It occurred to me that I was a lot bigger than he was, so I dropped to my knees, directly atop him, effectively trapping him. With a short squeal, the creature let go, and I tucked and rolled, coming to my feet a few yards away from the wight. He lurched toward me, but Camille was right behind him. Her dagger raised, she plunged it through his back and jumped away as he fell.

"Always playing big sister to the rescue!" I teased as she whirled to engage yet another wight headed her way.

"You know it!" I heard her call back. But another member of the living-dead brigade was on my tail, and I turned to engage, caught up in the battle again. The air hung thick with the smell of blood and carrion as sounds of screaming and the clash of blade on flesh echoed through the chamber.

My body weary, I could feel Hi'ran watching me. His spirit rested on my shoulder, smiling with those brilliant white teeth, and his passion for the kill raced through my body like fingers tripping their way down my back, setting off sparks. Gasping, I dispatched the last wight near me, as the Autumn Lord's breath whispered heavy on my neck. He embraced me, and a shroud of tendriling mist seeped through my clothes, coiling in my belly like a snake waiting to strike.

I reeled, but he was there to catch me up, to wrap me in his arms as he drew me inside his swirling cape. His piercing diamond gaze drove itself into my soul. I tried to push away but couldn't move as his lips fastened to mine.

He sucked my breath away, and my knees buckled as the most intense orgasm I'd ever had exploded through my body. Unable to move or breathe, my heart fell silent, and I knew I was dying. And then—when I thought my lungs would never work again, when I ready to step out of my body—Hi'ran gently exhaled into my mouth.

My life slowly returned to me, filtering in through my lips. As my chest rose and fell, sensation returned to my toes and fingers. My heart started to beat again, a staccato pulse, and I pushed away from him, staring with a terrible fear.

He laughed and stroked my face. "I told you, you're one of many brides—but you are my only *living* Death Maiden. You will be revered and honored for your position, and when the time comes, you will be the one to bear my heir." And then, before I could say a word, he vanished, leaving me whimpering as I sank to the floor slowly realizing just what his words meant.

CHAPTER 17

"Delilah? Delilah!" Camille's voice echoed through the fog encasing my thoughts. I blinked, realizing that I was on my knees, curled over with my forehead against the floor, hands tucked over the back of my head.

The Autumn Lord's words rang in my ears as I looked around. The wights were all dead, scattered around the chamber like so much debris. Everybody—except Smoky, of course—was covered with blood and muck. I moaned gently as Camille and Menolly helped me up.

"Can you stand?" Menolly asked, her gaze locked on mine. She knew. Maybe not what had happened, but that *something* had happened. She always knew.

I nodded. No way in hell was I ready to talk about what had just happened. Not when we still had a shade to take care of and the seal to find.

"Yeah. I got overexcited, I guess." I shivered and pulled away. "Let's just finish this and go home. I need to sleep." What I needed was something to shake me out of my thoughts. Something to make me forget about the Autumn Lord and death and spirits and children conceived from Elemental Lords. My gaze landed on Zach. What I needed right now was a blond, gorgeous werepuma.

He blinked, returning my scrutiny, and slowly smiled. He could smell my arousal. I knew he could, because I could smell the same scent of desire emanating off of him. He wanted me as much as I wanted him.

Menolly glanced at Camille, and they both shrugged.

"Okay, if you're all right, let's get this over with." Camille motioned toward the back chamber. The seal was in there and, no doubt, the shade.

As we waded through the blood and bodies of the wights, the cavern began to feel like it was closing in on me. I didn't like underground spaces nor small rooms. Claustrophobia, Mother had called it, and she blamed it on my being a werecat. Cats didn't like to be locked in, though they may like cozy corners. Mother had always said, "Never trap a cat, or they'll scratch you to bits. Cats want the option to escape, even if they choose not to use it." I'd always believed she was referring to me with her gentle, chiding manner.

I'd never been good at being a daughter, at least not the kind Mother knew how to cope with. I'd always wanted to be wandering through the woods, wearing boy's clothing, chasing bugs, and climbing trees. A *tomboy*, that was what she called me, though she said it with love in her voice. I'd always wanted her approval, and I always felt like I could never measure up, even though she'd never once told me so.

Shaking thoughts of the past out of my head, I hurried to the front, where Roz and Vanzir waited.

"Has either of you faced a shade before?" I was hoping for a yes, but I'd settle for a *No, but I know how to kill them.* I didn't get either.

"Nope," Roz said. He shook his curly ponytail. "I've seen a lot of ghosts over the years, and dealt with a few spirits from the Netherworld, but shades—they play with the big boys. They're usually found outside of ancient ruins and old battle scenes."

Vanzir added his shake of the head. "Neither have I, though I've seen a few. They can be quite fierce, I understand. But I know that they hate light; they can't stand the sun, and are seldom seen or felt during the day."

"Wonderful," I muttered. "We're in a cavern, in the middle of the night. Perfect time and place for them to play spook central."

Camille and Morio caught up to us. "Hey, we have an idea that just might work," Morio said. "If they hate light, let's fire up the sun. Camille has the unicorn horn; she can use it to heighten her powers with fire and lightning. If we send a shock wave of light through the cavern, it might give us the time we need to grab the spirit seal and run."

Menolly cleared her throat. "You mean leave the spirit . . . well . . . *alive*? Not attempt to send it back to Hell—"

"Technically, we wouldn't send it back to Hel anyway," Smoky said. "Shades are usually from the Netherworld. Hel rules over the icy depths of the *Underworld*."

"I wasn't speaking of the goddess, you fire-breathing lizard." Menolly shot him a withering look. "I was speaking literally, as in, Hell. You know, the place where the fiery dudes in red tights dance on the skulls of their enemies."

I snorted. "Yeah, right. You know as well as I do that Lucifer is a god, not a devil, and that most spirits have nothing to do with the Sub Realms. Besides which, Shadow Wing is far more dangerous than any entity any mortal could think up. Let's get serious here. If we can get out of this without a fight, so much the better. The shade isn't causing problems, not that we know of. It's probably bound to this spot. How many people do you think are going to come visiting? I, for one, just want to get the heck out of here, go home, and take a long bath."

"Might be, probably not . . . there aren't guarantees. The shade also *might* follow us, looking for the seal," Menolly said. "Who's to say it wasn't sent here to protect the seal and to track anybody who manages to steal it? The spirits can't speak. What do we do if it comes after us? Tell it we're sorry, but we gave the seal away?"

"Well, yeah, I suppose you might be right. If you think you can dispel it, great, but I don't want to get caught in a one-sided battle with it." I frowned.

"Ladies, we don't have time to quibble," Roz said, interrupting us. He pointed toward the chamber door, where a shadowy figure had emerged.

The spirit was a black silhouette, a lot like the revenant we'd fought earlier, except it had glowing eyes. Red, of course. These things always seemed to have glowing red eyes. As it stared in our direction, it unleashed a wave of malevolent energy that rolled at us like a tsunami heading toward shore.

"Crap, it's using some sort of energy drain," Menolly said, racing toward it. I tried to stop her but could barely open my mouth.

As she swiped at it, her hand went clean through as if she was batting at mist. Startled, she stumbled back. The shade ignored her. Hands on her hips, Menolly contemplated the creature. I struggled to keep my thoughts clear, but that was about all I could do, the focused hatred coming our way was so strong.

Menolly motioned to Smoky as the shade slowly began to move forward. "You got anything? Apparently, I'm not a threat."

Smoky frowned, gesturing for Zach, Roz, Camille, and me to move behind him. "I don't know," he said darkly. "I'll try, but I've never held much keep with spirits." He pressed his fingertips together and formed a triangle with his thumbs. "Spirit, oh spirit, the balefire burning, I call upon my forefathers. *Dracon, dracon, dracon*, send this creature cowering back to the Netherworld! Remove this spirit from my sight!"

As a blast of silver light burst from between Smoky's hands to beam directly at the shade, the spirit recoiled for a moment, then straightened itself. I stared. Not even Smoky could trip the thing up. Shit. A cold sweat began to form on my back as it hovered right in front of the dragon. Could it hurt him? Could he protect us from it?

Just then, Morio and Camille linked hands and stepped to the side where they would have a clear shot. They had already begun to incant, and the power they were building scared the crap out of me.

A low rumble echoed from beneath their feet, as a bluish mist rose from the ground to swirl around them. Camille had hold of the Black Unicorn horn in her right hand, and her left was linked with Morio's. In *his* left hand, he held an Oreo-sized silver medallion I'd never before seen.

Smoky stared at them for a moment, then pushed Zach and

me out of the way as he backed up. Menolly dove for cover, along with Roz and Vanzir. Apparently, everybody could feel the rising energy. I was relieved—and a little embarrassed—to see that I wasn't the only one who had no desire to get in the way. I peeked out from behind Smoky's long white trench to see what was going on.

"Reverente destal a Mordenta, reverente destal a Mordenta, reverente destal a Mordenta . . ." Chanting in unison, Morio and Camille stood strong, with wild, feral expressions on their faces. Their voices resonated as they punctuated each stanza with a tangible infusion of power. The mist surrounding them began to spin as Camille thrust the unicorn horn into the air. Sparks flew off the tip of it, gathering up the vapors that were rising from the floor into one giant vortex, a thundercloud hanging low over their heads.

The shade let out a shriek and moved toward them, then paused as Camille dropped out of the chant to say, "Don't you dare. Get out of here, sucker, or we'll make sure you're so much smoke and ashes."

Her voice was caught up by a sudden breeze. I wasn't sure where the gust originated, but the currents of air swept through, howling like a bean Sidhe, rushing in on some invisible freight train. The cloud over her head let out a low rumble—thunder. The tip of the crystal unicorn horn was glowing now.

The shade moved forward again, eyes glaring out of the dark shroud of its body.

"Reverente destal a Mordenta!" Morio shouted as Camille dropped her head back.

"Cover your eyes!" she screamed, and we barely had time to look away when their spell crystallized into a lightning bolt that came scorching out of the point of the unicorn horn. It plowed through the spirit like a jagged pitchfork, and the brilliance lit up the chamber. For a moment, all I could see were spots, and then the flare died away as quickly as it had come. The shade vanished.

Menolly moaned, and I raced over to her, where she was cowering behind a rock. She had a few scorch marks, but the singed bits of flesh—mainly under her eyes and the tips of her fingers—were already healing. I helped her up.

"Are you okay?" I asked needlessly. Obviously, she'd made it through relatively unscathed.

"Yeah," she said. "Thank the gods she used lightning instead of invoking fire, or I might be a pile of ashes now."

Camille rushed over, her eyes round and wide. "Oh Great Mother, I'm so sorry! Are you okay? I had no idea it was going to be that powerful," she whispered, staring at the horn in her hand. "Guess it's going to take some practice before I learn how to control it. Then again, I did stop a lightning bolt in its tracks when Eriskel tested me."

Eriskel was the jindasel of the horn, a guardian spirit, not unlike a djinn but not as powerful nor as nasty. The jindasel watched over the Elementals sequestered within the spiraling crystal horn. I didn't fully understand everything Camille had tried to tell us about it, but what I did know was that the horn was a powerful weapon. A hunch told me she had no idea *just* how powerful. Yet.

"Guess it's going to take you some practice. Just make sure I'm not in target range!" Menolly huffed, then stomped over to where the revenant had been. There was no sign of the spirit. As good as gone.

We all looked at each other, and I saw Vanzir eyeing the door of the chamber. A nasty and thoroughly uncharitable thought occurred to me. I raced into the back chamber.

There, on a pedestal made of granite, lay an open box, hand carved out of crystal. In the box was a pendant. A ruby, set in bronze. I slowly picked up the heavy talisman, and the light within the gem swirled, taking my breath away. The fourth spirit seal.

As I glanced over at the door, Vanzir stood there, staring at me. He was leaning against the arch, and when his gaze dropped to the spirit seal, I immediately reached for my dagger. He snorted.

"If I wanted to take the seal from you, your dagger wouldn't stop me," he said, a contemptuous tone fueling his words. "Trust me, nothing would stand in my way, *werecat*." For a moment, he seemed to tower, his eyes luminous and glowing. And then he faded and relaxed.

"I gave you my word. I've bound myself in the Ritual of Subjugation. There's little more I can do save slit my throat for you to believe me. But I'll try once more. *I do not desire the seal.* Nor do I desire for Shadow Wing to possess it. You seem to believe otherwise, but my kind's existence relies on humanity making it through unscathed. We have a very powerful motive in helping you."

With that, he turned and left the chamber.

I watched him go, wondering what he meant. I almost felt guilty for doubting him. But then Menolly's and Camille's voices as they approached the entrance shored me up. I let go of the guilt. We were in a war. I had to be suspicious. Even if Vanzir couldn't understand our concerns, he'd just have to learn to live with them.

The walk back to the car was interminable, and the drive home seemed to take forever. We were all exhausted. Camille conked out in the back, her head on Menolly's shoulder. Vanzir sat apart from them, silent.

Morio was zonked out, too, next to Smoky and Rozurial. Zach was driving, and I sat in the front, next to him. As he navigated the chilly spring night, I watched his hands on the steering wheel. I was tired—exhausted, really—but I was also hyped up on adrenaline. Sleeping would be difficult. I leaned closer to him.

"Will you stay with me tonight?" I whispered.

He glanced at me, then back at the road. "Are you sure?"

I nodded.

"What about Chase?"

Taking a deep breath, I forced the air out of my lungs and said, "This is *my* choice. I choose to be with you tonight, if you'll have me." My voice trembled a little. Would he still want me, after all this time and frustration? I wouldn't blame him if he didn't want to get involved.

But Zach merely smiled. "Delilah, I always want you. Never worry about that." And it was set.

We rode in silence until we arrived home, and then Smoky

and Menolly set off for the portal with the spirit seal. Camille and Morio were too exhausted from their magical work to help, and I was just too beat in general.

The lights were on in the living room. Iris had waited up for us, even though we had told her not to. As we came in, she gave me an anxious look. I gave her a slow smile and a nod.

"We found the seal, and it's on its way to . . . its new home right now." I still didn't like talking about Queen Asteria in front of Vanzir.

Roz seemed to sense my hesitation, because he clapped Vanzir on the shoulder. "Let's go. We'll hole up at the local dive I've taken a sublet on for the month. Girls, we'll be out of your hair for the night. Call us tomorrow when you want to talk. I've got my cell phone with me."

As we waved them out of the house, Camille shook her head. "Need sleep. I'm about to crash. Morio's not much better. Smoky has a key. Lock the door when you go to bed." Dragging themselves up the stairs, my sister and her fox demon disappeared for the night.

"Delilah, before you go up, there was a call for you while you were out." Iris handed me half her sandwich. I must have been eyeing the food with a little too much gusto.

"I don't want to hear it unless it's an emergency." I tapped Zach on the shoulder. "Go on up and wait for me." He obligingly left the room.

Iris shook her head. "It wasn't Chase," she said, frowning. "It was Sharah, and she said it was important."

"Did she say it was an emergency?"

"No," she said slowly, then frowned. "But she sounded worried. You're not going to call her back?"

"Tomorrow morning. If it's an emergency, she'll call again. Meanwhile, I'm going to go relax, enjoy myself, and sleep for a gazillion hours," I said, running my hands through my hair. I needed a shower, and then I needed something a whole lot more sensual than a bunch of nasty water splashing over my body. "Zach's staying," I added.

Iris smiled slowly. "We live in troubled times, Delilah. Don't deny yourself the luxury of companionship out of fear or misplaced guilt. You and Chase have a great deal to talk over again before you can make any final decisions, but until then, if I were you, I'd consider myself a free agent."

Free agent. Not sure I liked that term, I merely gave her a peck on the cheek and headed upstairs to the man who was waiting for me with open arms.

CHAPTER 18

As I approached my room, music filtered out from beneath the door. "Magic Man," by Heart. Zachary must be listening to the playlist on my MP3 player. I opened the door to find him sitting on the window seat in my bedroom, one knee pulled up to his chest. His other leg hung over the edge, and he tapped the floor with his foot, keeping time to the music.

The lights were off, and he was staring out the window, his regal profile framed in the glow from the hallway behind me. When he looked at me, his mouth beckoned, full and sensual, and the dusty summer wheat of his hair was tinged with gold, fringing his collar.

I caught my breath as the scent of his leather jacket flooded my nose. Even beneath the dusty coat, I could see every outline of muscle. The image of his puma self up on the mountainside burned in my mind. The memory of racing up the rocks by his side ran through my veins, and from somewhere, deep inside, Panther growled in recognition.

It had been a long time since we'd been alone together without a chaperone. I slowly moved toward him, skirting the bed, keenly aware of the covers falling to the floor, of stepping over my pajamas and the other dirty clothes that lay scattered around the edge. He swung his head toward me, silently waiting as I approached.

As I closed the distance between us, I thought about Chase. I could still stop before I screwed things up even further. I could call him and beg him to talk to me. I could tell him that I missed him. Hell, I could even go find Erika and kick her butt and scare the hell out of her.

But I didn't want to do any of those things.

I was tired of thinking, tired of dealing with hurt feelings and jealousy, and I hated the jealousy that had grown in me. It bordered on insecurity, and that was one trait I *didn't* want that I'd inherited from our mother. I didn't like the feeling it left in my heart. If Chase wanted Erika, he was welcome to her. Right now, I didn't want to deal with any of this crap; all I wanted to do was . . .

"Delilah," Zach's voice curved around me, husky and low. He was suddenly standing and with one stride, planted himself in front of me. He slowly reached out to caress my throat. I shivered as he ran his finger down my neck, over my shirt, between my breasts.

"Don't say a word. Don't ask about anything," I said. "Just kiss me."

Zach leaned down and slowly pressed his lips against mine. They were full, plump, and I started to shake as his arms slid around me, pulling me tight against him. I kept my eyes open, staring into his own unblinking gaze as we kissed, as breath passed between us.

"Oh Great Lady Bast, remind me of what I am," I whispered.

He stopped, pulled back, staring in my eyes. "What do you want? Just tell me, and I'll do it."

I could feel Panther stirring from within. I grabbed his wrist. "Come with me."

He followed me as I dragged him to my playroom, past the kitty condo, past the upstairs litter box, and shoved the window open. I crawled out on the roof and jumped the short distance to land in the fork of an oak outside the window. As my hands grasped the trunk and my feet met the branch, I began to transform into Panther. She came quickly, painlessly, and within seconds I'd descended through the branches and dropped to the ground. I waited at the bottom of the tree as Zach followed suit, shifting into Puma as he leapt out of the tree to land at my side.

The night was thick and dark, the moon on her way to black, but we didn't need her light. I raced toward the woods leading to Birchwater Pond, reveling in the feel of my muscles, in the feel of the ground beneath my paws, in the air that set my fur to quivering. Every sense stood at alert; every feeling was intensified.

The rustle of small animals racing through the brush caught my attention as we padded into the forest. The scents of spring loam and water and fungi and Zach's desire careened on the wind, an intoxicating whirlwind, pulling me deeper into my feline self.

I raised my head and let out a deep roar, the vibrations in my throat sending me into a frenzy of hunger. I wanted him, wanted him to hold me down, to drive himself deep inside. As if reading my thoughts, he circled me, emitting guttural grunts as we sized each other up. Weres, we were—neither fully human nor fully feline—but an odd mixture of both.

In puma form, Zach was as amazing as he was in human. Sleek and muscled, golden—tawny with brilliant eyes that flashed between topaz and light brown—he slid up behind me. Receptive, I lowered myself to the ground and presented, but he stepped back and in a flurry of sparkling light and blurred edges, transformed back into his two-legged form. Surprised, I followed suit just as quickly.

"What's wrong?" I asked. "You don't sense Demonkin, do you?"

"I'd hurt you if I took you that way," he said, his voice broken. "I know you've fucked other housecats, but it's far more painful in big-cat form. My cock is barbed, as are all male werepumas' organs, and I don't want to take you that way . . . not this time. Not now. Not till the moon is full and we forget everything but the feel of her riding our souls. But let me love you here, as a man, in the forest where we belong." He held out his arms, his gaze burning a hole in my heart.

And then we were frantic, struggling out of our clothes, but still his luminous eyes stayed fixed on me as he kicked aside his jeans and tossed his shirt behind him. I yanked off my top, my jeans, my panties, as a low rumble rolled out of Zach's throat. His nostrils flared, and he laughed, low and hard.

"I can smell you. Come here, pussycat."

My stomach flipped. He was naked and fully aroused. I ran my fingers along his ripped abs, across his wide-set shoulders, tracing a line down to the V above his penis, where he stood firmly, marvelously at attention.

"Now. Here. In the dirt," I said, barely above a whisper.

"As you command." He grabbed me around the waist, and we fell to the ground, into the soft moss, which tickled my skin and teased my senses with its scent. With one hand, he reached down to stroke me, his fingers knowing exactly where to move, where to touch. He lowered his lips to my breast and sucked, rough and with a laugh in the back of his throat.

I let out a short moan as a series of explosions began to fire, each one slightly larger than the last. I tried to catch my breath, but there was no pause, no respite, and I found myself shrieking as he moved his mouth down between my legs, replacing fingers with tongue. I held his head as he licked, the feel of his thick, curly hair between my thighs making me laugh with the sheer joy of the force driving us forward.

Covered in leaf mold and debris, I finally sat up, pushing him onto his back. "Your turn," I whispered, lowering my lips to his penis. Carefully—cautious to avoid the fang issue—I licked the length of him, circling the head of his cock with my tongue, teasing him harder by the minute.

"I want you," he said, suddenly grabbing me by the waist and pulling me up to stare in my eyes. "I want inside you."

I broke away, fell to my hands and knees, and he knelt behind me, grasping my waist as he drove deep inside, sliding in, spreading me wide. I raised my head and growled as he began to thrust, slowly at first, then faster, changing position, swiveling his hips, a white-hot match that reached right into my center to ignite my flame.

He leaned forward to lick the back of my neck, lightly biting as I pressed against him, digging my fingers into the dirt. If we couldn't fuck *as* big cats, we could fuck *like* big cats.

He was riding me hard now, and I lowered myself to the ground as he lay prone atop my back, grinding so hard that I couldn't tell where he left off and I began. My breasts pressed into the damp leaves as I moved beneath him, the moist soil clinging to my flesh, rubbing against my nipples as if Mama Earth herself was suckling them.

We were both filthy and wet, and bruised from the day, and I loved it all—loved the moss beneath my belly, the feel of the mud plastering my legs. All the while, Zach's cock explored me from the inside out, his finger stroking my clit as I struggled for that last push that would break open the dam.

And then I was there, on the edge, arms held out in supplication. A loud pounding filled my ears, the thundering rush of a waterfall from a distant land, and I jumped—soaring as I toppled over the edge and came.

I screamed as Zach roared out my name. Puma and Panther rose up, superimposed against us, rising from deep inside of our hearts like ghosts from the past, shadows of ourselves mating even as we mated. And then, as I exhaled, limp and sweating, the big cats climaxed, and their roars filled my ears like jungle drums in the night.

Zach gently rested his head on my back. He was drenched—sweating and damp and musky. "Are you okay?" he asked after a moment, rolling off of me.

I sat up. Every muscle ached. Every inch of me felt bruised through. But it was a good sore, the kind of sore that left me bone tired and ready for a long hot bath and a warm bed. The kind of sore that wrung every drop of tension out of my body.

"Yeah, I'm good," I said, yawning. The chill of the evening was descending, and now I felt cold and wet. I scrambled into my jeans and yanked my top over my head. So I was muddy. The clothes were dirty anyway and needed washing.

"I need to get inside," I added. "Come. Spend the night?"

He gazed down at me. "You really want me to?"

I thought about it. The only other man who'd ever slept in my bed was Chase. "Yeah, I do."

"Color me there," he said, sliding into his jeans and zipping up. He carried his shirt as we headed back to the house. As we jogged silently along the trail, I wondered how the hell I'd deal with this. I'd never had sex like that before. It was the first time I'd felt like both sides of myself—Were and woman—had been invited into the bed. I felt whole—wholly accepted and wholly desired. And I didn't ever want it to stop.

CHAPTER 19

Morning broke, and I opened my eyes to find Zach snuggled up against my back, his arm draped around my waist. He was snoring lightly, and the stubble on his chin rubbed against my shoulder as he murmured something in his sleep. The sun had broken through, and a lazy beam fell across the bed, bathing us in unexpected light and warmth.

I blinked, squinting at the clock. Eight thirty. Time to get up. Even though we'd gotten to bed late, I still preferred catnaps. A few hours here, a few hours there, and I was good to go. Especially after the sex and the hot bath we'd taken together afterward.

I didn't like water, but Zach had eased me into the tub full of bubbles, where I leaned against his chest as he reached around and washed my tummy, gently rubbing my breasts as he did so. As his hands glided over my flesh, the tide between us rose again, and he took me there, in the tub. I slid up on his lap, my knees straddling his hips. He slipped into me from below as I leaned forward to brace my hands on the bottom of the tub, and we'd quietly thrust our way into soapy ecstasy until the water cooled. The moment my head hit the pillow, I was out.

Now, awake but still blurry-eyed, I yawned and eased my way out of bed. Zach groaned, then pulled himself up to a sitting position. He gave me a goofy smile, warming me from the inside out, and held out his arms. I dropped my panties and bra, slipping back under the covers to plant a good-morning kiss on his mouth.

After a moment, he leaned back against the headboard and regarded me with a serious look. "Okay, we didn't talk about this last night, but we need to now. What about—"

"Chase?" I finished the sentence for him. I still wasn't ready to discuss the situation, but Zach wanted some sort of explanation, and I felt I owed him one.

"Yeah, Chase." He let out a long sigh. "Last night was incredible. I can only hope to God you felt the same thing I did. We're meant for each other, Delilah. Can't you feel it? We didn't just fuck. We *mated*."

I almost about swallowed my tongue. I knew exactly what he was talking about but had been hesitant to vocalize it, not knowing if he'd felt the same way. The sex had been fantastic, but even more, it felt like we'd merged, like he'd accepted me fully. All of me. Fae, human, weretabby, werepanther . . . every aspect of me had been involved in our lovemaking, and as much as Chase and I clicked, there were parts of my being where he couldn't—or wouldn't—go.

"I know," I said softly. "I know. But Zach, so much is going on right now. Chase and I . . . Chase . . ." I held out my panties, staring at them. They were green satin, and Chase had given them to me, a gift from Victoria's Secret. I suddenly couldn't put them on. I stuffed them back in the drawer and found another pair: pale pink, cotton, very simple. These were mine. *My* own, *my* style, *my* comfort. As I slid them up my hips and then fastened a matching bra, I turned around to stare at the werepuma who was stretched out on the bed.

A long drink of warm rum on a cold winter's night—that's what Zach was. Milk and cookies in the afternoon, oatmeal in the morning. Hiking boots and blue jeans and a leather jacket that smelled like heaven. He was everything I was, except Fae.

"I'm furious that Chase lied to me. I could have handled him sleeping with his old flame, because truthfully, I think I'd like to have both of you in my life. But he didn't tell me the truth, and I feel stupid because of it. Now I don't know what he wants or what he's thinking." I sat down on the edge of the bed, staring at the floor as I rested my head in my hands. "And I guess I don't know what *I* want. I don't even know what I'm *allowed* to want."

I turned and pointed to the mark on my forehead. "I haven't told anybody this yet, but yesterday, during the fight, the Autumn Lord said . . . he said that one day his plans include me being the one to bear his child. If he's serious, I won't have a choice. I'm bound to him. So where does that leave me? As much as Chase wants to be cool with our ways—with the ways of my father's people—there are limits to what he can accept. To what he will accept. And he'd never accept something like that. Would you?"

Zach stared at me. After a moment, he reached over to rub my arm. "I don't know if I can answer that right now, to be honest. I think if the Autumn Lord was okay with you having a mortal lover, that I could learn to be okay with you having an immortal child. The Puma Pride wouldn't be, though. But I don't necessarily listen to everything they say. Not anymore. My latest antics, as the elders call them, haven't been well received at all. I'm sorry. I can't give you a better answer than that."

I shrugged. "I'd rather have you honest about it than lying to me. That's good enough for now. So what have you been up to that's got the council in such an uproar?"

He gave me a sheepish grin. "I'm running for City Council. In Puyallup."

I stared at him. "You're what?"

"I'm running for City Council. I want to be a councilman. I'm running on an open platform as a Supe. As one of the Rainier Puma Pride members. Venus is backing me up, and his support is the *only* reason they haven't thrown me out of the council yet. But I'm facing a lot of anger back at the compound."

I nodded. The Rainier Puma Pride—especially the council of elders—were set in their ways. They didn't approve of my sisters and me, even though we'd saved their butts from the hands of a ruthless serial killer who turned out to be an ancient enemy. But we had at least two allies there. Both Zachary and Venus the Moon Child, their shaman, stood up for us. Thanks to the two of them, the Pride had assisted us on more than one occasion, but without their backing, we'd be persona non grata.

"Councilman, huh?" I snickered. "Hey, can you fix parking tickets if you get in?"

He laughed, a throaty laugh that made me want to bite those beautiful lips of his, but he rolled away, hopping out of the bed to stretch. His muscles rippled in the warm morning light. As he grimaced and held up his muddy jeans, I tossed him a terrycloth robe.

"Give me those dirty things."

He raised his eyebrows as he exchanged them for the robe. "It's *pink*. And not hot pink, either. This is bubblegum pink."

"Hey, I happen to like bubble gum. So deal with it," I said, grinning. "We'll just wash your clothes before you head home—"

A knock interrupted me. As Zach clutched the robe closed, I opened the door to find Iris standing there, a concerned look on her face.

"Sharah's on the phone again, and she needs to talk to you. She's on line one. Why don't you take it while I toss these in the washer? I think we have a spare pair of jeans and a shirt around here that will fit you." She pulled Zach's clothes out of my arms as he hastily scrambled to keep his robe from flying open. "Relax, Zachary. You haven't got anything I haven't seen before," she said with a grin, then quickly gathered up a basket of my dirty clothes from the floor and headed back downstairs.

I picked up the phone near my bed. We'd installed two extensions on both my floor, the third, and Camille's, the second. Now we didn't have to run downstairs. We'd also signed up for an extra line.

"Hey Sharah," I said. If Chase had set her to calling for him, I'd chew him out. There was no need to stick someone in the middle of our dispute. But she sounded frantic.

"Delilah, thank the gods. I've been trying to reach you since last night, but you didn't call me back."

I glanced over at Zach. "I had . . . other things to attend to. Sorry. What's up?"

"It's about Chase."

"What about him?" I didn't want to hear that he was upset or off moping. He'd brought this onto himself, after all.

"Chase hasn't checked in since around noon yesterday. He never just drops out of sight. I'm really worried something has happened to him."

Her words slammed into my heart. "What do you mean? You think he's in trouble?" A niggle in the pit of my stomach began to worm its way up to the surface.

"I mean just what I said. He hasn't come in to work yet. Last night, he left early and I called him later with a problem, but he wasn't home. I was a little worried but I thought maybe he had a family emergency or something, so I called you. Now I'm really concerned. He hasn't been in yet. I've tried calling, but there's no answer at his apartment."

I bit my lip, tasting blood as one of my fangs accidentally caught the chapped skin where I'd forgotten to use the lip balm Camille had bought for me. Sharah was right. It was unlike Chase to vanish without leaving a get-in-touch number. He had too much respect for his job. But then again, he'd been leading a double life for a while now. Maybe Erika had messed with his sense of responsibility.

"Have you talked to Erika?" I asked, the words jarring me even as they tumbled out of my mouth. "Maybe *she* knows where he is."

Sharah paused. She knew. And I knew she knew. After a moment, she cleared her throat. "I called her, but there was no answer. I'm sorry, Delilah. I don't know what to say—"

I could feel Zach's gaze fastened on me as my cheeks reddened. I hated blushing, hated feeling conspicuous and embarrassed. As tears welled up, I dashed them away before they fell and tried to focus on the matter at hand. The fact was—Erika or not—Chase wasn't one to shirk his duties. If he could have called, he would have. Which meant something was wrong. Maybe it was car trouble. Maybe it was something else.

"Did you have somebody drop by his apartment?"

"No," she said. "Not yet. I thought I'd make some calls before I did that. You wouldn't be willing, would you? I understand if you want to say no, but there's a bug going around, and we're shorthanded here."

I let out a long sigh. The last thing I needed to do was go chasing Chase, but something about the situation didn't sit right.

"All right. I'll drive over there and take a look. If he comes in before I get back to you, let me know so I can move on to my other errands for the day." There were three case files sitting on my desk that needed attention. Nothing urgent, but they would pay next month's utility and food bills.

"Will do, and thanks. Again, I'm sorry I had to call."

As I slowly replaced the receiver, Zach slid his arm around my waist. "I think I got the gist of what's happening. You need me to come with you?"

I shook my head. "Probably not the best idea. If I do find him, we have a lot to talk about. And if I don't, well . . ." Leaving the thought untouched, I motioned toward the door. "Let's go down and grab a bite of breakfast. What are your plans?"

He leisurely tied the belt on the robe and opened the door for me. "Oh, not a lot. Just talk to my campaign manager, get some head shots taken, and then this afternoon, there's a fence out at the compound that needs replacing. I'm overseeing the work crew on that." He paused. "Will you call me later and let me know how things went?"

I nodded. "Count on it. Let's go find out how it went last night with the spirit seal."

As we hurried into the kitchen, the only ones there were Smoky, Iris, and Maggie. Maggie was sitting on Smoky's lap, playing with a strand of his hair, which was teasing her, tickling her belly.

Iris handed Zach a pair of jeans and a shirt and he went to the bathroom to change. She pointed to the range; one pan held scrambled eggs and another, thick slices of bacon. There were melon balls on the table, along with a stack of toast. I grabbed a slice and promptly plowed into it.

"Serve yourselves, please. I'm doing laundry and house-cleaning today. Camille's already left for the shop, and Morio's off to do the shopping. Menolly's in her lair, of course, and I haven't seen hide nor hair of the demon twins today."

I choked on a crumb. Iris had taken to calling Roz and Vanzir the demon twins, much to their chagrin. The rest of us found it amusing, but they—Vanzir in particular—didn't appreciate her sense of humor.

"Knock yourself out. I promised Sharah I'd check on something for her. Chase has disappeared, and nobody can find him."

"Great Mother, I hope he hasn't come to harm."

"I hope not either," I muttered and sat down at the table, as Zach returned, dressed. I offered him a plate of eggs and bacon, but he shook his head.

Swiping a couple pieces of toast, he kissed me on the forehead. "I'd better head out. I'll call you later. Bye, everyone." Before I could see him off, he was out the door, and I watched at the window as he climbed into his truck and drove away. I turned back to Smoky, who sat there, watching me carefully.

"Tell me, how did it go with the spirit seal last night?" I returned to my chair and dug into the food, starving. We had high metabolisms, and Camille and I ate like storm troopers. Menolly would have, too, if she'd still been alive.

Smoky shrugged. "Your sister needs to work on her diplomacy, but overall, it went well."

Uh-oh. "What did Menolly do now?"

The dragon arched his eyebrows, and he seemed to be repressing a grin. "For one thing, she almost let it slip that we knew about Trillian. That would not be a wise move, considering the elves went to such lengths to keep the mission covert. I managed to cover her gaffe, but I'm not sure they believed me when I had a coughing fit."

Wonderful. We should have known better than to let Menolly take the helm on that little excursion. While she was one hell of a fighter and as dependable as Old Faithful, she had a problem controlling what she said and who she said it to. She'd never give away state secrets, but make her mad enough, and she blew way too easily. I blamed it on the vampire thing, even though I knew that she'd always been that way.

"So, what did Queen Asteria say?"

"The Elfin Queen was overjoyed to have the fourth seal. She's still terribly worried about the third seal and what Shadow Wing might be doing with it. The Dahns Unicorns have reported several troubling attacks on the outskirts of their lands. At first they thought the raids were from goblins, but on closer inspection, the wounds don't match the usual pattern for goblin strikes."

I polished off my eggs and bacon. "Well, at least the fourth seal is safe and secure, and we didn't have too hard a time finding it. I'm headed out now. I'll be back in an hour or two, and I'm on my cell if anybody needs me."

"I'm headed out to my land now, too. Here," he said, depositing Maggie in my arms. "You tend to your charge. If Camille asks, I'll be at my barrow for the evening. I've errands to attend to, and those blasted Fae Queens are cluttering up the edges of my land. I need to make sure they don't tear the place apart."

He grimaced. Over the past couple of months, we'd all been privy to exactly what Smoky thought of Morgaine, Aeval, and Titania reconstructing the Seelie and Unseelie Courts.

Torn apart in the Great Divide when Otherworld split off from Earthside, the Fae Courts had been decimated, and Aeval and Titania effectively banished. A couple months ago, thanks to Morgaine's meddling, they'd decided enough with that shit and were now rebuilding their kingdom with a little help from Camille. We weren't quite sure whether this was a good idea, but one thing was certain: It kept them out of our hair, and it pleased FBHs to no end. The big question now was where they were going to set up their actual court. Titania was trying to claim part of Smoky's land. He wasn't budging.

"Just be careful. Those three are dangerous, and I don't trust any one of them." I put Maggie in her playpen and made sure she had her favorite toy—Chase had given her a stuffed monkey named River—and her blocks.

"You're right to suspect them. They're up to no good. I wish Camille hadn't gotten herself mixed up with them, but then, I suppose when the Hags of Fate order you around, you listen." The dragon slipped into his long white trench coat and headed out the door.

He was right about the Hags of Fate, I thought. None of us wanted Camille mixed up with that crew. Although Morgaine technically was part of our family tree, we all knew blood didn't ensure loyalty. But Camille had had no choice. Grandmother Coyote had seen to that.

One favor the new Queens of Fae *were* doing for us, however, was taking some of the pressure off with the general populace. Ever since we crossed to this world, we'd been seen through lenses clouded with mystique, and we'd been both despised and revered.

Now, with Earthside Fae coming out of the woodwork, it evened the score. But I wasn't counting chickens yet. Once the FBHs realized that the Queens of Fae weren't going to chum up to the ordinary Joe and play footsie, the mood could change in the blink of an eye. And the three Queens were anything but jovial.

I scribbled a note for Iris, who was busy with the laundry, kissed Maggie on the cheek, and grabbed my keys. As I climbed into my Jeep, my thoughts returned to Chase. I really didn't think he was missing. He'd probably eloped with Erika or something equally asinine. In the back of my mind, I wondered why I was still so upset. After all, I'd spent the night with Zach and had an incredible time. And I was going to tell Chase about it. Not rub his nose in it, but be clear about what I'd done. Maybe I should cut Chase some slack.

Then again, another little voice argued, it wasn't just the lying that bothered me so much, or the lying by omission. Chase had put up a squawk about me seeing Zach on a friendship basis as well. So I'd focused on Chase, given him my exclusive attention. And then he went out and screwed somebody else.

Thoroughly confused, hot and cold running about equally, I sped along the freeway until I came to the exit leading to his apartment building in south Seattle. He actually lived around Renton, though his zip code still tied him to the city proper.

As I pulled into the parking lot, I looked around for his new SUV, and sure enough, there it was, in the lot. So either he was home and not answering his phone, or he was out with somebody else—namely, Erika. Or, a little voice said, maybe he *was* home, but unable to answer his phone. I jumped out of the Jeep and took the stairs two at a time. After two knocks, I dug out my key. As I stared at it, I wondered briefly if this was the last time I'd be letting myself into his apartment. If we broke up, I'd have to give it back, and the thought made me unaccountably sad.

But when I went to open it, I found the door was unlocked. I pushed it open, gingerly stepping over the threshold. The lights were on, though it was broad daylight. Chase got plenty of light in his apartment, and he was meticulous about turning off the lamp when he left the room. Bad sign number one.

Bad sign number two was in-my-face big. The living room looked like a tornado had raged through it. Books were scattered everywhere, everything on the desktop now littered the floor: pencils, pens, papers. His laptop computer was open and blinking. Somehow it had survived the fall. My heart in my throat, I slowly made my way through the mess. What the hell had happened?

Panic rising, I ran to the bedroom. No sign of a fight, no sign of suitcases, the closet was full, the bed was still made. Which meant he'd either had time this morning to make it, or he hadn't slept in it.

The light on his answering machine was blinking, and before I even thought about fingerprints, I hit the button and sat down to listen. The first was from the dry cleaners, telling him his suit was ready to pick up. The second was from Sharah, asking him to call her as soon as possible. The third was from Erika. I stopped short at that one.

"Chase, where the hell do you get off? I thought we agreed that this time, you were going to play things my way. I don't play second fiddle to anyone or anything—whether it's work, or that creeped-out *cunt* you're sleeping with. Call me as soon as you get this or don't bother calling at all."

Whoa. Was *this* the real face of the woman he'd been seeing on the side? I stared at the machine, wondering what the hell he saw in her. Sure, she was pretty, but her mouth put an end to anything I'd ever find attractive about her. I never—not once—had treated him to that sort of scathing attack. We'd argued, but I never played dirty. The fourth message came on and startled me out of my reverie. Sharah again, and the fifth was also from her, this morning. And that was it for the messages.

As I sat there, I noticed a picture on the nightstand and picked it up. Chase had taken it a few months ago, it was of me, curled up in a ball on the end of his bed, snoozing on his favorite Armani jacket. I'd left him a hairball there. Purely unintentional, but he'd laughed till he cried and wouldn't let me pay to have it cleaned. Before I could stop myself, I realized I was crying.

I tucked the picture in my pocket and wandered back out to the living room, looking for the phone. As I picked it up and dialed Sharah's number, I decided to see Erika next. I'd talk to her, because I wanted to face her down. I wanted to face the demon who had come between Chase and me. A demon from his past and from my insecurities.

And I prayed—for once, I prayed—dear Lady Bast, let Chase be there. Let him be safe and sound and with *her*. Because if he wasn't, then we really had something to worry about.

CHAPTER 20

I didn't know where to find Erika, but it didn't take me long to find Chase's address book. After that, it was a simple matter to scan through the entries until I came to her address and number. She was staying in one of those furnished hotel suites, which told me she hadn't fully made up her mind whether to move back to Seattle or not.

I scribbled the address and phone number in my notebook, stuffed it in my pocket, and then headed out. My fingerprints were everywhere, but Sharah knew that I'd been here. As I eased out of the parking lot, I met her pulling in. I waved to her, and she gave me a quick nod.

The route to Erika's took me ten minutes. She'd settled in as close to Chase's as possible. How long had she been in town? A week? Two? Four?

When I entered the luxurious hotel, it occurred to me that Erika had to have money. No way Chase could afford this on his salary. I sauntered up to the counter and leaned across the marble top, lowering the masks on my glamour. I usually avoided using the charm from my Fae blood, but right now, I wanted every scrap of insurance on my side that I could get.

While the clerk gave me the once-over—long and leisurely—I flashed him a slow smile. "I need some information," I said.

"What do you need, pretty lady?" He was breathless in a creepy sort of way, but I wasn't about to nitpick. I had him hooked.

"How long has Erika Sands been registered here?" I pursed my mouth, offering the promise of a kiss.

He licked his lips as he stared at me. I didn't even think he knew he was doing it. "She moved in about four weeks ago."

Four weeks. So that meant Chase had been fucking her for four weeks. "Has she ever stayed here before?"

The clerk shook his head. "Not that I know of. She's in her room now. Do you want me to call her?"

"No, just give me her room number," I said. And he did. And then, because I was never one to tease and run, I leaned across the counter and planted a quick kiss on him. He shuddered as I drew away. "Thank you, Cliff," I said, reading his name tag. "You've been a real help."

"No problem," he whispered, staring after me.

The elevator was sluggish, but for once, I didn't feel like taking the stairs. Within a few minutes, I stood outside the door to suite 403. Should I knock? Just barge in? Knocking would be the polite thing to do, so I nixed the idea. I grabbed the doorknob and twisted. Locked. Without missing a beat, I pulled out my lock picks and went to work. Within seconds, I'd sprung the latch, pushed open the door, and wandered in.

Erika wasn't in the living room of the suite, but nothing looked askew. The sounds of water caught my attention, and I crossed to one of the two closed doors leading out of the room.

The smell of lavender wafted out. Synthetic. I wrinkled my nose. She looked rich enough to afford the real thing, so she was either cheap or had shoddy taste. I frowned, then—taking a perverse delight in knowing I'd be scaring the hell out of her—slammed open the bathroom door.

Erika shrieked, prone in a tub filled with metallic-scented bubbles.

"You! What the hell are you doing here? I'm calling the

cops—" She started to stand up, then stopped and sank back in the tub. "Get out of here."

"Shut the fuck up," I said, ignoring her tantrum. "Have you seen Chase since last night? I know you left a message for him."

"What business is it of yours—"

"As I said, shut the fuck up unless you're answering my questions. I'm asking you politely, but I could drag you out of that tub and make you tell me, and trust me, you do not want me to get rough with you." A raw jealous streak had taken over. I wanted to shake her, to smack her a good one. Hell, I wanted an old-fashioned catfight, but in this case, I was top cat, and she'd come out the loser. Thank the gods, reason prevailed, and I restrained myself.

"Listen to me, and listen good. Chase is missing. We don't know where he is, so if you've seen him since last night, I advise you to tell me now, because as I said, I can *make* you tell me. Don't push me, Erika."

"Missing?" The blood drained out of her face, and she leaned back against the tub. "What do you mean, missing?"

"I mean missing as in he didn't show up for work this morning. Last night Sharah tried to reach him by phone, but he wasn't answering. His apartment's been trashed—at least the living room—and he's nowhere to be found. Now, are you going to get out of that tub or do I have to drag you out?"

I took another step toward her, and she scrambled, almost slipping as she stepped out of the oversized Jacuzzi and fumbled for a towel. I stared at her nakedness, decided that I was prettier after all, and turned away. "I'll wait for you in the living room. Hurry up."

Within less than five minutes, she joined me, dressed in a silk robe with her hair wrapped in a turban. She wore fuzzy slippers that looked like they were out of some 1950s glamour-girl movie, and it occurred to me that, even though she was probably in her early thirties, she looked dated. Old.

She headed toward the bar and poured herself a Scotch. "You want a drink?" she asked.

I shook my head.

"Suit yourself. After I answer your question, I want you to

get the hell out and never show up here again. I told Chase to break it off with you when I found out about you, but he wouldn't listen. So don't blame me for everything that's happened," she added, giving me a narrow look that could have either been cunning or wary.

"You made the choice to continue seeing him when you knew he was with me. You share some of the fault. But that's not what I'm here about. When did you last see him?" I let out a long sigh. Her calm, collected manner was getting to me. I didn't like being hysterical. I didn't want to be the hysterical one while she remained in control of herself.

"Have a seat," she said, slowly sipping her drink.

As I gingerly sat on the edge of the couch, she slid into the armchair and crossed her legs, restlessly dangling the slipper off the toe of her left foot.

"So, Chase has turned up missing? Well, I have no idea where he is. We had an argument yesterday, during lunch. He started for the door, and I told him that if he wasn't going to take me out dancing as planned, don't bother coming back. He owed me an apology, and I wasn't interested in hearing from him until he was ready to ante up a contrite 'I'm sorry.'"

She took another sip. "I never heard back, so I assumed he was still pissed, and I sure as hell wasn't about to be the first one to call."

I swallowed some of my irritation. She sounded just as angry as me. "What did you argue about?" I asked, forcing my tongue to form the words.

She gave me a faint smile. At first I thought she was being snide, but by the tone of her voice, I realized it was just one of those "we're both women, we both know men can be pigs" smiles. "Do you really want to know?"

I didn't, but with Chase missing . . . I sighed. "It might give us some clue to help find him."

Erika let out a snort. "Well, I doubt it, but hey, what the hell. I imagine you must be on top of the world knowing we had an argument. Whatever. Chase wanted to have an open relationship with *you*. I said forget it. He got pissed." She stood and slowly crossed to the window, where she stared out over the parking lot. "He blames me for this whole mess."

I blinked. Chase was interested in an open relationship? That was news. Chase had been staunchly against it when I'd ventured the idea because of Zachary. Had he changed his mind? "There's something I want to know. Did Chase tell you he was seeing me when you first came back to town?"

She didn't move, didn't turn around, but by the shift in her stance and the droop in her shoulders, I knew the answer. "He didn't, did he? You didn't know at first."

"Fine," she said, polishing off the booze. "I didn't know at first. Chase didn't tell me." She turned around, looking less confident. "I found out about you two weeks ago when I went to his office. He had slipped out for lunch. To kill the time, I started talking to the elf—Sharah? Anyway, she told me you were his girlfriend. She didn't know I'd been seeing him. When he came back, I had it out with him. He said that he thought you two were on the rocks. I told him to break it off with you, then. I didn't realize until this week that he was exaggerating. I should have expected him to do something like that, damn it."

Tears rose in her eyes, and even though I didn't want to, I felt sorry for her. "What do you mean?"

"Because *that's* why we broke up in the first place. Let me ask *you* a question now. Did he ever tell you about me?" She placed her glass on a coaster and dropped back into the armchair.

I shook my head. "No, he didn't. He told me . . . he said he'd never had a serious relationship before."

"I see," she said. Even though she was trying to keep a straight face, I saw the devastation creeping in around the edges.

"We were engaged for three years. I suppose, in his book, that doesn't qualify as serious. Or maybe it was just me. Anyway," she said, shaking her head. "Two months before the wedding I found out that he had fucked my best friend. He insisted it had been a one-time slip. I loved him, so I took him back. The night before our wedding I caught him with a stripper. In *our* bed. I left him. Moved away."

I felt like I'd just been hit with a brick. Chase had done this? My Chase? Sure, he was abrasive at times, but he always seemed to preach doing the right thing. And now I find out he had a history of being a slimeball?

She glanced up at me, her gaze flickering over my face. "Aren't you going to gloat?"

Shaking my head, I said, "Not my style." Which wasn't entirely true, but this time, I meant it.

"Thanks, I guess. Anyway, I thought . . . when I came back a month ago, he seemed changed. He apologized. He brought me flowers and told me he was happy to see me. I'd never really gotten over him so I . . . we . . . I fell for him again. When I found out about you, I knew he hadn't changed. So I decided to play him for as good of a fling as I could get. I'm not out to keep him, Delilah. I just wanted to build him up, then drop him like he dropped me. I wanted to *hurt* him."

Cripes! I stared at her. Revenge ran deep among FBHs as well as the Fae. Chase would have his own side of the story, no doubt, and the truth probably fell somewhere between the two, but whatever the case, the whole mess left me with a lot to think about.

"So you were arguing about me?" I asked again.

"About you—about responsibility. About doing the right thing. I don't give a flying fuck if you get your pussy bent over this. But I am angry that Chase still doesn't have the balls to stand up and say, 'Yeah, I did this,' and accept the consequences. Yesterday, when he blamed me for all the problems, I decided that I'm done. I'm too old to play head games with a spoiled brat. And I'm not interested in getting involved in a love triangle. Or a three-way."

She stood, arms folded, her exquisitely painted nails drumming a beat against the smooth silk robe. "My motto anymore is that when it stops being fun, I'm gone. And it stopped being fun. You wanted to know when the last time I saw him was? Yesterday, at Ruth's Chris Steak House. We were having drinks and appetizers. He walked out and stuck me with the bill."

With that, she turned to me. "I am going to get dressed. When I come out, I'd appreciate it if you weren't here. I'm leaving town today. He's all yours, honey. But I don't recommend you plan on any long-term commitments, because Chase is carrying a shitload of baggage in that trunk of his."

I watched as she disappeared into the bedroom, then slowly got up and left, making sure to lock the door on my way out.

So Chase had lied to me, several times over. If Erika was telling the truth, Chase had done to her what he'd done to me, only worse. The night before their wedding . . . even in Otherworld, that behavior wouldn't be acceptable for anybody except nobility. And only the kind of nobles that congregated around Lethesanar.

I slowly returned to my Jeep, rehashing the conversation over and over. Chase was missing. Chase played the field. Chase had lied to me, had lied to her, had a history of lying about women.

In some ways, it made me feel better that I wasn't the only victim. If only he could have accepted an open relationship from the start, maybe this wouldn't have happened. But he couldn't—at least not on his woman's side. I was beginning to get the picture. Chase needed to play the field, but he couldn't stand having the tables turned on him. So where did that leave us? Me? Him?

Erika said she was leaving, and I believed her. I now realized she wasn't the enemy. In fact, there was no enemy . . . there was only the gaping void left by my new inability to trust a man who insisted he loved me. A man who had introduced me to passion, to love, to my human emotional roots.

Now what was I supposed to do? Turn my back on him? Walk away? But I couldn't do that. We needed him because of his job, because of the demon problem. Could we pull back, be friends instead of lovers? The more I thought about it, the more it seemed like a good idea. At least until we got our heads sorted out.

Wondering where the hell he was, I took off for home, deciding to put any major decisions about our relationship on hold until we'd had a chance to talk.

* * *

As I pulled into the driveway, I had the feeling something was wrong. I parked the Jeep a ways down the drive, just in case, and slipped up to the house by skirting through the woods. I hurried up the kitchen steps and stopped, staring at the door leading to the back porch. It had been ripped off the hinges. Shit!

Racing inside, I kicked aside the basket of laundry that had been overturned. The kitchen was a mess, with broken dishes and upended food everywhere. A glance showed that Menolly's entrance to her lair was still closed; with any luck, whoever it was hadn't found it.

But Iris—and Maggie? I whirled around to Maggie's playpen. It was torn to shreds.

Fighting back a scream, I raced into the living room, which was also upended. An odd fragrance hit my nose, and I recoiled. Almost overpowering, it was like decaying fruit: oranges and sugar vanilla and jasmine . . . oh fuck. Oh hell. The scent of Rāksasa. Karvanak had been here.

I sank down to the floor, crouching as wave after wave of energy rolled through me. I wanted to transform, to run and hide under something where it was safe and dark and hidden. As I fought the urges that ate at me like a junkie craving a fix, I could only wonder if Karvanak was still here—and if Iris and Maggie were still alive.

CHAPTER 21

"No, no, no . . ." I whimpered. If only I could change into my tabby self and go find a safe corner in which to hide. I didn't want to be the one to find the bodies. I didn't want to see what Karvanak had done to our home. Where was Camille? She was better at this than I was. Why wasn't she here? She was my big sister, and it was her job to take care of us.

I rocked back and forth on my heels, holding my head in my hands, trying to blank out the destruction around me. By now, I should be shifting. Why wasn't my body taking over and forcing me to do what I wanted to do? For years, the involuntary shifting had been a refuge from fear and anger, a respite from arguments. Where was it now that I really needed it?

After a moment, I realized it wasn't going to happen.

Both relieved and chagrined, I looked around. The urge to shift had died down to a manageable level. Another moment, and I could breathe again. I stood up, swallowing my fear. I forced my shoulders back. I had no choice. I'd deal with whatever aftermath the Rāksasa had left in his wake.

My pulse racing, I flipped open my cell phone and dialed the Indigo Crescent, Camille's bookstore. As soon as she answered,

I said, "Get your butt home now. The demons have been here. And contact Smoky if you can. We might need him."

Pocketing the phone, I edged my way over to the stairs. I had the ability to move silently—creeping like a cat—and I used it for all I was worth now, gliding up the staircase until I came to Camille's floor. The doors were all standing open. I checked each room. Everything had been torn apart. There were clothes everywhere in her bedroom. I glanced in her study. Her magical oils had been overturned and spell components destroyed, but there was no sign of the intruders. Thank the gods she carried the unicorn horn with her.

As I made my way up to my own chambers, I listened carefully, trying to pinpoint any noise that stood out. When I reached the third floor, I found the same situation. Everything tossed, some things destroyed, but nobody around.

That just left Menolly's lair. Praying that she was okay— and that I'd find Iris and Maggie alive—I raced back down the stairs, only to run into Camille and Smoky as they appeared in the living room, Smoky's arm around Camille's waist.

"We came through the Ionyc Sea," she said, looking disoriented. "I left my car at the shop."

"Thank the gods you're here," I said. "I haven't found Iris or Maggie yet, but I searched both the second and third floors, and there's no sign of blood, bodies, or the demons. Can you pick up the scent? Karvanak was here."

She breathed deep, paling as the fragrance of the Rākasasa hit her. "Hell and high water."

"Let's check Menolly's lair." I slipped past her.

We stopped in front of the bookshelf. Smoky was standing behind us. I glanced at Camille and she shook her head. "He's bound to find out sometime. Open it."

So, for the second time since we had come here to live, we revealed the secret entrance to Menolly's lair. As the shelves swung open, Smoky said nothing but gave a little nod.

I slipped into the dark opening and flipped on the dim light that illuminated the staircase leading down to Menolly's nest. As we slowly descended, I struggled to pick up the demon's scent, but there were no telltale fragrances lingering to indicate that he'd found the lair.

"Iris? Iris?" Camille called softly down into the depths of the basement that we'd retrofitted for Menolly. As I set foot on the bottom step, I found myself staring at Iris, her brilliant blue eyes wide with fear and anger. Maggie was tucked behind her, and she held out her wand with the Aqualine crystal on it.

"Stop where you are," she said, raising the wand.

"It's us, Iris . . ." I stopped. She was right to worry. Rāksasas were masters of illusion. We could easily be the demon and his cronies, cloaked behind a mirage. "Go ahead. Cast your Dispel Illusion spell, and you'll know for sure."

She raised the wand, and I could see her hand was shaking, but she called out in a loud, clear voice. *"Piilevä otus, tulee esiin!"*

A wash of light splashed over us, and I felt a little odd, but nothing much happened except for a moment I thought I was going to shift into my tabby form. After the flare died away, she lowered her wand, sinking to the ground and gathering Maggie into her arms.

"Thank the gods, thank the gods . . . I thought . . ."

"You thought we were the demons," I said, running to her. Camille checked on Menolly. When Menolly walked through her dreams, she looked wan and pale, dead as the vampire she was. She neither stirred, nor breathed, nor made a single movement. Sometimes I wondered where she journeyed in her dreams, but she wouldn't tell us, although I knew she wandered through her memories at times.

I gave Iris a kiss on the forehead and was about to help her up when Smoky gently pushed me away. He gathered Iris and Maggie into his arms and, as if he were carrying two feathers, headed up the stairs. Camille and I followed, securing the bookshelf firmly after we entered the kitchen again. Smoky deposited Iris by the rocking chair and motioned for her to sit.

"Tea," he said to Camille.

She nodded, searching through the mess of pots and pans that littered the floor. She found the stainless teakettle—dented but still usable—and filled it with water, then set it to heat.

Our teapots were smashed, but I managed to find four intact mugs. The cupboards had been emptied, but I finally located a box of Celestial Seasonings Lemon Zinger and dropped a tea bag into each of the mugs.

Iris shivered as Camille sat by her side, holding Maggie. "Can you tell us what happened?" my sister asked.

"Shortly after you left, I was washing up breakfast dishes when I heard a crash from the living room. I didn't call out. First, I knew everybody was gone, and second, it sounded like someone overturning a shelf or something rather than the slam of a door. And then I smelled it. Orange and sugar vanilla and jasmine . . . and I knew that Karvanak was in the house."

She hung her head. "I was afraid to run out back. He might have had guards outside. So I gathered up Maggie and slipped into Menolly's lair. As the latch closed, I could hear somebody enter the kitchen. Another moment, and I would have been too late. There was a lot of noise, shouting and crashing. I crouched in the dark and waited. I didn't know what else to do. I didn't have my cell phone, and when I picked up the land line down on Menolly's nightstand, it was dead."

I picked up the receiver on the wall phone and listened. "No dial tone. They must have cut the wires outside."

Camille handed Maggie to Iris and wandered over to what had been the playpen. She removed a large skillet from the mattress pad, then pulled the cushion away from the debris, making sure no broken glass was stuck to it. She set Maggie on the cushion and dropped to the floor beside her.

Iris let out a long sigh as she looked around the room. "How's the rest of the house?"

"Just as bad as the kitchen. Except for Menolly's lair. We're facing a lot of cleanup. A lot of loss." The kettle whistled, and I poured our tea.

"Oh man, what about the Whispering Mirror?" Camille jumped up.

"I didn't notice," I said, and she took off for the stairs.

I pressed my fingers to my temples. A headache a mile wide was pounding out a frenzied beat in the back of my mind. *Migraines R Us,* I thought.

Smoky opened the refrigerator door. The demons had apparently ignored it. The contents were intact. He pulled out a loaf of bread, lunch meat, and all the fixings for sandwiches and silently set to work. I had to give it to him. When the chips were down, he did what needed to be done without urging or complaint.

Camille returned to the kitchen as Smoky finished making a platter of roast beef sandwiches. We looked at her.

She shook her head. "Shattered. We're going to have to send someone through the portal to Queen Asteria and ask her if she has a spare. All of my spell components have been trashed. Some are missing. And on the not-so-urgent but irritating side, my makeup's been upended and smashed. Thank heavens for hardwood floors. If I had a carpet in my bedroom, it would be trashed." She pulled out her cell phone. "I'm calling Morio and Roz. We need all the help we can get."

While Camille talked quietly on the phone, Iris dragged in a trash can from out back. I turned my attention to the mess on the kitchen floor. Sandwich in one hand, with the other hand I began tossing chunks of broken glassware and battered pans into the can.

Iris joined me, kneeling over a spot by the table where at least four place settings of our good china lay, smashed to bits. She gathered up the halves of a broken serving platter in her hands and hung her head.

"I'm so sorry, girls. I feel like I should have been able to stop them."

"Don't be ridiculous," Smoky said. "You're lucky you had time to hide. You saved yourself, and you saved the cub. Otherwise, you'd both be demon fodder by now. Rāksasas are cannibalistic, you know. They feast on anything that walks on two or four legs. Karvanak would happily munch you down for an afternoon snack and then follow up with Maggie as dessert. So don't even think that you were lacking courage. You did the smart thing. Now, sit at the table, and eat."

Iris flashed him a grateful smile. "Thank you for that, my dragon friend. I felt so helpless, sitting there in the dark. For about two hours, I wondered whether it was safe. Should I try to come up? Should I wait? What would happen if Delilah or Camille came home alone and found the Rāksasa in the house? It's been a soul-searching morning, that I can tell you."

I stared at the mess. Now that my worry over Maggie and Iris was quelled, a new, uneasy feeling began to grow. "Oh shit. Oh hell."

"What's up? What's wrong?" Camille asked, looking over at me from where she was sorting a few unbroken plates from the rubble.

"Chase! I went to see him at his apartment. The living room was trashed. I stopped in at Erika's, but she said she hasn't seen him since yesterday afternoon, and I'm pretty sure she's telling the truth." My gut twisted. Had Karvanak been there? I hadn't smelled the telltale scent of his fragrance, but then again, he had plenty of lackeys working for him.

"Do you think—" Camille dropped the bag. "You don't think the demons took him, do you?"

"I don't know," I said miserably. "There wasn't any blood— not any that I could see. Only the living room was tossed. I left just as Sharah arrived. But, could it be coincidence? Iris, do you have any idea what the demons were looking for?"

She shook her head. "No. The seal, perhaps?" With a loud sigh, she motioned for Camille to join us at the table, then wiggled her fingers. The whisk broom and dustpan Camille had been using righted themselves and went to work on their own. "There's no need for us to bother ourselves with this mess when I can set the tools to work by themselves."

"Or who," Smoky said after a moment.

"Who what?" I asked. Camille had found some potato salad in the fridge and was dishing it out to go with Smoky's sandwiches, which were so well-endowed with beef and cheese that the meat overshadowed the tomatoes, lettuce, and bread. I didn't mind. I was a carnivore. I bit into a second sandwich and closed my eyes as the taste of rare beef trickled down my throat.

"I mean, maybe the demons weren't looking for a *what*, but a *who*. What if they were searching for Iris and Maggie? All of your cars were gone except for Menolly's, and Karvanak knows she's a vampire. He knew she'd be asleep. You'll notice they didn't come during the night or early morning, when you'd all be at home and awake."

I didn't like where this was going.

"I think the demons have been waiting for a time when Iris would be alone and unable to protect herself," he said.

"You mean, they were out to *kill* her?" Camille asked, thudding into the nearest chair.

"Not necessarily—" Smoky stopped as my cell phone rang, cutting him off.

I flipped open the phone. "Hello?"

A low voice, masculine and throaty, answered. "Is this Delilah D'Artigo?"

"Yes," I said. Warning bells were ringing loud and clear in my gut. The energy coming through the line was so threatening that my hackles rose.

"Karvanak here. Shut the fuck up and listen. Your boyfriend's life depends on your ability to follow instructions."

Oh hell! They did have Chase. I hastily motioned to the others and held my finger to my lips, motioning for Camille to crowd next to the receiver so she could listen along with me.

"I'm here," I said.

"Good girl," he said. "Here's how this is all going down. I know you have the fourth spirit seal, so don't even bother lying about it. You hand over the seal and my renegade flunky to me. I hand over your boyfriend—relatively untouched—to you. Sound good?"

Shit, he thought we still had the seal. Of course. How would he, or any of the demons, know we were giving them to Queen Asteria? Shadow Wing probably thought we were gathering them to use for ourselves! I kept my mouth shut. I might be naïve sometimes, but I wasn't stupid. Camille glanced at me, her jaw set.

"How long do we have to find it? We haven't got the seal. Not yet."

"Sure you do. But just on the off chance that you've somehow lost track of the gem, allow me to be generous. Reflect on what your detective means to you. And you should know, if you decide to back out of our little deal, your boyfriend takes a one-way trip back to the Subterranean Realms, and I'll sell him into slavery."

Taking a deep breath, I asked, "How do I know Chase is still alive?"

"A logical question. One I'd expect, so tell your sister—or that damned sprite you share your house with—to go look on the front porch. I'll wait."

I motioned to Camille. She headed for the front door. When she returned, her face was ashen, and her hand shook as she held out a small, open box. In the box was the last knuckle of a pinkie finger and a ring. It looked like the fingertip had been bitten off. The ring was Chase's. I forced myself to swallow the bile that was rising.

"What the fuck did you do to him?"

"You like our little gift?" Karvanak laughed. "As a bonus, I'll even let you talk to him." There was a muffled sound as the phone changed hands, and then a familiar voice came on the other end.

"Delilah—Delilah—" Chase sounded both frantic and in pain.

"Chase! Oh great gods, are you all right? Your finger—" I wanted to ask him where he was, but Karvanak was smart. He'd kill Chase if he even suspected I was trying to cadge information out of him.

"Never mind my finger," Chase said. "Listen. I'm sorry about everything. I love you."

"I love you, too—" I said, breaking into tears. "We'll save you. Just hang on. Do what they say. We'll rescue you."

"No! Don't deal with them," Chase said, his voice raspy and fearful. "You can't let them have the seal—"

"Enough." Karvanak was back on the line. "Use the tip of his finger for scrying if you want to know it's his for sure. And meanwhile, think about this: There are a lot of demons who like to play with humans down in the Subterranean Realms. There's always a great call for slaves there, and toys. And we've perfected the art of keeping our prisoners alive, even when they'd rather die."

I kept my mouth shut. It wouldn't help Chase at all if I showed how upset I was. "We need time—"

Karvanak laughed. "I thought you'd see it my way. I'm in a generous mood. You have thirty-six hours. Don't expect any extensions, and don't let the charge on your cell phone die. Both would be very, very bad ideas."

As the line went dead, I closed my phone and looked at the others.

"You talked to Chase?" Camille asked.

I nodded.

"I assume Karvanak wants the fourth spirit seal."

"He wants a little more than that. He also demanded that we hand over Vanzir. If we don't, he'll sell Chase to the Sub Realms, into slavery." All of my anger at Chase vanished in a sea of worry. I broke down, lowering my head to the table as the stinging salt of tears washed over my face. "I can't let anything happen to him. I . . . I . . ."

Camille rested her hand on my shoulder. "You love him, even if you are mad at him." As I nodded, she rubbed my back, and Iris hurried to fetch me more tea. How the hell were we supposed to handle this? Unable to keep up pretenses any longer, I gave in to my fear and wept until there were no more tears to come.

CHAPTER 22

As soon as dusk hit, we gathered around the table. We'd managed to clean up most of the mess, though the house looked a lot more empty than it had that morning when we left. Most of our knickknacks were gone, and some of the furniture had been destroyed.

We'd already sent Morio through Grandmother Coyote's portal to Elqaneve, to tell them we needed a new Whispering Mirror. He returned a couple of hours later with the promise that we'd have one before the week was out.

Now, Smoky and Morio sat on one side with Camille. Zach and I sat opposite them. Menolly parked herself at the head of the table, while Iris and Roz took the other end.

Menolly had instructed Luke—a werewolf who was her head bartender at the Wayfarer—to take over for the night. I'd asked Vanzir to join us a little later. We needed to discuss matters before telling the dream chaser he was technically part of Chase's ransom. No telling what he might do once he found out that Karvanak had plans for him, and they probably didn't involve a welcome-home party. Not that I intended to hand him over. He knew too much about us and our operations by now.

"What do we do? We can't give him the spirit seal. For one thing, we already handed it over to Queen Asteria. Even if we did still have it, we couldn't trade it. Not even to save Chase." Camille had a strained look on her face. We all did.

I stared at my glass of milk. "I know. If we start making deals with them, we might as well just throw open the portals and invite Shadow Wing to go all Godzilla on us." Logic tasted bitter in my mouth, but there it was—the bottom line. Even if Karvanak had kidnapped Iris, we wouldn't trade the seals for her. And I wasn't about to hand over Vanzir, either. Terrorism thrived on positive results, and if we gave in now, we'd be admitting defeat.

"Collateral damage," Menolly said. "That's what it comes down to. It's easy to say no to striking a bargain when the victims are nameless. But when the bodies take on the faces of friends, that's when we're forced to make hard choices." She glanced over at Camille. "Like I had to with Erin."

"Erin . . ." I said. "You're right. She was targeted because of us, too."

Erin Mathews was the owner of the Scarlet Harlot, a lingerie shop Camille frequented. She was also president of the local Faerie Watchers Club, a nationwide group of Fae groupies. Members traded pictures, autographs, asked various Fae in to speak at their meetings, and generally were a harmless, enthusiastic bunch.

When Camille had befriended Erin, we had no idea it would turn out so badly. A few months back, when Menolly's sire had come to town to raise hell, he targeted the human woman, solely because she was our friend, and he knew that hurting her would hurt *us*.

He'd meant to turn Erin and use her against us, but we had gotten to her first. We couldn't save her life. But we found her in time for Menolly to offer Erin the chance to walk among the undead. Instead of a mass-murderer for a sire, Erin now called Menolly "Mother," and Menolly was now spending a lot of time helping her "daughter" adjust to life on the flip side.

"I fear we're going to see more of this as the battle for control over the portals continues. And with the new portals cropping up randomly as the grid breaks down . . . we're in for a rough time of it," Morio said. "We have to come to grips with the fact that we're walking in the fire now, and fire burns."

Camille let out a long sigh. "He's right. This isn't the worst of it. Having said that, what can we do about Chase? Obviously, we can't give them the seal. And we can't hand over Vanzir, either. So how do we save him?"

"Find Karvanak, and we find Chase. We have to kill the Rāksasa this time. He'll be on us like white on rice if we don't, and he won't stop till we're dead." I slammed my hand on the table. "Why didn't we take him out after he stole the seal? We just skirted him, hoping he'd go away."

"We've been busy," Iris said. "And once he stole the third seal, he wasn't an immediate threat anymore. You know full well that before we even thought about getting near him again, we had to bind Vanzir with the Subjugation Ritual. And that took a lot of energy and time, if you remember."

I sucked back a retort. Iris had worn herself out performing the ritual. Even with Morio and Camille acting as her seconds, it had taken every ounce of energy the Talon-haltija had in order to control the collar of subjugation.

The symbiotic creatures that formed the collars came lumbering in from the astral realm, summoned by force and won over by bribery. They would only agree to act as an agent for subjugation after offerings of blood had been made from all who would wield the *whip of the master*. Which meant the four of us—Iris, Menolly, Camille, and I—had spent two weeks siphoning off enough of our blood to fill a quart jar before we could even summon the creature. Iris had fasted during that time, which made it even more difficult on the sprite.

During the ritual, the creature, which looked like a translucent eel, swelled thick and fat on our blood, then slithered toward Vanzir's neck, ready to form the living chain of energy beneath his skin that would forever bind him to us.

As it bit into his flesh, he winced, but the manacles holding him down were strong, and he forced himself to relax. The ritual went against every bone in his body, but he seemed determined to go through with it. I was relieved. Our only other option would be to kill him. We couldn't let him go.

As the soul binder wriggled to enlarge the opening it had severed in Vanzir's neck, my stomach churned. And as the astral parasite began to burrow into muscle, I had to force myself to maintain control and not go running out of the room. But I managed to stand vigil with my sisters and Iris.

By the time the tip of its tail had almost disappeared, I could see the head had worked its way around his neck, a few layers beneath the skin. The soul binder's teeth broke through directly opposite the original bite, grabbed hold of its tail like an ouroboros, and then settled deep into the muscle as the skin quickly began to heal over the two narrow slits.

Iris began the chant to forever merge the soul binder and Vanzir. The chant would bind both of them to us. Once again, it felt like we were headed on a one-way trip, deeper into the rabbit hole.

There is no spoon, I thought as the grisly ritual played itself out. Everything was an illusion. It had to be, or I didn't want to be here. And yet . . . and yet . . . from where we stood, everything was terribly, horribly real.

And then it was over, and Vanzir was our slave. He would live or die by our whims. We were his masters. One more hat I didn't want to wear. One more title I didn't want tacked onto my name. But there it was, and here we were, chained to a demon by a blood ritual as old as the demons themselves.

"We should be able to locate Karvanak," Rozurial said. "And quite possibly, we can rescue Chase from him. But won't the Rāksasa be expecting us? You can't fault the dude on intelligence. I agree with Smoky. He was here, looking for more insurance. I'll bet you anything the demon figured there's no way in hell you'd back out of the deal if he had Iris or Maggie. Or both."

"Cripes," Camille said. "I bet you're right."

"Of course he's right," Menolly said, backing her chair away from the table. She began to float, hovering up near the ceiling. She'd always preferred sitting in trees when we were children. Now that she was a vampire, she had transferred her love of heights to floating in midair without any visible means of support. It impressed the hell out of the locals, that was for sure.

Iris jumped off her stool. "Well, he would have had me, too, if it weren't for my excellent hearing." She looked around at what was left of the mess, stuff the dustpan and broom couldn't pick up by themselves. "Delilah's right. If we don't dispatch this cretin, we'll never throw him off our back. And we must rescue Chase. He's part of the family," she added, looking pointedly at me. "Maggie adores him."

Silently thanking her with my eyes, I turned to Zach. He laid a gentle hand on my shoulder. "He's a good man, and he's given his all to your efforts. I'll do whatever I can to help."

Just then, there was a knock on the door. I slipped out to answer it. Vanzir had arrived. Silently, I led him to the kitchen and asked him to sit down.

"You look like you're going to a funeral," he said, glancing around nervously, then he licked his lips. "Something's happened. What's up? Did I do something wrong?"

"No, you didn't." I took a deep breath, then let it out in a shaky stream. Even though I knew he was on our side, my heart flinched. Dealing with demons like Rozurial was one thing. Roz wasn't evil, just chaotic. But I had no doubt that Vanzir had paid his dues when he was a member of the Sub Realms.

"It's nothing you did," I said, after a moment. "But Karvanak is on the move. He's captured Chase, and he's holding him for ransom." I held out the box with Chase's fingertip and ring in it.

Vanzir turned a paler shade of white. "Crap." He let out a long sigh and leaned back in his chair. "You're lucky it was Chase's finger he cut off, and not something more personal. Karvanak is a cold-hearted bastard. He's offering a trade for the spirit seal, am I right?"

"Yeah . . ." I wasn't sure quite how to tell him that he was on the menu, too.

"You won't get him back that way," Vanzir said, resting his elbows on the table and staring at the fingertip. "Even if you give Karvanak the seal, he'll carve Chase up in little bites and eat him. He talks a good game and specializes in the double cross."

"Do you think he'll kill Chase before we get there?"

"Not before he realizes you aren't going to hand over the seal. Let's put it this way: Karvanak keeps his options open till he's sewn up a deal. Then he gets rid of the evidence. Chase might not come back totally intact, but he'll be kept alive until the Rākṣasa realizes you either don't have the seal or aren't going to give it to him." Vanzir shrugged. "Don't ever underestimate him. He didn't get promoted to general for being stupid."

"There's something else," I said, not wanting to tell him. But sometimes, like with pulling a bad tooth, it's better to just get it over with. "Karvanak also wants you back."

That bought an immediate response. Vanzir jerked up, his eyes wide. "No! You can't—" He fell silent, then looked around at us, anxiously tapping his fingers on the table. "Are you going to hand me over to him?"

For the first time, his voice didn't grate on my nerves, and for the first time, I saw the raw fear on his face. He might be a demon, but he really *was* terrified of his own kind.

"No," I whispered. "No, we won't. For one thing, you know too much about our operations. For another, trading life for life? No. If you were our prisoner, if you were here under duress, we might. But you made the choice to switch sides, and we don't rat out our allies." The words stuck on my tongue like stray fur, but I had to reassure him. Maybe I didn't like him, but he'd fought by our side.

I looked over at Camille and Menolly. They both nodded. For once we were all on the same page. "But we have to find out where he is. Since Mordred burned down the rug shop, Karvanak's gone into hiding, and we need to know where."

Vanzir crossed to the kitchen window and stared out into the yard.

I followed him and tentatively reached out to put my hand on his shoulder. "Don't worry," I said. "We aren't going to turn you over to Karvanak."

"Of course you aren't. I know too much," he said gruffly,

shrugging my hand away. "Your lover's being held by one of Shadow Wing's most ruthless generals. At least, one that he dares send Earthside. There are far worse back in the Subterranean Realms."

He whirled around, his gaze locking with mine. "Do you *know* what it's like now, living in the Subterranean Realms? Life there was pretty good for a while, until Shadow Wing seized control. Now it's a desperate place. There are *thousands* of demons down there who would love to come Earthside if only to get away from *him*."

"Then why are they fighting for him? Why don't they band together and fight against him?" I couldn't understand the reasoning.

Vanzir snorted, leaning on the windowsill. He stared bleakly out into the yard. "Some do—and I know a few. But understand that Shadow Wing is a *Soul Eater*. He can control the masses because he can swallow any soul standing in his way, be it demon, human, or Fae. He rules with fire and fear, and there are thousands who kneel to him only to keep their heads." He folded his arms across his chest, rubbing his shoulders as if he were freezing. "There's something else."

"What? Tell us now. If you hold out on us—" Menolly swooped down, landing on his other side.

"I'm not holding out on you. I wasn't sure if my imagination was running amok or if what I thought was real, was. Not until I did some scrying this morning. And I'm *still* not sure I'm right. But if I am, then we have to do more than keep the spirit seals away from him. We have to hunt him down and destroy him." Vanzir was so pale I thought he was going to pass out.

"Tell us," I said. "Tell us what you think is going on."

He scuffed his boot on the Persian rug and turned around, sitting on the sill, looking for all the world like a young David Bowie. "The breakdown in the grid that's allowing new portals to open spontaneously? I think Shadow Wing's discovered a way to use what's happening. My gut tells me he's doing more than trying to rip open the seals. Shadow Wing is fucking crazy. He's not just power hungry. He's mad."

"How so?" The room was so quiet that I could hear every creak, every movement, every shift people made in their chairs.

Vanzir took a deep breath, then let it out slowly. "I think he means to *unmake* the worlds. Shadow Wing the Unraveller, he calls himself now. I think he's out to do more than conquer. I think he's out to totally annihilate."

"Motherfucking son of a bitch," Menolly said. She seldom showed fear, but she was showing it now and but good. Her eyes were bloodred and her fangs had extended. "What makes you think so?"

"I know a few rogue demons who've managed to escape and cross over," he said. "For the most part they lie low, keep their noses clean, and try to fly under the radar. They don't want anything to do with Karvanak and his cronies. Or with Shadow Wing and this war. We talk a little. And no, they don't know about the Subjugation Ritual. They think I'm just hiding out from Karvanak."

"Why don't you get your butt back over to the table? Delilah's tired and needs to sit down," Smoky said abruptly in that disobey-and-you're-toast tone that he had.

Vanzir gave him a withering look but promptly returned to the table.

I slumped in my chair, and even Menolly slowly floated down from the ceiling and sat beside me, scooting in next to Zach. She gave Vanzir a narrow look. "So what are your buddies saying? And I suggest you give us a list of their names. We'll want to keep them under surveillance."

"Bring me a paper," Vanzir said quietly. He couldn't refuse. "You won't kill them, will you?"

"Only if they turn out to be a problem. If they are, as you say, keeping their noses clean, we'll leave them alone. For now. But if they show any sign of being under Shadow Wing's control, then they can kiss their asses good-bye. And you *will* keep your mouth shut about the fact that we know about them."

Her eyes were glowing as she planted her hands on the table and leaned toward him. "You hear me, demon boy? If I even think one of them is going to slip, he'll be staring down at the tip of my fangs."

Vanzir shivered. He might not have a good track record of saying the right thing at the right time, but he wasn't stupid. He knew all too well how powerful Menolly could be.

"Got it." He shoved the list across the table to her. "Here. I know where four of them live. There are others, but I have no idea where they hang out."

She took the list and nodded. "Good. Now, what are they saying?"

"I only heard the latest news this morning, on my way here. A demon named Trytian managed to sneak over a week ago. He was slated to be executed—and believe me, executions are big business down in the Sub Realms—on the summer solstice. His father is some bigwig daemon who is leading a rebellion against Shadow Wing over there. Shadow Wing managed to capture Trytian and was going to use him as a pawn, but Trytian's father refused to bargain."

Demons and daemons were both on the Big Bad list, but they had subtle differences and didn't tend to like each other. Just like devils and demons came from different branches on the hellion family tree.

"So Trytian managed to do what our cousin Shamas did—pull a disappearing act before he hit the block," I said slowly. "Why didn't he go home to his father?" It seemed a little too coincidental for me, but then I'd been studying Suspicion 101 with Camille and Menolly.

"He did, but his father thought he might be more useful over here. You see," Vanzir said, growing quiet, "rumors are circulating around the Subterranean Realms about three half-Fae, half-human women who are thwarting Shadow Wing's plans, but your names are still undercover as far as the demons are concerned. I doubt if anybody over there knows who you are except Shadow Wing and his cronies."

Karvanak would have told him; it stood to reason. "Why would Shadow Wing keep our names secret? Seems more likely he'd slap a bounty on us."

Vanzir shook his head. "Think about it. Shadow Wing's power comes through fear. If he officially acknowledged you, it would be admitting he's vulnerable, and he cannot allow that to happen."

Menolly agreed. "Yes, that makes sense. There's much the same social structure among the Vampire Blood Clans, but we're not quite as paranoid. It's good to know that not every member of the Sub Realms is looking for a vacation getaway over Earthside."

"Well, whatever the reason, I think Trytian's father was hoping that his son would run into you and enlist you as an ally." Vanzir smiled. Wanly, but it was still a smile. "You have no idea how much I wanted to tell Trytian about you. But I didn't. His father commands a large force in the Sub Realms. They could be very useful to us."

"In theory, it's a good idea, but we can't form an allegiance with him," Camille said. "We simply don't dare get entangled in demon versus demon affairs. I don't mean to be rude, but Vanzir, let's face it, most demons don't play with an open deck. What if this Trytian's father is out for the seals himself? I'm giving you a blanket order: Don't tell him, or any other demon, about us or our mission unless we give you our permission. Period. Done deal." She took a deep breath, and Smoky laid a light hand on her left shoulder.

"Got it," Vanzir said, his eyes shifting with their constant kaleidoscope of color. He looked like he wanted to say something else but kept his mouth shut.

Zach pulled the cookie tray over to our side of the table and bit into an Oreo. "So now what? Have you heard anything about where Karvanak is staying?" he asked Vanzir.

"Yeah, that was the second thing I wanted to tell you. I hit pay dirt this morning. I keep my eyes open and my mouth shut. Amazing how much you can learn when people forget you're in the room. Anyway, you remember that djinn, Jassamin?"

I nodded. Jassamin had been a lesser djinn working with Karvanak. Vanzir had verified she'd been Karvanak's lover, as well as a source of power. During our battle for the third spirit seal, it had come down to a tense moment in a cave, when Jassamin was about to kill Chase. That's when Vanzir turned sides and ran her through with a scimitar. "Don't tell me she's back."

"No, but there's another creature running around with the Rākasasa. I don't think she's a djinn, but I hear tell Karvanak has her under his thumb. This morning, I caught sight of her near the burned remains of the shop. I tracked her as far as I could." He reached in his pocket and pulled out a map, slamming it on the table. As he unfolded it, I spotted a precise red line outlined along the streets. As I leaned in, he moved aside to give me room to look.

"I traced her route in red. I figured maybe there was some importance as to why she was taking the route she did."

"Thanks," I said, peering intently. "She took a lot of twists and turns. Do you think she knew you were following her?" I glanced over at him.

He shrugged. "I wouldn't be surprised. Karvanak is probably running on the cautious side at this point. He's been outed—at least to you—and he doesn't underestimate his enemies. In the year or so I was in his servitude, I began to understand just how vast his intelligence is. Rākṣasas are terribly cunning. No, it's his debauchery that's his downfall."

Zach broke his silence. "Why did you work for him if you don't like what Shadow Wing is doing?"

Vanzir arched his eyebrows and let out a snort. I grimaced. Iris, my sisters, and I'd heard the story. Zach hadn't. I wondered if he'd manage to keep his cookies down.

"Work for him? Try again, buddy. I was presented to him as a gift. Nakul, another general in Shadow Wing's army, won me in a gambling bet. I stupidly wagered more than I had during a game of q'aresh. I know I had the better hand, but Nakul cheated. When I told him that I couldn't pay up, he dragged me before Shadow Wing. Shadow Wing ordered that I serve Nakul for seven years. He got bored of me a year into the deal, and that's when he gave me to Karvanak, as a birthday present."

Zach looked queasy. He still didn't understand just how vile and cruel the world could be, which surprised me, given his background and heritage. It wasn't that he was such an optimist, but he preferred to hold onto more hope than was good for him. "Why not just free you?"

Vanzir snorted. "Every move in the Sub Realms is about gaining the upper hand. If you can ingratiate yourself through a bribe—or a gift—you do so, because it might save your butt later. Nakul knew that Karvanak has *diverse* tastes in his bedmates. He has a thing for women with magical energy and for hot young demon ass. The women he drains of power each time he fucks them, and the men he just brutalizes. When he wears out a new playtoy, he eats them. He did things to me that I'll never forget. I still owe him five years of my life, but I don't think I'd survive them. Karvanak is vicious in his fuck fests."

I grimaced, my eyes on the map. Next to me, I could feel Zachary tense. Even though he was a member of the most powerful Puma Pride in North America, and even though they could get downright nasty at times, they didn't hold a candle to the violence rife within the ranks of the Demonkin. Life in the Sub Realms was lived on a kill-or-be-killed basis. Look out for number one, or find yourself staring at the tip of a blade . . . or worse. Vanzir had plenty of reasons to hate Karvanak.

The twisting red line on the map led to a building in south Seattle, in the Industrial District. "Vamp club? She a vampire?" I asked.

Vanzir shook his head. "No, she's not. That's the Fangtabula. She entered, but I didn't see her leave, although I waited around for a while. I want to say she's a djinn, but she doesn't smell right. She does have demon scent on her, but I don't know if that's just because she's cuddling up to Karvanak." He reached in his pocket and pulled out a scarf. "The woman dropped this, though. It reeks of her." He laid it on the table.

Camille hesitantly picked it up, sniffed it, then shook her head. "Sex," she said. "I smell sex but can't fix any particular impression other than that."

The scarf made the rounds until it came to Roz, who gave it one whiff and dropped it like he'd been stung.

He glanced at Camille. "You're right on track. I can tell you exactly who this belongs to. I never thought I'd see her again, though."

"Who is it?" I asked.

He let out a long sigh. "Her name is Fraale. She's scary-ass freaky and one of the most openhearted women I've ever met.

Just the right type—if you prefer life on the edge. But I can't imagine her hiring on to assist the demons. Seriously. If she's there, she's in trouble, too."

Menolly stared at him, her eyes widening. "Fraale? Are you sure?"

"Who the hell is Fraale?" I asked. "You sound like you know her."

"I do know her," Roz said, a sheepish grin escaping onto his lips. "Before Fraale was turned into a succubus specializing as a dominatrix, she was my wife."

CHAPTER 23

Of course, all hell broke loose. This was way too *Jerry Springer* for me to keep my mouth shut.

"Married? You? You've got to be kidding," I said, staring at him like he had just grown another head. "I've got to hear *that* story—"

"Delilah, shut up," Menolly said softly. So softly that I jerked around. The look on her face was anything but joking.

I bit my tongue and said, "Yeah, okay. Well, then tell us this. Is she freakin' out of her mind, cozying up to Karvanak? Or just plain nuts?" The thought of a dominatrix succubus scared the shit out of me. My guess was she'd be tall, lean, wearing lots of leather.

Rozurial's smile faded. "Neither," he said softly. "Fraale and I . . . when we were . . . let's just say that if she's working for Karvanak, chances are she was sold into his hands, like Vanzir, and has no choice in the matter. Fraale may wield one hell of a whip, but she's never been one to raise her hand in violence unless someone's done her wrong. I think she might be in trouble."

Menolly pushed back her chair. "Then it sounds like we might have two people to rescue," she said. Roz flashed her a grateful smile, and I wondered just what the hell was going on. Roz was obviously worried, and Menolly seemed to know more than she was letting on.

I let out a long sigh. "Menolly, you ever been to the Fangtabula?"

She nodded. "Only once, and it was with Wade. Not the cleanest place in the city and definitely on the shady side. They run gambling rooms there, though every time the cops have raided them, the place seems to magically empty, and they can't find anything. Spooks the cops like crazy to go wandering around a bunch of moody vamps."

"I bet," I said, wondering if Chase had been in on any of the raids. If so, he hadn't mentioned it.

"Not only that, but I'll bet a month's pay they're running a blood-whore service under the table." She grimaced.

"Blood whore?" Zach looked confused.

Menolly gave him a nod. "Yeah. Vamp wannabes or fang girls and boys hang out. They trade blood for the sexual high that a vamp can give them. They get addicted to the high and end up wasting away unless their 'owners' treat them right. Some vampires take care of their pets, but not all of them. The whole situation is illegal, and with good reason. But it's like prostitution; there's no way in hell you're going to be able to prevent it. I think the government should legalize it and then tax the hell out of the clubs. At least then they could slap some regulations in place so the blood whores aren't drained or abused."

"Sounds delightful," Camille said as she refilled her cup with tea. "You and Wade ever think of setting up rehab for the addicts?"

"No," Menolly said softly. She squinted. "We've been arguing about other issues as of late. You might be onto something, though. I'll talk to Wade next chance I get. Anyway, back to the Fangtabula. I don't like the feel of the club though, and it wouldn't surprise me if Terrance, the owner, is getting down and dirty with a demon or two."

"Good." I stood and stretched. "Then you won't mind playing spy for us. Somebody's got to go in and talk to Fraale to see if she's a willing participant in Karvanak's game or if she's being forced against her will."

A faint look of disgust crossed Menolly's face. "Well, hell." She let out a sigh, which was deliberate, since my sister never had to breathe. When she took a deep breath or sighed or any one of those wonderful oxygen-related activities, it was purely for effect.

"Fine," she said after a moment. "But if I do, you're coming with me. You can be my pet for the night. You're used to wearing a collar, aren't you, Kitten?" She gave me a wicked grin, and I groaned.

"I'm coming, too," Zach said, but I held up my hand.

"No. Too dangerous, even for you. Roz, do you want to come with us?" I tried to soften my voice, but the question still hit home, that much was clear by the look on his face.

"Let me think for a moment," he said, abruptly heading into the living room. Morio, Zach, and Smoky took off after him. Camille joined Iris by the sink, handing her the tea bags as Iris brewed another pot. Menolly wandered over to the window and stared out into the darkness.

Vanzir glanced over at me. "You are a lot like me."

Not really feeling up to a heart-to-heart, I gave him a brief look. "What do you mean by that?"

"I said, you and I are alike, in some ways. You try but you never quite say the right thing, even though you mean to." He leaned back in his chair, lacing his fingers together behind his head. "I don't fit in my world, you know. I'm good at what I do, but I don't enjoy it."

That wasn't quite what I'd expected to hear. "Oh, come on. You're telling me that you don't like sucking the life out of people through their dreams? But isn't that what you do best? I thought demons got off on hurting people."

I couldn't help being snarky, even though I wanted to be polite. With all that had happened lately and with the demons holding Chase captive, I wasn't feeling particularly generous.

He frowned. "Now you're being deliberately insulting. I understand, though. Really, I *do*. Some demons are like that. Karvanak likes nothing better than to destroy the will of his subordinates, whether they've been captured, bought, or hired. Rāksasas are born mean, and they're arrogant."

"Yeah. I got that impression," I said, playing with my cookie. Vanzir had been one of Karvanak's victims, too. While it was harder for me to feel sympathy for him, I forced myself to stare him straight in the face.

He returned my look, open-eyed. Vanzir was wiry and lean. His eyes, glimmering like a prism, betrayed his heritage. I'd expected them to be bloodred like Menolly's eyes turned when something set her off. But they weren't. They were a rainbow of colors. Against the platinum of his shaggy hair, his eyes stuck out, brilliant and shining, and he'd outlined them in dark kohl. Still silent, I lowered my gaze to his lips. They were thin, like those belonging to a number of men, and pale as the night. Dimples punctuated his cheeks, even as gaunt as they were. After another moment, he hiccupped and broke into a slightly mocking smile.

"You finished, or are you still looking for signs of the dog-faced boy?" he said. Pointing to his head, he added, "No horns in sight. And I guarantee you, no pointed tail, either. Nothing's barbed. Not my fingers, toes, or *cock*."

As I blushed, he pursed his lips and blew me a kiss. "*Oh, poor puddy*. Did I embarrass you? How does it feel to be the butt of a joke? That's what Karvanak put me through every day. And he made me feed. I'd managed to go for thirty-five years without draining anybody's dreams, and *the motherfucker made me feed*."

Vanzir suddenly leaned across the table. I jumped, but he just slid his hand next to mine. He didn't touch me, just tapped his fingers on the table. "I'm like an alcoholic, you see. Once I taste the energy, I want more. But I don't like what it turns me into. The Rāksasa knew I'd taken a vow to stop, and he threatened to kill his—my—victims if I didn't drink from their souls. So I did, to save them. I siphoned their souls and fed on their hope and their love and their life force. But at least they were *alive* when I left their dreams. So, *Miss Delilah*, maybe you're right not to trust me. I can live with that. But stifle the wisecracks until you've walked in my world. You aren't as funny as you think you are."

I felt sick to my stomach as images from my childhood welled up to flood my mind.

. . . a ring of children dancing around my sisters and me, chanting, *"Windwalkers, Windwalkers, got no home . . . Nobody wants you, you're all alone!"* They kept it up all the way home until Mother heard them and came out, shooing them away. We didn't let her see us cry; we didn't want her to feel bad because it was her blood that made them taunt us . . .

. . . one of my uncles pointing at us as we walked into his home during his midsummer gala. He whispered to his lady friend, *"Those are the three I was telling you about. My brother's dirty little half-breeds . . ."* Camille and I forced Menolly to keep her mouth shut so Father wouldn't know . . .

. . . the neighbor boy racing after me with his dog, making me so afraid that I transformed. They treed me, and I couldn't come down for hours. Camille finally noticed what was going on and beat the living crap out of him, then climbed the tree to coax me down. We never told anybody . . .

And here I'd been, doing the same thing to Vanzir because of *what* he was. It wasn't as if he were still our enemy. The ritual had provided us with a safety net. We could kill him on a whim, and he couldn't raise a hand to defend himself against us. And I'd been taking advantage of that.

I glanced over at the sink, where Camille was studiously ignoring us, arranging more cookies on a plate while Iris checked the tea. Menolly had hovered her way up to the ceiling and was hanging there, midair, eyes closed. I knew she could hear our conversation, but she'd chosen not to interfere. Voices from the living room told me the boys were coming back.

Hurriedly, I leaned across the table to whisper in Vanzir's

ear. "I'm sorry. Truly. I've been an ass, and I apologize." I
swallowed my pride. "I've been through it before. We all have.
I guess sometimes it's easy to become the very thing you
hate."

His gaze still fixated on my face, Vanzir nodded. "Yeah, I
know. It's all too easy to slide into the slot you really don't
want to fit in. Been there, done that, don't want to go there
again." He stretched. His Death Zombies T-shirt was ripped,
safety-pinned in a few places, and his black leather pants were
dusty, but not dirty. He definitely had the rocker dude look
going, I thought.

At that moment, Smoky and Morio entered the room, Zach
and Roz trailing behind them. Roz turned to Menolly, his face
deadpan. Whatever the guys had discussed, I had a feeling
they weren't going to share it with us.

"I'll go with you. I want Zach to come, too. You may think
he's too naïve, but trust me, he'll be a good ally. And my ex-
wife likes Weres," Roz added softly, glancing at me. "Make
no mistake: She plays both sides of the fence."

"I guess we should head out," Menolly said. "Even if
Fraale isn't there anymore, somebody's bound to have noticed
her. Kitten, you need to change."

Wondering just what kind of getup she was going to stuff
me into, I slid out of my chair. "Coming. Camille, can you and
Morio try to pinpoint Chase with your magic? There are some
of his things in my room, if you need them."

Camille nodded. "We'll get right on it. Smoky's going to
head out to his land to see if the Triple Threat has heard
anything." We'd begun using the nickname for Titania,
Morgaine, and Aeval sometime back, but usually we only used
it between ourselves. Now, the guys glanced at her.

"The Triple Threat? And they *know* you call them this?"
Roz asked, grinning like a bean Sidhe.

"Of course not, you idiot," Camille bantered back.

"What about you?" Roz turned to Smoky. "You call them
that to their faces?"

Smoky let out a low harrumph. "They're a pack of kooks,
but I'm always a gentleman—"

As Camille, Menolly, and I let out a collective snicker, he

just arched an eyebrow. "At least you have to admit that I have more manners than my beloved wife." He leered at Camille. "Isn't that right? Anyway, I have nothing to fear from them. They aren't a threat to me."

"Face it, love, you're stuck with me," Camille said, fondly patting his hand as he laid it on her shoulder. "Rude, crude, and totally lewd."

"I wouldn't have it any other way," he said, leaning over to kiss her. "Even though I do have to share you with the fox. And the Svartan." And then, like a silent shadow in the night, he slipped out the back door and was gone in under a minute flat.

I whistled. "When the dude moves, he moves."

"You can say that again," Camille said, a sly smile on her lips.

"Oh for criminey's sake . . . I didn't mean it like that—"

"Kitten? Get a move on!" Menolly's voice echoed from the stairwell, and I headed toward the living room.

Menolly was waiting for me by my closet, looking disgusted. "Can't you be a little more girly? I mean, come on Kitten—your underwear's okay, but don't you own anything but tank tops and ripped jeans?" She held up my most comfortable pair of jeans, with the knees and the thighs ripped. "Don't you have anything with a little lace or some glitter?"

Oh great gods. She was nitpicking my wardrobe? "Are you serious?"

"You want to get into the club without arousing suspicion or not? You've got to look like my pet. And that means showing some cleavage, or leg, or whatever."

I grimaced. "You're going to laugh your ass off. I've never worn this," I added, digging through a box in the back of my closet. "I bought it in a fit of insanity. The moment I left the store, I knew I'd made a mistake, but I was too embarrassed to return it, so I hid it before you or Camille could find it and make fun of me."

I so did not want to show Menolly my secret shame, but she wouldn't rest now that I'd let the cat—metaphorically speaking—out of the bag. I pulled a plastic shopping bag from the bottom of the box and, rolling my eyes, tossed it to her.

She yanked it open. As she withdrew the gold lamé pants and the matching fringe halter top, she began to shake, the smirk on her face growing.

"I told you," I muttered, trying to snatch it back from her.

"No you don't!" she said, darting away. "You are so wearing this tonight! I know it . . . isn't exactly your style—"

"That's an understatement." Glaring at her, I flounced over to my bed and flopped down on it, bemoaning my fate. "Being caught out in public decked out in that getup is going to be the most humiliating night of my life . . . well . . . other than walking in on Chase when he was dipping his cock into Erika's pussy."

"Somehow, *that* strikes me as more infuriating than humiliating," she said. "You shouldn't feel embarrassed. If he needs some sniveling, snot-nosed debutante to make him feel like a man, it's not your fault. But . . ." She paused, looking hesitant, like she wanted to say more.

"What is it? You obviously have an opinion on the subject that you haven't shared with me." I sat up, waiting.

"Yeah, I do, but I don't know how you'll take it."

"Just say it, then."

"All right." Menolly stared at me. "If you want my opinion, Chase was looking for reassurance. It can't be easy, Kitten, to be an FBH and have your lover not only be stronger than you, but faster, more magical, and more sexual. Let's face it. Any one of the three of us is a handful for any man—or woman. It takes a strong person to stand beside a partner with Fae blood without feeling emasculated. Chase has been overwhelmed keeping up with both facets of his job. He sees you outfighting and outshining him all the time. I'm just saying, it's got to sting his ego."

I stared at the quilt on my bed, fighting back a desire to smack her across the face. I never treated Chase like he was subpar. Never. Then I stopped. We all did. Not intentionally, but there was no way around it. We were always telling him to get out of the way in a fight, or get behind us, or stay behind because it was too dangerous. But that was for his own protection, not because we thought he was "lesser" than we were. For the first time, I realized that he might not see it that way, though.

"Oh my gods," I whispered. "You're right. He was an ass for lying to me, but you're right. He might have turned to Erika because he needed to feel like the strong one for a change." I stared at the pattern on my quilt. "Mother never felt like that around Father. Do you think?"

I'd never once heard a word of complaint out of our mother's mouth about Father being so strong or long-lived. In fact, she'd refused the chance to grow far older with him than her life span normally allowed because she didn't think she could handle the extra years.

Menolly sat on the bed next to me and took my hand in hers. "There's no telling. Not now. But I do know this: Mother never wanted to be a Guardsman. She never aspired to a life outside of being a good wife and mother. Hearth and home was her domain, and Father didn't intrude, so there was no competition between them. We don't know if they had problems in the bedroom, but their dynamics were totally different than the dynamics between you and Chase. Why do you think I've been so hesitant about supporting your relationship?"

"I just thought you didn't like Chase," I said in a small voice.

"At first, I didn't, but no. That's not the reason. He's one of the good guys. Someone we need, someone we can trust. But he's FBH, and that makes him vulnerable. Since we're all embroiled in dangerous work, that puts the both of you on the same playing field. And it isn't level, Kitten. Let me tell you that." She shrugged. "Even if we manage to save him, I have no idea how you can overcome this obstacle. Not unless he can detach and not take it personally."

I stared bleakly at the floor. She was right. How could I have been so blind? But I didn't have much experience with relationships. I wasn't used to handling the nuances of sharing my life with someone else. This whole love thing was new to me, and now I wondered, was I cut out for it? I was a cat, for the sake of the gods. Cats were notoriously solitary.

"Kitten? Are you okay?" Menolly stood up and kissed me on the forehead. "We'd better get moving."

"Okay? I have no idea," I said softly. "But you're right. We've got work to do." I forced myself to stand as she stuffed the clothes in my hands. Right now, rescuing Chase took priority. "Are you sure that I have to wear this crap?"

She gave me a smile. "Brace yourself, but yes. If you're going in as my pet, you have to dress the part, and trust me, blood whores wear shit like this." The look on her face told me there was no wiggle room. "Change."

"I do not want to wear this." On my way to a whine fest, I pulled my best sad-kitty-eyes act, but even that didn't sway her.

"Tough. What about boots? Do you have any high-heeled black boots? Stilettos, not mud thumpers?" Menolly looked ready to paw through my closet, so I motioned her aside and pulled a box down from the upper shelf and shoved it into her hands.

"Camille talked me into buying these. They're cute, but they'll put me at six five. You sure you want a pet that tall? You're barely five one, you know."

"So what? You're tall, and I'm a vampire. Yes, these are good," she said, examining them. "These are really pretty. We want you to stand out, Kitten, and we want you to fit a certain mold. The Fangtabula caters to vampires who keep pets and blood whores. If I go in there with you dressed in jeans and a wife-beater, people are going to question us right from the start, because they cater to clientele who look a little . . . sleazy. I just hope nobody recognizes me. My work with Wade could put me at a disadvantage."

"I don't wear *wife-beaters*," I said, sliding out of my clothes. "I wear muscle shirts, okay? Tank tops."

"Whatever the hell you want to call them." She motioned to my panties and bra. "Those, too. You don't have Camille's boobs, so you can do without a bra. And you don't want a visible panty line. Doesn't matter if they're tight and anything else shows. Just nothing that even hints of normalcy."

"Trust me, I won't have even a nodding acquaintance with *normal* when you get done with me."

I worked my way into the skintight pants, holding my breath as they stretched over my hips and hugged my crotch. The material was scratchy and made me itch, and one look in the mirror told me that people were getting a free peep show under the flesh-hugging spandex. You could see my lips, and they weren't the ones I used liner and gloss on.

I tried to tug the crotch down a little, but the material was molded to my body. Finally, I gave up, slipped the halter top over my head, and tied it around my neck. The halter ended about six inches above my belly button, draping my midsection with long, tasseled fringe that tickled. Actually, it made me want to turn into my tabby form and have a field day batting at it, but I squelched that thought.

Menolly handed me the boots, and I slipped them on, zipping them up. After that, I twirled for her, feeling totally ludicrous.

She nodded. "Good . . . now you need a collar. Black lace scarf, tied with a bow. If you don't have one, Camille will."

"Oh for Pete's sake, is there a dress code?" I asked, digging through my dresser until I came up with a chiffon scarf. It was black, plain but sheer.

Menolly gave it her stamp of approval.

"Yes, there is, unwritten though it may be." She adjusted the scarf so the bow faced the back of my neck. "There, that's code for a switch-hitter. If you had the bow in front, no vamp—or anybody in the Fangtabula—would approach you, because it would mean I own you and hands off. To the left— I'll let you play with girls only. To the right—boys only. If the bow's facing the back, then anybody can ask permission."

I blinked. What rock had I been hiding under? "How the hell do you know all this?"

"I get around," she said, arching her eyebrows and giving me a wicked grin. "Remember, this code only applies in the vamp subculture." Menolly motioned for me to sit down and picked up my makeup bag. "You'll find ownership and domination symbology runs differently through each subcult."

She sorted through the pots of paint. I had enough of Camille's cast-off supplies to last me for years. "Let's see what we have—oh! This will do nicely."

Within moments, I was sporting brilliant red lips and wild chartreuse eye shadow. After outlining my eyes in brilliant liner the color of green velvet, she dusted me with enough powder to pale me down. "You can't look too robust if I've been feeding on you regularly." She stood back. "I think we're done."

I stared at myself in the mirror, blinking. "Uh, yeah, stick-a-fork-in-me done. I look like a drag queen. So, what's our story?" I asked, following her downstairs.

"We met in a lesbian club. If anybody asks, say it was at Sapphic Blue. I picked you up, took you home, made a meal off of you. You liked it so much you came back for more."

"So now I'm a lesbian? Works for me, I guess," I said. "Just don't expect me to French you one." As I let out a snort, Menolly whirled around and pushed me back against the wall.

"Fun and games are fine, but remember, *this isn't a joke, Kitten*. Don't screw this up. Chase's life depends on finding Karvanak. This little fiasco may well lead us to that demonic SOB. So work the story and play it for real if you want to find your boyfriend."

She looked so fierce that I stumbled and slid down to sit on the steps. "I'm sorry. You're right."

"Damned well I'm right. Okay, you want a story? Listen up. We're a couple. You're one of my pets—which means you're a kept woman. I drink from you, and we have sex. When I'm not using you, you hang out in the living room and watch TV and talk on the phone."

I swallowed. "So I don't have a job?"

"No job. I take care of you, and I pay wherever we go. So leave your purse and money in the car except for an emergency stash in your boot. I'm an easy mistress. You don't have to ask permission to eat, go to the bathroom, talk to people, but I make all the decisions. When you address me, do so as Mistress."

I coughed. "Mistress? Oh boy, this is getting better and better every minute. So what do we do first?"

"Our first goal is to attract Fraale's attention. Chances are, if she's new in town, she won't have had time to get a bead on us, and we'll be lucky. If Karvanak has filled her in, and she's working for him, we're going to have to switch gears. We may have to kill her. Roz assures me she'll be interested in you and want to try you out."

"But she's not a vamp—"

Menolly stopped at the bottom of the landing. "No, but vampire clubs are good hunting grounds for her play. And apparently succubus blood is tasty. I've never had it, so I don't know. My bet is that she offers a vein in exchange for an hour or so with the pet of her choice. She'll play for a while, give the vamps a drink, and then be off. We need to find out why she's hanging around Karvanak and where he's hiding. If we're lucky, she'll mention him. If not, then we make contact, play for a bit, and trail her home."

"Delightful. I might get a spanking out of this, you mean." It wasn't a question. I'd given up trying to fight the current.

"You might at that."

I shrugged. "Okay. Let's do it. I guess if Camille could face a dragon's bed for us, I can face seduction at the hands of a succubus. Just why do we always end up using sex to pay for help? Can't we just cook them dinner and take in a movie?"

It was Menolly's turn to let out a snort. She smiled at me, then sobered. "Let me tell you something, before we rejoin the others. Rozurial and Fraale were married before he was transformed into an incubus and she, a succubus. They loved each other dearly. She was the only family he had after Dredge killed his parents and siblings."

"They were normal Fae?"

"Right," Menolly said. "This happened when he was around ninety—still quite young. A traveling wizard stopped at their house and tried to seduce Fraale. As Roz stepped in to chase him off, the wizard's wife showed up and transformed Fraale into a succubus. That's when they realized they weren't facing a wizard and his deranged wife at all. It was really Zeus, who was trying to play the field again."

"Let me guess. Hera was the wizard's wife?"

"Bingo. And she was out for blood. Hera was pissed at Zeus, but she took it out on Fraale. Roz begged Zeus to change Fraale back, but Zeus couldn't, so he turned Roz into an incubus, somehow thinking that might help matters. Of course, it just made them worse."

"The gods can be real shits sometimes, can't they?" I let out a low growl. "They don't always play fair."

"The Greek gods have never played fair." Menolly let out a sigh. "I guess the dynamic duo forgot all about Roz and Fraale. As their new natures began to take over, they ended up separating. They couldn't stay together without traumatizing each other. They'd been monogamous, you see. Like Father and Mother. Rare among two full Fae, but it happens."

Cripes. "I'll try to be more sensitive. I noticed the look on Roz's face when he smelled that scarf."

"Good." Menolly gave me a little push. "Let's go find Chase."

As I stepped into the kitchen, all conversation stopped. Camille dropped the cookie she was eating and it splashed into her teacup. Iris stopped whatever she was saying midsentence. Smoky coughed and quickly tried to cover a smile, while both Morio and Zach looked horrified. A slow grin spread across Rozurial's face, and Vanzir just shook his head.

The only one to speak was Maggie, from her playpen, where she called out, delighted, "De-ya-ya!!!"

I scooped her up and nuzzled her, then handed her to a still-silent Iris. "Well, don't all speak at once. Do I look ready for the Fangtabula?"

Camille sputtered. "Where the hell did you find that getup? You certainly didn't nab it from *my* closet."

"I certainly hope not," Smoky said.

"Bite me." I rolled my eyes at the dragon. "I never thought anybody would ever see this. I should have thrown it away."

"It's perfect," Menolly said. "And now, we'd better get moving. The club should start hopping in about ninety minutes, and I want to be there before it gets too crowded. Hopefully, we'll pick up some information."

As Zach and Roz grabbed their jackets, I glanced back at the others. "I have my cell phone. Menolly has hers. You guys do what you can here. We've got to find Chase, before Karvanak . . ."

The thought of what he'd done to Vanzir, what humiliation

he'd put the dream chaser through, kept running through my mind. Chase couldn't survive that treatment. *He* wasn't a demon. And given what had already gone down, if he did survive, would he manage to recover?

"Let's move," I said. "We don't have any time to waste."

CHAPTER 24

~∞~

The Fangtabula was down in the Industrial District of south Seattle, not too far from where we'd fought the venidemons. It occurred to me that if the demons *did* have a foothold with some of the local vamps, then trouble was brewing big-time. And if the demons were taking over houses and setting up nests of their grotesque blowflies, what else were they doing, and where else had they infiltrated?

The fact that there was a portal to the Netherworld in the venidemon house worried me. Had the demons also forged contracts with creatures from the spirit realm? Were they attempting to gather armies on all sides? I mentioned my fears to the others.

"You might be on to something. The demons usually give the Netherworld a wide berth, but with all that's going on, old grudges and alliances aren't necessarily holding true. And if Vanzir is right, and Shadow Wing has gone over the edge, then we better be prepared for anything. But why would anybody in the Netherworld want to help him? What could they gain?" Menolly frowned as she maneuvered the streets in Camille's Lexus. Her Jag would be a tight squeeze, and my Jeep didn't fit her style. She'd changed into full leathers and was looking quite the mistress indeed.

"There are creatures in the Netherworld that hate the living," Roz said. "If they've taken corporeal form at any time, some of them resent having to give it up and fade back into the shadowed worlds. The demons might have promised them easier access to the physical world if they help."

"I don't know about any of that," Zach said, frowning, "but we've had some odd goings-on out at the compound. There's an unsettled air on the outskirts of our land, and we've doubled guard duty at night. If I didn't know better, I'd think the werespiders were back."

Shivering, I stared out the window. The werespiders had been a field day, all right. Kyoka and Karvanak might be evenly matched, now that I thought about it. Except Kyoka had been nursing a grudge against the werepumas, where Karvanak had his sights aimed directly on us.

"I doubt it. At least, I hope not," I mumbled. "We've got enough to worry about, but Kyoka isn't one of them. Maybe some werespider has taken his place, but I destroyed Kyoka and consigned his soul to oblivion." Flashing back to that night, I shivered. Hi'ran—the Autumn Lord—had given me direct orders, and I'd carried them out. I'd obliterated Kyoka and sent his soul spiraling back into the vast expanse that makes up the energy pool feeding the universe. Whatever essence he'd had was long gone, destroyed in the white fires of creation. There was no way he could still be in existence, but that didn't mean that the Hunters Moon Clan hadn't decided to re-form and cause havoc again.

As we sped through the rain-soaked streets, I opened the window a crack to get some fresh air. Spring in the northwest was cool, but the damp chill refreshed me, and I sucked in a deep breath, holding it tight in my lungs then letting it spiral out again. I might not like getting wet, but that didn't mean I lacked appreciation for the blessings the rains brought with them.

Rozurial was strangely silent, and I noticed there seemed to be some sort of communication going on between him and Menolly. I couldn't put my finger on it, but it was as if the two were talking. Whether they'd developed some secret rapport, or whether they'd just come to an understanding, there was a connection between the two. I wondered if they were sleeping together, then brushed the thought aside. Rozurial was many things, but reticent wasn't one of them. He wouldn't have been able to keep a secret like that to himself.

"When we get there, what should we do? Will Zach be one of your pets, too, and if so, why isn't he in a Speedo?" I grinned as he let out a grunt.

"Speedo? You've got to be kidding. I'm a boxers man all the way," he said, though I knew very well that at least some of the time, he went commando.

Menolly coughed. "Zachary in a Speedo leaves less to the imagination than I care to think about. No offense, Zach—you're handsome enough, but it just doesn't translate."

He laughed. "The thought of you eyeing my bare skin with those fangs hanging out doesn't make me comfortable either, so we're even. No Speedo unless we're swimming. In broad daylight."

She let out a snort. "Good thinking. And yeah, Zach better go in as one of my newest acquisitions, though you're right; he's really not dressed for it." Glancing over her shoulder, she shifted into the left turn lane, then turned onto Giles Boulevard. We were a few blocks away from the Fangtabula.

"Sounds good to me. I take it I walk in a few steps behind you, since you're my mistress?"

"Both of you, yes. And both of you make sure you never contradict me in public, or speak before I do unless it's with a request."

"Heard and understood," Zach said.

As she smoothly pulled off the street into the parking lot of the club, I saw that there was a number of cars already here. I glanced around the lot. Not many people hanging outside, but given the rain, that wasn't a big shock. The double doors leading into the warehouselike club were painted bright red, a shocker against the white and black stripes that patterned the walls. Three stories tall, the club was housed in what had once been—by the faded sign still propped against the back wall—a meatpacking plant. Leave it to irony.

As we climbed out of the car, I noticed the bouncers by the doors. One moment, there had been no one in sight. Now two very hefty, tall gentlemen were manning the velvet ropes gating off the entryway. We'd have to get through them to get into the club. The men were wearing PVC that looked almost as tight as my costume, and they had on motorcycle boots and dark glasses. They were carrying nasty-looking billy clubs that looked capable of breaking bones on first strike.

"Make a note," I said softly. "Don't let the leather twins get the first swing."

"This is not going to turn into a confrontational situation," Menolly said in a strained voice. "Those men are vampires. Get in a fight with them, and they won't need their nightsticks to take you out, Kitten. One of them feels old—very old. He's been around a long time, by my guess. And the longer the life, the more power he'll have. I wonder why Wade hasn't mentioned him."

"Maybe Wade doesn't know about him," I said, making sure my fringe was hanging straight.

Zach looked uncertainly at the door. "I so do not want to go in there, but I'm right behind you." His voice squeaked a little, and I detected the whiff of fear emanating off him. I didn't blame him. My stomach was having a butterfly party of its own.

"Don't worry." Menolly patted Zach on the back. "We won't let anybody get you. If Fraale approaches and introduces herself, let me speak first."

I took a deep breath and tried to get into the mind-set of what a vampire's pet would act like. Then it occurred to me. When I was in cat form, and when I wanted to be petted or brushed, I cozied up to Iris or my sisters and played the sweet and fuzzy card.

The domesticated puss is, as all cats know, just a ruse. Yes, cats most certainly love their humans, and yes, they cherish having a good home. But beneath that veneer of cooperation still lurks the tiny heart of a tiger. *I'll willingly walk into a gilded cage with my feet,* yodels the housecat at night, *but you can't imprison my spirit.*

I focused on Iris holding me, coaxing purrs from my

throat. I conjured up the memory of curling up on the pillow next to Camille, and her waking in the middle of the night to scratch behind my ears and tell me what a good girl I was. Yes, in tabby form, I'd willingly wear a collar if it meant love and protection and acceptance.

As I sank into the energy, I moved a little closer to Menolly and let out a small mew. She turned to look at me, then smiled.

"Good, girl. I see it in your eyes, Kitten. While we're in there, I'm calling you Desiree, so nobody hears your real name. You just call me Mistress. Are you ready?" She looked at me.

I nodded. "Yes . . . Mistress."

"Very good. Zach, you should really call yourself something else, too. Why not Jerry?"

He blinked. "Jerry? Where'd you come up with that? Okay, I'm Jerry. Uh . . . yes, Mistress." Sucking in a deep breath, he looked over at me. "Delilah—be careful. Please?"

I nodded. Roz indicated he was ready and then he broke off from our group. He'd go in separately and keep a low profile until he was needed. With one last look around the parking lot, Menolly led us toward the doors of the Fangtabula.

The bouncers were no problem, once Menolly showed her fangs. They backed away, gave her a curt nod, and eyed the rest of us as we followed her in.

The Fangtabula was *vampyr* to the extreme. In other words: They were hyping it up for the wannabes and tourists. The color scheme was red and black, with touches of silver and white tossed into the mix, and the vista that opened out before us looked like it was right off of an Elvira movie set.

The main room was huge, with a staircase descending from the entrance to the main floor, which had been tiled in a checkerboard of black and white. The ceiling stretched a good twenty feet overhead, and large cloth panels in black and red velvet draped down to produce a labyrinth of billowing walls.

The lights were dim and strobing, creating a vortex of light and shadow. It was like being in the middle of a gothic Cirque du Soleil tent. Only this was a warehouse, not a tent, and the acrobats here relied on supernatural powers rather than the strength of their mortal bodies.

Two grand stairwells led up to a second level, one on either side of the room, and in the center of the room I could see a railing surrounding three sides of an open area below, where yet another staircase descended into the underground levels of the club.

Drinks were served at a bar along the left wall that was surrounded by a number of tables and booths. On the other side of the enormous hall was a grotto, looking a lot like the "pit" back at the Collequia in Otherworld. The Collequia was a nightclub and opium den Camille used to frequent. She was never into the drugs, but she met a number of interesting men there, including Trillian, which pretty much summed up the kind of place it was.

The grotto was thick with conveniently placed divans and giant beanbag chairs, where several lovers' triads lounged. It was obvious that one woman was playing blood host for a vamp who looked like he'd just stepped out of a biker's version of *GQ*, though there was no way of telling if she was a blood whore or not.

The vamp was simply gorgeous, with brilliant red hair that draped down to his lower back. He wore skintight leather pants and not much else. He nuzzled her throat, and at first I thought he was kissing her till I saw the trickle of blood flowing from the blonde's neck. Her eyes were closed, a look of bliss on her face as his tongue coaxed the blood out, drop by drop.

As I watched, the vampire glanced up. His tongue never missing a stroke on her neck, he gazed into my eyes, and I couldn't look away. I stopped in my tracks, mesmerized by his absolute beauty. My breath quickened in my chest, and I started to blush. It felt like his gaze was peeling layers away, down to my skin, down to my muscle, down to my very bone. To my horror, I felt myself getting wet, and even though I tried not to, my hand slid toward my crotch.

I whimpered.

Menolly whirled around, took one look at me, then glanced over at the vampire. So quick she was only a blur, she opened her mouth, her fangs sliding down as she let out a loud hiss. Startled, he pulled his energy back, and I felt him receding out of my space. He gave her a courteous nod and returned his attention to the young woman on whom he was feeding.

"Shit," she said under her breath. "That was just lovely. Try to keep your eyes down, Kitten. You, too, Zach. Some of these vamps are very old and very powerful, and I might not be able to stop a few of them from coaxing you away. Don't look at any of them face on. You're supposed to be my pets, anyway, so you shouldn't be looking anywhere but at your feet unless I tell you to." She nodded to us and headed toward the center of the room. Zach and I swung in behind her, following about three paces behind. I could sense Roz near us, but couldn't see him anywhere. He cloaked himself well.

The farther we made our way into the heart of the club, the more I understood why Menolly wanted to get here ahead of time. For one thing, it would be easier to spot Fraale, but for another, the sheer energy of the club, even sparsely attended, was overwhelming. Intoxicating, frightening, pushing me to want to shift, the Fangtabula was a smorgasbord of emotion and hunger.

Suddenly, Menolly stiffened. She held her hand up ever so slightly. I almost ran into her but managed to stop in time, and Zach put on the brakes right beside me.

Just ahead, at a round black table with red chairs molded out of hard plastic, sat a woman. She wasn't a vampire, that much I could tell. But something about her told me we were bearing down on Fraale.

Fraale wasn't a beautiful woman. In fact, some people might call her plain on first glance. But on second look, they'd lose their hearts. One glance at her, and she seemed fair of face but not a classic beauty, and her hair was mousy brown. But then a second look, and she glowed, her hair took on a golden shimmer, and her lips seemed especially lush.

Fraale stood as we approached. She wasn't tall—about an inch or so shorter than Camille. Nor was she the lean, svelte woman I'd imagined. She probably wore a size twelve or fourteen. But her curves were delicious, and I followed them with my gaze, sliding over the supple, rounded breasts thrust upward by the hint of pink lace belonging to a push-up bra. My gaze lingered over the black PVC waist cincher that hugged her midriff, then flowed over the curves of her hips beneath the body-hugging red dress.

I stifled the breath that quickened in my chest. What the . . . ? I knew theoretically that I could—and did—find women appealing, but tonight my libido seemed to be on fire. First the vampire, now the succubus. Sex on the brain? Or did they spray something in the air here? Maybe an air freshener called Lust in a Can?

Menolly thrust her shoulders back. By her stance, I knew she was attracted to the woman, too. And beside me, Zach inched over to my side, one step at a time. I could feel the tension in his body.

Before Menolly could speak, Fraale beckoned us over. All our carefully laid plans flew out the window when she said, so low I could barely hear her, "I know who you are, and you put yourselves in danger by coming here. Don't even bother playing the game I see you've set up. And I know who's with you."

She glanced around. "Rozurial, do you really think you can hide from me? I know you're here, so you might as well show yourself. I recognize your scent even after all these years." Her voice was soft, almost wounded, and she tilted her head in a way that made me want to kiss away the pain that stabbed into her words.

Roz stepped from behind a nearby pillar. "I wouldn't have come if we didn't need your help. Tell me this—and if you have any memories of the honor we once shared, speak truthfully—are you in league with the Rāksasa?"

Fraale looked at us, one by one. As her eyes met mine, I thought I caught a sparkle of what looked like a tear. She blinked. "On my honor, on the honor of our wedded days, I am not his ally. He controls me, yes, but not by my choice."

"Then how?" Roz motioned for her to sit down, and we joined her around the table. "Speak to us."

She gave him a pained look and ducked her head. As she returned to her seat, the glamour seemed to fade for a moment, and I found myself staring into the all-too-sorrowful eyes of a woman in mourning.

"He's due to arrive soon. If he catches me talking to you—"

"We'll be gone before then," Menolly said. "Please, we need your help. If you aren't in league with him, then at least hear us out?"

Fraale considered Menolly's request. Finally she sighed and said, "Very well. What do I have to lose but my life?"

"It won't come to that," Roz said. "Now, what are you doing with Karvanak?"

"I accidentally crossed his path," Fraale said slowly. "I teased one of his young pets into my bed, and Karvanak found us. He was furious; the boy had been a virgin, and the demon had been looking forward to . . . to . . . deflowering him. I couldn't let that happen. The boy was young, barely eighteen. He was a poet, an artist. He wouldn't have survived Karvanak's treatment of him. Karvanak offered me a bargain. I let him source off my energy for a year's time, and he'd let the youth go. How could I say no? How could I send the boy to his death? He looked like my brother, Rozurial. He reminded me of Marion."

Roz pressed his lips together in a thin line. He hung his head.

"So you saved the boy at the expense of your own self?" Menolly asked.

Fraale nodded. "And a bitter price it is. Karvanak's loathsome. He orders me to come here, to find a playmate, and then to bring him—or her—back to his house. There, he ravages them. I've complied twice, but I can't do this time and again. I'd rather die. Is there any way you can help me?"

Her question ringing in my ears, I was about to answer when Menolly jumped in her seat.

"Karvanak. He's over there." She pointed to a table near the back. We couldn't see much but the back of his head. There was no mistaking that gleaming scalp of his, nor the expensive suit, nor the fragrance of jasmine, orange, and sugar vanilla that drifted over to us.

I cautiously slid out of my seat, trying not to attract attention. "I don't think he's seen us, but we have to get out of here. Fraale, you know this place. Where should we go?" If we made for the door, we'd be walking right by him, and the place wasn't full enough to give us cover.

She hesitated, then said, "The catacombs will be easiest. He'll never go down there. The Rāksasa doesn't like vampires and only comes here to finalize business arrangements. Come, follow me, and hurry."

Before he could see us, we crept to the descending staircase and headed down the steps. I prayed to every god that might be listening that she was telling the truth. Otherwise, we were in for a world of hurt.

CHAPTER 25

The lower levels of the Fangtabula were far more gloomy than the main floor. The color scheme was a monochromatic black and white set in a large checkerboard pattern across both walls and floor, making me almost dizzy with its squares. The staircase ended in a hallway, which in turn branched off into other hallways. The doors, evenly spaced along the wall, bore no markings, and all of them were the same size and color. For some reason, that gave me the creeps. Who knew what lurked behind them? And with no markings, how did their occupants know which door to enter?

I crowded closer to Menolly. "What the hell is this?"

She glanced over at Fraale. "The catacombs. Vampires come here to rest and to feed. There must be some way of assigning rooms, but I'm not sure what it is. I don't advise we randomly go opening doors, though."

Roz and Zach took up the back, Roz keeping his eye over his shoulder. He had barely spoken to Fraale, and now it seemed like he was looking everywhere but in her direction.

"We can't stand around here long," he said. "We're too conspicuous. What's our next move?"

I turned to the succubus, feeling inexplicably sorry for both of them. "Can you lead us to Karvanak's hideout? We have to rescue my boyfriend."

She stared at me for a moment, then nodded. "I'll help you. The hideout's in south Seattle, not far from here."

Her voice was weary, and I had the feeling she'd seen too much over the years. She didn't seem cut out for the life into which Hera had thrust her.

"You're taking a great risk," I said.

Fraale shrugged. "I don't care. If Karvanak kills me, then he kills me. It's not like I've got a family waiting at home. I can't go on; if I help him, I help brutalize his victims. I can't live with that." Though she spoke to me, her gaze was fixated on Rozurial, and I realized that she still loved him.

"Then we'd better get moving," Menolly said. "Is there an underground exit to this place or—" She stopped, holding up her hand. "I smell someone familiar."

"Karvanak?" I asked.

"No," she said. "It smells like—"

"Holy shit!" I let out a shriek as a door to my right opened and a vampire suddenly grabbed my arm. Wearing a simple black T-shirt and blue jeans, he yanked me to his side, his grip far too strong for me to break. I struggled, but he held fast. Menolly hissed, her fangs extending as the vamp sank his teeth into my shoulder.

I instinctively pulled away, and my skin ripped under his pit bull–like vise, but the vampire must not have been expecting me to fight him, because he let go, and I stumbled away, my neck bleeding from the puncture wounds.

Before I could move, Menolly was on him, and they were fighting. She hurled him to the floor, but not before a second vampire entered the hall. The new vamp looked older, and he reeked of power. He stared at Menolly, and she froze, returning his gaze.

"You belong to the Elwing Blood Clan," she whispered, warily circling him.

My touchy-feely vamp, who had already taken a good bruising and was obviously no match for my sister, took one look at the pair and slunk away toward the stairs. Smart man, he was. But as he reached the staircase, it occurred to me that one word from him would likely have the whole house down on us. I grabbed Roz by the arm and pointed.

"We have to stop him." I was set to run, but Roz held onto my wrist.

"You go upstairs bleeding like that and you're as good as drained and dead. Nope, I say we make tracks. Not only will he set up an alarm that will bring out the vamps, but he'll alert Karvanak."

Meanwhile, the vampire who was circling with Menolly let out a hiss. "Traitorous bitch. You killed our sire. You turned on your own bloodline and broke the oath. I'll see you in hell before I let you out of here alive."

With a leap, he was on her. Menolly managed to break away, and she lashed out with her foot, driving her stiletto into his chest, sending him thundering into the wall behind him. Unfortunately, she didn't hit center on his heart.

He let out a low roar and lunged for her again, this time taking her down. I wanted to rush in, to stop them, but I wasn't stupid enough to try. They were both in full form: fangs out, eyes bloody red, their inner demons unleashed. If I tried to pry them apart, I'd be torn to shreds. As they hit the floor, the hallway shook, and I could hear commotion coming from up the stairs.

I frantically motioned to Roz. "We have to leave!"

Roz took one more look at the stairway, then yanked open his duster like some crazed flasher. The gleam of metal from a dozen different weapons hanging from loops inside his coat shimmered in the dim hall. He pulled out something round and threw it on the floor next to the fighting vampires. Immediately, the stench of garlic filled the corridor.

Menolly and her attacker broke apart, both gasping. Roz took the opportunity to shove another one of the garlic bombs into the open mouth of Menolly's rival, and the vamp began to scream as the fumes poured out in a surge of white smoke. Zach and Roz grabbed Menolly by her underarms as Fraale motioned toward one of the side halls.

"There's an exit this way. I've been down here before," she said.

As we raced through the labyrinth of passageways, my

neck continued to ooze, and doors began to open. Brilliant-eyed vamps watched as we fled, hungry looks on their faces. From inside the rooms, I caught glimpses of half-clad men and women, languorously draped over beds and divans, their chests bare. Blood spattered down a chest, over breasts, as moans drifted out. Agony, ecstasy, it all ran together here at the Fangtabula. But no one gave chase—at least not right away. We managed a few moments' head start before we heard shouts from behind us.

We were almost to a small stairwell leading up to a metal door with a big red Exit sign overhead when the first wave descended. By that time, Menolly had managed to recover from the garlic, and she turned, blocking the way, Roz by her side. Zach and I were behind her, and Fraale was behind us.

A group of about ten vampires were headed our way, led by the one who had attacked me. Menolly's opponent was there, too, steadied by another of his brethren. One of the vamps was the hostess I'd seen near the bar. She stepped forward, and I groaned.

The woman had obviously been a bodybuilder while alive because she was built like a brick house: huge boobs and biceps, tiny waist, quad muscles way too big for comfort. To make it worse, she stood a few inches taller than me. Dressed in a pair of fringed white pants that laced up the sides and a cropped Hooters tank top—which she amply filled out—her mile-high stiletto cowboy boots were covered with orange rhinestones. Long blonde hair drifted down her back, and she looked like she should be sporting a California girl tan, but she was as pasty as the rest of them. She smiled, her fangs extended. In an offhand thought, it occurred to me that pale pink lipstick wasn't really her color anymore.

"You've just worn out your welcome," she said, staring at my sister.

"We're on our way out," Menolly said. "Let us leave, and we won't cause any trouble."

The Amazon vamp eyed my neck and licked her lips. "Too late." She lunged toward me, trying to dodge between Menolly and Roz.

Menolly let out a low growl as she head-butted the chick

and drove her back a few paces. Meanwhile, Roz pulled out a
string of what looked like firecrackers. He lit one end and threw
it into the crowd. As the crackle of gunpowder went off, another
smell infiltrated the hallway, and once again, the pungent scent
of garlic rose thickly.

I started to cough, choking on the vile mixture, but I
noticed the smoke's effects were a lot worse on the vamps.
Several of them pulled back, racing up the stairs. Steroid
Woman, however, seemed relatively unaffected, as did a few
of the others.

"Oh shit, she must have some sort of immunity," Roz
muttered.

The woman laughed at him. "What on earth do you think
we do around here? Leave the staff unarmed?" At that point,
she backhanded Menolly, who was getting ready for another
attack, and sent her flying back against me, which knocked us
both to the ground.

There was a sudden screech, so loud that I covered my ears
to stop the ringing. As I watched, Fraale leapt over us, landing
lightly on the balls of her feet between us and the vampires.
She sucked in a deep breath.

"Cover your ears," Roz warned us. We immediately obeyed.

Fraale opened her mouth and let loose, keening louder than
anything I'd ever heard. She was worse than a bean Sidhe.
Standing with legs spread, hands on her hips, there was
something very inhuman about her that scared me spitless.
Apparently, she took the vampires for a ride, too, because they
backed up as a group, eying her with a combination of hunger
and—fear?

Roz grabbed my arm and pushed me toward the stairwell.
"Up you go!" Menolly shoved Zach in front of her, and then
Fraale spun around and raced after us. We barely made it to the
door before a surge of movement told us they were on our heels
again. As we sprinted toward the car, Roz yanked something out
of his coat and tossed it over his shoulder right onto the hood of
a black car. We'd barely made it to Camille's Lexus when an
explosion rocked the parking lot, shoving Zach and me forward
to land on the hood.

"Holy crap! What—"

"Just move!" Roz dragged me around to the passenger side as Menolly opened the doors with the automatic control on the key. We leapt in. Zach, Roz, and Fraale tumbled into the back as I landed shotgun.

I glanced at the fire that was raging in what had been a brand new BMW. The vamps had pulled back, except for a couple who managed to skirt the deadly flames. The fireball sent a shower of sparks into the night air as it billowed on the updraft of wind, a roaring mushroom of flames and smoke.

Menolly started the car, and we screeched out of the parking lot at sixty miles per hour and climbing. The cops were either out on another case or were off at an all-night java joint. Although the sound of sirens echoed in the distance, growing louder, I didn't see any prowl cars. *Thank government cuts on spending,* I thought. Chase was always bitching about the lack of manpower, and I knew he wasn't kidding.

Menolly was up to seventy by the time we hit one of the main drags. Only then did she slow down a little and glance into the mirror. It was disconcerting for the others, I'm sure, to not see their driver's reflection, but I was used to it.

"Everybody in one piece?" she asked.

"I think so," Zach said. "One thing's for sure."

"What's that?" I said, leaning back against the seat, trying to calm my fried nerves.

"You guys are going to have to beef up your wards. Somehow, I don't think the members of the Fangtabula are going to take this lying down."

"Zach's right," Roz said. "They're mad as hell. Make no mistake; we almost didn't make it out of there. We were ten seconds away from being trapped. And that would not have been pretty at all."

"Especially not when Karvanak got hold of us," Menolly said. "Fraale, you can't go back to him. Let's hit his hideout and scram. Tell me where to go."

Fraale snorted. "Oh, I'm on his shit list now, all right. He'll eat me alive if he catches me. And I'm *not* speaking metaphorically. I've seen him do it. He was so mad at one of his servants one day that he turned into a tiger and bit off her arm. And you don't want to know what he did to her before that.

She bled to death, screaming." Her voice was so strangled, I knew she was telling the truth.

Shuddering, I grabbed my cell phone out of the glove compartment where I'd stashed it before we entered the club. I punched in Camille's cell number, and she answered almost immediately.

"We ran into trouble, but we're headed toward Karvanak's hideout with Fraale. Get Morio and Smoky and meet us there—and hurry the hell up. We need you. We may have vamps on our tail, too, so don't leave Maggie unattended. I don't know what you're going to do, but we have to be very careful out on our land from now on. Menolly ran into someone from the Elwing Blood Clan who wasn't overjoyed to see her."

"Mother of the gods, things are getting so fucked up," she whispered. "Okay, I'll figure out something. We're on our way. I'll have to put out a silent call for Smoky, but he should be able to pick it up and show up. What's the address?"

I handed the phone over to Fraale. "Give her the address, please."

"It's 23585 Forsythia. Smaller greenish gray house set back a little ways. Be careful about the yard—it's booby-trapped—so stick to the walkway." She handed the phone back to me.

"Got it?" I asked, glanced out the window at the side mirror. So far, no sign we were being followed, but that didn't count for shit. There were too many ways for vamps and demons to travel.

"Yeah, got it," Camille said. "Vanzir's here, I'm bringing him with us. We need every hand on deck for this one, and he'll just have to take his chances that Karvanak won't catch him. Not the best idea but I'm also . . ." Here, she dropped her voice and I knew she didn't want to be overheard. "I'm going to order him to—if he thinks he's about to be caught—kill himself."

I stared at the night as it passed by. The moon was on her way to dark, and the night seemed like one long hush at the graveside. "Yeah, that's probably best," I said after a moment. "You think we'll ever live a normal life again, Camille?"

She let out a strangled laugh. "Oh my Kitten, we could

walk up a stairway to the stars and never find normal again. No, I'm afraid that we're stuck in the nightmare. And you know what? That's okay, because our lives have meaning. And in this world with so much senseless anger and violence, I think we should be proud to carry the burdens we do. We're making an impact. At least, we have to keep telling ourselves that. Now, be careful, and we'll be there as soon as we can."

As the phone went dead, I looked back out into the night. As Menolly deftly swerved through the streets, driving us toward whatever disaster next awaited, the clouds parted for a moment, just long enough to let me look at the stars. They were beautiful, cold and stark against the velvet night. At least something would last forever, I thought. In this world of anger, of hatred, of insanity, at least the stars were—for all intents and purposes—eternal.

CHAPTER 26

~⚬⫩⚬~

Forsythia Street was tucked away in the Industrial District, cloistered from the main drag so you'd never know it was there unless you were looking for it. Before she turned right onto the street, Menolly flipped off the headlights and Camille's silver Lexus truly became a shadow in the night, ghostly and silent. We glided slowly down the street before Menolly parked a few houses down from where Fraale indicated the house was.

"I'd rather not park directly in front of the house," she said. "Too much chance for the car to be targeted and destroy our getaway." Menolly climbed out of the driver's seat and tucked the keys in her coat pocket, then zipped it shut. "Let's go. We want to get in there and out before Karvanak arrives home."

Karvanak. I shuddered. The more I learned about the demon, the more my stomach turned when his name was mentioned. Fraale's last comment about the servant who pissed him off had stuck in my mind, and I couldn't get the image out of my thoughts. And yet, I was part cat—and I'd killed as a cat. In hunger as well as from my basic nature. But this—this was spite. Pure spite. Surely, whatever she'd done, Karvanak's servant couldn't have been that out of line.

"What are we facing in there?" I asked. "Any demons other than the Rākṣasa?"

"Bloatworgles for sure. Several of them. A few full-grown venidemons. And I know he's got a few human warriors, too. There are some servants, but most of them are runaways he's picked up at the bus station and put to work or uses for his fun. They'll run the other way, hoping to escape."

She shivered, then slowly turned to face me. "I know I've done some terrible things over the years. It goes with the job. I've broken up families, broken men's hearts, and shattered women's dreams. But I've never seen anything quite so bad as the horrors that have taken place behind those locked doors."

"You can't help your nature, Fraale," Roz said. "But nothing you've ever done remotely resembles the hellhole that Karvanak has carved out for his victims." His voice sounded wistful as he added, "Don't ever compare yourself to him. You can't even begin to believe you're as bad as he is."

Fraale gave him an icy stare. "And just how would you know what I've been up to the past three hundred years? For all you know, I could be a raving lunatic who decided to play mass murderer. We've seen each other exactly four times since the gods chose to destroy our lives, Rozurial. And not once—not *one* time in all the centuries that have passed— have you ever thought to ask me how I'm coping with this. You always make up some excuse and hightail it out of my sight as soon as you can."

Rozurial bared his teeth. "Leave our life together where it belongs—in the past. There's no turning back. Regrets will only poison what memories we shared. I loved you when we were married, and I loved you after that bitch Hera transformed you. I wept as you changed. And I wept when Zeus did the same to me. But you know, as well as I do, that it never would have worked—not with what we were becoming. I cried until all the tears were washed away and there was only a hollow void."

Fraale's face twisted. "And then you left me. You left me alone."

"I had to. To save you. To save me. To protect what we had together." Roz sagged against the car. "Surely you can see why we had to move on. And this conversation only proves why we can't be near each other. Too many memories, too many regrets, and too much anger. *I couldn't save you then, and I can't save you now.*"

She stared at him. I thought she was going to try again. I thought for sure she'd pull out the love card and play it. And how could he resist her tears and her heartbreak? But after a moment, she just shook her head and turned toward the house.

"You're right. The gods won, and we lost," she said softly. "Let's get this over with, because the sooner we do, the sooner I can get the hell out of here. And I'd like to leave knowing I don't have to constantly look over my shoulder, wondering if Karvanak is going to come creeping up behind me to slit my throat."

She glanced at Menolly and, in a hostile tone, said, "It's obvious how he feels about you, but watch your heart. He's an incubus. He'll never be able to love anyone again without hurting them in the end. Incubi are born to fuck you, then walk out the door. And so are my kind. We're all just users."

Menolly wisely held up her hands. "Hey, color me Switzerland. I'm not involved in this," she said softly. "Whatever you think is going on between Roz and me, isn't. All I want to do is get in there and rescue Delilah's boyfriend before he ends up as cube steak on Karvanak's menu."

Fraale frowned, then shrugged. "Let's get a move on. Karvanak's bound to be on his way here."

"Should we wait for Camille and the others?" Zach asked, quietly touching me on the shoulder.

I shook my head. "We can't afford to stand around waiting. We're going to have to start this fight all by our lonesome and hope to hell it doesn't blow up before they get here. I just wish I wasn't wearing this crap. It's not going to provide a whole hell of a lot of protection." I tugged at the leg of my lamé pants.

The house was gray green, all right, and three stories tall, looking altogether way too much like the Munsters' mansion on Mockingbird Lane. But instead of the jaunty Herman, we were facing a ball-busting Karvanak.

The house was, indeed, set back on the property, with a

narrow walkway of broken concrete leading to it. Grass poked through cracks in the cement, and on both sides the yard had grown wild, a tangle of dead foliage from the winter mingling with new runners as the bramble bushes and ferns woke to spring.

"Where is he? What floor is Chase on?" As I stared at the place, it suddenly hit me full force.

Chase was *in there*. He was scared, with a mangled finger. The gods only knew what else they'd done to him. And we were the only hope he had. I sucked in a deep breath and started up the walk, remembering what Fraale had said about booby traps. Menolly and the others followed.

"I think he's in the basement. What better place to keep a prisoner you don't want escaping?"

"Guards?" I cracked my knuckles, gearing up for the fight.

She shook her head. "Just what I told you: bloatworgles, venidemons, and some FBHs. That's enough, I guess."

"Yeah, and more than I want to deal with. Damned bloatworgles are hard to kill. I found that out a few days ago." As we neared the door, I called back to Fraale, "The door? Booby-trapped? Rigged?"

"Not that I know of," she said.

"Good! That's enough for me." I ripped the screen door off its hinges, then landed a heavy blow with my foot to the doorknob. The latch broke, and I slammed the door wide. Fraale's pale tears had hit me in the gut. Rozurial had let his love slip away, had turned his back on her. The odds against them were overwhelming, and he'd caved and let the gods win. I wasn't about to do that to Chase. Not until I knew he wanted out for good. If he did, I'd step aside gracefully. If not, we'd find some way to make it work.

I pushed into the living room, which was expensively— though gaudily—furnished. The others crowded in behind me and immediately spread out.

"Where's the basement?" I asked but stopped short when three big, burly, fully leathered men stepped into the room. They didn't *look* magical, but looks could be deceiving. They were carrying swords that emanated a faint bluish glow. Enchanted blades. Good for controlling creatures like the venidemons, where guns might be useless. Also good for hacking off arms and legs.

I sucked in a deep breath and—oh shit! My knife! I didn't have my knife. I'd left it at home! How could I have—

"Kitten! Catch!"

I whirled as Camille, Morio, and Vanzir tumbled into the room.

Camille tossed me my blade. "Thought you might need this," she said, eyeing the men with delight. "Looks like we got us some playmates," she added and immediately froze. I could feel the energy spin around her like a vortex. Oh goody— faulty spells on the loose! But hey, when they worked, they worked with a vengeance.

I caught the dagger by the hilt and flashed her a brilliant smile. "Love you, too, babe! Let's get on with it!"

The men raced toward us, their eyes glinting with a perverse delight. I knew it was a perverse delight because I recognized the feeling and the look. My own adrenaline was pumping as I leapt forward, wishing to hell for jeans and a tank. But all thoughts of clothing were swept away as I entered the fray.

On my left, Roz wielded a nasty-looking serrated blade in one hand. On my right, Menolly moved in on one of the bikers, her fangs out and eyes glowing. As we engaged the three men, I could hear Morio tell Camille, "Rope it in—save the magic. They can take care of those three, and we'll need all our powers for Karvanak."

And then I was into the fray. My opponent's blade was long and curved and spattered with blood. As I raised my dagger and braced against his blow, I wondered how many men he'd killed. How many women? I put my weight behind my blade and shoved, knocking him back. He stumbled but caught himself and swung low. I leapt, playing jump rope with the sword as it passed beneath my feet. The next moment, I did a Bruce Lee and flipped over his head, landing behind him, my dagger at the ready.

He jerked around, startled. I took advantage of his confusion and leapt again, this time spinning to kick him solidly in his sword arm with my stiletto. The heel pierced his leather, pierced his skin, sank deep into the muscle.

Oh shit! My heel was caught in the tissue of his arm, and I couldn't pull loose. I shook my foot, ripping a long, jagged gash in his arm as I did so, and he let out a scream that echoed through the room. As he jerked away, I managed to free my boot and stumbled, rolling into a somersault, coming up into a squat.

"Bitch! Bitch!" My opponent was obviously in pain. He was losing it, and I aimed to drive him over the edge. One bit of battle wisdom: Push an adversary too far, and they often lose sight of common sense and make mistakes.

A slow smile spread across my face as I stood, tapping my blade against my hand. "Come on, baby. You gonna let yourself get whipped by a pussycat?" With a smirk, I blew him a kiss. "I'd offer to blow you, but your dick's gotta be smaller than my little finger and I just don't *do* shrimps."

Oh yeah, that did it. He came at me full-tilt, roaring as he raised his sword over his head, leaving his torso open to attack.

One thing about berserker rage, I thought, *it can make a grown man incredibly stupid.* I hauled back and sent my dagger singing through the air, to land right in his heart. As I danced away, he suddenly realized he wasn't going anywhere anymore. He lost his grip on his sword, and it tumbled to the floor behind him. He glanced down at his chest, at the blood burbling out from around the dagger's point, then at me, looking confused.

The coppery scent of blood filled my nostrils, making me salivate. As quickly as stepping through a doorway, I could feel *her* there, aware and awake; Panther wanted off the chain. The man was close to dying, and the Death Maiden in me reveled as he slipped away.

I grabbed my dagger, yanking it out of his chest as he started to topple forward. His gaze locked on mine, and I saw the shock and the bewilderment that accompanied whatever last thoughts had run through his mind. And then, just like that, he lurched to the ground and lay still. He was dead.

Staring at his prone form, I tried to summon up some feeling of regret, but the only thing I could think about was rescuing Chase, and how this man might have been the one to cut off Chase's fingertip. I wiped my blade on his back and turned to help the others.

Roz had cut down the man in front of him, and Menolly had taken care of her opponent. For the moment, we were alone again.

Camille walked over to their swords and picked up one. "These could come in handy. Not iron—but sort of alloy. The enchantment's to make them stronger and more deadly. I don't think its aimed at any one particular race or species." She tossed one to Morio, one to Roz, and offered the third to me. I took it, staring at the curving blade.

"I dunno, I'm used to my dagger. It would be hard to run with this. On the other hand, it's good for holding people at arm's length. Vanzir, you want it?"

Vanzir looked at the blade with a hunger I seldom saw on his face. "I'll use it to cut out his heart," he murmured, and I knew he was talking about Karvanak. He took the sword and swished it around. Obviously the dude had experience from the way he made it sing through the air.

I glanced at Morio. "You don't have any clothes that you could spare in that bag of yours, do you?"

He grinned. "Don't like looking like a hoochie mama? I have a spare karate outfit. The pants will be short, but it's got to be better than what you're wearing." He zipped open his bag and tossed me a pair of black pants and a white top, along with a belt, also black.

"Thanks," I said, yanking off my togs of torture. Everyone stared. I was buck naked beneath the lamé. "Look all you want, but right now, I don't give a shit. I just want out of that crap and into something that won't give me jock itch."

Camille laughed as I yanked on the pants, which came up to my shins, and belted the top. "Feel better?" she said.

"Much. The material's a lot heavier than that crap," I added, kicking the glittering hooker togs. "At least my skin can breathe now."

"Take them with you," Camille warned me. "Morio, put the

pants and halter in your bag. They've got her scent and essence on them, and there's no way in hell we want anybody who might work magic to get hold of that."

"Good point," he said, snagging them up. He stuffed them in his bag, then zipped it shut.

"Okay, let's find Chase. We've still got a bunch of bloatworgles and venidemons to deal with." I led them into the hallway that branched off from the living room. The house reminded me of the one in which we'd fought the venidemons, though it looked in better shape. I also doubted we'd find a portal here; the energy wasn't strong enough for that. At least, I hoped we wouldn't.

I opened each door as we came to it. In one room, we found stacks of expensive rugs: wool, hand-woven, and beautiful. The next was a bathroom, and the third was a bedroom. Lush and opulent, the room smelled like Rāksasa. I was about to cross the threshold when Camille stopped me.

"Wards—strong wards. You'll blow your head off if you go in there. Let's find Chase and get him out of here." She pulled me back from the door, and I nodded, looking around.

"Where's the basement, Fraale?" I didn't want to waste time running around like a chicken with my head cut off. Camille was right: Get in there, get Chase out, and then come back for Karvanak.

"See that door over there—the one that looks like it might lead to another bedroom?" She pointed to a door on the other side of the arch leading out of the hall. "That's it. The basement is unfinished, so it's cold and dank. I have no idea where the venidemons are. Karvanak was pretty clear about not letting them loose down there. The creatures are mindless and would have tried to use your detective as an all-you-can-eat diner."

But the bloatworgles weren't mindless . . . dangerous, yes. Disgusting, definitely. But mindless? No. I reached for the door handle.

"Be on your guard. My guess is that the bloatworgles are down there. Don't go in without your defenses being up. By the way, Roz saved me from getting toasted by the one on our property. Remember, they breathe fire."

As I opened the door, a fetid smell wafted up. Oh yeah, bloatworgle stench. Delightful. A pair of glowing eyes gleamed from the darkness below.

Those sure as hell aren't cat eyes, I thought. With a shout, I decided to play Han Solo and ran full tilt down the stairs, screaming at the top of my lungs and waving my dagger like a crazed berserker.

Apparently, blind and foolish courage has its advantages, because I landed right square on the stomach of the creepy critter before he could shake himself out of his astonishment and skedaddle.

It was a bloatworgle, all right, and he looked like he'd just swallowed his tongue. Before he had a chance to open his mouth, I raised my dagger and brought it straight down on his eyes. While his hide was tough, his eyes were not, and I drove the dagger deep. A spray of gray green mucus sprayed up on me.

"Ewww." I grimaced. Grungy and gross, yes, but there was no time to worry about the crap staining Morio's karate suit. No time to worry about anything. I was on autopilot: Seek and destroy the enemy. Rescue the valiant knight locked in the castle dungeon. Any sense of remorse or hesitance had flown the coop, and my body was chugging along on adrenaline and instinct.

I leapt to my feet as the others joined me. Where was the next little creep?

A flash of movement caught my eye, and I whirled just in time to see a second demon open his mouth and let loose with a scorching blast, hitting Vanzir straight in the stomach. Vanzir didn't seem to even flinch, and I wondered what the hell dream chasers were really made of. We'd never seen him in his native form. He let loose a low growl in his throat and moved in, his sword making contact long enough to carve a nice little niche in the bloatworgle's arm before the blade bounced away again. Man, those suckers were tough!

"Move," Morio said, sounding a little like Smoky. He was shifting. Within seconds, he went from five eight to eight feet tall, his nose and chin morphing out to a muzzle with drool dripping off the fangs. I stared, always impressed by his youkai form. Unlike Weres, he remained bipedal, though his head was vaguely vulpine. Though he was covered with a downy reddish fur, his hands and feet remained humanoid. Yet his eyes mirrored Morio's spirit, through and through. Altogether, he was one scary-looking mutha.

I jumped out of the way as he dove for the demon, catching the potbellied creature up in his arms. The bloatworgle let out a squeal and made a nosedive for Morio's muzzle, its mouth open to land a bite.

Before it could make contact, Morio grabbed the thing around the neck and sent it smashing against the wall. The house shook, and the bloatworgle let out a gurgle and slid to the floor. Morio turned toward Camille, who nodded.

It was then that I saw the door in the back of the basement. Chase was in there; he *had* to be. I raced toward it, heedless of whether there were any other demons in the room. As my hand touched the doorknob, I heard a scuffle behind me and glanced over my shoulder. Menolly and Morio were taking out another bloatworgle, playing volleyball with the demon as the ball. I ignored them—they could handle it—and yanked open the door.

I flipped on the light, and cockroaches scattered in every direction. The inside of the room was small, not much bigger than a utility room. A cage had been built in the back. A cell, really, with floor-to-ceiling bars. There was a bare incandescent lightbulb screwed into a ceiling fixture, giving off all of forty watts. The room was empty save for a chair near the door to the cell, and a layer of grime covered the walls. The place smelled like shit and blood and rotting food.

I swallowed the lump growing in my throat and stepped forward, my gaze glued on the cell. In the corner, huddled beneath a thin blanket on a mattress, sat my Chase. My sweet Chase.

He raised his head, his eyes glazed over. When he saw me, a look of disbelief crossed his face, and he began to cry.

"Chase! Chase!" I yanked on the cell door, but it was locked. "Wait here. I'll get someone to bend the bars." I ducked back out into the room. The third bloatworgle was dead. "Menolly, come bend these bars for me. I found Chase."

Menolly sailed to my side, her feet barely touching the floor. She raced inside the room. A grimace washed over her face as she looked around, but her focus was solely on Chase, and she grabbed the bars and began to bend them.

"Wait!" Morio rushed in, back in his human form. "Let me cast a Dispel Illusion spell just in case." A bright light filled the room as he conjured the spell, but nobody proved to be anything other than what they were.

Menolly immediately went back to the bars, and they screeched as she slowly forced them apart. Her hands were blistering—there must be iron in them—but she didn't show any pain or hesitance. After a moment, the bars were big enough for her to squeeze through.

"Let me do this. I'm stronger than you and can carry him out without a problem." She stepped through without another word and knelt by Chase, murmuring softly to him. He nodded as she gathered him up in her arms and, hoisting the man who was a good foot taller than she over her shoulder, she carried him to the bars.

Taking his arm, I helped him to step out of the cell. The bloody stump where they'd chopped off the tip of his finger looked like it might be infected.

I had to force myself not to burst into tears. I had to be strong for him. I had to be his anchor right now. The gods only knew how terrified and adrift he probably felt at this moment.

As he leaned against the bars, shaky and pale, he whispered. "Delilah, I'm so sorry—I'm so sorry—"

I pressed my fingers to his lips. "Hush. Just hush. There's time enough to talk later. The important thing is to get you out of here where we can treat your wounds." I wrapped my arm around his waist and led him out of the cramped room. Camille gasped, but at my look, she stayed where she was.

Zach moved forward.

Chase stared at him. His eyes were worn, he looked like he'd been to hell and back, and I could only pray that a severed finger was the worst that Karvanak had done to him. Chase glanced at me, then at Zachary.

"You—you . . . I understand . . ."

Once again, I pressed my finger to his lips. "Shush. There's nothing so important we have to discuss it now. We need to focus on getting you out of here before Karvanak returns—"

A bolt of fear washed through Chase's eyes. "He's still alive?"

I was about to speak when a voice from the stairs answered for me.

"No, they haven't been able to kill me," the voice said. "Just like you weren't able to fight me. You tried your best, Detective, but you couldn't do a thing when I was holding you down. When I made you kiss my feet."

Karvanak was standing there, in his Calvin Klein suit and polished shoes, his wraparound sunglasses hiding the cruelty in his eyes. The light glinted off his shaved head, and he gave me a soft smile.

"Mistress Cat, you've stolen my toy. Haven't you heard what curiosity does to kittens? I suppose I'll have to teach you. And Fraale, you dare to turn on me? Both you and Vanzir will live in my hell for a long, long, long time, and you're going to rue every moment of every day that you still draw breath."

And then, in back of him, a tall man appeared. Dressed in a long, black robe, he looked vaguely Chinese, but it was hard to place his background. This was no biker, no FBH thug. No, power drifted off of him in waves, setting off an internal alarm that shrieked so loud I thought I was going to scream.

And then I knew—somehow I knew. I stared at the creature who looked so human but was so far from humanity that there was no center point on the line where the two could meet. One of the Scytatians, summoned from the deepest bowels of the Netherworld. *A Scythe Reaper.*

Karvanak nodded, looking pleased. "Oh, yes, be afraid. I know who you are, Death Maiden, and I know that you're young. You can't hope to fight a Scytatian, and neither can your friends."

I stood frozen in my tracks, the tattoo on my forehead shifting and pulsating in response to the being's appearance.

Never moving my gaze, I said to the others, "Scytatians are from the realm of Death, the realm of the Harvestmen. I know this in my core. I can *feel* him. None of you can fight him—only me. And only because I have a direct connection to the realm of the Netherworld, so if I fall, get the fuck out of here. Because I guarantee you, if that thing touches you, it will rip out your heart and swallow it as a snack."

And so we stood for what seemed like an eternity, waiting for that moment when the dam breaks and the battle begins.

CHAPTER 27

Every battle is different. Every fight has its own spirit. Every haunted battlefield is rife with not only ghosts of the dead but the soul of the battle. And just so, every sword has a consciousness. Every blade, a name. Sometimes steel and silver remain silent until they are gently coaxed out of hiding. Sometimes they never reveal themselves. And sometimes, they wake up on their own.

My dagger tingled in my hand as I stared at the Scytatian. I sucked in my breath. Could it be? My blade had never spoken to me before, but now I heard the whisper of a woman's voice, delicate and ethereal and cold as ice.

"Lysanthra," she whispered. "I am Lysanthra. And I am your blade."

Without moving my gaze, I answered as silently as the message had reached my ears. "I am Delilah. I'm Fae, human, and Were. And . . . I'm a Death Maiden."

I might hate the term, but I had to face it. Not only did I belong to three realms—Fae, human, and the realm of felines—but I also walked under the shadow of Death. I followed in the tracks of my master.

And with that acknowledgment, the truth I'd been hiding from for months faced me square on. No matter how much I'd tried to avoid my fate, I knew I had to face—and embrace—the person I was becoming.

Delilah, the Death Maiden. Delilah, obliterator of souls. Delilah, harvest woman of the dead.

My blade sent a bolt of energy reeling through my hand, and her gentle laughter rang in my ears. "Your father chose well to give me to you. Wake me, Delilah. I will help you walk through the darkness. I will teach you how to grow strong and keep your soul intact when all around you is madness."

Destiny in action. Fate on the move. "How do I wake you up?" I asked. "And why have you never spoken to me before?"

Lysanthra's breath tingled through my elbow, through my shoulder, into my heart. "Only when I'm wielded by one who loves with the depth of her soul, and who fights to protect the one she loves, will I speak. You have been close to summoning me before, but today—today you fight with the desire to die rather than see the one you love destroyed."

Chase. It had to be Chase. I *was* in love with Chase. Despite the passion I felt for Zachary and the betrayal from Chase's lies, I still loved him. Fool? Maybe. But sometimes our hearts don't play the logic game. Sometimes the Hags of Fate like to see us squirm.

"Tell me what to do."

Lysanthra's voice was so delicate she might have been the tinkle of wind chimes, the delicate call of a night-roaming bird to her mate. "Say my name three times aloud. And then I am yours. But you will not be able to kill this creature using me. For that, you must use your own powers."

I raised the blade. The Scytatian waited, silent and brooding. Karvanak looked impatient but didn't seem in a rush to hurry things along. Smart move. The Scytatian could make mincemeat out of him in three seconds flat.

"Lysanthra, Lysanthra, Lysanthra!" I called out, raising the blade. A shaft of light burst from the tip, and I flushed, new strength flowing into my veins. Lysanthra fell silent, but I knew we were bound together.

Camille kept quiet, her gaze fixated first on my blade, then on my face. When Menolly started to speak, Camille shushed her and smiled gravely at me.

I turned back to the Scytatian and Karvanak. "You— demon scum. You're so sure of yourself, so get your ass over here and fight. The Scytatian's got your back. What are you waiting for?"

Karvanak let out a low snarl, then he shimmered, and his head took the form of a tiger, claws ripped from his nails, and he stepped forward.

At that moment, the sound of a freight train came whistling down the steps, and a blur of white and silver crashed into the room, knocking over the Rāksasa as the whirlwind whipped down the stairs. Straight out of the Ionyc Sea, Smoky landed in a crouch and rolled to straddle the demon.

Smoky promptly began to beat the crap out of Karvanak, but the Rāksasa was strong. He managed to get a hand free and clawed at Smoky, gashing the dragon across the face.

"Don't you hurt him!" Camille leapt forward, yanking out the unicorn horn. She'd used it once in the past few days. How much power did it have left?

My question was answered as a shaft of ice burst forth, like a frozen bolt of lightning, zigzagging out of the tip of the horn. The ice bolt struck Karvanak directly on the head between his ears, distracting the demon long enough for Vanzir and Menolly to dive in and help out.

Karvanak roared, lunging at Vanzir. He knocked the dream chaser down and stepped over him to get to Zachary, who was trying to protect Chase. With one hand, he backhanded Zach and sent him flying against a wall, then turned to Chase, who was still in shock.

Menolly raced across the room, but Zach was faster. He scrambled to his feet and, head down, charged directly into the center of Karvanak's stomach, driving him back. He was able to hold him off long enough for Menolly to grab Chase and pull him out of the way.

Karvanak growled and whirled, his foot squarely landing against Zach's lower back, sending him to the floor. Smoky dove in, but then my attention wavered as I noticed the Scytatian bearing down on me.

I had no doubt it intended to kill everyone in this room. Once we were all toast, if Karvanak was still alive, my guess would be that he'd find himself next on the menu. Summoning spirits—even for a demon—never worked out quite the way it was planned.

I sheathed Lysanthra and focused on the swirling energy that pulsated a staccato throbbing beneath my tattoo.

"Hi'ran," I whispered. "Help me. I need you. I need your power. I need your strength."

A faint laugh, carried on the wind along with bonfire flames and graveyard dust drifted by. "I'm sending you help. Let go and change. Only you can kill this creature. Your sisters will die if you don't."

And so I unleashed Panther. Hands to paw, spine lengthening, ears pointing, teeth growing long and sharp, fur coating my palms, coating my legs, coating arms and face and back . . . the world was bathed in gray scale as scents grew stronger, urges grew more difficult to control.

As the transformation fully took hold, I let myself flow into the opulent energy that imbued my Panther self. I sucked in a deep breath as mist rose around me, and I found myself facing the Scytatian. Everyone else had vanished, and once again, I was fighting alone, on the astral.

The creature had been cloaked in shadow—difficult to get a bead on when I'd been in my bipedal form—but now I could see him clearly for what he was: an avatar of Death. The shadows were gone, and he stood there in brilliant white, shining like magma working its way up to the surface of the world.

The Scytatian shone so brilliantly, he was difficult to look at, but my third eyelid shaded my eyes from harm, and I slowly moved forward. If I'd been a regular Were, my claws would not touch him, my teeth would bounce off. But with the energy of the Autumn Lord behind me, I had the power to defeat the being from the Netherworld.

I crouched as the Scytatian approached. One . . . let it get close enough . . . two . . . wriggle into just the right position and then—pounce! I grappled him with my front paws. For a fraction of a second, I felt my essence being coaxed out of my body as he sucked me into his energy field, but then I yanked myself back. He stumbled, just the briefest moment, but enough to tell me he hadn't expected my strength.

And then we were wrestling. He took me down, his strength phenomenal. It was all I could do to keep him from squeezing me to death. If he got his arms around my neck, I'd be screwed for sure. I leaned my head back and drove my fangs deep into his shoulder as we rolled along the floor.

And then I made a mistake. I let go of him to try for a better grip.

He chose that moment to flip me over so he was beneath me, one arm around my belly, the other around my neck. My paws pointing toward the ceiling, I scrabbled but couldn't free myself. He began to tighten his grip around my neck, his arm shutting off my windpipe. I squirmed but couldn't get loose, and I didn't dare transform, or he'd snap my neck like a toothpick. My tongue lolling out, I began to lose consciousness.

As the mist began to grow gray, I thought I heard a low growl from somewhere in the distance. I couldn't see—everything was going black—but I prepared to give up the fight. My sisters were depending on me, but I wasn't strong enough. I'd let them down. Menolly might escape, and Smoky and Rozurial, but this creature would finish the rest of them off, even Vanzir.

I began to spiral out of my body. Would I go directly to Hi'ran's side? Or would I have the chance to see my ancestors first? I'd like to see Mother, at least once, before I passing into the realm of the Autumn Lord.

Youch!

Something bit my tail. Hard. Hard enough to suck me back into my body. I opened my eyes, aware that the Scytatian had loosened his grip and I could breathe again. The next moment, he let go, and I sprang away as he leapt to his feet. Energy crackled around him as he began to summon something nasty.

I glanced around to see what the hell had saved me, and to my surprise, I saw a leopard standing there. As spotted as I was black and with a piece of material hanging out of her mouth, she—I could smell she was female—blinked at me, then let out a low growl. She seemed terribly familiar. Yet whoever she was, she was dead on the physical realm. But here, she was lean and strong and—holy hell, most important, she could affect the Scytatian! The rag in her mouth was from the edge of the Scytatian's robe.

Just then, the Scytatian let loose with a bolt of energy, and I recognized the feel of it. Death magic. It wouldn't affect my ghost-leopard friend, but it could affect me. I managed to dodge out of the way, and it hit directly where I'd been standing.

As I leapt to safety, the leopard gathered herself and charged toward the Scytatian. The creature from the Netherworld jumped to the side as I shook out the kinks. The leopard was going after him again, so I took the other side, and as the Scytatian lightly moved out of her way, I lunged behind him. The back of his legs met my body, and he went sprawling, crashing to the ground.

Ghost leopard dug her teeth into one arm, and I leapt on his chest. My paws holding him down, I stared down into the glowing white face. So beautiful, so brilliant I could barely discern his features. And then I went for the neck and bit deep. Ghost leopard raked at his gut, her spotted paw tickling my belly as she reached beneath me to get at the creature.

The Scytatian twisted, shrieking, and I tightened my grip on his throat, feeling his energy drain like air out of a leaking balloon. And then—just like that—he was gone. Vanished. Poof.

I stood there for a moment, staring at the ground where he'd lain prone. The ghost leopard wandered over to me and nuzzled me gently on the neck, then stepped back. I looked into her eyes. She was familiar, but I knew I'd never seen her before.

"Who are you?" I asked.

She let out a little growl. "You wouldn't recognize me, I suppose, though I've been watching you all of your life. Are you all right?"

"I'm fine, I think. You've been watching me all of my life?" I cocked my head to the side, the feel of my muscled body solid and comforting. I felt almost invulnerable when Panther came out to play, although I knew I wasn't.

She gazed at me, her eyes glowing. They were the same emerald as mine. And then I saw a glimmer of light surround her, and a flutter of golden hair, and she began to vanish. I raced forward, suddenly understanding.

"Wait, don't go! Come back!" As I loped over to where she'd been standing, I heard one last message from her.

"I'll always be here, Sister. I'll always watch over you."

And then she was gone. I stared at the empty spot as the scent of bonfire descended around me again, and then I closed my eyes and slid into unconsciousness.

When I came to, I was back in my usual form, with Camille patting my face. "Delilah, Delilah? Are you okay?"

I blinked against the sharp light that was filling the room and let her help me sit up. Where the hell was I? As I glanced around, I realized that we were in the FH-CSI medical offices, and I was sitting on a table.

"How long have I been out?" I asked, wincing. My head hurt like hell.

"About an hour. You hit your head on a pipe when you fell, but Sharah says you should be okay. How do you feel?" She pulled over a wheelchair and forced me into it. "No walking about until we know that you don't have a concussion."

"Chase—how's Chase? And Karvanak—" Panic took hold as I suddenly remembered how I'd gotten here. I tried to stand, but a whirl of dizziness forced me back into my seat. I must have really bonked my head, that was for sure.

As Camille pushed me into the hallway, images began to flood my mind. Karvanak. Chase. And—my sister. The ghost leopard. So it was true, I had a twin sister, and she died. As I tried to digest the knowledge, Camille guided me through a set of double doors. She pushed me through into a large room that held three beds and several chairs. We were in one of the recuperation wards.

Chase was there, sleeping in one bed. And on the bizarre side, Menolly was standing by his bed, holding his hand.

Zachary was in another bed, looking a lot like a mummy, wrapped in bandages. Smoky sat on a chair, and for the first time since we'd met him, he looked tired. Vanzir was there, too, sporting more bandages than I could count, and his arm was wrapped in a splint. Everybody looked covered in bruises, including Camille.

Morio and Sharah entered the room.

"Chase, Zach—how are they doing? Is Karvanak dead?" I motioned for Camille to wheel me over to Chase's side. Menolly stepped away, giving me a soft smile which—for her—translated into a yeehaw.

"Chase will be all right, though there's no way to ever reattach the finger," Sharah said. "It's his mind I'm more worried about. They roughed him up. I can recognize the signs of torture, including those that don't leave marks. He's been through hell. I've sedated him. Rest is vital to the healing process."

I stared down at my sleeping detective, wondering how we would weather this hell. How would he fight these new demons come to haunt him?

"And Zach?" I said softly.

She shrugged. "He'll recover, too, but it's going to take a long time for his back to heal. If Karvanak had kicked him any harder, he would have broken Zach's spine and left him paralyzed. As it is, he's got a broken tailbone, two fractured vertebrae, a broken hip, broken leg, fractured wrist, and he's taken a lot of soft tissue damage. I'm guessing he won't be walking on his own for at least six months, and he might always have a limp. It's too soon to tell."

"He was hurt saving Chase's life," Menolly said. "He threw himself between Chase and Karvanak."

I pushed myself out of the chair, ignoring Camille's entreaty, and cautiously made my way to Zach's side. Images of the fight were flooding back. Blood, so much blood on our hands. My pulse quickened, and I suddenly realized that now, instead of dreading the memories, my adrenaline was shifting back into high gear. I felt myself itching to continue the chase, to follow the enemy and tear him apart.

"You saved Chase," I whispered, leaning down to kiss Zach's forehead. "I remember now. Right before I shifted . . .

I saw you jump between Chase and Karvanak." I looked back at the others. "What about *him*? What about Karvanak?"

"In the end it took all of us to bring him down," Smoky said. He motioned to Camille, and she sat on his lap. He wrapped his arm around her waist and let out a long sigh. "He was a greater demon, but still . . . he was just *one* demon. There are thousands like him in the Subterranean Realms." He left the thought unspoken that was running through all of our minds. Thousands of demons, waiting for Shadow Wing to open the floodgates.

It was then that I noticed that Fraale and Roz were nowhere to be seen. When I asked about them, Menolly frowned. "They left after the fight. Roz said they needed to talk."

"Well, hell. We saved the seal this time, but we almost lost two of our own." I walked back to Chase's side and took his hand in mine. What would happen when he woke up? To him . . . to us?

"I take it everyone else is unscathed? More or less?" I asked, still holding Chase's hand. His other hand was bandaged, and by his color, I saw that they had the infection on the run. But infections and lost fingertips couldn't hold a candle compared to bad memories.

"Yeah," Camille said. She sucked in a deep breath, held it for a moment, then let it whistle out in a sharp stream. "And you—you saved us all. The Scytatian would have killed everyone there if you hadn't . . . well . . . done whatever it was you did to him."

I blinked. I still hadn't told them about the ghost leopard. About my twin. I tried to summon up the words, but this wasn't the time. Right now, all I could think about was the bone-weary pain that ran through my body. About the fact that both of my lovers had been hurt. About the fact that my sword had spoken, my dead sister had come to fight by my side, and that my master—one of the Harvestmen—wanted me to have his child. I felt so overwhelmed, I didn't know where to begin.

And then a miracle happened. Or maybe it was the Hags of Fate smiling on us for a brief second. Chase opened his eyes and gave my hand a squeeze. I motioned to Sharah.

"He's awake. You said you sedated him."

"No," Chase whispered as Sharah scurried over. "I need to tell Delilah something before I sleep. Please?"

Sharah stood back and nodded to me.

I leaned down and put my ear near Chase's lips. "What is it, sweetheart?"

He gave a slight shudder and then whispered, "I'm sorry. I'm sorry about Erika. I was an idiot. I thought . . . I don't know what I thought, but please, tell me you won't leave me? Promise me you won't leave?"

I stared into those deep brown eyes and fell. I fell so hard that I broke every chance I had to retreat, to walk away. "I'm here. I'm not going anywhere. When you're feeling better, we'll talk. We'll find a way."

A tear trickled down his cheek, and he pressed my hand to his lips. "It's you, Delilah. It's only you. And whatever it takes—whatever arrangement you want, I'll accept it. Whatever you want me to do to make up for lying to you, I'll do it. Even if . . . even if you want Zachary. He saved my life, and he almost died. How can I ever forget that? How can I ever repay him?"

I pressed a finger to his lips. "Shush. Save your strength. Sleep, and know that I'll be here when you wake up. We'll figure this out, Chase. My parents made it work; somehow we will, too."

His eyes drifted closed and a soft snore came whistling out of his nose. I smiled then. Everything was going to be okay. It had to be.

CHAPTER 28

I stayed at the hospital that night, sleeping in the bed next to Chase's. Camille and Menolly went home and took care of matters there. We had a lot of housewares to replace, and while Iris had already started the process, there was so much work to do. Camille and Morio wanted to strengthen the wards and figure out a way for all of us to know when they'd been broken.

I didn't think I'd be able to sleep, even as weary as I was, but Sharah brought me a mug of kettle-nap tea from Otherworld, and it did the trick. I was out like a light and slept until an unexpected sunbeam splashed on me. Shining through the window, it filled the room with warm light. As I stretched, yawning, I couldn't help but feel relief. We might be staring hell in the face, but at least this morning, we'd do so in sunshine.

"You're awake." Chase's voice echoed through my head, and I turned. He was sitting up, his hand gingerly resting on a pillow. Bruised, he looked exhausted, but his smile lit up the room.

"I'm awake," I said, padding over to curl on the end of his

bed. "And how are you feeling this morning? Where'd Zach go?"

"They took Zachary in for surgery on his back. He took one for me. Don't think I don't know that. How I'll ever repay him . . ." With a shrug, Chase leaned back against the pillows. "As to how I am . . . that's a loaded question. They were rough on me, Delilah. I took more abuse than getting my finger chopped off." He stared at the gauze-wrapped hand, shaking his head. "But you know what? I understand now."

"Understand what?" I blinked. I'd expected him to sound fragile, and he sounded the opposite: strong and determined.

"I understand what you're fighting for. What *we're* fighting for. I understand the nature of the Demonkin better. And I get why Menolly does what she does, why the rules no longer apply. I think I can do my job better because of this. I guess . . . I'm saying I've just enlisted in your army instead of standing on the fence." He gave me a hesitant smile. "If you're still willing to have me."

I lowered my gaze. This was not the Chase I'd expected to find. And I rather liked it. "We need you, Chase. Whatever happens between you and me—we need you."

Letting out a long sigh, he closed his eyes. "I hurt you. I can't believe I did that—"

"Don't. Menolly explained it to me. How you needed to feel strong and how I might be making you feel like less of a man because of my father's bloodline and how it makes me stronger—" I stopped. He was staring at me with a peculiar expression. "What? Did I say something wrong?"

"No, but you're way off track. I wouldn't take relationship advice from Menolly, if I were you." He snorted. "The blunt truth is that I did what I did because I've always been a pig. I'm not very good with relationships, Delilah," he added, leaning forward and reaching for my hand with his good one.

"This commitment thing is hard for me. I've always used women the way some guys use booze or drugs . . . even Erika, when we were engaged. I never took our betrothal seriously, and I hurt her. When she came nosing around, I screwed up. Plain and simple. No ulterior motives. No excuses. She's pretty, she was always a lot of fun before she dumped me, and

I decided to take a chance. I never thought you'd find out, and I never meant it to be anything more than a fling."

I stared at him, thinking that I'd liked it better when I thought it was some angsty crisis he was going through. "Not sure what to say, dude. It's not that you slept with her that pissed me off so much."

His smile dropped away, and he looked like a dog about to be beaten on the butt with a broom. "Go ahead."

"You *lied* to me. And you made me feel bad for wanting Zachary. You made such a big deal about Zach, and then you go out and fuck some woman I've never even met? If you would have told me you wanted her, we could have avoided this mess! I won't live with a double standard." I waited, wondering where the chips were going to fall.

Chase sighed. "Yeah. I know. I meant what I said. Whatever you want me to do, I'll do it. I'll take any promise or oath you want. If you still want to be with Zach, I'll be okay with it. Ever since you walked in on Erika and me, I realized just how much I love you, and how much I want you in my life. Maybe it's true. Maybe every relationship is different. If I stop expecting it to be like what I *think* it should be, we can have the relationship we're *meant* to have."

My detective had grown up a lot during the past few days. I reached out and flicked his nose with my finger and thumb. "Silly man. When did you finally get so smart? To start things off right, I'll be honest. I slept with Zachary again. I was so mad at you, and I was so pent-up from a fight . . . and I wanted him. But Chase, I love you. I care for Zach, I respond to him— our natures are similar. But I don't love him."

I watched Chase's face, carefully gauging his reaction. He pressed his lips together, and I could tell I might as well have punched him in the gut, but then he let out a long sigh and smiled. "Yeah. Okay. It's going to happen from time to time, and I can accept that. And if I . . . if I see someone . . ."

"Then you tell me first. Let's just take it one day at a time. How about that?" I leaned down and pressed my lips to his. His tongue slid into my mouth, searching, and then his good hand was on my breast, and I moaned, wanting him, wanting my love inside me.

"Are you up to it?" I asked, glancing back at the door.

He nodded, an eager light in his eyes. "Oh, yeah, just take a look and see how up I am for it." He raised the sheet, and I saw that he was rigid and waiting. I licked my lips, and he laughed. "No biting! Just climb up here for the ride, ma'am, and I'll show you the sights."

I grinned, stripping off my panties, and slid into bed with him as he took my right breast in his mouth and sucked. As the warmth spread from the tip of my head to the bottom of my toes, I lowered myself onto him, sliding down over the deliciously hardened cock, hungry to reconnect, hungry to feel him inside me again. We matched rhythms, my hips rocking to a slow, steady beat, and he reached down to finger me with his good hand, sending a ripple of sensation through my body. Gasping, I drove down so that he filled me to the hilt, making me so wet that it felt like I could never get enough of him.

In our haste, he must have forgotten to move the call button, because just before I was about to come, the door opened and Jessila, one of the elfin nurses, rushed in.

"You rang, Mr. John—oh!"

I glanced over my shoulder as she stood there, shaking her head and grinning from ear to ear. I know we should have stopped right there, but I was so close, and Chase felt so good, that when he touched my clit one more time, I let out a little scream and came, waves of orgasm rolling over me, sending me reeling as Chase followed suit.

"Carry on, then," Jessila said, laughing as she shut the door behind her.

Chase broke out in loud guffaws as we disentangled ourselves, and I crawled under the sheet next to him. "Man, did you see her face?"

"You are a bad, bad man," I said, snickering as I cozied up in his arms. I brought his injured hand to my lips and gently kissed the gauze. "You're a bad man, and I'm going to have to punish you. How about if I order you to fuck me again?"

But he said nothing. My sweet detective was asleep, snoring soundly. I shook my head. He needed his rest, and so did I. I slid out from the bed to give him more room, pulled the covers up to his chin, then let myself go and transformed into my tabby self. One quick leap, and I curled up on the pillow next to his head, sleep beckoning like a warm, lazy day.

For the moment, everything was right with the world.

CHAPTER 29

❧

Three nights later, we gathered what turned out to be quite a conclave in Smoky's barrow. Among the invited: my sisters and me, Iris and Maggie, Chase, Morio, Vanzir, and Roz, along with a medley of humans and Supes.

Venus the Moon Child from the Rainier Puma Pride was there, and Wade from Vampires Anonymous. Shamas, our cousin, and Lindsey Cartridge, the director of the Green Goddess Women's Shelter, showed up, along with Tim Winthrop, a female impersonator–computer guru FBH who was instrumental in helping us build the Supe community database.

But our most daunting guests were the three Earthside Queens of Fae, Titania, Morgaine, and Aeval. As we sat there, a tangible energy raced through the air.

"They should be here any moment," Camille said during a lull in the conversation. "Trenyth, Queen Asteria's assistant, sent word via Grandmother Coyote's portal that they were planning on attending. There have been new developments, apparently, in the war at home."

She sat beside Smoky at the head of the table, with Morio on her left. An empty chair to the right indicated the place they were saving in hopes Trillian would return.

Every stick of furniture, every glass or plate that Smoky owned was exquisite. *Figures,* I thought. Dragons love fine goods and money. There was nothing ostentatious, just an incredible array of unbelievably expensive possessions, most likely gathered over a thousand years or more. The furniture was old-world and hand carved, the crystal hand blown, and the wine from the best years and best vineyards.

I glanced around the barrow, amazed by how much room an innocuous mound of dirt could have beneath it. This molehill might as well be a mountain. Smoky's barrow extended far into the earth as well as into other realms. No wonder Camille had said she felt like she was in some bizarre Alice-in-Wonderland sunken castle.

The ceiling of the barrow was a good thirty feet over our heads, while the walls enclosing us were granite on three sides. The fourth side opened into a huge ravine, and from below, I could hear the sound of water running. A stream or river wound through the bottom of the channel, but it was so deep and dim that I couldn't see which. I wanted to go exploring but reined in my curiosity. Right now, we had more important things on the agenda.

Chase had just been released from the hospital. We were officially back together again. Though we hadn't quite decided on the terms on which we were going to establish our relationship, we were determined to make it work. I sat there, his hand in mine, blessing the fact that he was alive.

I glanced around the room. I still hadn't told anybody about meeting my sister yet, and I wasn't entirely sure why. There was just something that kept me silent, some desire to keep the experience mine for as long as I could before I let anybody pick it apart and dissect it.

At that moment, a knock resounded from outside the barrow, and Smoky crossed to open the door. He stood back, bowing gracefully as the Elfin Queen—Queen Asteria—entered. She was followed by Trenyth, her assistant. I noticed Smoky staring outside, a look of surprise on his face. He said nothing, however, just shut the door and followed them back to the table.

After the round of introductions, everyone presented their news.

Venus went first. "Zachary will recover, but he's out of the game for a while. His plans to run for councilman are on hold, so we're pushing Nerissa to run in his place. I've marshaled the Elders and put my foot down. They agree to sponsor her, and they agree that it's in our best interests to offer you whatever help the Puma Pride can give you. We've spoken to some of the other tribes who are going to sign the Supe Community Treaties. Within a month, we'll form a militia. Let's just say reading about the troll incident with Camille, and then Zachary being attacked by the Rāksasa spurred them into action."

Tim stood up. "I've almost completed all the programming for the database, and we'll have an expansive phone tree printed out soon. This will go to the elders of every tribe participating, as well as to individual members who are heading the different committees."

Venus leaned forward. "Sounds good. What about privacy?"

Tim nodded. "I've managed to rig it to maintain a degree of privacy while still allowing us to reach everyone on the rolls within an hour, providing they're near their phones. But the *only* people who will have access to the entire organization's files will be the council, once it's elected, and Camille, Menolly, Delilah, and me."

Camille nodded and turned to Lindsey. "What do you have for us?"

The newly pregnant—and thoroughly delighted—newcomer to our group gave everyone a timid smile. Lindsey had been so much help with Erin Mathews, and she was a well-known priestess among the FBH witches, so we'd decided to bring her into the fold. She'd been terrified when we told her about the demons, but she was more than willing to help.

"As you know, most human pagans and psychics are a scattered lot and not taken too seriously, but I've managed to convince several of the larger magical orders that there are dangerous energies around, and that you're trying to help deflect these. We're working together to seal areas of the city with protective runes. It's too early to tell, but we should keep an eye on the crime rates in those areas. Several of the Fae you recommended we talk to are working with us to strengthen our own magic. Kind of scary, but we're with you."

"Then it seems," Menolly said, "that we're building our allies."

"Good. Speaking of allies, we have much to discuss and little spare time, so if you will allow me to go next," Queen Asteria said, "then I can return to Elqaneve before morning."

She glanced around the table, her gaze lingering on the three Earthside Fae Queens. "First, I have important news about the war in Y'Elestrial. Tanaquar's forces have breached the city, and she's claimed the crown."

My sisters and I let out a cheer, but Queen Asteria held up her hand. "Lethesanar is on the run, but she and her armies are murdering everyone in her path as she attempts her escape. The city is burning. She decided to raze it rather than hand it over to her sister."

My stomach lurched, and Camille blanched. Menolly stared at the Elfin Queen, her eyes dripping bloody tears. Our home, our beautiful home. Our family was missing, and now the city of our youth lay in ruins.

Camille let out a long breath. "At least Tanaquar has taken the city. If she can destroy Lethesanar, then perhaps Y'Elestrial can be rebuilt."

Queen Asteria nodded. "Yes, it's very good news indeed. Though there has been so much destruction that it will take a long time before Y'Elestrial returns to its former glory."

"Will Tanaquar help us out, when she gets the city back to order?" Menolly leaned forward, resting her elbows on the table. "Or are we still on our own?"

Queen Asteria let out a long sigh. "The death threat on your head has been rescinded, but the OIA will be a long time in re-forming. Tanaquar made it quite clear she intends to overhaul the entire structure of the government. I've tried to impress upon her the gravity of the situation, but she is as strong-willed as her sister. And . . . there's something else. Something that may present a problem in the future."

She paused and looked over at Camille. "My dear, I know you did as the Hags of Fate required, but the fact that you broke the spell holding Aeval in stasis is causing quite the concern, as is the fact that you now bear the horn of the Black Unicorn. I've kept both bits of news quiet, but somehow, rumors have filtered back to Otherworld. You and your sisters—but especially you—are fueling debates all through the cities there."

Camille flushed, looking so downcast that I wanted to wrap my arms around her and hug away the pain.

"Wonderful," I said. "We're over here busting our asses to protect our home, and we're being singled out for controversy? Let *them* put *their* pussies on the line and see how quickly they talk."

Queen Asteria smiled at me. "Easy, child. While only the Elemental Lords and the great Sidhe lords who commenced the Great Divide can punish Camille for breaking their spell, there are magicians aplenty who wonder how to claim her powers for themselves. You must all be careful. The enemy is no longer just the foe you see in front of you. It might just be the friend you thought was backing you up."

"You see?" Aeval said, shaking her head. "This is the thanks you get from those who ran away. Stay here, you are part of our world, too."

"Hush!" Queen Asteria rose and glared at the Queen of Darkness. "Be silent. Quit making things worse. These are but tidings I bring. My main reason for coming is to discuss how we can make a concerted effort to help these girls in their fight against the demons. They seem destined to lead the army against the damned, so we must back them up."

Aeval let out a long sigh. "Oh very well. We'll put aside petty grievances for now. I will speak for the *Triple Threat*." Here she gave us all a dark smile. It was my turn to blush.

"Come the summer solstice, we play host to the first gathering of Earthside Fae this world has seen in thousands of years. At that time, we will coronate the new Courts and establish our sovereign state. We will align ourselves with no one nation but will fight against any foe who might seek to harm this world."

Titania smoothed her hair and flashed a gracious smile around the room. "In return, we've claimed autonomy. We've purchased a parcel of land on which to establish our palace within this dimension, and it will host our sovereign state. While most of our work is done between the worlds, our land will be considered sanctuary for the Fae, and we will be choosing an ambassador to represent us to the world."

Everybody broke into conversation at once.

Titania rose, holding up her hand. "Our Fae militia will also be at your service, should you need it. We intend to host both magical and military brigades. Think of us as a Special Forces unit. The warriors will be connected to the FH-CSI, by the way. So, Detective Johnson, you may have reserves at hand sooner than you think."

The room grew silent as we digested all of this. My heart began to soar. Good news at last. One month, and we'd have allies. One month, and we'd have help to fall back on.

Queen Asteria broke into a smile then. "I have another tiding to add. As soon I can make arrangements, we will be sending over more of our people from Elqaneve to work in the medical unit here. I'll also be assigning an ambassador to Earthside on a permanent basis. And so will Tanaquar. Meanwhile, she bade me to introduce you to her new chief advisor."

Why would Tanaquar want us to meet her advisor? Unless we were going to be reporting to him.

Trenyth glanced at the Queen. "May I have the honor, Your Majesty?"

"Of course," she said, gracefully resuming her seat.

Trenyth turned to Camille, Menolly, and me, beaming. "After all the bad news I've brought you, it gives me the greatest pleasure to introduce you to the man who will be working alongside the new Court and Crown of Y'Elestrial."

Smoky silently walked over and opened the door.

A man stepped through, clad in the rich blue and gold of Y'Elestrial. As he pulled back the hood of his cape, Camille gave a little scream, and Menolly's eyes widened. I rose, unable to believe what I was seeing. As my gaze fastened on the face of my father, I trembled and started to cry.

"Delilah—what is it—" Chase started to say as I broke away and raced across the room. All three of us converged on him, though Menolly hung back, waiting. He caught Camille and me in his arms, looking weary and tired but alive. His hair was tied back in the raven-blue braid he always wore it in, and his smooth cheeks gleamed with tears.

"My girls. My girls. Oh how I've worried . . ."

I buried my face on his shoulder, never wanting to let go. Father was here. Father was alive and safe, and everything was going to be all right.

After a moment, he let go and stepped forward, staring at Menolly. Bloody tears stained her face as they trickled from her eyes. Our father—Sephreh ob Tanu—had always hated vampires. In fact, he despised them. When we parted, his relationship with Menolly had been strained. He wanted to love her, but we'd all seen the struggle in his face.

But now he hung his head and held out his arms.

"Please forgive me, my child. Forgive me for everything. I was wrong. You are my daughter, through life and death and life again. And I beg you to forgive me. I love you. I accept you as you are, fangs and all."

As he waited, Menolly glanced over at me, looking ready to panic. I could see the hope and disbelief warring in her eyes. And then Roz stood up and pushed her forward. Just enough so that she stumbled into Father's arms. As they stood there, embracing, it occurred to me that bleak as the future was, at last we were finding our way. Forging allies. Laying plans.

I glanced at Chase. The odds were against us, all right. But with help, maybe we had a chance, after all.

Camille, Menolly, and I sat by the edge of Birchwater Pond. Dawn was an hour off, and we still had a little while before Menolly had to retreat for the day. Iris and Maggie were snuggled asleep, and Father was sleeping in the parlor.

"We're outgrowing the house," Camille said. "Morio and Trillian can stay with me, but I think we need to build a studio or something on the land. Roz, Shamas, and Vanzir can sleep there when they need to. Sort of like a stable." She smiled softly, staring at the water as it rippled under the fading stars.

"Sounds like a plan to me," Menolly said. "Did Queen Asteria have anything to say about Trillian?"

Camille shook her head. "No, and I didn't ask. I'm not supposed to know about his secret mission, but now that Father's safe, we should be hearing from him soon. I only hope that he can adjust to all the changes." She let out a long sigh, looking a little nervous. "I guess we start searching for the fifth seal now. At least Father's safe."

Our father had been captured by a party of the Goldensün, or the golden Fae as they were often known. With gilded skin and jet eyes, they were xenophobic and lived high in the mountains. They'd imprisoned him when he accidentally stumbled into their lair. They hadn't harmed him, but it had taken him a while to escape. The information he managed to deliver to Queen Asteria had turned the tide in the war and allowed Tanaquar to route Lethesanar. Our father was a hero. And he'd always been one in *our* eyes.

"Whatever happened to Fraale?" I asked. "I lost track of her during the fight."

"She returned to Otherworld. Roz says they can't be around each other without arguing. She still loves him. He doesn't think they can make it."

"Maybe he should give it a try," I whispered softly. And then, under the stars shining so brilliantly, and the moon deep in her dark cups, I knew it was time. "I met my twin sister." And I told them about her, about the fight. "She didn't give me her name, though. I'll ask Father. He'll have to be straight with me about what happened."

"So we had a fourth sister," Menolly said. "It feels odd to think about."

"What are you going to do about Chase?" Camille asked, after a moment.

"We've decided to give it a try. We aren't promising exclusivity, not right now. But Chase asked me about something and I didn't know what to say."

"What is it?" Menolly gazed at me.

"He wants to know more about the nectar of life. I think he wants to stay with me—with us—for the long haul." In the depths of my heart, I wanted him to. "I'm going to talk to Titania about it. She'll understand, and maybe she'll be able to help prevent what happened to Tam Lin from happening to Chase. If he only takes a small dose—enough to let him live with me through my allotted span . . . maybe it would work."

There wasn't much to say after that, and thankfully, my

sisters didn't even bother trying. We watched the water lap on the shores for another few minutes, and then Menolly took my hand and pulled me to my feet.

"Come on, Kitten. I think it's time for *Jerry Springer.* I've still got an hour or so. I'll join you, and we can feed Maggie while Iris and Camille rustle up a big breakfast."

Suddenly lighthearted, I pushed worry to the side and let loose, racing along the path. Camille and Menolly ran full tilt behind me, all three of us laughing under the solemn moon. We were heading home. Home to our father. Home to our lovers. And home to our family.

GLOSSARY

Calouk: The rough, common dialect used by a number of Otherworld inhabitants.

Court and Crown: The *Crown* refers to the queen of Y'Elestrial. The *Court* refers to the nobility and military personnel that surround the Queen. *Court and Crown* together refer to the entire government of Y'Elestrial.

Crypto: One of the Cryptozoid races. Cryptos include creatures out of legend that are not technically of the Fae races: gargoyles, unicorns, gryphons, chimeras, etc. Most primarily inhabit Otherworld, but some have Earthside cousins.

Earthside: Everything that exists on the Earth side of the portals.

Elqaneve: The Elfin lands in Otherworld.

Elemental Lords: The elemental beings—both male and female—who, along with the Hags of Fate and the Harvestmen, are the only true Immortals. They are avatars of various elements and energies, and they inhabit all realms. They do as they will and seldom concern themselves with humankind or Fae unless summoned. If asked for help, they often exact steep prices in return. The Elemental Lords are not concerned with balance like the Hags of Fate.

FBH: Full-blooded human (usually refers to Earthside humans).

FH-CSI: The Faerie-Human Crime Scene Investigations Team. The brainchild of Detective Chase Johnson, it was first formed as a collaboration between the OIA and the Seattle Police Department. Other FH-CSI units have been created around the country, based on the Seattle prototype. The FH-CSI takes care of both medical and criminal emergencies involving visitors from Otherworld.

Great Divide: A time of immense turmoil when the Elemental Lords and some of the High Court of Fae decided to rip apart the worlds. Until then, the Fae existed primarily on Earth, their lives and worlds mingling with those of humans. The Great Divide tore everything asunder, splitting off another dimension, which became Otherworld. At that time, the Twin Courts of Fae were disbanded and their queens stripped of power. This was the time during which the Spirit Seal was formed and broken in order to seal off the realms from each other. Some Fae chose to stay Earthside, others moved to the realm of Otherworld, and the demons were—for the most part—sealed in the Subterranean Realms.

Guard Des'Estar: The military of Y'Elestrial.

Hags of Fate: The women of destiny who keep the balance righted. Neither good nor evil, they observe the flow of destiny. When events get too far out of balance, they step in and take action, usually using humans, Fae, Supes, and other creatures as pawns to bring the path of destiny back into line.

Harvestmen: The lords of death; a few cross over and are also Elemental Lords. The Harvestmen, along with their followers (the Valkyries and the Death Maidens, for example) reap the souls of the dead.

Ionyc Lands: The astral, etheric, and spirit realms, along with several other lesser-known noncorporeal dimensions, form the Ionyc Lands. These realms are separated by the Ionyc Sea, a current of energy that prevents the Ionyc Lands from colliding, thereby sparking off an explosion of universal proportions.

Ionyc Sea: The currents of energy that separate the Ionyc Lands. Certain creatures, especially those connected with the elemental energies of ice, snow, and wind, can travel through the Ionyc Sea without protection.

Melosealfôr: A rare Crypto dialect learned by powerful Cryptos and all Moon Witches.

OIA: The Otherworld Intelligence Agency; the brains behind the Guard Des'Estar.

Otherworld/OW: The human term for the UN of "Faerie Land." A dimension apart from ours that contains creatures from legend and lore, pathways to the gods, and various other places like Olympus. Otherworld's actual name varies among the differing dialects of the many races of Cryptos and Fae.

Portal, Portals: The interdimensional gates that connect the different realms.

Seelie Court: The Earthside Fae Court of Light and Summer, disbanded during the Great Divide. Titania was the Seelie Queen.

Soul Statues: In Otherworld, small figurines are created for the Fae of certain races and magically linked with the baby. These figurines reside in family shrines, and when one of the Fae dies, their soul statue shatters. In Menolly's case, when she was reborn as a vampire, her soul statue re-formed, although twisted. If a family member disappears, their family can always tell if their loved one is alive or dead if they have access to the soul statue.

Spirit Seals: A magical crystal artifact, the spirit seal was created during the Great Divide. When the portals were sealed, the spirit seal was broken into nine gems, and each piece was given to an Elemental Lord or Lady. These gems each have varying powers. Even possessing one of the spirit seals can allow the wielder to weaken the portals that divide Otherworld, Earthside, and the Subterranean Realms. If all of the seals are joined together again, then all of the portals will open.

Supe/Supes: Short for Supernaturals. Refers to Earthside supernatural beings who are not of Fae nature. Refers to Weres, especially.

Unseelie Court: The Earthside Fae Court of Shadow and Winter, disbanded during the Great Divide. Aeval was the Unseelie Queen.

VA/Vampires Anonymous: The Earthside group started by Wade Stevens, a vampire who was a psychiatrist during life.

The group is focused on helping newly born vampires adjust to their new state of existence and to encourage vampires to avoid harming the innocent as much as possible. The VA is vying for control. Their goal is to rule the vampires of the United States and to set up an internal policing agency.

Whispering Mirror: A magical communications device that links Otherworld and Earth. Think magical videophone.

Y'Elestrial: The city-state in Otherworld where the D'Artigo girls were born and raised. A Fae city, currently embroiled in a civil war between the drug-crazed, tyrannical Queen Lethesanar, and her more levelheaded sister Tanaquar, who is trying to claim the throne for herself. The civil war has escalated to other lands, and many races are taking sides in the fighting.

Youkai: Loosely (very loosely) translated: Japanese demon/ nature spirit. For the purposes of this series, the youkai have three shapes: the animal form, the human form, and then the true demon form. Unlike the demons of the Subterranean Realms, youkai are not necessarily evil by nature.

And now . . .
a special excerpt from the next book
in the Otherworld series
by Yasmine Galenorn . . .

DEMON MISTRESS

Coming soon from Berkley!

"Could you at least wait until I open the window to shake that thing?" Iris shot me a nasty look as I yanked the braided rug off the floor and started beating it against the wall. "I can barely breathe, there's so much dust."

Chagrined, I dropped the rug to the floor and gave her a sheepish look. "Sorry," I said. "Open the window and I'll shake it outside."

Rolling her eyes, she lifted the sash and pushed it up as far as she could. I took over, finishing the job. A wash of warm summer air filtered through the open window along with the sounds of horns honking, blaring music, and laughter from a gang of street kids who were smoking weed in the back alley behind the Wayfarer. The air had a happy-go-lucky feel to it, a stir of excitement, like a street party about to spontaneously erupt.

I leaned over the sill, waving to one of the boys who was staring up at me. His name was Chester, but he went by Chit, and he and his buddies had become a fixture around the bar over the past few months. Too young to come in, they hung around out back, and every now and then I'd make sure they got a good meal from the grill. They were good kids—a little at loose ends, but they never caused much trouble and they weren't gangbangers or druggies. In fact, they kept some of the less desirable elements from hanging out in the alleys.

Chit waved back. "Yo, Menolly! What's shakin', babe?"

I grinned. I was far, far older than he, although I didn't look it. But like a number of the younger FBH men I'd met, he flirted with every woman who looked to be under forty, especially if they were Fae. And even though I happened to be only half-Fae, and a vampire to boot, he treated me like I was just another one of the locals.

"Just getting around to some long-overdue cleaning," I called down to him, waving again before I turned back to Iris, who was poking around an old-world trunk that had been hiding in a corner of the room.

Since I now owned the entire building the Wayfarer Bar & Grill resided in, I decided it was time to clear out some of the rooms over the bar and turn them into a paying resource. My sisters and I could furnish them, rent them out to Otherworld visitors, and make a nice chunk of change.

Even though we were back on the Court and Crown's payroll, money was still going out faster than it was coming in. Especially since we were paying Tim Winthrop for the computer work he was doing for the Supe community.

The Wayfarer's second story held ten rooms—two of them bathrooms. And it looked like all of them had remained untouched for years. Piles of junk and thick layers of dust permeated the entire story. Iris and I'd finished one room, but it had taken us two nights to sort through the boxes filled with newspaper and old clothes.

I stretched, arching my back, and shook my head. "What a mess."

The room had obviously been turned into a storage room, probably by Jocko, who wasn't the cleanest bartender the Wayfarer had ever seen. Unfortunately the diminutive giant had met an untimely end at the hand of Bad Ass Luke, a demon from the Subterranean Realms.

Jocko had lived in one of the OIA designated apartments in the city and I was pretty sure he'd never slept at the bar. Or, at least, we hadn't found any giant-sized clothes hanging around.

At least not yet. But it was obvious that *someone* from Otherworld had stayed here at one time—or at least she'd left a bunch of her things here. I recognized the weave on a couple of tunics. They certainly hadn't been sewn over here Earthside.

Iris snorted. " 'Mess' is certainly the word, isn't it? Now, if you'll get your albino butt over here, I could use some help moving this trunk." Hands on her hips, she nodded to the wooden chest she'd uncovered from beneath a pile of newspapers.

Shaken out of my reverie, I lifted the trunk with one hand and effortlessly carried it to the center of the room. Being a vampire had its perks and extraordinary strength was one of them. I wasn't all that much taller than Iris—skimming five one, I towered over her by a mere thirteen inches, but I could have easily lifted a creature five times her weight.

"Where on earth are your sisters? I thought they were going to help."

The Talon-haltija—Finnish house sprite—brushed a stray cobweb off her forehead, leaving a smudge mark from the grime that had embedded itself on her hands. Her ankle length golden hair had been pulled into a long ponytail and she'd carefully woven it into a thick chignon to get it out of the way. Iris was wearing a pair of denim shorts and a red and white gingham sleeveless blouse, with the ends tied together under her breasts. A pair of blue Keds completed her country-maid ensemble.

I grinned. "They are helping, in their own *special* ways. Camille's at the store buying more cleaning supplies and dinner. Delilah's out scrounging up a pickup so we can haul away some of this junk." I'd left running the bar to Chrysandra for the evening—she knew where I was, and she was my best waitress. Luke was bartending and he'd take care of any jerks that stumbled in. Tavah, as usual, was guarding the portal in the basement.

"*Special* my foot," Iris mumbled, but she flashed me a brilliantly white smile. She had good teeth, that was for sure. "Let's see what this old chest holds. Probably dead mice, with our luck."

"If it does, don't tell Delilah. She'd want to play with

them." I knelt beside her, examining the lock. "Looks like we need a skeleton key if you don't want me to bust it open."

"Forget about keys," Iris said. She leaned over and deftly inserted a bobby pin into the oversized hole, then whispered a soft chant. Within seconds, the latch clicked. I gave her a long look and she shrugged. "What? Simple locks I can pop. Dead bolts, not so much. Life is easier when you don't have to worry about locks and bars."

"I would have to agree," I said softly, opening the lid. As it softly creaked, the faint odor of cedar rose to fill the air. Even though I didn't need to breathe, that didn't mean I couldn't smell—at least when I chose to—and I let the aroma filter through my senses. Mingled with the fragrance of tobacco and frankincense, the scent was dusty, like an old library thick with leather and heavy oak furniture. It reminded me of our parlor, back home in Otherworld.

Iris peeked over the edge. "Pay dirt!"

I glanced into the trunk's belly. No dead mice. No gems or jewels, either, but there were clothes and several books, and what looked like a music box. I slowly lifted the box out of the soft cushion of dresses in which it had been nestled. The wood was definitely harvested from Otherworld.

"Arnikcah," I said, peering closely at it. "This comes from OW."

"I figured as much," Iris said, leaning over to examine the box.

Wood from an Arnikcah tree was hard, dark, and rich, with a natural luster that shimmered when polished. Easy to spot by the rich burgundy tones, the color rested somewhere between mahogany and cherry.

The box was fastened by a silver hinge, and I flipped it open, gently raising the lid. A small peridot cabochon, inset on the underside of the lid, flashed as the sound of tinkling notes fluttered out. Not panpipes, but a silver flute, sounding the song of woodland birds at the close of sunset.

Iris closed her eyes, listening to the melody. After a moment, it stopped and she bit her lip. "That's beautiful."

"Yes, it is." I examined the contents of the music box. "My

mother had a box similar to this one. Father gave it to her. I don't know what happened to it, though. Camille would know if anybody does. The tune's a common one, used to lull children to sleep."

The inside of the music box had been lined with a rich, velvety brocade. I'd seen it used in the skirts of women who belonged to the Court and Crown. A deep plum, the cloth had absorbed the scent of the Arnikcah wood.

I shuddered, finding myself unaccountably sad as I touched the glowing gem fastened to the underside of the lid. Once more, the melody began to play, lightly trilling through the dusty room. I closed my eyes, transported back to the long summer nights of my youth when I would dance in the meadow as Camille sang her spells to the moon, and Delilah chased fireflies in her kitten form. We'd come a long ways from those days.

Iris peered into the box. "There's a locket inside."

I gently set the box onto the floor and picked up the heart-shaped locket. Silver, embossed with a scrollwork of roses and vines, the heart sprang open as I touched the hinge, revealing a picture and a lock of hair. The photo was definitely Earthside in nature, and was of an elf. A man. The lock of hair was so pale it was platinum. No dye had ever touched these tresses. I held it out to Iris.

She closed her fist around the hair and squinted. "Elf, by the feel. What a pretty pendent. I wonder who it belongs to?"

"I haven't the faintest idea," I said. "What else is in the trunk?"

Iris lifted out the books and the pile of clothes. The books were Earthside—*The Idiot's Guide to Living Earthside*, and *American English for Elves*.

The clothing had belonged to a woman. A tunic, several pair of leggings, a belt and jacket, a brassiere. I held up the undergarment. Whoever owned this had small breasts. The cloth was elf-weave, that much I recognized.

Beneath the clothes, in the bottom of the trunk, we found a journal. I opened it to the first page. The inscription read *Sabele*, written in a scrolling hand. The name was written in

English, but the rest of the journal was in Melosealfôr, a rare and beautiful Crypto language from Otherworld. I could recognize it, but not read it. But Camille could.

"This looks like a diary," Iris said, flipping through it. "I wonder . . ." She stood up and looked around the room, rooting under the towering piles of debris. "Hey! There's a bed here, and a dresser in the corner. Want to make a bet this was a bedroom—perhaps for whoever owned this locket and diary?"

I stared at the piles of old magazines, newspapers, and faded liquor boxes. "Let's clear away everything that's trash. Just haul it into the next room for now. We'll see what we find." As I replaced the music box and clothes within the trunk, laughter echoed down the hall from the stairs and within seconds, my sister Camille stood at the door, two of her men in tow.

"Pizza!" Camille entered the room, gingerly stepping over a rolled up rug. As usual, she was dressed to impress, in a black velvet skirt, a plum bustier, and stilettos. Morio was right behind her, carrying five pizza boxes, and behind him— Smoky towered over everybody, looking bemused but not entirely thrilled to be tagging along.

Iris jumped up and wiped her hands on her shorts. "I'm so hungry I could eat a horse."

"Hush or Smoky might oblige," Camille said, wrinkling her nose as she gave the dragon a playful look.

He might look like six feet, four inches of manflesh with silver hair down to his ankles, but when he transformed, he was all dragon under that snow-white veneer. He ate horses, cows, and the occasional goat. On the hoof. He joked about eating humans, too, but none of us took him seriously, although I suspected there might be the occasional missing person we might attribute to him. Whatever the case, Smoky wasn't just a dragon who could take human form. He was also my sister's husband. *One* of her husbands.

Morio, a Japanese youkai-kitsune—fox demon, loosely translated—was her other husband. He wasn't nearly as tall as Smoky, but he was good looking in a sleek, lithe way, with a ponytail that hung to his shoulders and the faintest hint of a goatee and thin moustache.

Camille had a third lover. Trillian, a Svartan, had been missing far too long for comfort and I knew she was worried about him.

"You just hush up about my eating habits, woman," Smoky said, gently patting her shoulder. He indulged behaviors in her that would earn most people a one-way ticket to crispy critter land. Love was supposed to be blind, but I had the feeling in Smoky's case, he'd come to accept that he'd better develop patience with my sister, or end up miserable.

I frowned at the pizzas. I'd give a lot to be able to eat pizza. Or anything, actually. My ever present diet of blood kept me going, but I wasn't particularly thrilled with it. All salt, no sweets.

Morio's eyes gleamed as he pulled out a thermos and handed it to me.

"I'm not thirsty," I said. Bottled blood wasn't exactly a tasty treat. Kind of like generic beer. It did the trick but in no way or form could you call it haute cuisine. When I wasn't hungry, I left it alone.

"Just drink," he said.

I cocked my head. "What are you up to?" But when I opened the thermos, the blood didn't smell like blood. Instead it smelled like . . . pineapple? I hesitantly took a sip. If I ingested anything but blood I'd get horrible cramps.

But to my shock and delight, though it was blood that flowed down my throat, all I could taste were coconut milk and pineapple juice. I stared at the thermos, then at him. "By the gods, you did it!"

"Yes, I did," he said, a victorious grin spreading across his face. "I finally figured out the spell. I thought piña colada might be a nice change for a first try."

Morio had been working on a spell for some time that would allow me to taste foods I'd left behind when I died.

"Well, it worked!" I laughed and perched on the open windowsill, one knee pulled up to my chest as I leaned back against the frame. As I drank, my taste buds doing a Snoopy dance, it occurred to me that this was the first time in more than twelve years that I'd tasted something other than blood.

"I could kiss you for this."

"Go ahead," Camille said with a wink. "He's good."

Snorting, I set down the thermos and wiped my mouth carefully. More often than not, I ended up with a few spatters around my lips and I preferred not to look like some blood-crazed monster.

"With all due respect to your darling husband, I think I'll leave his kisses for you. Not really my type," I said, winking at Morio. "No offense intended."

"None taken," he said, grinning. "Next time we'll try for some sort of soup flavor. What's your poison?"

"Hmm . . . beef vegetable would hit the spot."

Happier than I'd been in a while, I glanced around the room. "While you guys eat your pizza, I'll start clearing some of this junk out of here. Iris and I found something curious. Don't trash anything that looks like it might have belonged in a bedroom or to an elf."

I piled a stack of magazines in a box and carried them out, dumping them into the room across the hall. Smoky ignored the pizza and pitched in, helping me, as did Morio. Iris and Camille perched on a bench, digging into the Hawaiian-style pie.

As we worked, Camille alternated between eating and filling me in on what I'd missed during the day. With the summer solstice so close, the time in which I could be awake and active had been severely curtailed. I was down to around eight hours per night between sunrise and sunset. I'd sure be happy to see autumn and winter again. It sucked having to be in bed by five thirty in the morning.

"We finally got the wedding invitation from Jason and Tim. They're holding it during the night just so you and Erin can make it." She picked up another slice and held it overhead, letting the strings of mozzarella trail into her mouth.

"I'm glad they're finally getting hitched. They make a good couple."

Tim had won my respect a hundred times over when I'd had to turn his best friend, Erin. I'd sworn never to sire another vampire, but Erin would have died otherwise, and she made the choice. That's how I ended up with a middle-aged human vampire daughter. Tim was her best friend. He'd come through when Erin and I'd needed him most, and my respect for him had soared.

"By the way," I said, "Erin's selling the Scarlet Harlot to Tim. She can't work there during the day, so he's taking over. He'll open a computer consulting business on the side, now that he's graduated from college. He's decided to give up his job as a female impersonator altogether and focus on other things."

"I know. He told me," Camille said. "I'll be sad to see Cleo Blanco fade away, but then again, I never did think he made a very convincing woman. He's much better looking as a man. Although, he did a good job lip-synching to Marilyn Monroe's songs."

She licked her fingers and then added, "Oh, yeah, Wade called shortly before we left home. He said he has something he needs to talk to you about. I told him to drop by the bar, so he'll be over in a bit."

Shit. I didn't want to talk to Wade. We'd been arguing a lot lately and distance definitely helped the heart grow fonder in this case. Whether it was the summer heat, or the overdose of sleep, I didn't know, but we'd been getting on each other's nerves and the problem wasn't showing any signs of easing up.

"Great," I mumbled. "Smoky, can you help me carry this rug? I can lift it, but it's so long it's unwieldy for one person."

Smoky obligingly propped one end of the rolled up Persian rug on his shoulder and I did likewise to the other. We carted it across the hall and tossed it onto the ever-growing pile of debris.

"Where's Delilah? We need to get some of this crap out of here before we end up with a fire. One stray spark and this place would go up like a match." I kicked at the rug and it shifted.

"Patience, patience," Smoky said. "Let me cast a frost spell in here. I can saturate everything with a layer of moisture and make it harder to burn."

I groaned. "And turn it into a breeding ground for mold. Oh, go ahead. At least I won't worry so much about fire then."

An hour later, we'd cleared the bedroom of everything that didn't seem to belong there. We'd uncovered a bed, dresser, trunk, writing desk, bookshelf, and rocking chair. Everything pointed to the original occupant as being a female elf.

"Who lived here?" Camille asked, picking over the remains of the second pizza. Smoky and Morio had settled into eating, and I could see that the other three pies were about to become history.

I shrugged. "I haven't the faintest idea. Nobody at the OIA filled me in on whoever it was that held the job before Jocko."

Iris sat in the rocking chair, rubbing her hand over one of the polished arms. "Would the OIA have that information if you asked them?"

Camille shook her head. "Chances are, even though the organization's back up and running, the files were most likely lost during the civil war."

I had to agree with her. "Yeah. Most of the personnel have either been fired or arrested, depending on their loyalty to Lethesanar. Except, interestingly enough, the director of the Otherworld Intelligence Agency. Father told us he was a double agent, but I didn't know whether or not to believe it. Damned if the information wasn't correct, though."

"Jocko's dead. *He* can't very well help us," Camille said. "Any of your waitresses might know?"

"Doubtful, but that gives me an idea." I jumped up and headed for the door. "I'll be right back. Meanwhile, you guys search the room and see what's in the closets, in that desk. Look for whatever you can find. Check under the mattress, too."

I hurried down the stairs. While Chrysandra and Luke had come to work for me *after* Jocko's death, there was still one person who remembered the gentle giant. Peder, the daytime bouncer, had been around during Jocko's time. I flipped through the address book that we kept behind the counter and then picked up the phone, punching in his number.

Like Jocko, Peder was a giant. But where Jocko had been the runt of his family, Peder was smack in the middle of being height-weight proportionate for his race. After three rings, he picked up.

"Yef?" His English was still limited and his accent was atrocious, but I knew Calouk, the common dialect used throughout the more uncouth members of Otherworld, and I switched to it immediately.

"Peder, this is Menolly," I said, my lips tripping over the rough words as I translated my thoughts into Calouk. "I know you worked for Jocko, but do you by any chance remember who was the bartender before him? Did an elfin woman run the bar? Her name would have been—"

"Sabele," he said. "Yeah, Sabele was the bartender before Jocko. She went home to OW, though. She vanished one day. Never said nuthin'."

Vanished? That seemed odd, considering the locket and diary left behind. "What do you mean, vanished?"

"She quit. That's what Jocko told me when he came here."

That didn't ring true. I was fairly certain Peder wouldn't lie to me, but that didn't mean that what he said was accurate. Giants weren't the brightest bulbs in the socket and Peder wasn't the on the gifted end of the spectrum.

"Are you certain? I found a few of her personal things upstairs while cleaning out one of the rooms. Items I doubt she would have left behind."

"That's what Jocko told me. He said . . . he said the OIA told him that Sabele deserted her post. She was really nice, though. I liked her. She never made fun of me."

His tone told me that—like Jocko—Peder was sensitive to ridicule. Giants were surprisingly emotional, not like trolls or ogres. Oh, they acted like oafs, but they could be caring oafs.

"Do you know if she had any friends around here? A boyfriend, maybe? Or a brother?" The image of the male elf's face from the picture in the locket drifted to mind.

"Boyfriend? Yeah, she had a boyfriend. He used to come into the bar a lot. I thought they went back to OW together and got married. Lemme think . . ." After a moment, Peder sighed. "All I can remember is that his first name was Harish. And her family name was Olahava. That help you any?"

"Yeah," I said, jotting down the two names. "More than you know. Thanks, Peder. And by the way, you're doing a good job. I appreciate it." Everybody needed strokes sometimes. Even giants.

"Thanks, boss," he said. I could hear the glee in his voice.

As I replaced the receiver, the door opened and I looked up to see Wade wander into the room. His shocking bleached-blond hair was even whiter thanks to a dose of peroxide, and he'd given up the glasses he used to hide behind. He was wearing a pair of PVC jeans—gods know where he got hold of those—and a white T-shirt. I blinked. When had he gone glam?

A psychiatrist until he'd been bitten and turned, Wade Stevens was the leader of Vampires Anonymous, a support group for the newly undead. He'd become my first vampire friend when my sister Camille insisted I join the group.

Lately though, he'd been on edge and snippy and I had no intention of wasting the energy to find out why. I had enough problems to deal with, without adding a moody vampire to the list. Anyway, I wasn't the coddling type. His mother did enough of that.

In fact, his mother was one of the primary reasons I'd stopped dating him. A vampire herself, she was the perfect antidote to any spark of attraction I'd had to Wade.

He leaned across the bar. "We need to talk."

"I'm busy," I muttered. Avoidance wasn't my usual M.O. but I had no intention of ruining my mood. "Can we do this later?"

"No. We need to talk *now*," he said, his eyes shifting toward red.

Whoa. Touchy, touchy.

"Fine. In the back, where the customers won't overhear us." I led him into the office and closed the door behind us. "All right, what's so damned important that it can't wait for a few hours? Or days?"

I waited, but he remained silent. Irritated, I started to push past him, intending on returning to the bar but he stopped me, barring my way with his arm.

"Fine. I'll just tell you straight out, because I don't know how else to do this. I've thought this over and over for the past few weeks, but there's no way to get around it. I have to put some distance between us or you're going to ruin any chance I have of becoming regent of the Northwest Vampire Dominion."

I stared at him, unable to believe what I was hearing. "You've got to be joking."

"No." He waved me silent. "I'm asking you to quietly withdraw from Vampires Anonymous. Don't show up at the meetings. And don't contact me in public . . . keep all of our communications in private. You've become a liability to me, Menolly. And to the group."

Don't miss a word from the "delightful...series
that simmers with fun and magic"* featuring
the D'Artigo sisters, half-human, half-Fae
supernatural agents.

By **Yasmine Galenorn**

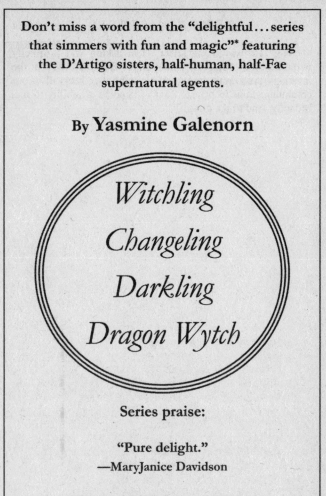

Witchling

Changeling

Darkling

Dragon Wytch

Series praise:

"Pure delight."
—MaryJanice Davidson

"Vivid, sexy, and mesmerizing."
—*Romantic Times*

penguin.com

M192AS0508